MEET CAROLYN STEELE—SUPERLADY OF SEX!

"How does it feel to be the Queen of Sex Advice?" he asked, smiling slightly.

"Silly," I told him, and it really did.

At least the centerfold of the month can justify her title by her body. What did being the Queen of Sex Advice mean in measurable job terms? That I could look up the answers in Kinsey, Masters and Johnson, et al., to any sex question faster than the next writer? That I didn't mind saying "penis" or "cock," for that matter, in print or aloud?

"You must intimidate a lot of men," he said, pressing his lips against my hairline.

"Do I intimidate you?"

I straightened out my legs and leaned back against the pillows and closer to him. I was still wearing the buttery soft lavender leather suit I'd selected for the press conference that morning. Women back home have belts wider than this skirt was long. My panty hose, the only underwear I had on, were a deeper shade of lavender. I had, of course, kicked off my lavender heels.

"Do I look intimidated?" he asked, grinning.

He put his hand on my thigh, and the fingers curved possessively around my flesh. My breath came faster. Before climbing onto the bed, he'd removed his socks and shoes; his feet, I suddenly noticed, were as long and slender as his hands. He was tall, thin, elegant, and graceful. His penis, I imagined, was average length. . . . If he'd kept his hand on my thigh much longer, I might have written an epic poem to it, sight unseen.

"No. You don't look intimidated. That's what I like best about you."

I knew as Charles caressed my thigh with his long sensitive fingers that we were going to have sex that night. . . . I would [illegible] him by morning.

FEMALE SUPERIOR POSITION

SUSAN CRAIN BAKOS

ZEBRA BOOKS
KENSINGTON PUBLISHING CORP.

ZEBRA BOOKS are published by

Kensington Publishing Corp.
850 Third Avenue
New York, NY 10022

First Hardcover Printing: June, 1994
First Paperback Printing: July, 1995

Printed in the United States of America

This book is for Tamm above all, and also for Rich, Mike and Dan, Barb and Gary, JDK and CK, and Kim.

Part One

TALKING SEX

Chapter One

Looking back, I wish I could say that an anticipatory shiver passed through my soul as the makeup brushes drifted across my face, but I was aware of nothing more cosmic than a vague tickling in my nose. I was being made-up in preparation for an appearance on the Olive Whitney show. Olive was number one in the ratings, but to me it was just another talk show, a routine event in the life of a frequent guest. I had no clue that my life was about to change.

As a makeup artist was stroking brown shadow across the outer third of my left eyelid, I was obsessing on eyelids, not life. My left lid is larger than the right and thus requires more shadow so it won't appear to droop on screen. It's surprising how much the camera sees that the eye misses. I was thinking about cameras and eyelids, not about the first threat on my life received only hours before the show in an express mail envelope delivered directly to my apartment.

It never even occurred to me to wonder if any other members of WIP had received, or would receive, death threats. At that point, I wasn't what you would describe as "close" with any of the members of my support group, Women In Porn—or the WIPs, pronounced "whips" by Tim Price, one of the three men with whom I was more or less involved at the moment. The other

WIPs called me "The PTA Mother of Porn." While nobody ever said it to my face, I think they thought I was *"cute,"* just a degree or two to the not-so-respectable left of Kathie Lee Gifford. The WIPs tend to divide women into two groups: Those who have fucked in front of a camera; those who haven't. And I haven't—which is all it takes in their set to type you as a distributor of tea and cookies, not that I haven't been on the serving end of tea and cookie trays in the typical life of a suburban wife I led before becoming a sex journalist.

"You know, honey, you should never wear any other color lipstick," Olive's makeup artist, José, said as he filled in my lips with "peachy-pink, the color of Georgia clay" or so he claimed it was. I've never seen Georgia clay. Joan Rivers's makeup person said I should never wear any other color than rose-pink. Who to trust? "It's perfect for blondes," José cooed. "And you're sooooo blond. It's natural, isn't it?" he asked, peering suspiciously into the roots.

I said "Yes" through my lips scrunched into the semirelaxed open "O" makeup artists prefer for lip work. It is natural—naturally blond, fine, thin, and limp. WASP hair. Have you ever seen a real blonde who didn't have a bathroom full of hair-thickening products?

"You're lucky, you know. Women would kill for hair this shade of blond. And the blue, blue eyes, too, lucky you. Sooooo perfect!"

In addition to making you look as good as possible for the camera, makeup artists psych you up for the ordeal ahead. A really good one, like José, can make you believe you're beautiful, exactly the way a really good lover can. A really bad one can leave you convinced he'll be laughing backstage about several of your least attractive facial features even as you're being introduced to a probably hostile audience.

"Just a teeny touch of blue eyeliner on the lower lid.

Now, don't look at me that way." He put his hands on his narrow hips, affecting a queen's posture. *"Everybody* knows nothing is more outré than blue eyeshadow. I said liner, not shadow. Don't you be thinking José is that down-home!"

I wasn't thinking down-home. No. I come from down-home, southern Illinois; nobody like José ever grew in the cornfields back there. I was wondering if he is gay, bi, or merely an effeminate straight guy playing into the prevailing stereotype about the sexual preferences of makeup artists and hairdressers by sending off gay vibes.

My mind wandered while he worked. When I shut my eyes briefly, I could see the letter I'd pulled out of the express mail envelope. On cheap white typing paper, letters apparently cut from magazines spelled out: "Superlady, You must pay for your life with what you have done." Nothing more. The letters, with capital and small letters randomly mixed running first up, then down the page, were innocent in themselves, like a child's plastic letters tossed out of the container onto a flat surface. What kind of nut would choose to arrange them in that way?

When José was finished, he rested his hands lovingly on my shoulders and smiled with genuine joy into the mirror above my head. Our eyes met. Gay. I can always tell in the eye clinches. I nodded in the affirmative, sharing his happiness. He'd given me peaches and cream skin to go with the peachy-pink lipstick. My eyes looked huge, alluring, yet intelligent. All in all, it was the best TV makeup job I'd ever had, even though he couldn't really hide the fact that I was forty years old. What do you do with those major grooves running from nose to corners of mouth? Some artists fill them in with gunk, which only runs by the first commercial break, making it look like you're losing your face which must be following the mind you'd already lost when you agreed to be there in the first place. Rather than trying to fill in the craters, José put the blush high on the cheekbone and shaded it upward to direct the observer's eye away from the fact that everything from my nose down was going south. It worked fairly well. Thirty-seven or -eight. I could pass for that.

In the "green room," which was not painted green, I joined the other "guests"—a talk show industry code word for the human offerings presented five days a week to audiences composed largely of fat, frigid, and frumpy wives defending the state of dependency with their carefully applied polyurethane claws. Each time I euphemistically agree to be a "guest" on a talk show, I assume the experience will be better than the ones before. I don't know why I assume this. It never is, *I* never am. In countless appearances representing the "pro" side of sex issues, I have failed to distinguish myself in "talk"—industry code word for the stilted monologues exchanged by opposing forces each armed with well-barbed rhetoric—but somehow I don't remember that until I am seated in a preshow waiting room, the "green room," *never* painted green, facing the opposition over a tray of donuts and Danish no one dares eat for fear of messing up our lipstick or getting greasy crumbs on ties.

"Hello," I said, smiling at the younger blonde across the table. She barely acknowledged me with a slight inclination of her head in my direction. Obviously this was not the other Easily Orgasmic Woman or if she was, her ease of bodily response didn't extend to smiling. "Elizabeth Thatcher, I presume?" Another slight inclination of the head.

"Oh!" squeaked a trim and prim little brunette in her late twenties, obviously one of the show's many producers, as she came through the door. Why do the women behind the scenes in talk TV look like they've never been laid? "You two shouldn't be in here alone together!"

The producers believe opposing sides lose their edge if they're allowed to fraternize without supervision over coffee. What, Goddess forbid, if we should discover we go to the same hairdresser in civilian life? Or, that we both buy garlic bread twists from Balducci's in Greenwich Village? Could we still glare effectively at each other on camera if we shared such intimate details of the other's life?

"Where's our expert?" she asked. "Where's our other Easily Orgasmic Woman?"

"Makeup," said the young and beautiful gay man, clearly the PA, or producer's assistant, prancing two steps behind her and carrying a clipboard. "José is doing everyone today, so he's backed up."

"I'm Amy McHenry," she said, extending her hand first to me and then to Elizabeth Thatcher, public relations officer of Women Worried About Wantonness Among Women, the WWAWAWs, a right-wing conservative group recently formed as an offshoot of Women Concerned For America—the group who backed that Wisconsin husband after he had his wife charged with adultery as a criminal offense under an old law still on the books. Women Concerned For America are loosely allied with Women Against Pornography—the group started by Susan Brownmiller back in the late seventies when feminism and porn were both briefly "in" at the same time, shortly after Jackie O was reportedly seen leaving the theater showing *I Am Curious Yellow*.

The WWAWAWs are more blatantly antipleasure than the other two organizations. Concerned Women imply they don't mind your husband having an orgasm. WAPs imply they don't mind lesbians having an orgasm. WWAWAWs come right out and admit they would prefer that nobody ever had one, the exception being men when impregnating women to whom they are wed in the eyes of God and under the law; if anyone could figure out a way for men to ejaculate without enjoying it, these girls would be for it. They have elevated the traditional woman's statement of sexual piety—"I don't really need an orgasm to enjoy lovemaking"—to a credo. If my threatening letter writer—or is "letter assembler" a better term?—belonged to an antiporn group, I would have bet on the WWAWAWs. The WAPs could never have said it in so few words.

One of the new breed of post-Schlafly conservative women who are young—this one might have been late thirties, probably younger—pretty, articulate, and invariably clad in a bright red or floral print silk dress, Thatcher got the attention of talk show producers everywhere when she answered Joan Lunden's question, "Why another antiporn group?" on "Good Morning, America," by saying, "We can't be comfortable as members of WAP because it's infiltrated with lesbians. We have no objection to lesbians as long as they aren't sexually active. If they are fighting their lusts, we support them in their struggle against their sex demons. But, we have reason to believe many of these lesbian WAP members are indeed having active sexual relations, which breaks God's laws." She was a gift from talk show heaven: A natural and definite "anti" for any sex story.

Somewhat reluctantly, Elizabeth Thatcher shook McHenry's limp hand as the gay PA nervously brushed a sweep of hair so black it had to be dyed back off his forehead. The door opened again, admitting our expert, Dr. Adrian Prescott, author of *Any Woman Can Be Easily Orgasmic: How To Get More Pleasure With Or Without A Man,* his arm protectively around the shoulder of the other Easily Orgasmic Woman, Lisa X, who was keeping her last name secret so her husband wouldn't be embarrassed by her appearance on national TV. At the eleventh hour, she'd been talked out of enforcing her initial proviso—that she appear in silhouette only behind a screen with a muted voice like a member of the Federal Witness Protection Program, who had recently testified in a Mafia trial. But, she was still adamantly insisting on the X behind her first name.

"Carolyn, you look wonderful!" Adrian said, taking my hand and raising it to his lips. Every talk show segment has an expert on the panel, usually the author of a book and preferably a therapist. Adrian is both. Though I am not a therapist, I am, as a columnist, often billed as an expert, too, but today I am a combination expert and regular person confessing something about my life. Absolute bona fide experts, the PhD types, don't ever confess. They explain the confessions of others.

"It's been too long, darling, I've missed you," he said.

Gratefully, I leaned toward his soothing presence. Though Adrian looks the part of the stereotypical TV expert—major hair, pancake tan marred only by crinkly smile lines at the eyes, blue-tinted contacts, pearly white smile, quiet tie—he is a likable guy. We met as guests of ex-porn star/erotic video producer/erotic photographer/performance artist Tiffany Titters (Tiffany has many "careers" because nothing she does is sufficiently financially lucrative for her to do that one thing alone) at the Carnival of Sleaze, a performance art evening at The Kitchen, a dark and dank space in the Village where the audience either stands or sits on the floor. Whenever I go to The Kitchen, I put a roach trap in my handbag to be sure the ones who will inevitably accompany me home are dead or dying, not alive. For the uninitiated, a performance art happening is where a collection of people who have little recognizable talent, but don't mind exposing themselves in some way most observers find discomforting, do just that for minimal fees. Karen Finley, the most famous performance artist, got her start at The Kitchen by shoving yams up her asshole, but that night she accepted her check on stage and left without performing, labeling it "the sleaziest thing I could possibly do."

As the only two people backstage who were even slightly embarrassed by Tiffany's large and naked breasts bobbing around all over the place, Adrian and I had something in common. She had unleashed them for the Booby Ballet, a dance of the mammaries punctuated by much swishing of tasseled pasties, and never put them back in harness. When Adrian told me about his research for a book on easily orgasmic women, I told him about my multiple orgasms; that's how I became part of his book.

"I don't know," Lisa whimpered, and Adrian drew her closer to his side. "Oh, God, I don't know." He rubbed her arm up and down. She probably hadn't had this much attention since the last time she'd given birth. "If Owen knew I was doing this, he'd kill me."

"But, who'll ever tell him?" McHenry asked, all innocence, accentuated by a hint of blusher, pink lip gloss, and mascara.

Talk show producers wear minimal makeup, the better for projecting sincerity among the overly made-up guests. Yeah, right. Who would possibly tell her husband she was on "Olive" talking about her orgasms? My guess was someone would have it on the TV at his office, even if there was no TV normally kept in the office, ten minutes into the show, max.

"Believe me, even people who know you don't pay the slightest attention to who you really are on TV," McHenry said. "They're caught up in the dialogue, in the topic of the moment. I was once a guest on a talk show panel, and my own mother watched without realizing it was me."

"Are you sure?" Lisa said, lisping slightly.

Another blonde, though definitely bottle, she was in

her early thirties, maybe as young as twenty-nine, presenting the possibility of the three of us looking like the aging of the blondes if they seated us in chronological order. Her skin under the thick makeup wasn't great, but the camera would smooth it out thanks to José's skill with the brush. Maybe her husband wouldn't recognize her without the visible pimples. McHenry nodded vigorously and patted her arm.

"Okay, okay, I said I would so I guess I should. What do you think?" Lisa asked, turning to me.

"Uh . . ." I was aware of Adrian's other hand pressing gently into my arm. He was capable of playing coach simultaneously to two women with differing emotional support requirements, a more impressive feat really than fucking us both simultaneously would have been.

"Well, I'm not worried about it, personally," I said.

What makes these ordinary people spill their guts—or, "share," as the process is more popularly labeled—on Oprah, Geraldo, Phil, Sally, and Joan? The free make-overs? The airfare and hotel rooms for out-of-town guests? Did they really believe Andy Warhol when he said we all are going to be famous for fifteen minutes?

"I'm sure it will all be fine," I said. "You're doing good, really. Think of all the women out there who rarely if ever reach orgasm. You can help them."

She nodded thoughtfully, a modern Joan of Arc headed toward her martyrdom.

"Really, it will be fun," I finished in that relentlessly cheery voice of the aging Valley Girl, a voice I hate but too often use as a hiding place. I should have put my arm around her from the other side and said: Does fifteen minutes of fame really compensate for the ignominy of having your home video shown at family reunions for life? No? Then, we're out of here.

"Okay," she said, "if you're not worried, I'm not."

I thought she was incredibly naive. Of course, *I* wasn't worried about appearing on national TV discussing *my* orgasms. For me it was all part of the job. And, *I* didn't have a husband at home who might consider the discussion an invasion of his privacy, too. No, at the moment I had three men in my life who were never in the same room with me when I was having an orgasm. What would they care?

Looking back, *I* was incredibly naive. So, what is the fleeting wrath of a husband who, after all, has just been identified by his adoring wife as a gonzo orgasm giver, compared to what I was going to face? The "Olive" show changed my life. It merely gave her something to talk about for the rest of hers.

"Carolyn," McHenry said, beaming at me. I looked at the heading on the paper in her hand. Today's show was titled: "Women Who Enjoy Sex Too Much." She caught my eye and hastily covered the title line. Conned again. She'd told me the show was "Why Some Women Like Sex More Than Others Do." She smiled winningly. "How do you want us to introduce you?"

"Our first guest is the Superlady of Sex, Carolyn Steele!" Olive said; the audience tittered. "Carolyn's sex advice column has appeared in *Playhouse* magazine every month for the past five years; she's an ex-pert"—she drew out the word and ended it on an up note—"on *sex*," she finished on the downbeat. The audience tittered more loudly. "Yeah!" Olive squealed. "Okay, Carolyn, what makes you an expert on sex?"

"Well," I said solemnly, as if I'd just been asked to explain the meaning of life, "I have a master's degree in math, which makes me a good research person. I keep up with all the latest studies, and interview sexologists and therapists from around the country, the world even, to answer readers' questions." I continued, sounding sillier and sillier.

"O-kay," Olive said. "Audience, what about that? A math major who knows about sex!"

Once on a local show in Seattle, I answered the What Makes You An Expert? question, "I like sex; I'm comfortable with sex. I'm good at it." I liked that answer. I felt good about it. Three hours later, while wandering through Pike's Market looking for Market Tea, Seattle's own blend of orange spice tea, which turned out to be too sweet, I walked into a tiny shop selling herbs and spices. The aging hippie owner, long hair nearly reaching his waist, single earring in left ear, sandals, tie-dyed shirt—yes, the entire nine-yard cliché—said, "I saw you on television this morning. I thought, 'Oh, Christ another expert. What makes this one an expert.' But, I liked what you said. It was honest." I wish I'd felt more comfortable about his endorsement.

". . . but what she's got to tell us about herself probably isn't what you ever expected to hear from your math teacher . . ." Olive was saying. Math teacher? "Tell us, Carolyn, how many *orgasms,"* she lowered her voice deliciously on the "O" word, "can you have at one time?"

"Well," I began. I caught my reflection in the monitor. My nose was already greasy, and the camera had given me chipmunk cheeks, the fate of those who have no bones. The tag line at the bottom of the screen under my inflated face read: "Easily Orgasmic Woman." I looked back at Olive. Her face was even fatter than mine. What were we doing in a place like this? Why not radio for us? "I don't count them."

"Then how do you know you're really multiply orgasmic?"

"Well, I *have* counted."

"You *have* counted," Olive said, coming in for the

kill. "When you *have* counted, how high did you count?"

"A couple dozen, but then I stopped counting."

The audience gasped. A few women groaned. I heard one hiss something that included the word "disgusting." Olive's mouth opened wide. She was certainly putting the weight back on, but she's still surprisingly beautiful.

"Good-ness!" she said, and the music came up, signaling an imminent commercial break. "We'll be back in a minute with another Easily Orgasmic Woman and the man who knows more about these women than any man in America, Dr. Adrian Prescott, author of *Any Woman Can Be Easily Orgasmic: How To Get More Pleasure With Or Without A Man."* She held the book up. "And, maybe Carolyn will tell us if she had those couple dozen orgasms with or without a man!"

The commercial rode in on a gale of audience laughter.

". . . and, it was almost a religious experience for me, having my first orgasm finally, with my husband, after all those years," Lisa said softly. Adrian, who had just finished explaining how easily orgasmic women get that way in part by thinking about sex before they do it (a concept he calls Pre-Sex Mental Foreplay), had one arm around her shoulders. He was beaming proudly at her. The camera caught the glint of tears in her luminous green eyes. The pimples didn't show, and, since she had prominent cheekbones, her face didn't even look fat. The audience loved her, because she had *worked* to become easily orgasmic. I was just born that way, which made them angry. They kept getting hung up on the word "easy" which they translated as "promiscuous." Nothing gets an American TV audience more outraged than sexual pleasure. "Adrian's book changed my life," Lisa lisped. "It saved our marriage."

"And, you really believe *any* woman can learn to have orgasms as easily as you do simply by reading this book?" Olive asked—again, waving the book.

"Oh, yes," she said, the lisp quite pronounced. In the front row, a woman was dabbing the corner of her eyes with a tissue. "And, I really believe every woman owes it to her husband to become multiply orgasmic."

"All right, audience," Olive said, squelching their applause. She spotted the woman with the tissue, ran over to her, and put an arm around her shoulders. "Sister," she said to her. "It's okay. Almost every woman in America has had trouble having orgasms at least once in a while." The audience laughed and clapped delightedly; she had to silence them again by waving her mike. "Now, you've heard from two Easily Orgasmic Women. For Carolyn, having an orgasm is as easy as falling off a log, but Lisa had to learn to have them easily and in fact had her first *just . . . last . . . year* at what age, Lisa? No, girl, I'm kidding. You don't have to tell your age! Now, audience, I get the feeling you're a little uncomfortable with Carolyn. Why is that?"

Olive stuck the mike in front of a white woman with a bad perm, who said, "She doesn't say anything about love! What about love? I don't think it's right to be having all those orgasms with someone you don't love. She's a slut." Accepting the applause, she grinned for the folks back home. "Besides, she writes for *that* magazine."

"Okay," Olive said. "Okay. That magazine bothers you, does it?" The bad perm bobbed vigorously up and down. "Why is that, girlfriend?"

"It exploits women. I think. . . ."

But, Olive had turned away from her. "Okay, audience, is that what you think? Does Carolyn's magazine exploit women?" Resounding applause. "Well, Carolyn—"

"Olive," Adrian interjected. "I don't think that's our point here. Our point here is orgasms and how every woman can have them easily and often. Our bigger point here is how orgasms can improve a woman's relationships with men."

"Even if she has them without men as your book promises she can whenever she wants?" Olive asked.

"Yes, of course, even having them without men improves her relationship with men. In my book I teach women how to become orgasmic through self-pleasuring, which is, as you may know, the most reliable learning path to orgasm." In private, among friends, Adrian calls female masturbation "woman's own whanking." On air, he says "self-pleasuring" in tones so civilized, he should be holding a teacup in the digits often used for such activity. "Self-pleasuring is good for relieving tension as well as teaching women how to have orgasms. Can you honestly tell me you don't think a relationship is improved when a woman is relaxed?"

"Well . . ." Olive said, lowering her voice, playing into the titters. "I don't know what to say about that. But, stay tuned! When we come back, our next guest, Elizabeth Thatcher, spokesperson for Women Worried About Wantonness Among Women is going to tell us what *she* thinks of all this pleasuring going on!"

I looked over at Thatcher, her face set in an accusatory mask. I knew she was going to crack, but I didn't know how wide the fissure would be . . . or how deranged the woman was behind the mask.

". . . thank you, caller," Olive said firmly, and the woman with the nasal Jersey accent was sent to oblivion after congratulating Elizabeth Thatcher on the "fine work" she's doing to save America from female wantonness, which, of course, is responsible for everything from teen pregnancy to AIDS. Olive was standing in the audience, her arm tightly around a sobbing woman who had just confessed she'd never had an orgasm. "Okay, Elizabeth, you and the caller and a lot of our audience agree that you don't need an orgasm to enjoy sex." She hugged the sobber. "And, that's fine! That's great! But, are you saying you think there's something wrong with a woman who *does* need an orgasm to enjoy sex?"

"Olive, if I may interject," Adrian said. "It isn't okay to say you don't need an orgasm to enjoy sex if in saying that you really mean you don't believe you deserve an orgasm."

"Thank you, Adrian. I hear what you're saying. You don't want women to feel guilty about desiring sexual pleasure. Elizabeth, how do you feel about that?"

"I am not opposed to sexual pleasure for married women," she said, carefully choosing her words, "as long as it doesn't become a separate goal in itself. Orgasm," her lips seemed to go numb around the word, "should be a by-product of the loving communion between husband and wife. It shouldn't be a goal. Too many orgasms can cause a couple to focus on their carnal feelings, not their higher love for one another. Before you know it, a woman is trying to have more and more orgasms to the exclusion of showing her love and tenderness for her husband. Making sexual pleasure a goal denigrates the marital relationship."

"Now, how does it do that?" Olive asked.

"Marriage, Olive, is a union blessed by God. Its purpose is higher than our navels." An outburst of laughter and applause greeted that obviously well rehearsed bon mot. "When you strive for sexual pleasure in marriage, you lose sight of its higher purpose."

"So, you're saying orgasm is okay if it happens, but don't try to make it happen?" Olive asked. Elizabeth

Thatcher smiled and nodded enthusiastically. "Then you think Lisa's marriage didn't need an orgasm to save it?"

"I think Lisa is misguided and misinformed. If she had come to me, I would have sent her to the scriptures for solace, not his book. But, I don't condemn her for what she's done," Thatcher insisted, smiling beatifically on the sinner to her left. Adrian appeared to be winking at the audience. "She's been brainwashed by a sex-mad media. *Her,*" she said, indicating me, "I most certainly and soundly do condemn."

"Well, I guess by your definition, Carolyn is part of the sex-mad media, isn't she?" Olive asked.

"Most assuredly," Thatcher replied. She turned in her chair, leaned across Adrian to face me. The hairs in my nose stood on end.

We were in the last segment of the hour, the place where I lull myself with the thought, *It's almost over, and I'll never do this again.* I start making bargains with the Goddess to whom I rarely otherwise converse. *Get me out of here, Goddess, and I swear I'll never say yes to a producer again.* During the preceding commercial break, José had whispered into my ear when he powdered down the grease around my nose, "Madame X's husband is on the phone, and he is not amused." Adrian was making the connection between early masturbation and women who are easily orgasmic without the help of his book.

Olive asked Lisa X if masturbating had helped her, and she blushingly said, "That's too personal."

Adrian said apropos of nothing, "Some women in my study have orgasms with extragenital stimulation." Olive nodded, but I don't think she got his point. "For instance," he continued, "they can achieve orgasm by having their breasts or other nongenital body parts stimulated."

"I once had an orgasm in the subway when my lover

nuzzled my ear," I said, and I saw Elizabeth Thatcher quickly cover her left ear with her right hand.

"Your ear?" Olive shrieked. "Girl, you're putting me on!"

"She's not," Adrian said.

"I'm not."

A significant percentage of the audience was glaring at me. It was true, but why did I choose that fact to share? If I had said to these women, "Look, I haven't had partner sex since my lover left me for a twenty-year-old seven months ago," they would have taken me into their collective heart with its arteries clogged by cholesterol and sentimentality. I would have been one of them, a female victim. But, no. I had to tell them about the time I orgasmed on the 1 train. I had to set myself apart from them, didn't I? My fierce and misguided sense of pride which wouldn't let me admit I shared many of their same fears and sorrows was standing in my way again. I couldn't see past it. Why, I'd never admitted childbirth had been painful, so great was my need not to be like other women.

"I was already aroused from thinking about the sex we were going to have when we got back to his apartment," I said, attempting to soften the blow.

"That's Pre-Sex Mental Foreplay in action," Adrian said.

"Wow!" Olive said. "That's some action! How old were you when you had your first orgasm anyway?"

"Eleven. I was shimmying down a tree. I didn't know what it was, only that it felt good. I asked my older sister, and she said I'd had an orgasm, and I didn't need the tree to do it again." The audience laughed and hooted, except for the sobber who started crying again. I saw Elizabeth Thatcher's face go red with fury, but, perversely, I continued. "Think of the splinters I could have gotten if she hadn't told me."

"That's disgusting!" Thatcher snapped.

"Olive, if I may interject . . ." Adrian began.

"Now, just a minute!" Olive said to Thatcher, ignoring him. "She's describing a perfectly normal and natural physical response . . ."

But, Thatcher couldn't take her eyes off me. I wiggled my middle finger at her, the one I use to masturbate. Before any of us knew what was happening, she had leaped from her chair and had her hands around my throat. She made me famous.

Chapter Two

Dear Superlady of Sex,

I am a forty-year-old white woman having an affair with a twenty-five-year-old black man, my first adventure into the heart of darkness. Frankly, his penis is a disappointment. It isn't any bigger than a white man's—and it's NAVY BLUE! Is he an exception or is that stuff about big black cock not really true? I haven't told him I'm let down, but maybe he can guess.

Also, on the subject of stuffing, he doesn't get very hard. No matter what I do, he seems semi-hard to me, so I get tired of trying and just stuff him in as best I can. Is this normal for a man so young? I've had to stuff old guys, but never someone so young.

I was going through the mail in bed, which is where I normally read, eat, sleep, watch TV, talk on the phone, and do any work not performed on the computer. Modern urban life does that to people. When not on the streets engaged in the combat of daily life, dodging the homeless with their hands out, avoiding eye contact with the crazies while being careful not to step in dog shit, and schlepping each day's necessary purchases because we have no cars with trunks to fill on a weekly basis, we retreat to our beds surrounded by

Chinese take-out cartons, newspapers, magazines, and the assorted chaos of our own "stuff," by which we imprint our style on our surroundings. My stuff is largely books, novels from Trollope to Atwood, and mysteries, especially with female detectives, and the occasional volume of feminist literary criticism. Piles of books leaned into the bed on either side.

How I envied the letter writer her navy blue penis. I knew I could make it hard. How much longer would I be able to stand this job without getting laid? It was like being a food writer on an eight hundred calorie a day diet.

Dear Disappointed, You Bitch,

Over forty years after Kinsey told us the average black penis measures approximately two-tenths of a centimeter more than the average white penis—hardly enough to get excited about—the myth of the BIG Black Penis still lives. And, most men at twenty-five rarely need to be "stuffed." But, a woman who regards your navy blue penis as something short of spectacular could have that effect on a man.

Okay, this answer would need a little more work, but I was only playing. It didn't surprise me to see the Georgia postmark on the letter writer's envelope. Nobody buys into the big black penis myth like a southern white woman—unless it's a black man. The average black man does seem to have more sexual confidence than the average white guy. Could it be all the positive PR his penis has gotten?

Paying minimal attention to the telephone conversation I was having with Tim, I put the letter aside and picked up another.

"And, how does that make you feel?" Tim asked. It was his favorite question of me. My favorite question of me was rapidly becoming: Why do I put up with him and The Question? Listlessly, I put down a letter requesting advice on the etiquette of asking a woman who's had a mastectomy to leave her blouse on during sex. *(Make wild passionate love to her on the sofa, removing only the necessary items of clothing. But, make sure she's convinced you couldn't stop long enough to get to the bedroom.)* I sighed and let my thoughts stray to my clit, the source of my greatest pleasures in life. I was lying on my back, knees up, legs open, accessible. I have strong, taut thighs from riding the exercycle in the corner of my bedroom. I love my thighs. Somebody has to love them.

"This has to be arousing some powerful feelings in you," he prompted. "I know it would in me. Jeez, this is big stuff. Big stuff."

"It doesn't make me feel that great, okay?" I said crossly. I was losing patience with him. During the first two months I'd dated Tim, I took pains to answer The Question as carefully and honestly as if he'd been a real shrink and not the editor of *The Journal of New Age Psychology,* an obscure quarterly published in the basement of a sagging brownstone in the East Village.

The first two months of dating Tim were like the first two months of dating any man in my post-35 dating history: I invested him with qualities he didn't have to justify my interest in him. When it started to become painfully obvious that he, like the ones before him, was simply the product of my overactive romantic imagination, I grew irritated with him. After irritation, comes embarrassment and the horrible question: *What did I ever see in him?*

I'll tell you what I saw in them: They weren't engaged, married, or living with another woman. Availability was the deciding factor which explained why my recent past was littered with geeks, losers, wimps, nerds, lying womanizing sleazebuckets, and just plain jerks.

Dating at forty is like shopping for a good wool dress at a department store clearance sale the last day of January. It's okay if you have a closet filled with dresses at home. But, imagine how you'd feel if everything you'd owned had just been lost in a fire?

I was tired of The Question and the condescending yet pseudo-therapeutic tone of voice in which Tim asked it. He has a bachelor's degree in psychology and, at forty, was still trying to decide if he wanted to go back to school and become a psychologist. Really, he wants to be paid for earnestly asking, "How does that make you feel?"

"That's good," he said enthusiastically. "That's valid. It doesn't make you feel great. Sometimes, we know what we do feel by eliminating what we don't feel first."

I sighed again. He spends all his discretionary income, what little there is of it, on therapy himself. For the past four years he'd been seeing a Jungian who treated him at a discount in exchange for Tim rewriting his papers which were then published in the journal. And, for two years he'd also been in a therapy group run by an MSW who combined Freud and "body work," something involving exercises of the nonaerobic variety. During the first session each member stripped to underwear or a bathing suit to have his body "read." In a typical session, talk alternated with bizarre mat activities, in which someone ended up on the mattress in the middle of the floor with the "expert" helping him or her let go of blocked emotions. According to Tim, the mat interludes could get so "intense" that barf bags were kept handy for participants who let go of lunch as well as old emotions.

"I know how I'd feel if my picture were on the front page of the *New York Post* with the headline, 'Sexpert Nearly Expires of Pleasure!!'," he said smugly—smugly because, of course, nothing so tacky would ever happen to him.

"Tim, please." I groaned, shoving the *Post* under the down comforter with my left foot. Why had I called him anyway? What kind of woman would find emotional solace in a nutcase like Tim? "I can't stand it."

"That's good, that's good. Let it out. Let your feelings out on this one."

Now *he* sighed; more deeply than I could ever sigh, of course, thanks to his body work breathing exercises which, with daily practice, had taught him to sigh from his gut. Too bad he doesn't practice other things with his gut, like regular sit-ups. Tim is medium height and build, except for the soft, expansive middle. With his thinning brown hair and sparse facial and body hair, he is far from a sex object. I only wanted him because he was hard to get. If he'd tried to seduce me on the first date, I would have hastily declined, bolted the door behind me, turned on the answering machine, and never returned his phone calls.

Instead, he'd announced, "We aren't going to have sex right away," over the first cappuccino we'd shared, and I was hooked temporarily. As my best friend Morgy says, I only want what I think I can't have. Why didn't it occur to me that his sexual position was probably fear of being with a woman of my assumed experience?

It didn't occur to me because I was in the midst of a midlife crisis which had temporarily left me unsure of myself and seeking validation, and masochistically accepting the refusal of it, from the geeks of the world.

"You must be feeling really out there right now, really alone," he said. "Yes, that's it, out there and alone, a visible target for women's anger. I know how you feel."

"You should know how I feel. You've been a visible target for the anger of every woman you ever dated."

The last woman left him when he failed to renew his driver's license so he could share the driving on a trip they'd planned to take upstate. It was, she said, the "last straw," the last of many times he'd let her down in many ways ranging from the insignificant, like forgetting to buy her a corn muffin one Saturday morning when he went out to get *The Times,* to the incredibly important, like wearing a shirt that reeked of stale sweat and smoke when she introduced him to her kids. It was, he said, only an excuse she'd used. The real truth: They were playing out their scripts. She was a leaver; he, who feared abandonment, always chose leavers. Oh, get real, Tim, what woman worth having wouldn't eventually leave you?

"My ex-lovers adore me," I continued, my turn to be smug. "They send flowers on my birthday. My ex-husband still calls on our wedding anniversary." True, but why is this so important to me? Tim was right about one thing: It was time I asked some questions about my life. It was time I asked, but I wasn't ready to answer. "Your exes return your Christmas cards stamped, 'Refused!' "

"Okay, take it out on me if it makes you feel better," he said. His voice, which is deeper than you'd expect it to be, given his general wimpiness, sunk an octave lower. "I'm strong. I can take it. I can handle it. I want to handle it for you. I want to be there for you, *want to,* as opposed to *have to.*"

Tim, who, of course and you probably guessed this, considers himself a new sensitive man, talks a lot about needing to get beyond the "feeling of having to," which, he claims, paralyzes him. That, his fear of abandonment, and his Oedipus complex are his "big issues," which taken together form his "complex." He can't, for example, clean his apartment until cleaning is something he "wants to do as opposed to has to do." His apartment does look like the kind of place described in newspaper articles about elderly recluses found dead amidst their roaches and newspapers, those articles accompanied by photos of cops in gas masks carrying out scrawny, mean cats—the kind of place that lends credence to his theory only a sick person would live this way. But his mother, a tough old Texas gal, says he's "just plain 'ole lazy," an explanation I tend to endorse.

I scanned another letter, this one from a man who just wanted to tell me what a great time he'd had with the twin sisters, big of boob, blond of hair, who had picked him up in their convertible while he was hitchhiking in the Texas panhandle. They loved rubbing his "jism" into their nipples. Or, so he said. Personally, I would bet he saw Texas from the window of a Greyhound bus where he fantasized this encounter. Irritably, I pushed the pile of letters aside.

"This feels right for me," Tim said, though I didn't know, and wasn't going to ask, *what* felt right for him. "Yes, it's feeling good. I need to get past this point of having to and reach the point of really wanting to, and I feel it coming with you. It's good. It feels good. I feel it coming."

"Tim, let's talk about something else, okay?"

Sometimes I thought of him as Jeff Goldblum turning into The Fly. He was repulsive—positively oozily yucky—yet I kept going back to stick my fingers in his goo. Figuratively, of course. Something about him compelled me. Or, maybe it was just my secret self-loathing that motivated me to be involved with him.

"Can't you ever just be my friend and say, 'There, there'?" I asked.

"Okay," he said with petulance in his voice.

He cleared his throat, giving me time to change my mind. I waited, imagining him lying on his moldering bed in his studio apartment across the hall from Clarissa, who introduced us. Never allow yourself to be fixed up by a lesbian who shares a three-room apartment with her pregnant lover and six female cats which have not been spayed. What a woman like that knows about men wouldn't take up a corner of the litter box.

When I didn't weaken, he said, "But I want you to know I'm here for you whenever you want to talk about this. It's big stuff. You can't shove it back down. Well, you can, of course, but if you do . . ." As he launched into his familiar monologue on how "stuffing"—and he wasn't referring to something done with a limp penis—had kept him emotionally weighed down, I began to touch myself, sliding my finger back and forth around the slick shiny protrusion that was the source of so much joy . . . and since yesterday, a fair amount of media attention. Jeremy Mitchell had called that morning. Jeremy *himself.* I closed my eyes and wiggled farther down into the nest of pillows in my bed. Sometimes I masturbate to meet an immediate need for release generated by something I've thought or heard or read or written . . . and sometimes because my hand is there anyway.

"What did you say, Carolyn?" he asked sharply. "Are you gasping?"

"Uhmmm . . ." I said.

Initially the world intrudes. Gradually it doesn't anymore. The finger that was only tapping the surface is pulled deeper, connecting with the longing inside me. Whatever minor stimulus led me to this place is overshadowed now by the greater need. I am inside myself, enveloped in layers of undulating satin tissue. Within seconds, I can get from the point where the erotic spell can be interrupted to that place where nothing can stop me and any interruption is incorporated into my private lovemaking. The ticking clock or ringing phone or the voice disembodied in my ear are carried along as if they were so many twigs in a river headed for the falls. Tim was an interruption, not the erotic catalyst, but I would incorporate him. I bore down on the fingers inside my vagina while massaging my clit with my thumb.

"Uhmmm . . ." I said, sucking myself inside.

"You're breathing harder, Carolyn. Talk to me!"

"Jerk yourself off. Don't tell me your cock hasn't been outside your pants for the past fifteen minutes." He loved it when I talked dirty, though afterward he swore he didn't. Like so many of the men who wrote to me, he loved it; so I did it, one last time. Superlady couldn't stop me anymore than he could.

"Do it, Tim. Pretend you're ramming it up my ass. You know you want to." I wanted him too. I fantasized him taking me anally, effecting entry in short hard thrusts and then plunging rhythmically inside my bowels as far as he could reach. A woman is never as submissive as when she offers a man her ass to plumb, and my recurring fantasy lately was one of submission. "Do it, Tim. Fuck me hard."

"Carolyn," he said. "Carolyn . . ." The masturbatory narration was definitely my department. "Oh, Carolyn . . ."

"I'm kneeling with my ass in the air, Tim. My head is down. My ass is open for you. I feel erotic dread grow in the pit of my stomach and wash through my loins as you spread my cheeks apart with your hands. I am hot, aching, and panting. I want it, fear it. The head of your cock is poised against my asshole. It's so big, Tim, so big. You grasp my hips with your hands and push hard. Oh, my God, Tim, again, harder . . . my God, you're inside me so far. I feel your testicles slapping against my pussy lips. Over and over again, Tim, I feel you fucking me, a hard, driving, burning force opening me up, leaving me vulnerable. . . ."

Tim snorts when he gets excited to the point of almost coming; he was getting there. I put the phone down on the pillow, so I couldn't hear him. I replaced him with a sexual memory of a man who was so far superior to him, no comparison should even be made.

I was in my mother's bathroom, on my last morning

of a visit home, carefully shaving off all my pubic hair in preparation for a reunion with this man. I had never shaved myself there before, and it felt strange. Walking through airport lobbies, the air striking my naked skin, because I wasn't wearing panties under my skirt, I felt more sexually vulnerable than I had in years. It was exhilarating. My nipples were erect from St. Louis to Philadelphia.

In his car, parked at the end of a row in the Philadelphia International Airport, he put his hand up my skirt and discovered what I had done. No man had ever touched my skin in that way before. He pushed the seat back as far as it would go, unzipped his pants, and lifted me up. Wet and swollen, I sat down on his erection and rode him. His hands on my hips accepted rather than controlled my movements. My third orgasm released his; afterward, I sat on his lap for many minutes, while he held me. My shaved pussy made me feel so close to him, so open to him, that I came again, just sitting there quietly in his arms.

As I thought about him, I moved my fingers faster and pushed farther down into the bed; my foot slid inside the pages of the *Post.* Eyes closed, I saw myself alone, totally exposed, with no space left unexplored. The orgasm crescendoed around my fingers, reverberating into little sucking noises that I could barely hear beneath my moans.

When I brought the phone back to my ear, Tim was breathing heavily; I was still having orgasmic contractions.

"Whew!" he said. "Whew! That was good." Then he let out one of his little yipping noises, which he says are part of his body work. "So, dinner in an hour or so? At Winston's?"

"Yeah. Sure."

"I love you," he said. Tim prided himself on being a

feeling man. He said "I love you" a lot, almost as often as, "How does that make you feel?"

"Love you, too," I said, a very large lie.

"I wish it were different, Carolyn," he said. "But you know it wouldn't be healthy for me if we had sex. You could drive me so far into my complex I would never be able to climb out again." Then his voice brightened. "I'll bring my research into the psychology of the WWAWAW type. I think it might change your mind about whether or not that woman is seriously dangerous."

Tim's new favorite hobby was psychoanalyzing the authors of my hate mail. He had a psychological profile worked up for every one of them. Now, he had the WWAWAW workup, too.

As he'd outlined it to me on the phone, the typical WWAWAW members were religious zealots, programmed by leaders who delivered the same messages over and over again. They claimed they "loved," not "hated," but Tim said they weren't programmed to deal with anyone who wasn't brought over to their side by the power of their "love." Failure to convert left them confused and laden with repressed anger, enough, he said, in some cases to render them capable of violent acts.

"I still think you should take that threatening letter to the police," he said.

"Why should I go to the police with a little piece of paper? Madame Zelda took some letters to the cops several weeks ago and they more or less said, 'What do you expect? You solicit mail from sex perverts?' Why would it be any different for me?"

"Did she get the same kind of letter?"

"I don't know. I never saw them. Look, I'm tired of talking about it," I said, hanging up on him.

When would I have an affair with someone I wouldn't be embarrassed to recall had aroused my lust six months or a year later? I knew I was definitely going to be embarrassed remembering phone sex with Tim after he was no longer in my life. Pressing my hand against the last of the contractions, I already felt a little nauseous about it.

I took a quick shower, applied minimal makeup (mascara, blusher, lip gloss, a sponging of ivory foundation) and put on black garter belt and stockings rather than panty hose under my short black skirt. What other color is there for skirts and stockings? Then I spent forty-five minutes putzing around the apartment, pulling dead leaves from plants, organizing magazines, clipping coupons, unloading the dishwasher. I'll always be a housewife in my heart. I wasn't answering the phone. The machine was set on two rings with the volume all the way down so I wouldn't be tempted to pick up. I'd already talked to Morgy and Johnny Badalamenti, the jazz drummer I was sometimes dating. Anyone else could wait.

I was living on Wayne Street in Jersey City, in a newly renovated two-bedroom apartment in what was once a splendid art deco building located on the block that served as the dividing line between the barrio, the Puerto Rican ghetto, and the Van Vorst Park area recently claimed by the upwardly mobile young transplants who couldn't afford, or wouldn't spring for, New York City rents. Only the hallways had survived the Yuppie-azation. Their black and white tile floors gleamed; turquoise carpet runners danced up marble steps. The walls, washed pale turquoise, were topped like slices of wedding cake heavily and decoratively iced by ornate cornices. Chandeliers and wall sconces bloomed in tulip shaped leaves. But, inside the apartments, all was industrial off-white from the carpeting to the bathroom and kitchen tile and the Eurostyle cabinets—pale wood or some reasonable imitation thereof with off-white accent strips. My apartment on the fourth floor had a loft over the kitchen and bathroom that could be reached by a narrow nearly vertical "staircase," which was really a ladder. Even I, at 5′2″, couldn't stand up straight in the loft.

Morgy (Morgan Harris Carter, a ravishing and rich strawberry blond stock trader) said "too bad you can't live in the halls" on her one and only visit. Not that Morgy's Manhattan apartment, a large one bedroom with wood parquet floors and terrace with panoramic view, on the Upper East Side was exactly a decorator's dream. Her bedroom contained an enormous nineteenth century cherry bed she hadn't assembled. She slept on the mattress on the floor surrounded by sections of the bed, like the oversized pieces of a child's wooden puzzle. Her underwear lined the walls in little piles. What with making money and spending it on worthless men, she didn't have time to shop for anything but clothes. Anyway, I loved my apartment, with its tiny boxy rooms. It was filled with light for my plants. From the loft, I could look down on my high-ceiling living room lined with bookcases, rich in trees, and spare in modern furniture, all gray and black, leather and glass, and pretend I was in a *New York* magazine layout. I couldn't see the drug dealers lounging on the front stoops of the neglected brownstones across the street from that vantage point.

I was hanging up some clothes in the bedroom closet when I remembered the *Post* and pulled it out from under the floral peach down comforter. The bedroom was my retreat into the past, shamelessly feminine in shades of peach and ivory and turquoise, laden with needlepoint pillows, small pieces of antique oak furniture, framed photos of my son and daughter from infancy through young adulthood, similar photos of nieces and nephews, and a collection of feathered, sequined, and beaded Mardi Gras masks. My face on page one was wrinkled in the middle from where I'd kicked the paper in the throes of orgasm. I smoothed it out and turned to page three, where my brush with death was the big story.

"Sex Writer Nearly Dies For Her 'Sins' On Olive!" The picture splashed half the length of the page was of Elizabeth Thatcher with her hands around my neck. My mouth was open, eyes popping, as security guards were converging on us from all edges of the shot. An inset photo of Olive, who was also openmouthed and wide-eyed while standing frozen with her mike in front of the sobbing woman, was in the upper right-hand corner. The copy read:

> *A trembling but dry-eyed and otherwise composed Elizabeth Thatcher, spokesperson for Women Worried About Wantonness Among Women, was led away from the stage of the Olive Whitney show in handcuffs yesterday following her assault on another guest, Carolyn Steele, sex advice columnist for* Playhouse *magazine.*
>
> *The topic of Olive's show, "Women Who Enjoy Sex Too Much," brought together Steele, an Easily Orgasmic Woman Who Enjoys Sex Too Much; Thatcher; Dr. Adrian Prescott, author of the controversial bestseller,* Any Woman Can Be Easily Orgasmic: How To Get More Pleasure With Or Without A Man; *and a woman who called herself "Lisa X, Easily Orgasmic Woman," and was later identified as Lisa Pollack, wife of a Cincinnati orthopedist, who was said to be "distraught" over her involvement with the program.*
>
> *After Steele admitted to having orgasms with a*

stranger on a subway train, Thatcher, according to witnesses, jumped out of her chair and began strangling the blond bombshelldropping sex writer.

A spokesperson for Whitney said, "Elizabeth Thatcher appeared to lose self-control for a period of time during the show. We regret this incident deeply and are grateful that the quick thinking of security personnel averted a more serious tragedy." Only live markets saw the altercation, which was cut from the tape sent to other markets. The spokesperson would not say if the program will be included in those scheduled for rerun during holiday time periods.

Steele is said to be a member of a subversive underground group of women pro-pornography activists. The Pro-Porners, according to reliable sources, are bent on making pornographic materials more widely available. They include legendary X-rated actresses Tiffany Titters and Gemma Michaels. Following the attack, Steele was taken to Chicago's Mercy Hospital, where she was pronounced shaken but unharmed except for minor external bruising. A cadre of bodyguards provided by Whitney hustled her to O'Hare Airport where she boarded a charter jet for New York City. She was unavailable for comment upon her arrival and was whisked into a limo, also provided by Whitney.

Law enforcement officials declined to say whether or not charges would be filed against Thatcher, who was escorted by her husband Phillip, a Memphis attorney, last night from police headquarters.

In a statement to the press, he said, "My wife has been under a great deal of stress lately."

At a Brentano's bookstore in Chicago where he was autographing copies of his books for a record crowd, Dr. Prescott labeled Steele "a near martyr to America's fear of sex."

Subversive underground group of Pro-Porners bent on making pornographic materials more widely available? All we did was meet for lunch once a month and discuss how hard it is to get laid when men are sexually intimidated by you. How did I feel about this?

I glanced at my watch. Ten minutes before I needed to walk down the block to Winston's to meet Tim. I flipped the pages of the *Post.* At the bottom of page sixteen another story captured my attention. The headline read: "Porno Pretty Pays Price." Tanya Truelust, or Julie Beckman, as she was known to MasterCard and a very few others, a former porn star turned independent producer, had fallen to her death when one of her high-heeled shoes had caught in the rungs of the fire escape outside the window of her Chelsea office. She was, according to the *Post,* apparently sneaking out the window to avoid creditors lurking in the lobby.

The moral was: Don't skip out on your creditors if you're wearing high, high heels and your back door is a fire escape.

Was something wrong with this story other than its condescending tone? I felt a queasiness in the pit of my stomach. Tanya, whose erotic specialty had been exuberantly faking orgasms, had died shortly before my appearance on Olive, even perhaps as the threat to my life was being shoved under my door. Was there a connection? Or, was it only coincidence that Tanya was lying in a metal drawer in the morgue, an identifying tag around one toe, likely painted fuchsia, her signature color, as Elizabeth Thatcher's hands encircled my neck?

I shoved the *Post* down the incinerator chute on my way out of the building.

"You probably should have expected to find a reporter or two standing outside your door today," Tim said. He patted my hand, then glanced covetously at the two reporters, who'd followed me and were sitting at the bar drinking beer, to see if they were watching him comfort me. He ran his finger up and down my hand from wrist to knuckles, familiarly, seductively. Rather than look into his eyes, I scanned the room. Winston's is a tasteful blend of dark green and glowing wood, the bar a genuine antique salvaged from a local pub in which it is said the young Frank Sinatra drank back when he lived in Hoboken. Too bad the food, with the exception of the burgers, which they only serve at lunch, is so mediocre. I've often been tempted to go inside Tony's, the little Puerto Rican bar on the other side of Wayne Street, to see if they do any better.

"I know being hounded by the tabloid press doesn't feel comfortable for you, but they're only doing their job," he said in an excessively reasonable tone of voice that makes me nuts. "Do you know what I was thinking as I read this article? You are a person who elicits strong responses from people. No one reacts to you in a neutral way. You have to ask yourself, is this soliciting of strong response a behavior that I want to keep?"

"Oh, will you please stuff it? I didn't expect them to be hanging around outside my front door," I said, pulling my hand out from under his. I glanced discreetly around the room to see how many Winston's regulars, predominantly white, under thirty-five and Wall Street, were watching us. Several. "That was yesterday's news."

"We've talked about this before. You know that by doing certain things, you open yourself up for certain reactions from others. I'm not saying those reactions are fair or just," he said, raising his hand to fend off another one of our usual conversations, this being the one in which I tell him he makes me feel like there's something wrong with what I do and who I am, to which he replies, "I can't make you feel anything. You feel it; that's all."

"They just are. Reactions, that is. They own their reactions as you own your actions. And, you open yourself up to them, don't you? Besides, it isn't exactly yesterday's news. Jeremy called you today, so it's still today's news. Are you going to do his show?"

"Two glasses of white wine?" Marti, our waitress, asked. We nodded. She was staring so hard at my neck that she didn't notice we'd given the order. I had my throat swathed in an imitation Hermes scarf, green and gold saddles on cream background. She couldn't see the bruises. Tim put his hand over mine again, and again, I pulled free. "Two glasses of white wine?" she repeated.

"Yes," I said, staring her down, forcing her to look up into my eyes. "Two glasses of white wine." To Tim, I said, "I don't know about the Jeremy show. I have a meeting with Vinnie at the magazine tomorrow." Vinnie Mancuso, owner and publisher of *Playhouse* magazine, *himself* called only minutes after Jeremy, controversial star of "The Jeremy Mitchell Show," *himself* called. "He'll probably want me to do it. I'm sure that's the point of the meeting. Vinnie doesn't do meetings."

"Yo, guy, can you handle her?" a man on a barstool called out to Tim, who grinned and ducked his head. I wanted to smack him.

"How does that make you feel?" he asked.

"What? Meeting with Vinnie? Or, having that guy think you're actually fucking me? It makes me feel like telling him the truth."

"Okay," he said, blushing. "I want you to read these," he hurried on, putting a folder on the table between us. "Women like Elizabeth Thatcher shouldn't be underestimated. These articles explain the brainwashing techniques used by the leaders of these groups.

And these," he said, pointing to the second half, "describe the pathology of the participants. It's fascinating stuff."

"Uh-huh," I said, signaling for the check.

"Yee! Yee! Yee!" Tim yelped. The reporters, who'd accepted my "no comment" with grace, were nevertheless following us back down Wayne Street to my apartment, maintaining a not very discreet distance of less than six feet. "Yee! Oh, that feels good. I needed that."

"I wish you wouldn't yelp in public."

"It's good for me, sweetie. It gets my energy up. It releases that pent-up tension. You should try it. I wish you'd let me teach you a few body work exercises. You won't give it a chance."

"I'm not yelping in public, thank you."

"You don't have to—"

"I know," I said, deliberately cutting him off. We'd had this conversation too many times before. The story of my life, or lives, with men was rife with repeated conversations. It was a different conversation with each man, but always the conversation was repeated over and over again. We worried it like two old dogs with the same bone. Was it them or me? Morgy says, "Well, whose the one person who has been a part of every bad relationship I've ever had? Me!" Ouch!

"I'm sorry. I feel tense," I said to Tim, knowing this gift of a feeling, any feeling, would send him home satisfied.

"I hear what you're saying," he said. Holding me close, he tenderly kissed me good night. "I love you, sweetie," he said.

"Superlady!" yelled a man slouching in a doorway across the street. "I saw you on TV! Lookin' good,

Mama, lookin' good! You keep on doin' it to yourself, Mama!"

When I looked back over my shoulder once I was safely inside the double-locked lobby doors, Tim was waving; the reporters were right behind him, also waving . . . and so was the fan across the street.

I unlocked the three locks on my apartment door, stepped inside, and turned on the light. When my eyes adjusted, I saw it. An envelope had apparently been slipped under the door. I picked it up and opened it, expecting some communiqué from the management office. But, it was another one, the same as the first, the letters cut from glossy magazines glued on the cheapest variety of typing paper.

This one read: "Superlady, You have failed to change and you will pay with your life. You had your chance."

I started shaking as if it were January and I was on a street corner at night trying to flag a cab.

Chapter Three

Dear Ms. Steele,
How much longer will you continue to be a collaborator in the rape of your sisters? Pornography is part of an ideology of cultural sadism promoting violence against women, particularly rape. How much longer will you lend your name to a masthead led by a sexual imperialist who built his lavish lifestyle on the pain of women? You degrade yourself and all womanhood by your participation in this tawdry endeavor you call a magazine. Wake up! Refuse to be a part of the wholesale humiliation of your sex!

The letter writer had printed "member of Women Against Pornography" beneath her name, as if I couldn't have figured that out for myself. Her diatribe ran on for seven pages, a fairly typical length for a communication by a militant feminist, in tiny precise script, the kind one associates with nuns. She'd probably sent the same letter to publishers, editors, and columnists of other skin mags this month; she saw no difference in any of our products as she licked her stamps. Wouldn't she be insulted if I told her I couldn't differentiate between her and a typical WWAWAW?

Pornographic images are more varied than any of

these women like to admit. Some, like the airbrushed pets and videos which seem to be shot through a steamy mist, are idealized. Some are crude and graphic. A few are even witty. While aimed primarily at men, the erotic visualist sex, who require visual images for arousal, porn images appeal to many women—me, for example. I am aroused by pornography, by the glistening cocks moving in and out of moist and tender vaginas, by the beads of sweat, the drops of moisture on the ends of tongues poised to perform fellatio or cunnilingus. I am aroused and not ashamed to admit it.

In *Playhouse,* the women are more often than not the sexual aggressors . . . and they're always satisfied. A fantasy, yes. A *male* fantasy. What our reader really wants is to be desired by a woman whom he then satisfies beyond her wildest imagining. Under all that throbbing cock and dripping pussy terminology is the modern man's version of Sleeping Beauty and Cinderella. He wants his fairy-tale heroine to awaken him so he in turn can awaken her. But the women of WAP see nothing in material meant to arouse men except *The Story of O* carried to its ultimate climax, her death. The end point of pornography, they insist, is the violent degradation of women, possibly to their death.

We are living in censorial and confusing times. The antiporn activists seem to believe we can end rape and violence against women by censoring sexual imagery. In the Scandinavian countries and other places where "porn" is openly consumed, the national rates of rape and violence against women are far below our own. Normal, healthy heterosexual lust is constantly under attack by a strange coalition of New Sexual Puritans, who stand diametrically opposed on their other important issue, abortion.

Ironically in the same batch of mail I received a catalogue for lesbian S&M aficionados. Strap-on dildos in regular, large, extra large, and XXX. Nipple clamps.

Chains. Leather harnesses, collars, handcuffs. Whips. The usual paraphernalia also found in catalogues aimed at the heterosexual S&M market. Plus hot videos and steamy novels featuring women doing it to women the hard way. The women of WAP are strong defenders of the rights of lesbian pornographers to promote their literature and their sex-play products.

Can someone explain why lesbian S&M is okay, while men who spank women are the worst kind of sadists? Why any erotica aimed at arousing women is okay while material meant to cause an erection is not? Why lesbian women can masturbate to the smut of their choice, while if men or heterosexual women with pornographic tastes do, we're all being degraded and humiliated?

I dumped the letter and the catalogue into the trash together—there was a pleasing symmetry in the act—and shut down the computer in the tiny second bedroom I used as an office. In no other part of the country would this be considered a bedroom. I doubt a twin bed would fit into the space between these walls, but if it did, one would only have to walk into the room and fall forward onto it to be tucked away for the night. Vinnie probably didn't have a closet this small, but, lined with white shelving attached to wire mesh grids, it was perfect for my workspace.

Picking up the two threatening letters made from cut-out letters and shoving them into my bag, I turned off the light and hurried out the door for my appointment with Vinnie.

"I can't believe Vinnie's going to cut our budget," Clarissa said to the five of us through bites of cold Szechuan noodles with spicy sesame sauce. Four *Playhouse* editors were taking me out to lunch, a ratio of editors to writer which indicated my sudden importance to the organization. "I mean, it has to be just a rumor, don't you think?"

Only twenty-nine, Clarissa, a *Playhouse* senior editor, talks and looks like someone who was smoking grass in the sixties rather than playing in it in a safe New Jersey suburb. Her long, stringy brown hair, which falls forward into her face when she gets excited, missed her fork by millimeters. She paused to push hair aside, then straightened her plain wire-framed glasses on the bridge of her nose with the thumb of one stubby hand. What a little mascara and blusher wouldn't do for Clarissa.

We had been discussing Tanya Truelust's untimely death and unfortunate financial situation when Clarissa, as she is wont to do, personalized the issue.

"This couldn't happen at a worse time for us," she said. "Miriam's due practically any minute now. I haven't even told her there might be budget cuts because I'm afraid the stress of worrying about whether or not I'll get my next raise might send her into premature labor." She narrowed her eyes meanly in my direction. "But, like you don't have to worry, of course, since you're free-lance."

"If she's due any minute, then labor won't be premature," David said. "Next week you'll be begging us to break the news to her over the telephone to hurry things along."

Editor-in-chief, he paused for the predictable laugh which was his due from me and Cynthia, also a senior editor. Rhumumba, the new hire, sat at one end of the table, isolated from the rest of us who sat beside and across from each other, silently shoving moo goo gai pan into her wide mouth. She did not laugh.

"You might show a little remorse over the loss of a human life, Clarissa, a life known to most of us at this table," David admonished.

"Oh, David," Clarissa moaned, allowing a tendril of

noodle to escape from her mouth and slither down her chin. I averted my eyes from the sight and looked upward into the glowing orbs of a white dragon. These dragons with fiery eyes highlight the black and white decor of Shun Lee's, my favorite Chinese restaurant though the food critics say Shun Lee's Palace on the East Side has better food. "You always make me look like a jerk."

"I couldn't do it without your help," he responded in the most clipped and haughty tones he could interject into his pseudo-English accent while preparing to bite into a spring roll. "You lend yourself fully to the endeavor."

David Keltner, my longtime friend, despised Clarissa Chase, who along with Cynthia Moore-Epstein did most of the real work at the magazine. He would have fired her two years ago if firing her hadn't meant he'd have to edit the damn thing himself. An exceptionally intelligent man, David was not, at this point in his life, particularly ambitious. And, there was too much work for one woman to handle alone, even a woman like Cynthia of the sleek shining brown hair and double Seven Sisters backgrounds, Smith College and *Mademoiselle* magazine. It was too soon to tell how helpful Rhumumba, the epitome of the strong, silent type, was going to be. Frankly, even David, who could devastate almost anyone with one of his targeted verbal onslaughts, seemed intimidated by her, but then lesbian bodybuilders who've renamed themselves have never been his favorite people. Grumbling "the last thing the magazine needs is another lesbo writing cunt line copy," he'd agreed to hire her as a favor to somebody in the accounting office to whom he no doubt owed many favors. David abused his expense account, using it to cover family dinners and sometimes even weekend getaways for him and his wife. Vinnie's tolerance for fiscal irregularity was legendary.

"I'm not a bad person because I'm worrying about money, you know?" Clarissa whined.

"Do you think there's any truth to the rumor that Tanya was pushed?" Cynthia asked. "Tiffany Titters told me on the phone this morning that she'd heard Tanya's death may not have been an accident. Who would have wanted to kill her?"

David shrugged. For a group of people who were, however loosely, involved in the pursuit of journalism, we spent a lot of time wondering about rumors, but little time tracking them down. Like the rest of America, we were waiting for someone else to confirm our facts.

"I'm not a bad person," Clarissa repeated.

She put her fork down and crossed her arms over her chest, where surprisingly ample breasts were bound beneath a man's shirt and baggy jacket. She hides a truly spectacular body under men's clothing. I only knew about her hidden assets because I'd helped Miriam undress her once after she'd thrown up all over herself in a cab we were sharing back to Jersey City from a Christmas party at Vinnie's mansion. Vinnie frowned on excessive drinking or excessive eating for that matter. In her nervousness at being in his presence, Clarissa had put away enough of his expensive champagne to be quite spectacularly sick. She was drinking, while the rest of us wandered self-consciously, discreetly sipping from our champagne flutes, as we admired the downstairs art. The upstairs was off limits to us, protected by one of Vinnie's bodyguards at the top of the massive marble staircase, a case of decorator overkill if there ever was one. I hated the art, too heavy on religious themes. How many Virgin Mothers does one man need?

Perhaps Clarissa drank to avoid seeing in clear focus the Madonnas and cherubs lining the walls. Anyway, she couldn't get out of the cab and inside the apartment without my assistance; once there, how could I refuse to help strip her? Neither of them so much as hinted at a threesome, not that I would have. But, wouldn't you think they'd have asked?

"I'm not a bad greedy person," Clarissa said, again directly to me. "You were with me last week when I chased a homeless person to give him my leftover pizza slice. I ran after him for six blocks and he called me a 'cunt.' I'm a good person. I've never been a father before. I don't know how I'm going to afford all this. Will the cats have to go? And, on a strictly personal level, will Miriam be so busy with the baby she won't even bring me a Pepsi when I come home from the office?"

She and Miriam had the most old-fashioned marriage I'd seen since leaving the Midwest. It was, she said, patterned after her parents' marriage. Clarissa is the only person I know who claims to have had a "Leave It To Beaver" childhood and genuinely adores her parents. Miriam, who didn't work, considered herself the "wife," in the traditional sense of the word. My lesbian friends were appalled by their behavior.

"You've done it five times, David, and don't tell me you didn't have the same concerns," she said.

"I did it the old-fashioned way by shooting my own sperm directly into my wife. We didn't have to go to a clinic where she was basted like a turkey," he said with a contemptuous sniff for the artificial insemination procedure which allowed Clarissa and her lover Miriam to become parents.

"Like it was the only way to do it when you were doing it," Clarissa retorted. She had a point. David, at forty-five, had a twenty-eight-year-old daughter. His last one had just turned twenty-one.

Turning dismissively away from her, he said to me, "The meeting with Vinnie went exceptionally well, I gather?"

The meeting with Vinnie had gone well . . . and

predictably. (I hadn't shown him my threatening letters because protocol, even if your life is on the line, demands David see them first.) He'd frequently clasped my wrist by encircling it with his hand and pressing gently downward, his way of making a friendly point, as we sat side by side on the gray leather sofa in the office he rarely uses. Vinnie conducts most of his business from "The House," an Upper West Side brownstone, actually two brownstones joined in a remodeling process that created, among other splendors, the largest indoor swimming pool in the city, filling the entire basement level, where a huge bust of Caligula is the prominent sculpture.

Without once reminding me I was, at $5,000 a month, a well-paid columnist, he'd used every persuasive technique short of offering to loan me his gold chains to wear on Jeremy's show. The gold chains, worn for TV appearances only, in multiples against his mat of chest hair, clearly visible since he didn't button his shirts on these occasions higher than three inches up from the navel, were his worst fashion habit. Otherwise, he was impeccably groomed and dressed in handtailored and fairly conservative suits. He'd been using the same London tailor for decades.

How could I refuse him any request? I had an easy gig. I wrote what I wanted to write from home, coming into the office once or twice a week to get the mail and schmooze. I had plenty of time to do occasional articles for the women's magazines on sex and relationships, articles like the one I was working on for *Women Today,* which I was calling, "Why He Won't Eat You Out—And How To Make Him." They would, of course, change that to "Sex Secrets Every Wife Should Know," the title of approximately half the articles I write for the women's magazines. Without the *Playhouse* column, for which I owed David, life would be leaner.

Therefore, I once again agreed to be a "guest" on a talk show doing my part in the war against the forces of sexual repression, its battles fought mainly by women: women in silk dresses or, like me and the new breed of female X-rated video producers, short black skirts and dark stockings, or militant left-wing lesbians who never mention their sexual partner preference on their frequent "Donahue" appearances. At least, the Jesus freaks aren't leaving out the crucial part of their bios.

"I regret I can't join you and the others, Carolyn," Vinnie had said, referring to the lunch he'd arranged for me to share with my editors at Shun Lee, where Woody Allen sometimes dines. Rarely do four editors take one columnist out to lunch. The last time I'd been feted by more than one editor was the day before I began a ten-city tour representing the magazine on local talk shows from Boston to San Francisco in the wake of the Southland Corporation's decision to remove *Playhouse* from their 7-Eleven stores. Clarissa, Cynthia, and David took me to The Ginger Man to fatten me for the media kill on warm duck salad.

"This kind of controversy is good for the magazine," David said, nodding his approval. "I know you're tired of being on television, but I'm glad you're doing it. Shows admirable team spirit on your part." Unlike Vinnie, he didn't call us a "family." "Team" was his guilt-inducing noun of choice.

He turned again to Clarissa and said, "Only men can be fathers. Remember that. You may wear the pants in your family, but you can't fill the crotch."

"So what exactly did happen to Tanya?" I asked David. We were all walking back to Broadway to get a cab to the *Playhouse* offices on East 86th and Lexington, where I planned to kill an hour discussing my sex life, or lack thereof, with David behind his closed office door while Clarissa, Cynthia—and who knew if Rhumumba?—worked. Afterward, I was going to meet

Morgy for drinks before we joined her latest Eurotrash boyfriend, Georges, and Johnny Badalamenti, the drummer in my life, for a Jamaican dinner at Caribe in the West Village. David, over six feet tall and most of it in his legs, was in the lead; I scurried on high heels, burning the balls of my feet, to keep up with him. He was moving so fast, the strands of hair combed over his bald spot were rising rhythmically up and down. They couldn't blow in the wind. He used too much hair spray for that to happen.

We hurried past the regular antiporn protestor who sat at her little card table displaying the same poster she'd been using for at least two years: a nude woman, from the waist up, mouth tightly gagged and arms bound to her body, electrodes attached to her nipples. It was, according to our lawyer who after exhaustive search found the original photo, a blowup of a torture victim from the files of Amnesty International, but the good lady of the crusade would have you believe it was last month's centerfold.

"Women," she yelled, compulsively brushing the sweep of short blond dirty hair off her forehead with the hand that wasn't waving the poster, "what are you going to do about this? Men are masturbating to this every day! They're masturbating to it right now! What are you going to do about it, women?"

We were well past her when her voice got even louder and she yelled, "Hey, Superlady, you're responsible for this! Women are in pain because of you! What are you going to do about it?"

"Do you suppose she's ever had an orgasm in her life?" I asked David, who ignored the question. "She hasn't got any boobs at all. I remember noticing that last summer when she was not hanging out of her men's sleeveless ribbed undershirt, not that boobs have anything to do with orgasms."

Clarissa and Cynthia, well behind us, were picking up

speed as they approached the protestors who operated between two street vendors, one selling hot dogs and another selling used books and magazines, including several back issues of *Playhouse.* Bringing up the rear was Rhumumba, who, when viewed fleetingly over my shoulder, moved like a Russian tank, slow, placid, and formidable by reason of sheer bulk. She was wearing the tattered jeans popular with rich young West Siders, but the holes in hers revealed pieces of jumbo muscled flesh grinding as she strode.

"David?" I interrupted his concentration, obviously on something other than me. "What really did happen to Tanya?"

"Jesus, she's ugly," he said in a sotto voce voice. "I feel her back there. She feels ugly." He giggled. David is one of the few men I've ever known who genuinely giggles. "Tanya, as far as I know, fell down the fire escape. No mystery."

"You're talking about Tanya," Clarissa said, coming up behind us. "Like maybe I should write an editorial eulogizing her. What do you think? Could I submit a separate free-lance bill for it?"

I glanced at David who was rolling his eyes. Behind me, Rhumumba had narrowed hers to slits only big enough for the steam to pour out. Maybe she didn't like us talking of the dead with so little compassion. Or, maybe her jeans were cutting off the circulation in her crotch.

David and I were alone in his office, a nine by twelve square of gray and mauve, gray industrial carpet and desk chair, mauve sofa and vertical blinds. Photos of nude circus people matted on gray and mauve paper lined the walls. I particularly liked the tattooed man with the rosebud on his flaccid penis. I wondered if the rose bloomed when he got an erection. The view was of Lexington and the new HMV music superstore on the corner at 86th Street. David liked to watch the store entrance for the celebrities who frequently shopped there. He compared it to birdwatching in the wild, claiming it alleviated the boredom.

"So, what do you know about the proposed budget cuts?" I asked.

"Nothing, it's boring." He was peering out the window at the entrance to HMV. "Dr. Rita was in"—Dr. Rita, meaning Weinberg, the famous tiny sex therapist, "in" meaning shopping at HMV—"this morning. She certainly relishes her celebrity. I watched her stand outside long enough to collect a few curiosity seekers who followed her in. Tourists from Iowa, no doubt." He turned his gaze toward me. "Rhumumba is creepy. She gives me the creeps. What do you think of her?"

"Creepy."

"Exactly," he said and nodded, satisfied with my reinforcement of his critical character assessment.

"What's happening with your Hispanic?"

"Nothing."

"If you can't lure him between your thighs, he must be gay."

"I don't think he's gay." I stuck my tongue out at him. Well, maybe I was beginning to wonder if Manuel was gay, but I wasn't ready to concede the point yet. "I don't like her," I said, getting back to Rhumumba.

"I don't either." He giggled. "Maybe she won't last long."

"Does she do any work?" There was a knock at the door. "Clarissa," I whispered. "Cynthia would call from her desk."

"Come in," David said, and Clarissa did.

"David, you have to look at this, like now, because it has to be in Art, like yesterday." She manages to convey the impression of wringing her hands even when they're full, as they were then, of blue line copy. "I'm running late again. Consuela is threatening my life." She put the pile on his desk beside his propped-up feet. "So, Carolyn, what's going on with your love life? Any new action? Here," she said, tossing me a fat gray envelope stuffed with my mail. "We threw out the ones that were ticking or oozing semen."

"Sit down, Clarissa," David said, and she joined me on the sofa. No one is allowed to stand when he is sitting. They might see the bald spot on top of his head.

"Same three guys," I said breezily answering her question about my so-called "love life." Only David and Morgy knew I wasn't fucking any of them. "Nothing new."

"I miss those days," she said. "Being married is wonderful, but it has its ups and downs. Sometimes I feel really trapped. I'd like to go to a party and pick up someone, you know. I want to experience the thrill of seduction, the head rush of first-time sex. I want to light up a cigarette afterward. I can't smoke in bed anymore because Miriam's pregnant. Her stomach runs our life."

"Uterus," I said. "Her uterus runs your life, not her stomach. Didn't they teach you anything at NYU?" I begin to sound like David when I'm around him for longer than an hour. "I thought you played around in California last year when you went out to cover the lesbian S&M convention."

"She did play around," David said, not looking up at either of us from the copy in his hands. He grimaced. "Jesus, Clarissa," he said, running his pen through a cutline, as the sentence identifying a photo is known. This particular photo was of two women masturbating each other while a man, cock in hand, happily watched. Clarissa had captioned it: "Luckily, he just said, 'Well, enjoy yourselves!' "

"What a dumb line," David said. "Change that to 'Stick your fingers in the dykes, girls!' "

"Oooh," Clarissa said, "oooh, gross, exploitive, demeaning to lesbian women everywhere, oooh," running through the groaning and grimacing routine she presumably believed David expected of her in response to his editing. Then, "Oh, what's the difference," she told him, her perfunctory protest out of the way. To me, she said, "I didn't exactly play around. I flirted a lot. You know me, all talk and no action."

"What do you think of Rhumumba?" I asked.

"No fisting?" David asked Clarissa, referring to the practice of fist fucking, which is, exactly what it sounds like it would be, rough lesbian sex. "I thought that's all one did at a lesbian S&M conference."

"I'm not into S&M, you know that. I only do it to Miriam on occasion because she likes it. Like that's her taste, not mine. What am I supposed to do? Say no? If I say no, she'll get it elsewhere. Isn't that what you tell those women who write and ask you if they should suck their husbands' dicks? We don't do anything rough now with the baby and all. It changes your life. It really changes your life."

"Maybe the baby will just fall right out after years of fisting," David said, handing the copy back to her. "Get it to Consuela before she makes good her threats."

"I'm in trouble again," she said to me. "Did he tell you? He sent me another warning letter for being late." She shifted back and forth from one foot to the other and clasped her hands prayer-like in front of her chest. "But, like, I can't help it. Miriam is sick in the mornings, and she doesn't get me up on time. I don't trust her, Rhumumba, that is. There's something very weird about her. She won't tell me her birth date so I can cast her horoscope. I don't like her vibes. Something isn't true about her. Do you think she might be a corporate spy? I can see Vinnie putting someone in here to check up on us. And, like why did she give herself that name? It sounds African. She looks Irish. She's so pale, she'd look sickly if she weren't built like Mr. Universe. *Rhumumba.* I mean she sounds like a poisonous snake. Do you think she might be a transsexual?"

"Goodbye, Clarissa," David said, waving her out of the room. "Shut the door behind you." After she did, he said, "Where were we?"

"Do you think Clarissa is really putting us on with her imitation of Ward and June Cleaver doing rough sex?"

I've learned from my gay friends that a lot of swishing is done for the benefit of straights. They do love to tweak us, not that we don't deserve to be tweaked more than occasionally. He shrugged his shoulders.

"David, I have to show you something. The first one came in an express mail envelope the day I did Olive. The second one arrived the next day. And it was slid under my door while I was out."

I handed him the letters and watched him study them. If he'd seemed overly concerned, I would have panicked. He didn't.

"Damn," he said, whether in response to my hate mail or the ringing phone, I don't know. He picked up the phone. "Hello. Yes. Yes. Okay, I'll come down and look at it." To me, he said, "Five minutes. I have to check a layout."

Once a month, when the magazine closed, he almost had to work, and he hated it. He left the door open. Rhumumba's cubicle was directly across from his office. She was staring intently at her computer screen. Clarissa, the sniveling hypocrite, was standing behind her, one hand on the lesbian bodybuilder's massive shoulder. But that's Clarissa, one minute talking about someone, the next minute rubbing their back and cheering them on. She could be so irritating, but I loved her anyway, the way some people love family members in spite of their peccadilloes. I don't love any of my family members, except my kids.

Last year she sent me flowers after I'd embarrassed myself on a talk show, subject AIDS. I'd written an article for *Playhouse* based on research provided for the Center for Disease Control in Atlanta explaining exactly how AIDS is transmitted, either by blood to blood or semen to blood, making it a difficult disease to catch unless you're involved in sharing needles or rough, most likely anal, sex or have an open STD lesion. The other "guest," who won audience sympathy, was an AIDS victim claiming he caught the disease during heterosexual sex with a prostitute.

Two minutes before airtime, the host told me, "The prostitute was menstruating, and he had an open herpes sore." There we had it: Blood to blood transmission. "But he won't say that on camera, and we can't violate his confidence without being sued," the host added.

Why, except to appease the ratings god, would a journalist be a part of such deception? If people know exactly how AIDS is transmitted, aren't they more likely to take precautions to avoid it? Instilling fear of sex never stopped anyone from having sex, only perhaps from having safer, or at least more informed, sexual relations. In the last century, people died of syphilis, and women have always risked death by childbirth in having sex. Fear has never proven a path to celibacy. I was furious at the host, and I came across on TV as someone who was pissed off because her theory was being refuted. Clarissa's note enclosed with the flowers had said simply: "I understand exactly how you feel."

Waiting for David, I pulled a letter out of the envelope and opened it.

Dear Superlady of Sex,

I like to fantasize that I am petite and beautiful. In reality, I am over six feet tall, weigh almost 250 pounds, and have a very hairy body. This, I think, is why ladies' lingerie looks so strange on me . . .

Most transvestites ask one of two questions: Where can I buy lingerie in my size? How can I tell my girlfriend/wife about my secret passion for panties? My advice in general is shorter, snappier, and sassier than Zelda's ever was. It is frequently backed by the findings of sexologists and also more practical. In some cases, I provide shopping or acquisition information. I have more female readers too than she ever did.

When I advised a panty sniffer (a man whose fetish, upon which his arousal and ejaculation is dependent, is used women's panties) to stop raiding his female friends' laundry hampers and suggested he pay someone to provide him with her worn panties on a regular basis, I was inundated with letters from women readers offering their panties via the mail.

Letter Number Two.

Dear Superlady of Sex,

Can you tell me once and for all the proper way to measure a penis? Along the topside to the tip? Or, along the underside? And, do you measure that flaccid or erect?

Penis size. The American male obsession. Measured topside when erect, end to tip, five to seven inches is the norm. I sifted through the envelopes. Out of approximately one hundred, there would be at least ten about penis size. Half would want to know if they were too small. *Does she fail to have an orgasm because I'm not big enough? (No. The almighty penis has little or nothing to do with the female "o." Haven't you guys ever heard of the clitoris?) Do those penis enlargers work? (No, Vernon, there is no penis enlarger.)* The other half would tell me their whoppers of nine, ten, and twelve inches were more than their women could handle. (According to Kinsey, less than two percent of American males have a penis measuring more than seven inches when erect. Isn't it funny they all write to me?)

Then, I saw the envelope, with the familiar handwriting. Something wasn't quite right about it, but at the time I didn't notice what it was. Starred Man had been writing to me for over a year, approximately one letter a month. We called him Starred Man because he drew a careful five-point star before each paragraph.

I opened the envelope and pulled out five sheets of lined yellow legal pad paper, his stationery. The first paragraph was always the same:

Dear Superlady Carolyn,

**Do you like hairy chests? I have a very hairy chest. I like your picture. I touch my hairy chest and then I touch my hairy balls and then I jerk off while I look at your picture.*

Mentally I was wrinkling my nose in distaste. Philosophically, I endorse the right of perverts everywhere to have an outlet for their sexual expression, as long as they don't hurt anyone physically or psychologically. I understand how isolated from the family of American heterosexuals who do it on Saturday night in the missionary position the transvestite, the fetishist, even the lesbian S&M aficionado must feel. Having been isolated from my own frozen WASP family shortly after discovering my clitoris, I identify with them. But, personally, I don't like getting mail from convicts who masturbate to my picture. This is the existential paradox of my career as a sex advice columnist.

My correspondents are too often even less appealing than the high-school retard who ate his own boogers. Imagine how you would have felt at sixteen if he had a crush on you. Then imagine how you'd feel to discover he took your yearbook photo to prison with him after he'd bashed his grandmother's head in . . . and you'll have a glimmering of the feelings Starred Man aroused in me.

In the back of my mind is a tiny seed of paranoia, the fear I'll find myself sitting across from one of these guys on the subway some day. I would never want to be that close to someone who masturbates to my picture. I shoved his letter to the bottom of the envelope as David came back into the office.

"Starred Man?" he asked. "Copy it before you go so I can file it." David had a file of "strange" mail; to be qualified as "strange" among our readers took some doing. He kept the file, he said, in case some pervert ever came after any of us. Then, he would have something to turn over to the police. Comforting thought. "Where were we?"

"I can't remember," I said. We were both looking at the two letters in the center of his desk. "Talking about my sex life, I guess."

"What sex life?" We giggled. "Tell me about your latest favorite masturbatory fantasy," he ordered, sitting down in his chair, propping his feet on the pristine desk. His eyes were on the entrance to HMV. "Did I tell you Madonna was in last week? I wouldn't have recognized her without the binoculars. Her hair's black now. Without makeup, she's not much. The bodyguards around her tipped me off. Now, talk."

He'd already heard my anal sex fantasy. I decided to give him oral. I always wondered if he got an erection listening to my erotic tales, but he would never tell me if he did or not. Either answer could be, he said, construed as an insult. Anyway, before we were halfway through my projected monologue, Steve Martin showed up at HMV and then Clarissa burst into the room.

"You won't believe this," she said. "I've heard the most bizarre and wild rumor. Vinnie's new operations manager is planning massive staff cutbacks. I can't believe it, can you? That's even worse than having our raises on the line and no free lunches. Now, it's our jobs. I feel so threatened—not, of course, that you have anything to worry about."

"Clarissa," David said, frowning, shooing her back out the door as he spoke, "no one is indispensable."

A few minutes later as I got up to leave, he put his hand over the two letters and said, "You'd better let me keep this. Vinnie has to be informed."

Chapter Four

"I know who you are," said the young Puerto Rican woman, and she pronounced "you" like "Jew."

She'd been eyeing me curiously since we both got on the train at 86th Street. Dressed in high-heeled black ankle-strap shoes with open toes, a skintight hot pink sweater, and equally snug white ankle-length pants, she was sitting across from me on the Lexington Avenue train going downtown. Didn't her mother ever tell her not to wear those pants in November even if it is unseasonably warm? Normally people are packed tight in the aisles of the subway car during rush hours, but this train was only comfortably full. We passengers had the luxury of viewing in addition to inhaling each other. Damn the luck.

"You were on the tel-e-vi-sion," she said, separating the syllables of the word in the pleasingly melodic way New Yorkers of Puerto Rican descent often talk. "I know you were. You were on that Olive show where the lady got choked."

I didn't say anything. She looked harder at me. I pulled the letter I'd been reading closer to my body, while keeping it angled so the rotund bald white man beside me with the garlic breath couldn't read it. Do only white men get bald and fat in the middle and wheeze garlic, or does it just seem that way?

"Weren't you on that show?" she asked. The people on either side of her, a young black woman with huge triangle-shaped golden earrings in her ears and a middle-aged white woman dressed in typical Evan Picone black and white separates and black patent leather flats, were watching me now, too. "You could answer me, you know," she said, which came out, "Jew could answer me Jew no."

"No," I said. "I wasn't."

That appeared to satisfy the others, who averted their gaze, but not my interrogator. She stared me down. I could feel her eyes boring into me as I, the first to look away, continued reading the letter in my hand. Thank the Goddess we were at 23rd Street. Only two more stops before mine.

Dear Superlady of Sex Steele,

My girlfriend has a gorgeous body but she is shy about showing it in public. It turns me on to see other men watching her strut her stuff in high heels, tight, short dress exposing plenty of cleavage. I would really like it if she would go out sometimes in garter belt and stockings without panties and sit on a bar stool so she can flash guys at my command. She thinks I'm sick . . .

There was more, but the writer basically wanted to know how to persuade his girl to act out his erotic fantasy. *(Buy the clothes you want her to wear in public. Bring flowers when you give the clothes to her. Tenderly dress her and later, just as tenderly, undress her; then make wild, passionate love, paying particular oral attention to her clitoris. And, not to worry, you aren't sick. Many men are aroused by the sight, or fantasy, of other men lusting after, or even making love to, their women. Men are erotic visualists, primarily aroused by what they see. But, you may not get her to go along with the flash-*

ing, at least not the first time up on the bar stool.) A lot of my mail falls into the category of How Can I Get Her/Him To Do What I Want? In one way or another, I tell them: You have to give to get.

"I know I saw you on tel-e-vi-sion," the young woman persisted.

You know what they say about Puerto Rican women: They dress hot for the street, but act cool in the bedroom, because their men like it that way. In other words, they are the flip side of the ideal WASP woman. Or, so I hear. The women beside her looked back at me, their interest growing. Suddenly I recognized them for who they really were: typical members of an "Olive" audience after a few months on Ultraslimfast. Recognizing the look of the judgmental woman in their eyes, I began getting nervous. By this point, my accuser and I had the attention of nearly everyone in that end of the car. A motley crew, they looked back and forth from one of us to the other. If she'd pulled a knife, they'd have watched her stab me.

"I know it," she said firmly. "I am never wrong about a face."

"You have me confused with someone else," I said, stuffing the letter back into the gray envelope. My heart was beating faster, and my palms were beginning to sweat. I felt my neck begin to itch beneath the red, black, and gold imitation Hermes scarf wrapped around it. You never want to be identified as a woman who likes sex, for whom sexual pleasure comes easy, in any public place in America, unless security guards are present. Americans get very angry at women who like sex. You particularly do not want to be identified as such on a subway train. "You're wrong," I said.

"No, I'm not," she insisted. The chime sounded; and the doors closed, making a sucking noise. Eighteenth Street. I debated getting out. I stayed in my seat. I should have gotten out. "You were the one who got choked."

Looking straight ahead, I didn't say anything. I wanted to pull the scarf closer to my neck. Were the bruises showing? I wondered. I sat stiffly, feeling the sweat bead above my upper lip. Though I deliberately didn't focus my eyes on any of them, I knew they were watching me. I could smell their collective body temperature rising. The train squealed to a halt at 14th Street, one stop away from my destination. Should I get out here anyway? I should have gotten out, but I didn't. I was afraid someone would intuit that I was forced off the train before my stop by fear. Show fear, and they'll go after you.

"She was the one who got choked," the Puerto Rican woman said conversationally to the white woman beside her like they'd been chatting on a daily basis all their lives. I wiped the sweat away from my upper lip before it ran into my mouth, discreetly masking the swipe as a scratching of my nose. "She was, I don't remember, some kind of sex maniac. And this other woman, she went *loco* because *that* one"—out of the corner of my eye, I saw her finger pointed at me—"drove her *loco* with sex talk. And then this other woman, she choked *that* one!" Again, I had to dab my upper lip. My head was sweating, and I was afraid trickles would begin to pour down my face at any moment. "It was some show," she finished. "You didn't see it?"

"No," the woman replied, her eyes, like all the others, fastened on me.

"A sex maniac, huh?" said a white man clasping the strap almost directly over my head. He leered at my legs, encased in black stockings, exposed to almost midthigh in black leather miniskirt, my legs crossed high above the knee, Mary Hart fashion. "Whoa! How about that?" he said. The "Whoa" came out on a rush of bad breath; he didn't look like he'd been draining the city's water supplies with long hot showers lately. "I'm a sex maniac, too!"

The train pulled into my station, and I stood, pushed past him, and hurried toward the door. On my way out, I looked into the eyes of the Puerto Rican woman. She hated me.

"Whore!" she yelled. "Fucking high-class white whore!"

"Aren't you somebody?" the waitress at Caribe asked when she put the banana daiquiri down on the bar in front of me. Morgy laughed. "Sorry," said the waitress, tall, slender, Jamaican, and gorgeous, probably an aspiring actress or model or actress/model like most of the Village waitresses. She put another banana daiquiri down in front of Morgy. We removed the chunks of banana from the edges of the glasses. Morgy discarded hers, and I ate mine. "I guess everybody is *somebody.* Haven't I seen you somewhere?" she quizzed me. "In the movies?"

"No," I said through a mouthful of banana. "I come in here a lot."

"Oh," she said dubiously. "Sure. You want your privacy."

"Front page of the *Post* yesterday," the bartender said from the other end of the bar. He was coming back from the tiny hallway containing the two unisex johns and a phone. "The sex woman who got strangled on 'Olive.' "

"Oh," the waitress said, obviously disappointed, because she was savvy enough to know you don't have to be somebody to get on "Olive." She turned to the bartender and said, "Two more of these things for the couple down there," and went back to waiting tables. I love the West Village.

"I knew it was you right away as soon as I saw the picture," the bartender called. "I said to my buddy who was with me at the time, 'She's a regular at the restaurant. Can you believe it?' My buddy said, 'She almost wasn't a regular anywhere anymore.' "

He laughed, so I felt obliged to join him in a tepid chuckle.

"Well, Carolyn, you really did it this time," Morgy said in a perfect imitation of the line I usually give her when she's reached the crisis point in a romance, delivered the way Donna Reed spoke in that smarmy old TV sitcom, like words popping out of bubbles from the mouth. "Yes, you really did!"

She unbuttoned the jacket of her tastefully small-patterned black and white check suit, exposing the elegant red silk blouse beneath, kicked off her three-inch black and white spectator slings, and hooked her black stocking clad toes around the bar stool we'd left between us for Georges. Johnny, who was having new still photos made, was going to arrive last; we'd agreed to sit at the bar until Georges joined us where we would all drink banana daiquiris, specialty of the house, until Johnny got there when we would get a table. Johnny doesn't sit at bars. Leaving my shoes on, I put my feet on the other side of the bar stool so she and I were facing each other.

"We aren't going to talk about it anymore," I said. We had relentlessly analyzed every detail of the "Olive" episode in a two-hour phone conversation the day before, which was more time than we'd devoted to the meeting of Georges, if you can believe it. "I'm sick of the whole subject."

"Right," she agreed, casting a covert glance over my shoulder at the bartender who was conversing with the couple at the end of the bar. "They are all looking at us.

But, it's New York. Next week somebody else will be Dead Meat of the Week and you'll be forgotten."

"Thanks. I feel better."

"What are friends for?"

She took a huge sip of daiquiri. Morgy eats and drinks with wild abandon, yet remains a perfect size six. I have never seen another woman eat food the way Morgy does. She makes love to it, then devours it. I can imagine what she must be like with a penis in her mouth. I'm her only real female friend. Other women hate her, both for her ability to eat and drink without gaining weight and the effect she has on men. Morgy's face is so beautiful she renders the rest of us invisible to the male gaze. I took a smaller sip of my drink.

"Georges is titillated by this," she said. "He was afraid you'd cancel out of dinner tonight. When I told him you weren't, he goes, 'Oh, Morgan, that is so excellent!' *Excellent.*"

She put her first finger in front of her open mouth in the simulated gagging signal, normally reserved for her descriptions of first date experiences with the kind of men who would probably become devoted and adoring in two dates or less. They make her sick. She breaks dates with them or stands them up. Standing people up, usually men, but sometimes even women friends, is a bad habit we share. I have gone through periods lasting up to several weeks of standing up more men than I've actually met for dinner. You don't know the true meaning of the phrase "Feeling like a jerk" unless you've ever sat beside your answering machine listening to a man call for the third time from a restaurant pay phone asking what happened to you. Yes, we know it's passive-aggressive behavior. We've had therapy. And still I had the urge to slam bills on the counter to pay for our drinks, grab Morgy's arm, and drag her out of there. We could be quietly eating Italian food two blocks away by the time Georges arrived at Caribe.

"I want to hear him speak in French, but Georges loves our slang," she complained. "Does he think I'm dating him so I can talk to an American college kid?"

"Why are you dating him?" I asked.

"The same question could be asked of almost everyone either one of us has ever dated," she said, signaling the bartender for another round though I was only one-quarter down on my drink. "Remember the older man I dated who sat on the edge of the bed taking his pulse after sex? Or, Ron—we both dated him, remember?—who had a two-inch penis and a size triple large sexual ego?

"Georges is good in bed."

"Well, yes, that is a consideration," I said; we both laughed at the implied reminder of my lack of sex life. "I can remember when I dated men for sex. I can almost remember when I *had* sex."

Actually, I could remember very well. I'd had some wonderful sex, just not lately. Orgasmic ecstasy had ended for me at thirty-nine. There was Ray, whose exquisite technique of lightly flicking his tongue across my clitoris reminded me of being ravished by butterflies. And Gordon who ate pussy with so much relish he could leave even me limp from orally induced orgasms. And Jack, a much younger lover, who had surprised me the first time we were in bed by positioning himself so he could eat me out as he simultaneously angled his beautiful large penis into my mouth. Many men have tried to pull off that maneuver so adroitly, but few have succeeded. And, there was . . .

Shifting uncomfortably on my bar stool, I turned my attention back to Morgy. She was at the beginning with Georges. Her relationships are confined to two groups of men: "bad boys," men with dangerous drinking, drug, or sex habits who don't earn money but do spend hers, or "losers," men who lose substantial sums of other people's money, including hers, in entrepreneurial schemes. These adventures in sex and adversity typically last less than six months and are followed by brief celibate periods in which she verbally flagellates herself for "being wild." Her two major love groups, which sometimes overlap, have lately been composed largely of Eurotrash, like Georges recently of Paris, Rome, and Madrid, beach bums like the Portuguese sailor she picked up on vacation in Bermuda, or garden-variety users with strong manly profiles and the desire to be a beach bum or have a Eurotrash accent, like the graphic designer who cost her $10,000 last year. Her affairs begin on a pheromone high. Initially, she says, "It's only going to be sex. It's only going to be fun." Then, she gets *involved.* Morgy has a lot of sex, the kind of wild sex people assume I'm having, but I secretly think she feels guilty about most of it. Why else would she get *involved* with those guys? Why else submit herself to the post-romance punishment cycle?

"It's getting intense with Georges," she said. "But, I'm trying to keep things moving at a slower pace than usual for me."

"Tornadoes move at a slower pace than you do."

"Right," she said, taking another huge sip of daiquiri and holding it in her mouth before swallowing, the way a smoker holds the smoke from a joint before exhaling. "I'm learning at The Forum that I rush into relationships because I don't value myself enough. I give away my power."

"And your money," I reminded her.

She nodded enthusiastically and launched into an explanation of how giving away your money was part of giving away your power was part of giving away yourself. Or, something like that. Recently she'd fallen victim to The Forum, Werner Erhard's new, improved version of Est, the training that is "not an answer, but an opening," "an inquiry into being human," and the "path to excellence." Now she had her own new set of buzz words, verbal playthings with which to impress listeners with her newly acquired self-knowledge. I wasn't impressed. In fact, I was only half-listening as she said something about "the conversational tape playing in my head that keeps me from achieving my full potential," followed by how her "act," the way she presented herself to the world, was keeping her down. Or, holding her back. One or the other.

Less touchy-feely, primal-scream oriented than Est, Forum is a philosophy of how to get more out of life acceptable to baby boom professionals looking less for inner serenity than a kinder, gentler version of the Gordon Gecko Creed from *Wall Street:* Greed is Good. They encourage professional success at The Forum. How else could you pay for all those seminars? At least, she wasn't into something really disgusting like body work.

"You aren't listening," Morgy accused. "You think just because you dated a guy who did The Forum that you know everything there is to know about it. You don't. He did it wrong."

I nodded and continued not listening. Maybe he did it wrong, and she was doing it right. But they both sounded like they'd swallowed the same "conversational tape." Following the first "intense" weekend seminar, in which the participants are allowed minimal sleep opportunities and only periodic trips to the rest room, the better to convince them they've had a tremendous experience because it feels so good when it's over, the neophyte self-improvers signed up for additional seminars and begin hounding all friends and acquaintances with expendable income to attend a Monday night meeting as a "guest," subject to a high-intensity sales pitch from a Forum group leader that makes a Baptist revival preacher's "Come down to the altar and take Jesus as your personal saviour!" look reserved. (I know. He conned me into going with him once.) Yes, the whole process had much in common with AA or a WWAWAW "commitment to life and purity" weekend.

"I wish you'd come with me as my guest to a meeting," she said for perhaps the fifth or sixth time in recent weeks. "You didn't give it a fair chance."

"I'll get my self-improvement for a few dollars from the women's magazines, thank you very much," I said.

"Anyway," I continued, changing the subject while her mouth was full of daiquiri, "I told you Tanya Truelust is dead, didn't I?" She nodded affirmatively. "There are rumors it wasn't an accidental fall, which is ridiculous, of course. But, it makes me feel more vulnerable knowing that Tanya Truelust met with an unpleasant end while I—and, is it a coincidence?—have received two death threats. Maybe a cosmic force is at work."

"You know the most interesting people, Carolyn," she said, patting the gray envelope next to my handbag on the bar and graciously relinquishing her new favorite subject for the moment. "Any good mail?"

"Another letter from Starred Man," I said, and she winced. Morgy was convinced he was going to break out of prison some day and come find me. I had real problems and she was focusing on the danger presented by a drooler behind bars. "I've only opened a few, but nothing particularly amusing yet."

"Let me peek," she said, and I magnanimously waved her on. I sipped delicately while she opened envelopes and scanned letters for something good. "Who are these women who don't do anal sex?" she asked. "I do anal sex. I always do anal sex. It happened right away with Georges. He sort of slipped it in that way without even asking, and now it's all he wants to do. I like it, but, I mean, something else would be nice, too."

"Uhmm," I said noncommittally. The bartender was hovering nearby; I'm sure he was eavesdropping.

"Okay," she said, waving a letter triumphantly, "here it is! I'll just read the good parts.

" 'Dear Superlady,' she began reading in a low voice rippling with suppressed laughter. " 'My husband is a foot fetishist. I have accepted this until now, but it's gotten worse, and I want to become pregnant. The problem is he only ejaculates on my feet. When we got married, he began lovemaking with my feet but moved into my pussy. Now, he has gotten lazy and just stops at the feet. What can I do to get him where I need him to be to make a baby?' " Morgy looked at me. "Well, Superlady, what are you going to tell her?"

"She has to bring her foot closer to her pussy, of course, and then maneuver him inside her before he ejaculates. What could be easier?"

"Divorce," Morgy said. She was already looking for another letter suitable for reading out loud.

"I'll also suggest sex therapy," I said.

"Carolyn," she said, "look at the envelope to Starred Man's letter."

She held it up in front of my face. And then I saw what had only registered subliminally when I'd opened his letter in the office. In place of the usual prison stamp in the right-hand corner was an ordinary postage stamp. His most recent letter had been mailed from somewhere other than the safe confines of a state prison.

"This wasn't mailed from the prison," she said. "He's *out!* And look it was mailed ten days ago. He could be sending you those death threats. The time frame works."

I took it from her and checked the postmark, Albany, where the prison was located. Maybe he gave it to a friendly guard to mail on the way home for him.

"You should have listened to Tim when he researched the pathology of sex criminals," she said.

"We don't know that Starred Man is a sex criminal.

He's never told me why he's in prison, Morg. Maybe he's an armed robber, not a sex criminal."

"Would he be writing to you if he wasn't? Look, you ignore Tim's research, because you think he's a geek, which he is, but, like, he does have some point to make. If Starred Man is a sexual deviant who's obsessed with you, which he clearly is, he may come after you as soon as he has a chance, which apparently now he does."

I was about to say something meant to reassure both of us when I felt a hand on my shoulder. Jerking away, I almost fell off the bar stool.

"Carolyn, darling," Georges said. "I'm so sorry to disconcert you. After what has happened to you on that television show, I should have never approached you from behind."

Surrounded by huge tropical trees in various stages of leaf loss, we were the kind of dinner foursome a charitable person labels "interesting," a mismatched and eccentric group largely speaking at, rather than to, each other. If I were going to do a modern art rendition of us, I would title it, *Egos at the Trough.* Georges, who radiates the kind of raw sexuality I associate with men who won't perform cunnilingus, peppered his speech with sexual innuendoes and foreign phrases in French, Spanish, and Italian. Morgy was so anxious for Georges to enjoy himself and make a better impression on me than he had the first time we'd dined together that she was babbling, much of it in Forumese.

More silent than usual, I was preoccupied with myself. Was Starred Man stalking the streets of New York or New Jersey in search of me? Could he possibly be responsible for the death threat letters? Did that couple at the next table recognize me? And was my scarf slipping? As his contribution to the evening's hilarity,

Johnny told a lot of corny jokes, always prefaced with, "Have you heard the one about . . . ?"

I met Johnny Badalamenti when I was sitting at a table near the stage one night at The Blue Note with my visiting nephew, the jazz aficionado. Johnny reminded me a little of Harrison Ford. I smiled at him a lot; he smiled back. He sweat profusely as he drummed. When he took a bow, he sprinkled me with the moisture from his brow, which, I'm embarrassed to admit, I found sexy. During their break, he sent me a note via a waitress. It read, "Do you ever go out with men your own age? If so, give me a call," and he'd put his phone number on it. Thoroughly charmed, I called him. That, however, was the only clever and original thing he ever said to me. Thirty minutes into our first conversation, I suspected he copied the idea from some other band member who'd once used it to pick up an older woman sitting with a younger man.

On our first date, we spent six and a half hours at Arturo's on West Houston where, after saying, "I knew you were thinking I looked like Harrison Ford; everybody tells me that," he told me the story of his life. He was forty-five, and he took both his life and the retelling of it one day at a time. The question I'm still asking myself: Why did we ever have a second date?

"Have you heard the one about the midget with the big balls?" Johnny asked, a forkful of jerk pork poised above his plate.

I had to smile encouragement, because no one else was listening to him. He launched into his joke, which he would conclude by saying ba-da-da while air-drumming. While smiling at him the way Nancy Reagan smiled at Ron, I listened to Morgy and Georges.

"All people are secretly afraid of rejection," Morgy said to Georges. "Do you know how liberating it is when you realize an entire roomful of people are just as secretly afraid of rejection as you are?"

"You know," he replied, "I once lived with a woman in France who wore her hair the way you do." Morgy's haircut is a short cap of blunt-cut hair shaped to her head with a full sweep of bang worn to the left. Is that French? "Utterly delightful, *mon chéri amour.*"

He took one of her hands and sandwiched it between both of his briefly, then lifted it to his lips and kissed. That would surely have her reaching for her wallet when the bill was presented.

". . . ba-da-da," Johnny finished, air-drumming the space between us.

"You'd understand me better if you came to a meeting with me," Johnny said again. "I know you think it's all about God, but it isn't. It's about a higher power. Your higher power can be the group. It can be a light bulb if you want. You just have to accept your own powerlessness and put your faith in the higher power."

He was pouting. We were in a cab headed toward a church on Bleecker Street where an open AA meeting was being held. Recovering alcoholics are allowed to bring guests to open meetings. Johnny had been a recovering alcoholic for five years, and he still attended five or six meetings a week. He knew this particular meeting was "open" because he'd excused himself during dinner to make a phone call to find out. While he was still on the phone, Morgy had excused herself to use the rest room, but she'd actually settled the bill with the waitress. Caribe only takes cash, and she hates to put down cash rather than her gold AmEx because she thinks cash embarrasses her dates. Gold cards send "clean, neutral messages," she says.

While Johnny and Morgy were both gone from the table, Georges had told me, "I've wanted to spank you from the moment I met you, Carolyn. Tell me you have been thinking of this, too."

I was whispering savagely to him, "I haven't been thinking of this at all," when Johnny and Morgy came back to the table. They didn't seem to notice anything awry. The four of us hugged goodbye like two suburban married couples and split for two separate cabs.

"I'm tired, Johnny," I said as our cabdriver gracefully swerved to avoid rear-ending another cab. "I'll drop you off at the meeting, then go to the PATH stop. It's been a long day."

"You know," he said, grasping my hand fervently, "we could have fallen into bed. That would have been the easy thing to do, but I want us to get to know each other. I want a relationship. Sex can get in the way. It can be an addiction like booze. It can mess up your mind and lead you into stinkin' thinkin' again."

"I understand," I said.

"I want you to know me," he said, but I already knew him.

I already knew, for example, after six months of sporadic sexless dating that he seethed with thwarted ambition. He was damned mad because Harrison Ford *was* Harrison Ford, and he wasn't. I also knew he swam at the Y daily to keep in shape, auditioned for bit parts in movies, and had recently acquired a library card and checked out only large print books because he could read them faster than the other books. More to the point, I didn't have to attend a meeting to hear his "drunkalogue," the story of how low he'd sunk before surrendering to his powerlessness over the bottle. He'd told me, and there wasn't much more to know about Johnny than this paltry accumulation of facts. I wanted to fuck him, but I didn't want to know any more about him.

"I'm flattered, Johnny, I really am," I said. "And I do want to know you, but not tonight."

The cabdriver pulled over in front of the church. Johnny kissed me passionately. Then, he leaped from the cab like a character in a movie which is, of course, what he wanted to be. I was left holding the tab.

The PATH (short for Port Authority Trans Hudson) is the subway running beneath the Hudson River connecting Manhattan with Jersey City and Hoboken. It's cleaner and generally considered safer than the New York subway. Its bell has a slightly different chime. Rarely do I feel uneasy riding it, but I did that night.

I cast surreptitious glances at the other riders, particularly the women. They were mostly wannabe Yuppies, probably entry level financial district workers, women who surely didn't watch "Olive." I relaxed a little. Then the thought occurred to me: They might watch "Olive" if they were home with the flu, and everybody reads the *Post* sometimes. Clutching my gray envelope of mail to my chest, I discreetly kept my eye on them.

I wasn't exactly depressed, but I was feeling subdued. And why not? A deranged right-wing woman had tried to strangle me on national TV. A pervert and fan was possibly out of prison. I'd been insulted by a young woman on a subway. My best friend's latest repulsive boyfriend harbored fantasies of spanking me. I'd received two letters threatening my life. A woman I knew slightly was dead in unpleasant circumstances. It would have been easy to make fun of Tanya/Julie dying because she was delinquent in paying her bills, but who hasn't been delinquent in paying their bills?

By the time I got off the PATH at Grove Street, I felt sufficiently paranoid to walk fast to the point of nearly sprinting until I was safely inside my apartment building on Wayne Street. Or was I safe here? Somehow someone had broken the sanctity of my double-locked building to leave one of his or her acid missives. I held my breath on the last stretch of stairs and didn't let it out until I'd opened my apartment door and found nothing waiting on the carpet for me.

Feeling as bad as I did, I knew there were only two things I could do to feel worse: eat an entire carton of deep fudge peanut butter Steve's Gourmet Ice Cream . . . or call Tim.

"How did that make you feel?" he asked me after I told him about the Puerto Rican woman who'd called me a "whore" on the subway.

"Unpopular," I said, sighing.

"That's good," he said, "that's real."

After a few more minutes of listening to him feel, I hung up the phone mid-feeling and ignored the immediate ringing afterward. I felt sick to my stomach. Maybe it was the banana daiquiris and conch fritters. No, it was Tim.

"I'm never going to talk to him again," I promised myself, and I kept the promise. I'm really very good at eliminating people from my life. According to my older siblings, nobody does it better or worse, depending on how you feel about the process of elimination.

Resolutely, I rewound the tape on my answering machine and played back my messages. David. Clarissa. My sister, Jenny.

And this one is a high, tight voice that could have been a woman's under duress or a man's if he were trying to sound like a woman. She, or he, said: "You are going to pay with your life. I will see to that. Don't think you will get away with what you have done, because you won't."

Chapter Five

Dear Superlady of Sex,

My boyfriend likes to do it to me before I wake up in the morning. He says I shouldn't mind because coming is a great way to wake up. What makes him think I come? What should I do about this little annoying habit of his?

Dear Sleepyhead,

Unless you are faking in your sleep, I don't know why he would think you are having an orgasm. Maybe the orgasms you have with him are real snoozers, and he can't tell the difference, awake or asleep. This is not my idea of an annoying little habit. His forgetting to put the cap on the toothpaste is an annoying little habit. This is extremely selfish behavior. Tell him if he wants morning sex, he will have to wake your pussy first. And, insist he brush his teeth. Morning mouth is offensive everywhere.

I'd just added the "Morning mouth is offensive" line when Clarissa called. It had been a successful morning in which I'd pushed the afternoon's taping of "The Jeremy Mitchell Show" out of my head as I worked and also decided to dump Johnny Badalamenti before I did end up at an open AA meeting listening to numerous drunkalogues as long and monotonous as his, told by men who all end their stories with "ba-da-da." Sometimes Johnny didn't call for days anyway. He would barely notice he was being dumped, especially if he had a few good weeks where he happened to be walking past a lot of mirrors or clean and large plate glass windows, equally good at giving him back what he most needed from the world. I could keep putting him off until he had forgotten my phone number, a matter of weeks at most, probably more like days.

"What?" I asked irritably as soon as I recognized Clarissa's voice.

"You aren't going to believe this. Madame Zelda is dead."

She paused long enough for my brain to provide a cause of death. Heart attack. It had to be a heart attack. The author of *The Classy Call Girl's Guide To Pleasing Men,* the first modern sex guide, published in the late 60s, Zelda was America's first celebrity hooker. Her advice column, written for the past three years by Clarissa who didn't even run the copy past Zelda, had been in every issue of *Playhouse* since the magazine was born, accompanied by the original photo of her as blond, young, and gorgeous. In the last five years of her life, she'd doubled her body weight, shaved her head, given up men, and gone into a seclusion that was only interrupted by visits from lesbian lovers and her clients, the men she whipped. She was a dominatrix. Perhaps that had been too strenuous for an overweight woman.

"Well," Clarissa prodded, "aren't you going to ask for the details?"

I did, but Clarissa's details were sketchy. Zelda had been found dead in her hot tub, apparently drowned. End of details and on to the real issue: How does this affect Clarissa?

"Heart attack in the hot tub?" I asked.

"Do you think her column has to die with her? Like

I need that money, you know? Maybe Vinnie can keep it out of the papers. Wouldn't it embarrass the magazine? And who cares that a three hundred-pound lesbian dom with a shaved head died in her hot tub? As far as the world has to know, she was Stella Mae Parks, not Zelda. Zelda can't die. She's an institution." She paused and added meanly, "Not that you care. Now you'll be the new Queen of Sex Advice."

The call waiting signal beeped; knowing it was David, I told Clarissa I'd get back to her.

"She was cooked," he said. "Can you imagine that? Cooked. All that fat boiled. The man who tends the plants found her floating like a bright red beached whale." I closed my eyes, feeling momentarily nauseous. I'd been to Zelda's house, an A-frame overlooking the Hudson with a huge hot tub in the greenhouse. "It's disgusting, isn't it?" he asked.

"Was she alone when she died?"

"Rumor has it she'd been involved in a heavy S&M scene before the hot tubbing. Maybe whoever she'd been whipping left before they got into the tub or ran away in a panic after she got in and died. Apparently the combination of exertion, heat, and overweight killed her. There was also something wrong with the heating unit. The water was too hot."

I was relieved that I had to hang up to dress for television before David began to speculate on the temperature at which human flesh begins to cook. More the fool, I. What Olive had launched ten days before, Jeremy supplied with additional rocket fuel.

Dear Superlady of Sex,

For the longest time, my boyfriend asked me to suck him while he was driving on the freeway. I didn't want to do it because of the danger involved. What if he lost control of the car as well as his sexual responses? But I finally did. He loved it so much, he wants it every time we drive. Also, now he wants me to not wear panties and put my feet up on the dashboard, hike my skirt, and let the passing drivers see me flashing them. Next he will want me to masturbate in the car. What do you say?

"What will you tell her?" asked Tina, Jeremy's makeup person, a skinny gum-popping brunette, early twenties, with the kind of "high hair," large and teased up, up, up, and away, favored by Staten Island and Jersey girls. Her own makeup was minimal, except for the kohl-lined eyes framed by lashes which had been individually coated with some kind of miracle lengthening mascara. She was reading over my shoulder as she applied my blusher. Was she using too much? Would I look like I was highly embarrassed for the entire hour?

Jeremy's producer had asked me to bring some letters, "Not to read on air, of course, just for him to wave at the camera during his intro of you." If I had to bring them, I might as well be reading them and formulating the answers in my mind.

"Yes, he will definitely want the masturbation scene next," I said in reply to Tina's question. "And she should not try this when the pavement is slick."

"Men! Do you get a lot of this sort of question?" She dipped her fingers in gel she'd thinned with water and attempted to create curls around my face. The tiny curls began to go straight almost as soon as her fingers moved away from them. Later, I would feel like a border of hair was glued to my face. "I'm glad I don't live where you have to drive to get places. It's bad enough they want you to fuck in the back of cabs. I can't see having some guy's dick in my mouth while he's got my life in his hands."

"A profound sentiment," I said, and she nodded thoughtfully.

I tucked the letters back inside the gray envelope

before she started working on my eyes. Imagine being blinded by a mascara wand because the woman wielding it couldn't take *her* eyes off a letter from some guy in Omaha who wanted to know why his wife didn't like the way he ate her out.

Made-up in thick ivory pancake and lipstick the color of "an overripe watermelon," the shade I should always wear according to Tina, I winced at the sleaze king's intro to the show.

"Stay tuned for 'Crimes of Passion,' what some people have done for love or at least for what was considered love in their eyes."

Crimes of Passion? They'd told me the theme was "Fear of Sex." My hand went involuntarily to the lavender, green, and sapphire blue print scarf at my throat. Love? Letters in hand, Jeremy was beaming at me and the hand-holding middle-aged married couple to my left. I swallowed. The more benevolently a talk show host beams in the seconds preceding the first segment, the worse it's going to be for the guests. To my right, a large TV monitor was blank. It would soon be filled with the image of a man in prison, the fourth "guest." And, to the right of the screen, sat a woman, bleached blond, deeply tanned, and scrawny. By forty, she would be as wrinkled as a linen suit after being packed in a suitcase and sent to the wrong destination before finally arriving at your hotel twenty-four hours later. Men will be far less happy to see her than the suit. She was going to marry the man in prison via remote hook-up on live TV. Was this really legal? Could she be sane enough to enter into the state of wedlock? More importantly, what was I doing here? It was the all-purpose question of my life asked on dates, in front of TV cameras, and in the makeup chair.

"With us today," Jeremy said, as the commercial faded out, "is Carolyn Steele, the Superlady of Sex, an advice columnist for *Playhouse* magazine who very nearly lost her life recently in a crime of passion. This stack of letters in my hand is only a small sampling of the mail she gets each and every day from men and sometimes women, detailing their sexual obsessions from bondage to even kinkier, more painful pursuits. Carolyn, I know you don't mind if I share with our audience this fact. [*How* could he know that? Did he ask? No, not any more than he'd read the letters he waved, which from my quick perusal weren't particularly kinky at all!] That lovely scarf around your neck is hiding bruises made in an attempt on your life. I assume the marks must be about the same color as the silk, though probably not as bright—bruises, which attest to one woman's warped obsession with other people's passion.

"And, next to Carolyn, the Kleinfeldts, who made national headlines two years ago when she shot him in their marital bed. Obviously"—Jeremy paused to chuckle—"he survived the attack." The audience chimed in with their chuckles; the Kleinfeldts grinned and squeezed hands. They looked exactly like the typical middle-aged couple in next-door America: a little chubby, not fat; twinkling fondly, not passionately, at each other. Looking at them, you wouldn't guess either excited the other as much as the prospect of dinner and a solid night of favorite TV shows ahead.

"And finally," Jeremy continued, "Shelley Cornell, who will later be joined, through the miracle of modern technology, in holy matrimony to John Marshall, who is currently serving the third year in a six to twenty-five-year term in prison for the murder of his wife, Melanie. He killed her when he caught her in bed with another man. But he wouldn't have pulled the trigger, he said, if she hadn't told him, while wrapped in her lover's arms, 'You never gave me an orgasm. What was I supposed to do, not have one all my life?'

"Crimes of passion. Who commits them and why? We'll start with you, Carolyn, a victim. Just last week on the Olive Whitney show you suffered a vicious attack by another guest, and the Kleinfeldts and Shelley Cornell have assured us nothing like that will happen here!" He paused for the audience group chuckle. "A spokesperson for Women Worried About Wantonness Among Women was so inflamed by what she considered your anti-love, pro-sexual and licentious comments, she wanted to kill you.

"If you didn't see it, ladies and gentlemen, this is what happened on 'Olive.' "

Suddenly the TV monitor was filled with the same bug-eyed replay of events that had been on the news shows last week, with the line, "Courtesy of Popeye Productions," running across the bottom, bisecting my feet and ankles from the rest of me. Jeremy gasped. The audience gasped. The Kleinfeldts gasped. Shelley Cornell gasped. Each chiming in a beat behind the other, they sounded like a grade-school class doing a round of "Row, Row, Row Your Boat."

All eyes were on my scarf as the monitor dimmed and Jeremy asked in a hushed voice, "Can we see beneath your scarf?"

Give me credit for some dignity. I said, "No," and then he put forth his conspiracy theory.

"We understand your reticence," Jeremy soothed. "Perhaps later in the show," he said huskily, as if he were suggesting a private meeting in his dressing room when the theme music faded away for the day. Then, turning his back to me, he said to the audience, "The recent deaths of two former porn stars make us question whether or not the attack on Carolyn was an isolated incident. Was the attempted strangling of the

Superlady of Sex merely the freak reaction of one angry woman?

"Or, could it be in some way related to the deaths of Tanya Truelust and Madame Zelda, the Queen of Sex Advice, known around the world as the Classy Call Girl, who was only just this morning found dead in her home?" He briefly gave the known facts surrounding both deaths, then turned back to me and asked: "What about you, Carolyn? Do you think there's a connection?"

"No," I said firmly. "They were accidents. I cannot believe Elizabeth Thatcher or any of the women from WWAWAW would commit a premeditated murder."

Actually, I was lying. I *could* believe it, but I didn't.

Jeremy persisted. "But don't their deaths make you feel a little more vulnerable than you did before? Don't you feel like a highly visible target for anyone, or any terrorist group, bent on ridding America of what they call 'smut'?"

"No," I lied.

Mercifully, he moved on to the Kleinfeldts, who happily described, in medical detail, her shooting of him in the left buttock. She had been, she said, aiming for his penis, but she wasn't a very good shot.

"I was in terrible pain, but conscious," he said. "I reached for the phone to dial 911, but she pulled the plug on it just as I had the receiver in my hand."

"I started crying and telling him all the evidence I'd found proving his affair. Telephone bills. Credit card receipts. Her smell in his car. The usual things. I said, 'Do you dare deny it?' "

"I didn't," he said, "because she still had the gun in her hand, pointed at me."

"I asked him why," she said.

"I told her it was to see if the grass was greener on the other side, nothing serious. She shot me again. The bullet went through my side."

"I finally broke down and called 911 from the kitchen phone," she said, the tears in her eyes overflowing and cascading down cherubic cheeks, "when after half an hour I noticed there was a puddle of blood on the floor where he was dripping over the side of the mattress. I thought, 'He's almost dead. You have very nearly killed your husband here.' "

"I knew then," he said, "she still loved me after everything that had happened between us."

During the first commercial break, Shelley Cornell asked me to be her maid of honor since her best friend, waiting in the green room to perform the duty, had sent word by a producer's assistant she was "too shy" to go on. We had matching bouquets, sprays of pink, green, and mauve baby orchids entwined with fresh baby's breath and lacy fern. Shouldn't hers have been all white? A three-tiered wedding cake was placed on a table beside the Kleinfeldts who cast covetous glances at it. A second monitor was wheeled in so Shelley could see her almost husband and his best man, both attired in prison blues and needing haircuts, while the audience, at home and in the studio, could watch the entire proceedings on a split screen. A cameraman's wife sang, "We've Only Just Begun," in a surprisingly pleasant voice. The minister, a woman with a southern accent, skipped the preliminaries and went straight to the "Do yous?" as if she were presiding at the funeral of a deceased she'd never seen in life. When it was over, the bride and groom kissed the monitors before them. On the split screen, I saw their lips miss each other by inches.

Following the last commercial break before the end of the show, Jeremy's assistant cut the cake and began, with the help of aides, distributing it to the people onstage and in the audience. With a few minutes remaining, Jeremy returned to his conspiracy theory. As the credits rolled and the Kleinfeldts munched, he almost had me convinced that Tanya Truelust and Madame Zelda had been my very best friends in the whole world, and that their deaths under "mysterious circumstances" and the "attack" on my "life" were somehow linked in a plot to get *the women of porn.*

I shouldn't have been as surprised as I would be in the weeks ahead when the *Post* ran an ongoing "investigative" series of "the plot to pull the plug on the women of porn."

"I liked the way that couple, the Kinders or whatever, held hands all through the show," Tiffany Titters said, tossing the stray end of her hot pink feather boa back over her shoulder.

We were having a Women in Porn lunch at some bland Japanese restaurant in midtown where they had put us in a separate room from the other diners and made us take off our shoes and sit on the little flat straw mats. Stephanie, an exotic Oriental call girl with delicate features who also wrote erotic fiction, had chosen the location for the day. The members included: me; Stephanie; Tiffany; Clarissa; Vera, former porn star, who dabbled at directing X-rated films and ran a transformation salon with Tiffany where both men and women were taught how to become sexier women; Carola, the most successful former porn star turned video producer, whose motto is, "The VCR put porn where it really belongs, in people's bedrooms"; Gemma, another former porn star, now publisher of a group of magazines considerably raunchier than *Playhouse;* finally there's Bobby, of course. Bobby was a transvestite or TV and past "queen" of Au Chante, one of the famous houses portrayed in the documentary about transvestite balls, *Paris Is Burning.* According to the rules, David, the only man ever allowed except for

Bobby, had to leave after cocktails, because he could never be a member only an honored guest. No one ever questioned the right of Bobby, who looked better than we did, to belong to the group.

"It was sweet, don't you think?" Tiffany said of the Kleinfeldts' tabloid-style devotion, a subject I suspect she found safer for the moment than the obvious one, Zelda's death. "The power of love can do awesome things."

Adept at finding the sweetness in life, Tiffany sometimes, however, mistook saccharine for the real thing. She was the kind of person you'd think my older sisters back home would be: innocent, naive, simple, good, and trusting. My sisters aren't like that at all. In fact, I don't know a single woman over thirty in Easterville, my hometown, who does fit the description.

"Awesome," Bobby said reverentially, his eyes on Tiffany's breasts, which, though pendulous and drooping when released as they so often are, were encased in the sort of décolleté Liz Taylor favors, even if Taylor wouldn't likely choose the leopard print stretch mini dress Tiffany had chosen. Though Vera, her best friend and sister in porn, was his "transformation guide," Bobby clearly loved Tiffany best.

"The power of love," he added, patting his purse which looked like a tiny black patent leather lunch box. "Awesome. How else can you explain why that woman would marry a man in prison?"

"Nuttiness?" I asked.

The only "awesome" aspect of the Kleinfeldts' story was its theme of sex reversal, upon which Jeremy had not pounced. After she'd been arrested, tried, and convicted for attempting to murder him as "punishment" for his multiple affairs, he visited her every day of the three years she'd spent in prison and insisted they renew their wedding vows the evening of her release. They'd proudly shown Jeremy, and all of America, the photograph of him meeting her at the prison gate, her wedding dress in a clear plastic bag draped across his arm. Thanks to three years in the slammer away from her own homemade blintzes, she was able to get into it again. Granted, this is unusual behavior for a wronged male. However, women who've been nearly killed by spouses do that sort of standing by your tormentor thing all the time without making the news. As for Shelley Cornell, she unfortunately was not the first woman to marry a convicted criminal while he was in jail. If only I'd announced my engagement to Starred Man on the show, it would have been a perfect wedding theme day.

"I found the entire program quite distasteful," David sniffed. "The Kleinfeldts were the worst of it. Not only did she shoot him, she failed to call the paramedics for three hours. It's a miracle he lived."

"She cured him of his problem, didn't she?" Gemma asked, her eyes sparkling mischievously. Tall, blond, and shapely, Gemma, like the equally gorgeous brunette Carola, wore her hair closely cropped to her head. Could their severe hairstyles be a reaction against all those years of having long hair, the better to fit the male fantasy of womanhood? "That nasty little problem of keeping his pecker inside his pants. He doesn't have any trouble keeping it tucked away now, does he?"

"Maybe that's the part we didn't get on Jeremy," Stephanie interjected. "Maybe she shot him in the chest *and* the balls, and his pecker don't peck no more. Maybe he stood by her side because he couldn't get it up for anybody else after what she did to him. I don't think I'd be having sex this afternoon at four if someone had put a bullet into my twat."

Stephanie always referred to that section of her anatomy as her "twat" as in, often lately, "I have to have my twat zapped again," referring to treatment for a recurring STD. Her best customers, she said, hated to use condoms. David pretended to frown at our laughter. The waiter came in with our menus, and he stood up to leave.

"Maybe the Kinders are just more evolved than other people," Tiffany said. "If they can't have intercourse anymore, they might be having better sex than they ever did."

Tiffany, who believed she had elevated pornography to a feminist art form, considered herself "the Shirley MacLaine of porno." A practitioner of New Age Tantric sex, she considered "sexual spirituality" more important than fucking. I'm not sure what that means because I always zoned out when Tiffany tried to explain.

"Be careful," David whispered in my ear as he bent down to kiss my cheek in farewell. I knew he was worried about me because he always said, "Call me later; don't forget the juicy parts."

"I heard what he said," Bobby whispered loudly in the other ear, "and he's right. I wish Jeremy hadn't ended his show by saying, 'Carolyn, I hope this public attack hasn't made you a visible target for all the sex haters out there.' "

"Oooh," Clarissa said, wringing her hands. "You're right. He was almost, like you know, setting her up for every paranoid schizophrenic crazy person out there."

"Yes," Bobby said, "like she's wearing a sign now that says, 'Attack this woman if you believe in Jesus.' " He adjusted his cleavage beneath the purple knit dress he wore. We should all have cleavage as delicious as Bobby's. His augmentation surgery was a brilliant success, better than any I'd ever seen. Of course, the first few times I'd seen men who'd had breasts augmented and penises intact, I'd been too startled by the full effect to critique the boob job adequately. "If anything happens to her, it should be on the head of Jeremy." And with that, he prettily tossed his own head of red-blond curls that contrasted beautifully with his *café au lait* skin.

There was an uncomfortable silence as everyone except Rhumumba—and who in the hell had invited her?—appeared to be considering my possible death by unnatural causes. Probably she had tagged along with Clarissa, who'd been too polite, or intimidated, to refuse her admittance to our circle. She was only interested in the menu; in fact, she looked as if she might consume it if the waiter didn't soon return. The woman's aura, as Tiffany would put it, was sinister.

"It's those WWAWAWs I'm worried about," said Vera, who like David, testified before the Meese Commission and was our most politically active and astute member.

When asked by a senator if the publication *Vera in Tight Bondage* wouldn't encourage men to "brutalize" other women against their will, she'd parted her full red lips and replied: "Senator, my purpose in posing for the photographs was to explore my own bondage fantasies. I do not consider myself a victim. I think we should be free to explore our own fantasies." When he persisted with the questioning, she'd read him a poem, which had begun, "I am your love toy," and ended: "Through the purity of my surrender you become my captive too." As she read, her breasts heaved and the amethyst pendant resting in her cleavage sparkled, reflecting light back into the senator's glasses. I was there. David's testimony, following hers, got a lot less rapt attention from the gallery.

"I got a copy of their hit list," Vera said, pulling several stapled sets of paper out of her black canvas carryall. "We're all on it. I made a copy for everyone. Take one and pass it on."

"How literally do you mean the word 'hit'?" Gemma asked.

"I didn't think they meant it literally until that woman tried to strangle Carolyn," Vera said.

"She was probably a crazed lone gunman," I said. They all looked at me, but no one laughed. "You know, like J.F.K.'s killer."

"We got it, sweetie," Bobby said. "We just didn't want to, if you know what I mean."

The hit list was seven pages long and titled: *Groups Or Individuals Whose Existence Threatens The Sanctity Of The American Family And The Purity Of The American Woman.* And, yes, we, including the recently departed from among us, were all on it.

"I can't believe it," Tiffany said. "They don't know anything I've done lately. Listen to this, 'Got her name from her perverse specialty of stimulating her partners to orgasm between her breasts. Self-described as Queen of Kink. Prostitute.' It's a natural variation on a theme. 'Perverse!' They have no idea how many men want to come between a woman's breasts. It liberates them from the pressure of intercourse. Besides, that's in the past. And that's all they have to say about me? Nothing about my work in tantric sex, the transformation salon, my videos, photography, the—"

"I know," Vera said, cutting her off. "They have us packaged and labeled, as if we had no other dimensions beyond the most noticeable one. For me, of course, it's the bondage films. And Carolyn, sex advice. They don't acknowledge her work as a journalist at all."

"They could have sent for our curriculum vitae," I said, and they looked at me again. This was not an easy room to work. "Okay, let's chill out. I don't think these women really mean to kill us one by one," and here, I must admit, my eye wandered restlessly to the names, Tanya Truelust and Madame Zelda, "only to picket, boycott, or debate us into oblivion. I mean, really, they are, middle-class women in silk dresses after all."

"Never turn your back on a middle-class female fanatic in a silk dress," Gemma said, "but you're probably right. Let's order."

While we sipped wine and waited for food, Tiffany invited me to her book party in an East Village gallery. Her collection of erotic photography was being published in two weeks. I'd seen the photos for the section on male piercing; what is done to earlobes, noses, nipples, bellybuttons, and vaginal lips is also done to penises. But, not for Tiffany's book, the discreet ring through the foreskin. Her subjects had rows of decorative pins, most in the shape of fat needles, some studded with diamonds, from base to tip. Sex, Tiffany had explained, was no longer the point for these men. Or, the possibility?

"I'm using an actor in a video now who's high as a kite on coke most of the time," Carola said. "He's a sex machine, but he can't come, of course. Yesterday he asked me to bottle some of the fake 'come' for him for his own personal use. Now, you tell me if he ever comes with *anyone,* off-camera or on."

While she, Gemma, and Vera discussed the merits of various mixtures of fake "come," the frothy stuff which either enhances or substitutes for male ejaculate in the films, Tiffany told me her plans for a new series of workshops, the Goddess and Slut seminars.

"The point is," she said, "you can be a goddess or a slut depending on what you wear and how you fix your makeup. Nobody looks like a porn star. Porn stars are created, not born." Most days, Tiffany didn't look like a porn star herself. Her typical uniform was black tights in winter and beach thongs in summer, T-shirts with sayings like "Anarchy in high heels," and denim skirts. But no panties. Tiffany, like Marilyn Monroe, never wore underwear, which always made me wonder if she never had those days when the tampon leaks. "I'll take before and after Polaroids, which the participants get to keep," she added. "I want to demystify porn and also give women a sense of their inner goddesses."

Tiffany's porn had become a statement about porn, rather than porn itself. While I nibbled at my first course, something raw and fishy and wrapped around a glob of rice, she told me about a film she was making in which a genie would pop up in the bedroom while a couple was having "mechanical" sex to an old Tiffany Titters video. The genie, the new Tiffany, would show them how they could use tantric sex, health food, focusing energy, and belly dancing to put "meaning into that meaningless sex."

Meanwhile, Bobby was finishing a story I hadn't heard with the comment, "Really, I'd rather have sex by mutual masturbation than any other way now. I've swallowed so much come in my life, my insides must be bleached."

Everybody laughed. Even Rhumumba had a thin smile on her face as she dipped one fat index finger into a bowl of salty, fishy sauce. I watched her lick it clean. She worried me; she really did.

"Hey, Superlady, I got one for you," the cabdriver said. Our eyes locked in the rearview mirror. He was a white guy, unusual for a cabdriver in New York City, on the stout and grungy side. He smelled of stale tobacco, stale sweat, and staler ideas. "Didn't think I recognized you, did you? Saw you on TV. Never forget a face. Had a lot of celebrities in my cab.

"So, hey, I got one for you. It's a real situation. Friend of mine. His wife won't do it anymore since she found God. She could be one of those WWAWAWs you and Jeremy were talking about on the TV show.

He's beside himself with wanting to get it. Would you tell him it's okay to get it somewheres else being the circumstances are the way I've just described them?"

"Oh, absolutely," I said, suspecting I was giving him permission to cheat on his wife and hoping he didn't for a second fantasize it could be with me.

"That's exactly what I told him. Don't that beat all, you'd agree with me. Wait 'til I tell him that. It'll make him feel better. You've done a lot of good here today, I can tell you that."

I would also tell him: Shower, shave, deodorize, use mouthwash, lose thirty pounds, do sit-ups. Then, maybe your wife will decide God isn't a full-time lover after all. Why do men think it's okay if they're fat and smelly?

I was so relieved to get out of his cab at the PATH station on 23rd Street, I forgot to feel uncomfortable about being recognized until I got off the train in Jersey. Then, as I was hurrying along Grove Street past the newsstand and King Donut, I realized someone, taller and much heavier, was moving at an equally quick pace in an effort to keep up with me. When I turned the corner at Wayne Street, I saw him: mid-thirties, over six feet tall, heavyset, particularly in the gut, thin dirty-blond hair. He was wearing a cheap dark suit topped by a gray raincoat in a shiny polyester material, blue shirt, red print tie, black thick-soled shoes, the kind mailmen wear. He looked like a retired Secret Service agent.

And I'd seen him before, but where?

I didn't think about it for long after I got inside my apartment, because there was another message on the phone machine from my androgynous caller. All it said this time was: "Carolyn. . . ."

Chapter Six

Dear Superlady of Sex,

Recently I discovered my boyfriend with a pair of my panties up to his nose. He was not checking out the quality of my fabric softener as these were dirty panties straight from the hamper in the bathroom. I was disgusted. He denied doing what I clearly saw him doing. And, he refuses to talk about it. What would make a man do such a sick and perverted thing? Is this as weird and unusual as I think it is? Is there any hope for our relationship?

Dear Hampered Relationship,

I have received dozens of letters from men who have a used panty fetish. They become aroused from sniffing those panties which have recently been close to the intimate flesh of a woman. Some of the men who write to me request my used panties for their personal enjoyment. Of course, I cannot respond to these requests. This is not a panty fulfillment center. Your boyfriend has responded to your disgust, however, by retreating into silence. Perhaps knowing more about fetishes would help you handle the situation. I recommend the book Love Maps *by Dr. John Money. He explains how some men who are sexually or psychologically damaged in childhood can only get in touch with their erotic selves through the use of a fetish, in this case, worn panties. This may be your boyfriend. Or, he may simply have an occasional urge to sniff panties. If you can approach him without disgust, perhaps he will be able to tell you how often and why he sniffs panties.*

If I caught my boyfriend inhaling my underwear, I'd tear up his Rolodex card immediately after rushing him out of the apartment. That is not, however, an acceptable Superlady answer. I shut down the computer. Manuel would be arriving soon to take me out to dinner and, I fervently hoped, back home to bed. In another few weeks, I would be writing about sex purely as an uninvolved observer, the memory of "penile thrusting"—a phrase I once had to define for a *Ladies' Weekly* fact checker—only a dim one.

I missed intercourse. I missed cunnilingus and fellatio. My mouth watered with the desire to wet a penis and hungrily, tenderly embrace it with my lips and tongue. Sometimes at night I remembered sex play, like taking Roger's penis, Cocky, between my breasts, rubbing his silkiness against my skin, squeezing my breasts around him until he grew hard and the first drop of seminal fluid slipped out of him.

No one caresses my clitoris like I do, but there's more to a sex life than personal clitoral stimulation or "autoeroticism," as talk show hosts prefer. Lately, I had taken masturbation to a new high. After giving myself several orgasms, I felt a new peace, a clearer understanding of why I, and all of us, are so desperately seeking salvation, intimacy, and sexual release. At those moments, I felt I'd reached satori, the Zen Buddhist state of sudden enlightenment. Then I fell asleep and woke unable to remember exactly what I'd suddenly realized. So, masturbation was enlightening me, but the effect lasted not as long as the feeling of fullness following a Chinese dinner.

I yearned for sexual contact with a male, for a penis inside me and masculine arms around me. How I missed Cocky, the best I'd ever known. Could the young woman who had him now possibly appreciate him as much as I did? Often, while tenderly touching myself, I envisioned him, seven inches of glowing rose-pink flesh, rising beneath me. His complexion turned a delicate lavender when he was hard, which was often. I dubbed him The Perfect Penis and used him as the model for my *Playhouse* article of the same name.

But, I preferred my sexless dates to what Morgy had with Georges. We'd just spent one hour on the phone discussing *that,* following the hour I'd spent on the phone with Clarissa trying to convince her I hadn't told Jeremy that Stella Mae Parks was Madame Zelda and Madame Zelda was dead. I hadn't. Jeremy had found out about her on his own.

"I mean, give the man credit," I'd told Clarissa. "Digging up dirt is his specialty."

"You planned this," she accused, "so you could be the new Queen of Advice, when you know I desperately want to keep Zelda alive. Why does she have to die with Stella Mae? It's like they're twins, not the same person. We're throwing her on top of the funeral pyre."

Finally, knowing this would silence her and induce lingering guilt at the same time, I told her Starred Man was out of prison. It worked. She was immediately contrite, but as soon as I'd hung up with her, Morgy had called.

"You're the expert," Morgy began, without asking if there had been any more threats to my life. I knew she was going to detail her new man's perversion for my analysis.

Her last lover had worn a penis ring and would only fuck her if her pubis had been cleanly shaved. When she'd asked what I thought she should do, I'd said I thought she shouldn't do anything with him. I told her about the risk of contracting AIDS through broken skin, a distinct possibility when you fuck with penis rings or shave. She'd done it anyway.

"So, I want you to listen to this and tell me, like, is it really abnormal . . . or is he braver than most men in admitting his fantasies?" She cleared her throat in preparation for reading. "He came in and handed me this letter while I was taking a bubble bath last night," she explained.

Morgy had a huge pink and ivory marble tub, which I coveted. Fitted with a Jacuzzi, it was deep and wide enough for me to float, the kind of tub in which it is possible to have a true sensual experience or a good fuck. There was a skylight overhead and a surrounding marble ledge wide enough to hold all of her expensive bath oils, beads, bubbles, soaps, and creams. She could keep Georges. I wanted the tub.

"Okay," I said, encouraging her. "It can't be anything I haven't heard before. Read."

She read. He'd detailed everything he wanted to do with her, starting with "light slaps to the buttocks, leaving them rosy and quivering" and finishing with a wooden hairbrush. Not an uncommon fantasy until he got to the part about wanting to scrub her pussy with the bristles until she "screamed in orgasmic agony." That was something I hadn't heard before.

"Well?" she said.

"I'll never look at a hairbrush again in quite the same way."

"Is he that sick?"

"Get out of it, Morgy," I told her. "Get out of it *before* he hurts you."

After her tearful reading of his letter, she'd confided that the sex, sans vaginal brushing, was so good that she couldn't possibly get out of it, not just right now.

Though he didn't like it when she touched herself during intercourse to reach orgasm, he hadn't minded when she clasped her thighs around his and vigorously squeezed herself to orgasm after he was finished. He'd even laughed, she said, at the stickiness when they'd pulled apart. Georges—what a sport!

How does she find these guys? Why does a powerful businesswoman allow herself to be dominated by a man who couldn't touch her in hand-to-hand corporate combat? Inevitably I asked the questions, which always led me to other questions.

What do any of us find so compelling in the unsuitable, and often downright distasteful, men we pursue? My own collection of geeks, losers, men who fear sex and embrace therapy, all the self-involved and noncommittal men of my recent past is matched by the assortments assembled by my friends, though Morgy's choices are a few degrees worse than ours. Are we using them to punish ourselves? Or, do these men truly represent all that's left for us after a certain age?

My friend, Claudia, once sent me a card picturing a collection of unappetizing men hanging from wire coat hangers on a mark-down rack. Inside, she wrote: "At this point in life, you fuck down or you don't fuck."

Remembering the futile conversation with Morgy, I sighed. Thinking about my own sex life, or lack thereof, I sighed again, more loudly this time. I was not exactly happy with my life. Maybe the problem was my work. I was sure I would have been happier writing long profiles for *Vanity Fair* about the rich and famous, many of whom dabble in S&M discreetly and most of whom have fucked indiscriminately in their prime. Doesn't the same perversion as described by Dominick Dunne and practiced by expensively clad characters sound more interesting and less tacky than it does in letters from *Playhouse* readers, whom we assume are not rich and/or famous?

Upscale panty sniffers are, after all, breathing the mists from only the finest scented silk. The stories Stephanie, Tiffany, and Zelda had told me about the sexual proclivities of the "beautiful people" would shock the devotee of gossip columns which name names and describe dresses in lush detail. Politicians, movie stars, models, designers—they whip and are whipped, dressed in the softest leather bondage gear. Male and female, they've had so much anal sex it's surprising they aren't all dead of AIDS or at least unable to hold their feces inside their bodies. They do things even I have to look up in the *Encyclopedia of Erotic Wisdom.* But they have cachet. Georges, that little piece of Eurotrash who reminded me of a greasy food wrapper littering the street, had more class than Starred Man.

Resisting the urge to sigh again, I wandered around the apartment, picking off dead leaves from trees, straightening magazines on the coffee table so their edges were perfectly parallel to one another. If I didn't get laid soon, I would turn into an anal retentive—or was that anal compulsive?—personality, one of those people who tidies a room to death. With a tissue pulled out of my pocket, I dusted the head of my bronze penis statue, the first piece of art I'd ever purchased.

I love my penis, which stands about six inches tall and has a delicate flapper girl from the twenties riding his balls, her arms wrapped adoringly around him, her cheeks resting on his head. And, ironically, I found it back home in a tiny antique shop across the river in St. Louis, where I successfully bargained the price down from the $800 tag to $400 cash.

I remember clutching my penis to my chest in a brown paper bag and dashing into a restaurant where I was meeting my sisters for lunch the very afternoon I'd bought it. Proudly, I showed them my treasure, a unique signed bronze casting from the Art Nouveau period. Surely, they would see the wit in the sculptor's splendid work. Well, they were aghast, mortified as the waitress, giggling, asked, "Life-size, isn't it? Don't you wish they all were?"

"How disgusting," Billie Ann, the oldest, said, while Jenny Lee blushed her disapproval. Then they, who are shaped somewhat like Chinese steamed dumplings, asked me, almost in unison, if I'd been putting on weight. Had they asked "Why are you trying to shock us?," I would have been impressed by them for a change. In my family, no one says what they mean, which makes conversation more interesting afterward when you're alone and can dissect it than when it's actually taking place. And no one, except me, ever talks about sex. Are my sisters orgasmic? I don't know.

Never mind, penis, darling, I love you. I patted his head. Restlessly, I went back to the mail. Letters from women who couldn't have orgasms. Letters from men who loved women who couldn't have orgasms. Letters from men who were cheating on women who couldn't have orgasms. Letters from men who blamed themselves because women couldn't have orgasms. Sometimes I think the American woman is inorgasmic by definition. Letters from religious nuts and sexual perverts. I picked them up and let them fall back down on the desk, pieces of the twisted American psyche, our legacy from those religious zealots who stole the country from the Indians.

Think about it. Would you have fled the relative comfort of civilization in Europe to spend weeks—or was it months?—on a fusty leaky boat with people who'd never heard of deodorant soap, headed toward an uncertain future so you could be "free" to live life as a Puritan, perhaps spending large chunks of your new life in the stocks as punishment for minor transgressions? Puritans were so named because they wanted to purify the Church of England, which was too spiritually lax for them. These people were goofballs, and we're only a few generations away from Early Goofball ourselves.

The buzzer sounded. Manuel, a man not even descended from the Puritans. What was his excuse?

"Caro, querida," Manuel said softly, the lilting musical quality of his voice the only aural giveaway to his Puerto Rican ancestry. His English was better than mine. He brought my hand to his lips, dragging my sleeve through my paella. Tenderly he kissed my fingers. *"Querida,"* he sighed.

"Manuel," I said, taking my hand back and brushing grains of rice off my sleeve with my napkin. I was wearing a black silk minidress, with a discreetly plunging neckline that stopped at the top of the cleavage, and full sleeves, which I thought conveyed a hint of modesty. I'd covered my bruises with Dermablend, the makeup women use to hide varicose veins. In a dark restaurant, it had worked. My earrings were designer originals, bought from a Soho artist, little connected strands of multicolored beads, alternated with black metal arrows, gold stars, and silver moons. They tinkled when I talked. "This isn't working anymore," I said irritably.

"What isn't working anymore, *caro?* Don't you like the food?"

"The food is wonderful, darling. I'm not talking about the food." Truthfully, I was no longer thrilled by his deft ordering in Spanish. I was beginning to suspect he kept coming back to this Spanish café with its predictable white stucco walls, black wrought iron fixtures, and red tile floors because his command of the menu's native language gave him an excuse for placing "the lady's" order. "I'm tired of having only my hand kissed," I snapped.

"I thought you loved having your hand kissed," he

said sadly. I noticed the space between his middle front teeth, almost big enough to spit through, as they say in southern Illinois. And he was short, probably two or three inches shorter than the 5′7″ he claimed to be. Short men lie about their height the way women over thirty-five lie about their age.

"Only if there's the real possibility it will lead to a kiss to my lower parts later on."

"Caro," he said; he was actually blushing.

"I've made you blush again."

"It's just that you say things Spanish girls would never say. It's refreshing! I like it!" He looked nervously around at the people seated near us. "But it sometimes makes me a little nervous," he whispered. "I've never known a woman like you. Spanish girls—"

"Manuel," I said firmly, hoping to stave off another attack on Spanish girls, particularly his ex-wife, who was apparently the ultimate Spanish girl. They didn't, according to Manuel, have sex for the last five years of their marriage. Yet, he was shocked when she left him, pregnant with her lover's child. He hadn't, he swore, had sex with anyone else during those five years. How could she betray him by going to bed with another man? And what had he done about his sexual needs for five years? Masturbated, or so he said.

"Manuel," I repeated. "We have to talk."

"Of course, *querida,* we will talk about anything you like. Why are you looking at me so strangely?"

There was something different in his voice when he lowered it. The more softly he spoke, the more he sounded, yes, like a woman. Could his voice have been the one on my answering machine? After all, it is an unlisted number.

"No," I said. "Not *talk.* That's not what I really meant. We have to do something other than talk and kiss hands. What's wrong with you, Manuel? What's wrong with me? I'm a sex writer, and I can't get laid. This is ridiculous."

"Is it me you want then, *querida,* or merely the conquest?"

"The conquest?"

"I think you confuse your life with your work. You think, because you are a sex writer, you must have sex."

There it was, that androgynous note in his voice again. What had he told me when he'd first read my column in *Playhouse?* Something about his "concern" for my safety if I continued to "provoke" people by writing that way? Had he actually said, "Someone might make you pay for what they perceive to be a commission of sin." Or did I only remember him saying it now?

"No, I would think I must have sex if I wrote a column on orchid growing," I said.

"I don't know about that, *querida.* All this constant studying of one thing must have its impact on your mind." He reached over the paella and stroked the back of my hand with his finger. Could this tiny little man with the gentle touch be sending me threatening letters? "I worry about you. Your career almost got you killed. I can't believe what you do is worth dying for."

"Remember the Transit Authority worker who was killed in the token booth last month in a robbery? Was selling subway tokens worth dying for? I'm tired of having what I do for a living put down."

"I'm not putting you down, *querida.* I know in my heart that you have many conflicts about your work yourself. Don't blame me for expressing what is held silently in your heart."

I shoved a forkful of rice and shrimp into my mouth before I could sigh or say something that would let him know what kind of man I was beginning to suspect he could be.

Then he asked, "Why are you in this business anyway?"

The question was his version of "What's a nice girl like you doing in a place like this?" I'd answered it before: money, freedom, I like sex, I'm comfortable with sex, why not sex, what's wrong with sex.

I wasn't going to answer it again.

Dating Manuel was like stepping back into adolescence. I was sixteen again in Easterville where Daddy insisted my dates come inside, shake hands, and promise to return me safely before midnight. Manuel picked me up, opened the car door for me, drove me home, opened the car door again, and didn't fuck me. I didn't even know another man in the New York City area who drove a car. Typically, we made out until the windows fogged before he walked me to my front door, where I almost expected to find my father's ghost waiting inside, looking at his watch.

"Caro," he sighed, turning off the engine in front of the former church with Corinthian columns which was now a community center and frequent site of Alcoholics Anonymous and Narcotics Anonymous meetings. It was, however, dark that night. "I desire you so much, my *querida,"* he said huskily, putting his arm across the back of the seat, inviting me into his arms.

"Manuel, you can have what you want," I said, snuggling closer to him. His scent was both orange spicy and sweet, like Constant Comment tea, only sharper. "Why don't we go inside?"

"No one will bother us out here. I'm a brother," he said, lifting my chin with his finger, the way they do it in old movies, the better to kiss my lips. "Uhm," he murmured, as he kissed me softly at first, his lips like butterfly wings floating across my own. Then, gently he parted my lips with his tongue. After kissing and sucking each individual lip as though it were the source of life's honey, he thrust inside me, fucking my mouth with his tongue.

Manuel could kiss, but, to tell you the truth, his penis (the one time I experienced it) was a disappointment. I touched it, through his pants, in the backseat of a cab in the West Village, on our first date after we'd seen Spanish director Pedro Almodovar's film, *Matador*. We were kissing and suddenly I put my hand on his crotch, only to discover his short, thin penis standing hard at attention like a little boy whose short legs stuck straight out to the edge of his baby chair. It seemed eager, excited, like it wanted me to take it out for a romp. He'd tensed in shocked surprise, then taken my hand from his lap and brought it to his lips for the first of those interminable hand kisses.

We tell men penis size doesn't matter, but it does. The best position for a small penis is me flat on my back, legs up and braced against his shoulders. From that vantage point, he can thrust without falling out too often. The problem with little penises is the fallout factor, and I hate being distracted by having to worry about keeping it in. Big ones, on the other hand, require some forethought before you make a move. Like Goldilocks, I don't want them too big or too small, but just right. Given the choice between big and small, I will take big.

I didn't reach for his penis in the car parked in front of the church on Wayne Street. Instead, I put my hand between my legs, squeezing my thighs around it as Manuel kissed me. With my thumb, I massaged my clit. Holding me by the shoulders, he kissed and kissed and kissed; I reached orgasm in a matter of seconds.

Is this man secretly gay? Does he hate women? Fear us? Or is he only afraid of sex?

* * *

Walking up the steps, admiring as I always did, the beauty of the halls, I knew it was over with Manuel. He was beginning to give me what my sisters would call "the creeps." There was something not quite sane about his dating me when he disapproved of me. Yes, there was something not quite sane about me allowing it to happen. No more. The third man out, not down, in less than a month. I was alone. I had no one. But who and what had I had when I'd had these guys in my life?

The phone was ringing as I inserted the first of three keys into the three locks of my apartment door. By the time I got inside, David's voice was on the answering machine. I picked up.

"You were monitoring your calls?" he asked.

"No. I just got in from my last dinner date with Manuel."

"No sex again? It's time you dumped him. He's probably gay."

"Uhmm," I said noncommittally. I wasn't ready to admit my suspicions though I surely would next time I was on the couch in David's office. Don't women always accuse the men who don't want to sleep with us of being gay?

"I was out walking the dog," David said, "when I picked up the early edition of the *Post.* It's one of the advantages of not living in Jersey," he reminded me.

"I'm not sure getting first peek at the *Post* is a real-life advantage," I said, not for the first time either.

"You might change your mind and hop on a PATH train tonight so you can see this for yourself," he said. "May I read?"

"Please," I said, kicking off my high heels and sinking to the floor, where I could listen from my favorite phone position, flat on my back, legs raised and crossed at the knees. "Do read."

"This article is labeled the first of an ongoing investigative series on the plot to pull the plug on the women of porn, written by the hot-shit new columnist Barry Renfrew. Got that?"

"Fucking Christ!"

"Yes, well, between you good sisters of the pink, he may be the only man you *haven't* fucked."

Then, all joking finally aside, he read me the following Page Three story:

IS THERE A PLOT TO PULL THE PLUG ON THE PRETTIES OF PORN?

It's not often the Post *takes its cues from Jeremy Mitchell, but a recent Jeremy show inspired these questions:*

Was the death of Tanya Truelust truly an accident?

Was the death of Madame Zelda another accident?

Tanya Truelust, alias Julie Beckman, died in a fall from her own fire escape when the heel of one four-inch-high backless shoe caught in the open grillwork of a step. The former porn star turned video producer lost her balance and fell eight stories to her death. Insiders say she was hurrying down the fire escape which served as the "back door" of her X-rated video production company office in Chelsea to avoid creditors in the waiting room. Tanya was noted for her exuberant orgasms in the 130 films she made. Reportedly, her company was in financial trouble.

Not two weeks later, Madame Zelda, alias Stella Mae Parks, was found dead floating in her hot tub in her upstate New York mansion by the gardener. Few connected the three-hundred-pound and bright red corpse of Stella with the legendary blond beauty whose photo graced her monthly advice column in Playhouse *magazine. Author of* The Classy Call Girl's Guide to Pleasing Men, *Zelda, a former prostitute, had in recent years gained a great deal of weight and worked exclusively as a dominatrice, whose male clients pay for the pleasures of being whipped and humiliated. Cause of death was attributed to heart attack possibly induced by her weight and the failure of a heat pump in the hot tub.*

According to the gardener, "Steam was rising from the tub, and she looked like a cooked lobster. It was a terrible thing to find in the morning." When told of her real identity and her career, he said, "She was a quiet private person who kept to herself. I am much surprised."

Perhaps the deaths of two of porn's most famous female names coming within days of each other are nothing but a coincidence. But, the Post *has learned that yet another of porn's former pretties met a sudden and violent end in the past several months. La Passionata, alias Domina Rodriguez, starred in thirty-seven X-rated flicks, including the best-selling title of 1988,* Hot Girls in Chains. *Bondage films were her specialty. She was able to convey sensuality while only able to heave her bosom.*

Six months ago La Passionata was found dead in the garage of her boyfriend's Fort Lee, New Jersey, home. Her charred body had been tightly bound. The death, his defense claims, was a bondage accident, which, in panic, he'd tried to cover by moving her body to the garage and setting it afire.

But in his one and only statement to authorities, Spiker claimed not to know what happened to La Passionata on the night of her death. "We had a glass of wine, and I passed out. When I came to, the garage was on fire and she was gone."

Fort Lee authorities didn't accept his version of

the story, and he was charged with second degree murder. His trial begins Monday.

Is there a connection between the deaths of La Passionata, Madame Zelda, and Tanya Truelust? Could Anthony Spiker be telling the truth? Could someone else have been in his house that night while he was passed out? The possibility that a plot against the women of porn exists is given added credence by the reported threats on the life of Carolyn Steele, Playhouse *magazine's Superlady of Sex and heiress apparent to Zelda's crown, who was choked nearly to death by an enraged antiporner on Olive Whitney's show recently.*

Is someone out to get these women? I mean to find out.

"Well," David said, clearing his throat. "Awesome, isn't it, how they can turn something into nothing? They've made a patchwork sow's ear out of three unrelated silk purses."

"I never even met La Passionata," I said. "How long has she been out of the life?"

"Several years. Her last film, the one that hit big, sat in a can for a few years before it was released in 1988. The distributor ran out of money, sold his company to someone else, and it was resurrected. Last I heard she was a housewife in New Jersey. Apparently she got divorced, since the article doesn't mention a husband."

We talked for several more minutes. After we said goodbye, I kept my finger on the phone, holding the receiver in one hand, deciding whom I should call when I released the little lever. I let it go. The dial tone sounded. I listened to it for several seconds before hanging up the phone.

I called no man with whom I was, however peripherally, involved. This was, as Tim would say, "new behavior" for me. Instead, I played back my messages. While I was gone, Vinnie had called.

"Carolyn," his distinctive voice boomed from the machine. "I have good news for you. I want you in my office tomorrow morning at eleven. Dress to meet the media. I've scheduled a press conference for you and me at noon. Then, we'll have lunch."

Obviously, I was going to be crowned.

I was thinking about that when I heard the faintest rustle. The envelope slid slowly under the door like a snake which had flattened itself out. Mesmerized, I watched it. Why didn't I run to the door, throw open the locks, and chase after my tormentor? I was unable to move, terrified by this latest invasion. Manuel?

After what seemed an hour but must have been only a few minutes, I walked down the hallway and picked up the envelope. My fingers were shaking as I tore open letter number three, composed as before of glossy letters on cheap typing paper.

"You do not listen, and you will pay with your life."

Part Two

SEX EQUALS DEATH

Chapter Seven

"I hate having my picture taken," I told Charles, running my finger along his wrist as I spoke.

His skin was velvety, dark and rich and thick, black man's skin. Touching it was a pleasure. We were sitting side by side on his bed, our backs against the headboard, legs outstretched, so that we only had to face each other and slide down to be in position to fuck.

"Uhmm," I said, moving closer to him and nuzzling his neck.

He put his arm around me and massaged my neck and shoulders with one hand. His fingers were surprisingly strong. I wanted to take off my clothes and see what he could do with them on the rest of my body.

I liked the way he smelled, the mixture of dark skin, a green scented soap, and YSL. Liking a man's smell is important to me. It is not politically correct to say so, but black skin does smell and feel different. I love the difference. He was the most touchable man I'd been near in a long time; I had been touching him all day, stroking his arm, rubbing his back, making the physical overtures he hadn't been making. Charles's approach to seduction—lie back like a sleek cat and let her do it—may have been dictated by the fact we'd met while he was working or by the racial difference, but, I guessed, it was more likely his sexual style.

"Uhmm," I repeated, looking up at him.

The pitch of his breathing had changed, his eyes were melting into mine. Charles had the sexiest eyes set in the most serious and proper face. You could swim in his eyes; it would be exactly like wading into a muddy creek back home, warm and welcomingly oozing up into all your body crevices. I loved those eyes. I even liked his bald head. I wanted to see the top of it glittering with sweat between my thighs. It had been so long, a year almost; I didn't feel like I could wait much longer.

"I know you hate having your picture taken," he said, touching my chin with his other hand. "I knew that right away."

Charles was a free-lance photographer. He appeared to be somewhere between thirty and fifty. Who could tell with such beautiful unwrinkled skin? Vinnie had hired him to shoot the press conference that morning because Vinnie liked to have official shots of everything. He wanted "only the best" photographs for our "family" photo album. Charles would no doubt make me look a lot better than any photographer from the tabloids.

"You better get used to having your picture taken," he said. "You're gonna get your picture taken a lot more often now."

"You have beautiful skin," I told him, as I unbuttoned the top two buttons of his shirt and stroked his fine skin with my finger.

I didn't want to think about hate mail and crazy people. I didn't want to think about how my new status increased my visibility and, possibly, my risk factor. I didn't want to think about the proliferation of Carolyn Steele faces in tabloids across America. Still shots are somehow so much worse than being on TV, where you can look bad one moment, but enchanting the next, depending on the camera angle, with no single frozen facial expression identifying you in the minds of millions forevermore. I prefer being a moving target, but I didn't want to think about any of that. I felt special, safe, and secure in Charles's arms. Maybe it was an illusion, but that's what I felt.

"Your skin is like velvet, so luxurious," I whispered in his ear before I licked it.

"I know," he said. "And, I don't do anything to make it nice. I'm just lucky."

Maybe this should have been my first clue, but it wasn't, not at the time. Such moments are only heavy with portent in retrospect, when we relentlessly analyze everything the former beloved did, searching for the first hints of the fatal flaws which had eventually surfaced. His black cat leaped upon the bed and settled on his lap, eyeing me warily. I wasn't making too much of the fact we were sitting on the bed after having met that morning. In some New York apartments, the bed is often the only place to sit, and this was one of them. I wasn't making too much of it, but I was hopeful Charles would do what is considered the obvious thing to do with a woman on a bed in most parts of the country.

He had a one-bedroom apartment in Chelsea, but the living room was filled with photographic equipment, still and video, a computer, several file cabinets, and the general detritus of a small business. The bedroom was the natural choice for guest seating, and there were no chairs. Only a king-sized bed, teak dresser, an overstuffed walk-in closet with the door standing open, two televisions, some editing equipment, and a black enameled Japanese screen printed with bright red flowers blocking the windows that were probably barred and grimy. Magazines on scuba diving and photography were the only reading material in either room.

"How does it feel to be the Queen of Sex Advice?" he asked, smiling slightly. From the vantage point of hindsight, was it sardonically?

"Silly," I told him, and it really did.

At least the centerfold of the month can justify her title by her body. What did being the Queen of Sex Advice mean in measurable job terms? That I could look up the answers in Kinsey, Masters and Johnson, et al., to any sex question faster than the next writer? That I didn't mind saying "penis" or "cock," for that matter, in print or aloud?

"You must intimidate a lot of men," he said, pressing his lips against my hairline.

"Do I intimidate you?"

I straightened out my legs and leaned back against the pillows and closer into him. His sheets and pillowcases were a tasteful navy and maroon print, with which I happened to coordinate nicely. I was still wearing the buttery soft lavender leather suit I'd selected for the press conference that morning. Women back home have belts wider than this skirt was long. My panty hose, the only underwear I had on, were a deeper shade of lavender. I had, of course, kicked off my yet deeper lavender heels. Lying on the floor beside the bed, they looked like something Tiffany might have worn to a funeral.

"Do I look intimidated?" he asked, grinning.

He put his hand on my thigh, and the fingers curved possessively around my flesh. My breath came faster. Before climbing onto the bed, he'd removed his socks and shoes; his feet, I suddenly noticed, were as long and slender as his hands. He was tall, thin, elegant, and graceful. His penis, I imagined, was average length, but would look longer because it would be thin, as lean as he was, a glowing ebony godhead preceding him in nakedness. I could picture it shiny with drops of seminal fluid on its regal head prior to entering me. If he'd kept his hand on my thigh much longer, I might have written an epic poem to it, sight unseen.

"No. You don't look intimidated. That's what I like best about you."

I knew as Charles caressed my thigh with his long sensitive fingers we were going to have sex that night . . . and I would be in love with him by morning. I was a little bit there already. Maybe I was falling in love with him because at last I'd found a man who wasn't putting off the sex until I'd listened to every sentence of every paragraph of every chapter of his life story.

Whatever the reason, the soft, erotic pressure of his fingers on my flesh switched off the part of my brain which typically registers, caustically remarks upon, and then catalogues the unacceptable behaviors of men. It's an evaluation process continually taking place even when I'm not letting it stop me from trying to get them into my bed. With other men, I carry on this running critical dialogue in my head listing what is wrong as I smile, nod sweetly, and undo my top buttons. Mentally, I don't let them get away with one false word. With Charles, I allowed the batteries in the bullshit detector to run completely down. I was smiling, nodding sweetly, and breathing deeply, the better to show my already visible cleavage . . . and not thinking at all, except about his penis.

"Babe," he said, moving his lips farther down my hairline, against my ear.

Yes, he called me "*babe*." What would you call a woman who'd allowed herself to be picked up at her own press conference, then dragged along on two other photo shoots? You wouldn't call someone who watched a man perform his work "Ms.," would you? I mean, what about my work? Or, what about discussing my precarious life situation before it became more so with Vinnie's P. I.? All forgotten. I'd hurried out the door with Charles.

Briefly, I wondered if Vinnie would forgive me for cancelling out on lunch with him, and if anyone else had ever left him alone with his sushi in favor of leaving with someone he'd hired to do a job. At least I would always have the memory of him, his mouth open, the bright lobby lights bouncing off his gold chains as I said, "Another time."

"Babe," Charles repeated. He called me "*babe*," and I didn't bristle, that's how much trouble I was already in. "What would you like for dinner? Do you want to go out, order in, or shall I cook for you?"

"Uhmm," I said, closing my eyes, after I had surreptitiously checked out the large framed photo on his dresser. *Mother.* She looked like him, down to the wire-rimmed glasses, but she had hair. "Cook for me."

In one fluid motion, he was on top of me. I didn't open my eyes, but my mouth reached instinctively for his and found it. He kissed me long and slowly, his tongue probing me; I felt the heat of his body on top of mine opening me up. He slid down, squeaking against the leather, until his chin was resting on my pubic bone. Buffered by the leather, he gently ground into me, then raised my skirt with both hands and kissed me through the lavender panty hose, which were already damp from wanting him. My throat closed up.

"I am going to slave over a hot stove for you," he said, his own voice higher than it had been as he raised himself up on his elbows to look into my eyes.

Not trusting my voice, I nodded. I opened my arms, and he moved back up my body to hold me. We kissed again, our eyes open this time, because we needed to see inside each other before we made love. After we stopped kissing, I took his face in my hands and kissed each eyelid, then ran my tongue down each side of his face from the corner of his eye to his chin.

"If I don't get up now, we aren't going to have dinner," he said.

He went into the kitchen, and I went to the bathroom, where I sopped up some of the excess moisture with a tissue. The litter box, I noted, needed to be changed.

Something happened in the kitchen. It made me feel like a cat whose tail has suddenly swollen to twice its normal size. Something spooked me. Was it something he said, or I did? Was it the way he said something I perhaps didn't want to hear anyway? I don't know. It's happened to me in the past. Suddenly I want a man so much and, with equal passion, I am sure he won't want me back. Things are said to me; reading more or less into them than was actually meant, I say things back, which I don't mean at all. I look back later and can't remember the words, only the confusion and the feelings of overwhelming desire and fear of rejection washing over me like shame.

Whatever happened, I wasn't being the woman I wanted to be nor the woman I really was. My invisible swollen tail stood out from my body, creating a force field around me. I wanted to let him in, but I couldn't even believe he wanted to be there. Across the room, a thin knife glinting in his hand as he worked, he had to feel the emotional frisson I was creating around me; no, around the two of us.

He was preparing shrimp scampi (with not nearly enough garlic), rice, and a salad; he wouldn't let me help.

"Have a seat," he'd said when I came from the bathroom, indicating a stool next to the breakfast counter across from where he was deveining shrimp at the sink. He turned back to his task. From the back and clothed, he looked like an Armani model.

"I poured you a glass of wine while you were in the bathroom."

I picked up the goblet of white wine and sipped. A

good chardonnay, my favorite. His kitchen was compact, black and white, galley style. He had a stacked washer and dryer unit of which I was covetous. I walked from the fourth floor to the basement with my laundry basket. He was going to put raddichio in the salad. I could have guessed that within thirty seconds of meeting him. Maybe I was frightened by all this domesticity.

"How long have you lived in this apartment?" I asked, a typical New York question. If you know when someone moved into a place, you can gauge what they paid for it or, if they're renting, the amount of rent they pay.

"Twenty-four years. Since I first came to New York. I'm the most stable guy I know. I've had the same phone number for twenty-four years."

"Oh," I said. What do you say to that? Is stability really a function of one's phone number? "So, you must be older than you look."

"Forty-five. Do I look that old?"

"No, not nearly," I told him, and he preened. The man was vain, but I didn't care. He didn't look forty-five, and I wanted him. "Have you been a photographer since you came here?"

What I really wanted to know was: *Why aren't you married?*

Isn't that what women always want to understand about the man we instinctively know we'll want and never be able to have? Every woman has dated this elusive male at least once in her life. Handsome, successful, charming, he cooks dinner, sends flowers, gives her the first orgasm via cunnilingus. Spend a few hours alone with him and he'll tell you how much he wants to find the "right" woman, marry, and raise a family. Charles had told me over lunch that he wasn't married, had never been married, and wanted nothing more than to be married and have children. Men seduce with words; this particular configuration of words is a popular one.

"I don't get that much out of sex anymore," he'd said. "Sex doesn't mean anything to me unless I think there's a possibility I might be making a baby."

Have you ever heard a better sexual challenge to a woman than that? It's on par with her announcing to him, "Don't try to give me an orgasm. I've never had one. I never will. Just go ahead and enjoy yourself and don't mind me."

"I've done everything there is to do sexually with a woman," he'd said. "Now I want to settle down with the ideal woman and have the whole package, the house in the country, the kids, the station wagon."

Then *why isn't he married?* Excuse me, but there is no shortage of wonderful women, only of wonderful men. How could he not have found one? I didn't want to get married; I only wanted to get laid. But when faced with the elusive male, I was like a woman standing at the bottom of the stairs ready to dive when the bride tosses her bouquet. Catch those wilted flowers now; analyze your motives later. Charles was adept at creating this frenzied mood in a woman.

"Yes," he said. "I've been a photographer since I dropped out of college in my last year. I was studying engineering."

"I can't see you as an engineer," I said. The cat had entered the kitchen and was rubbing against my foot. I reached down to pet him, and he moved away.

"I couldn't see me as an engineer either, so I quit. The photography had always been a hobby. I thought, Why not try it? What have I got to lose?" Without looking behind him, he'd sensed the cat and flipped a raw shrimp onto the black and white tiled floor for him. "I had a few lean years, but it's been pretty good for me since the beginning."

He'd told me at lunch he'd worked for five years as

a fashion photographer. I asked him, "Did you sleep with the models?"

"Yes," he said, turning around to grin at me. "I slept with a lot of models. Photographers and models. Shit like that happens all the time."

He washed his hands after deveining the shrimp and poured more wine into my glass. I opened my arms and he walked into them. As he nuzzled my neck, I looked past the top of his head at the bowl of pink glistening shrimp. For a second, they resembled miniature mounds of pulsating vulvas, the liquid flesh of many beautiful women he'd had before me. I was intimidated.

"You smell nice," he said. "What is that scent?"

"Chloe."

"I knew it," he said with satisfaction. Of course, he did.

"I don't cook."

Laughing, he said, "I don't know many women who do, especially white women. I learned how to cook when I was living with a white woman. I figured we were going to starve if I didn't."

We ate the shrimp and salad on his bed, black-rimmed white stoneware plates balanced on our laps, the bread basket between us, while he talked about what he wanted in his life. Why do women spend so much of our time listening to men talk about what they want in life? Maybe it's because we still tend to forget our wants and needs when we're around them.

Anyway, he wanted, he said, a woman who could be lover, best friend, partner, mother, father, sister, brother—but he didn't want to commit to her until she'd proven her ability to get pregnant. He wanted children, he said, because he didn't want to grow old alone. Children, I wanted to tell him, determinedly biting down on the advice as I bit into shrimp, won't necessarily take care of you in your old age, and they certainly can't keep you from feeling lonely. Children, I wanted to tell him, aren't the idealized beings of your romantic fantasies.

"You could always adopt."

"It wouldn't be the same," he said, brushing the idea off as if it were a discarded shrimp tail. "I want the experience of having my own."

"I don't understand why you haven't found someone to marry," I said, picking up a leaf of lettuce with my fingers. I like picking up food not meant to be eaten with fingers. Cold pasta can be a sensual experience. "It seems to me a good relationship with someone you love is the best hedge against loneliness, whether you're old or young, or have children or don't."

Who would have guessed I'd be standing up for the old-fashioned way: Marry the woman you love and then have the babies.

"They didn't want to have kids," he said, breaking off a piece of the French baguette and sparingly buttering it. "A lot of women are selfish. They don't want to mess up their bodies or take time out from their careers or they think they're too old now."

If they were my age, they were too old. Don't tell me about the joys of motherhood over forty. I don't care how many celebrity older mothers make the cover of *People* magazine, I don't buy the concept. I had my babies at eighteen and nineteen, and I'd delighted in the little darlings every step of the way. Now, they were both studying in Europe; the daughter in Paris, the son at Oxford, where they were mercifully spared the story of their mother's climb to the top of the sex advice mountain. Few children grow up with the dream of their very own mother replacing Madame Zelda in the hearts and minds of men who want to know how to get their wives to have sex with another man while they watch, preferably with video cam in hand.

"I must know a dozen quality women in their thirties bemoaning their ticking biological clocks," I said.

"There's something wrong with the ones I meet. I've met a lot of crazy women."

"You could surely find someone sane enough to have a baby with you. Maybe you won't get the life partnership of your dreams, but it isn't like that for most of us anyway. My marriage didn't work, but the kids turned out great. We had joint custody. It can be done," I said, curling my tongue around a shrimp.

"You were lucky."

Why did I let him get away with that? Luck had nothing to do with it. We'd made it work. Why didn't I call him on his phony, romantic idealism over the raddichio which could have used more fresh cracked pepper? He wasn't married because he is an incurable "romantic," ever in search of the perfect woman, who can elicit the perfect emotion inside of him, thus making him the perfect man. Idealism is a powerful shield against intimacy. Why didn't I say that instead of murmuring in a falsely reassuring tone of voice, "Well, maybe someday you'll get everything you want," as if he were a child who was expecting the electronic game store to relocate to his bedroom on Christmas morning?

"Maybe I scare women off, because I jump right in," he said, wiping the shrimp butter from his mouth with one of those thick paper napkins that almost feel like cloth. "I meet a woman and if she has everything I want, I say, 'Let's make a baby together.' "

"It won't do you any good to say that to me. I had a tubal ten years ago."

"Can it be reversed?"

I didn't answer. He put the nearly empty plates on the floor and unbuttoned my leather suit jacket. If he needed to believe in the possibility of babies, let him believe. I wanted him so much then I would have agreed to babies, the house in the country, the station wagon, anything. I ached for him inside. Dimly through the delicious pain of wanting, I knew it was time to reach for the condoms. Where had I left my handbag?

"I love your breasts," he said, his voice catching in his throat as his hands lovingly encircled them. "They're perfect."

He took my left nipple into his mouth and gently sucked as he reached around my waist for the snap on my skirt. I raised my hips; he pulled down the leather and the panty hose at once.

"You've got a bitchin' body."

Not taking his eyes off my breasts, he sat on the edge of the bed and removed his shirt. No chest hair. I love chest hair, but I wasn't disappointed in his sleekness anyway. Then he stood and took off his pants and red bikini briefs; there it was, exposed, standing straight out in front of him like the Washington monument lying on its side. It was the biggest penis I'd ever seen. The standard-size condoms I carried at all times, just in case, would never have fit him anyway.

"Oh, my God," I said. It would surely measure ten inches, maybe more, a number many *Playhouse* readers claimed to reach on the yardstick, though statistically speaking, few of them really could. "Oh, my, God," I repeated. "It's magnificent."

"Is it more than you expected?" he asked, grinning.

"It's huge," I said, reaching for it as it was coming toward me at eye level. "We should use something," I said, my voice lacking conviction. No wonder he ignored my one veiled reference to condoms.

He straddled my chest and massaged my breasts while I took roughly the first third of him into my mouth. I sucked briefly, then holding his penis in my hands, plunged my face into his pubic hair and inhaled his scent. I ran my tongue experimentally up and down the shaft of his penis.

"Is it really big?" he asked, his voice a little strained. "Well, you should know. You're the expert. I always thought it was just average."

Right. I took him back into my mouth, pulling him deeper as he fondled my breasts; his hands were like velvet gloves smoothing the skin in lines radiating out from my nipples. Flicking my tongue around the head of his penis, I felt his body convulse. I thought he was going to come in my mouth. I wanted him to come in my mouth, wanted to taste and swallow his semen, but he pulled out and moved down my body. Gently he spread my legs open, then parted my vaginal lips with two fingers he'd dampened in his own mouth. As soon as he put his tongue on my clitoris, I was gone. My first orgasm came in waves around him.

"God, you're something," he whispered.

He pulled me up so that we were sitting in the center of the bed facing each other, my legs over his. Grasping my buttocks, he pushed into me. I moaned with pleasure. I had never been so filled by a man; it felt wonderful. I held onto his shoulders as he plunged in and out of me. Again, his body convulsed, and he pulled out.

"Touch yourself," he said. "Come for me. I want to watch you come."

I leaned back against the pillows, my legs open and bent at the knees. He sat still in the middle of the bed and watched as I put my hand against my own vagina.

"Come for me, babe," he said.

I wet my fingers in the juices and touched myself. Raptly, he watched as I masturbated. I kept my eyes on his face as I pulled the first orgasm out with my fingertips offering it to him. He was panting.

"Again, babe," he whispered. "Come again."

This time I arched my back, throwing my head back so I couldn't see his face. I lost myself in another orgasm, this one a long shuddering spasm that he broke when he pulled my hips off the bed and pushed into me. He thrust slowly and so deeply he seemed to penetrate my soul. I came again, biting his shoulder; this time he couldn't stop himself. I felt his ejaculation strong inside me. His whole body convulsed in spasm in time with his penile contractions. I came again. He pressed hard into me, to feel my orgasm, and covered my mouth with his.

"The trouble is," he said, after we had lain silently in each other's arms for several minutes, "I'm going to want more."

More what? More *of* me? More *than* me? I chose to believe he meant the latter, and it hurt. I nourished the hurt, letting it help me build a distance between us following the lovemaking.

Is it me or does my profession inspire sexual confessions from my lovers?

We napped in each other's arms for an hour or so. When I woke, he was still sleeping, but within seconds he opened his eyes and smiled at me. I felt a stirring in my groin and a corresponding movement in his penis which was lying against my thigh. I am a petite woman. It was lying against most of the length of my thigh.

"My work makes it hard to have a relationship," he said. "Sometimes I'm on the road three and a half weeks out of four."

"Uh-huh," I said, then cleared my throat. "Look, we've had sex once. It's a little soon to talk about a relationship anyway. I hate that word relationship."

It's true. I did. I do. It's also not true that I wasn't already thinking about having one with him.

"I know," he said. Was there anything he didn't know?

"You know," I said, "we're like the meeting of the

myths. You and your big black penis, the ultimate stereotype of the black male, and me, the sex writer."

"Yeah," he said, stroking my cheek. "Were you disappointed?"

"Not at all. Were you?"

Why did he dispense with the reassurances so quickly I can't remember exactly what they were? Or was he wonderfully reassuring, but I've chosen to forget his words? I don't know. I can't remember.

Somehow we plunged into his sexual history before I could even feel good about his sexual present and, hopefully, short-term at least, his sexual future. He enumerated the major women in his life for me. Dianne, black, educated, sophisticated, beautiful, smart, successful, married to someone else. When she finally left her husband for him, it was too late; his love for her, gone. Dianne came after the six-year living-together relationship with Mindy, the Jewish artist, who inspired him to take up cooking. She had followed the promiscuous period—not that he was faithful to Mindy in the not so promiscuous period he shared her bed—which had followed a love relationship with a young white woman, ending in her aborting his child, his "only" child. After Dianne, Barbara, white twentysomething, also married.

"She's married," he said. "She doesn't want kids. It ended. There hasn't been anyone serious since then. I can get a sense of what women want quickly. They haven't wanted kids."

I licked his nipple. It was so black, it was almost blue. What was I supposed to tell him now that it was my turn to share sexual details? Well, babe, there was Tim, the geek, who wouldn't fuck me; Johnny, the dry drunk, who wouldn't fuck me; Manuel, the possibly gay and undoubtedly repressed Latin non-lover, who wouldn't fuck me; of course, Roger, who left me for someone almost as young as my daughter.

"Dianne was the love of my life," he said, "and my sexual obsession. We were obsessed with each other sexually. She's still after me, but all she wants to do is sit on my dick."

"She must have a very long vagina."

He laughed and hugged me close to him. I guided his penis inside me; lying side by side, with my leg thrown over his hip, we made love again.

"I'm going out to get the morning papers," he said. "See what your press coverage looks like."

I groaned and pulled the sheet up to my chin. It wasn't morning. It was only a little after midnight. He pulled on his clothes, slipped his bare feet into topsiders.

"It's December out there," I reminded him.

"Only goin' a few blocks, babe."

"The morning papers really could wait until morning," I said.

He kissed me and tousled my hair. His eyes had that still familiar (despite all these months of celibacy) glazed expression of a man in deep lust. I sighed happily.

While he was gone, I replayed the morning conversation with Vinnie in my head.

"I want you to take a more public role in representing and promoting *Playhouse,* Carolyn," he'd said, sitting beside me on the gray leather sofa, his hand encircling my wrist. "It's good for the magazine to have a woman out there now. You're good for the magazine. I don't want you to worry about those letters and phone calls. I've got a good man on it. We'll find out who's responsible, take it to the police, and press charges."

I hadn't asked him if Zelda had gotten letters like mine and, if she had, why hadn't they discovered who was behind it before it got to be my turn? And we hadn't talked dollars, but he'd implied they'd be substantially more than I was getting now. It would be left to David to get the figure from him and report it to me. Or, not report it to me. Typically, I knew about my raises when I got my check because David had forgotten to tell me.

"You made front page of the *Post,* babe," Charles called from the entrance door, "but you're not going to like it."

"The picture's that bad?"

"Picture's okay," he said, standing in the bedroom door. "Not as good as the ones I took, but not bad." He held it up. At least my eyes were open wide, so the droopy left lid didn't make me look drunk. "Read the headline."

"SUPERLADY—NEXT PORN PRETTY TO DIE????"

"No. I don't like it."

"I knew that."

Chapter Eight

Dear Superlady of Sex,

Can you help me with an embarrassing problem? I am nineteen years old, but have very large sex organs. My testicles are about the size of eggs, and my penis is just at eleven inches and appears to be still growing. And the problem is even though I don't get full erections, I keep ejaculating just walking down the street and standing at the workplace. I have tried wearing a condom, but they are too tight and not long enough and leave me sore and red. My question is, how much more will I grow? And could I take a female hormone to stop me from ejaculating so much?

This was almost certainly a phony letter. If it were real, then the writer had no concept of how to use a measuring tape and also had a severe case of premature ejaculation. People ask how I can tell the fakes when the real ones are often so bizarre. I just can. After reading the mail for a week, I could tell. The prose of the jokers resonates with their self-congratulatory chuckling. Sometimes I answer the fakes anyway because they give me an opportunity to be more wicked than I would be with a genuinely confused and troubled soul. *(How much more will your penis grow, son? Reread*

Pinocchio *for clues.)* I put this letter in a folder marked "Possibles," which I saved for the day when the mail ran dry.

Thanks to the tabloids, would my mail ever run dry?

The morning *Post* reported I'd been receiving threatening mail for several months. They failed to add, however, the threats emanated from antiporn women's groups, both from the left and the right. Instead they made it sound as if I were in danger of being snuffed out by some poor panty sniffer, a man too timid in real life to come from behind his hamper.

"Ms. Steele is cooperating with authorities," the article said, which was news to me; I saw me sexually surrendering to a burly young man in blue, not necessarily bad news.

It was the day after the press conference, the day after I had been well and truly fucked. I was catching up with real life: the mail, phone messages, the water requirements of my plants. Dressed in black leggings, a large white sweatshirt, white socks, and tennis shoes, I did not look every inch the Superlady of Sex, but, for the first time in many months, I felt it. I was happy in the way one can only be happy following a night of great sex.

I was luxuriating in the sensual memories, but, physically removed from his intoxicating presence, I wasn't kidding myself about the man who had inspired them. He said he wasn't "involved" with anyone. I'd counted five different brands of shampoo or conditioner in his bathroom, which seemed excessive for a man with so little hair. And what did he do with that can of mousse and tube of gel? A great lover makes you feel like the only woman in the world; in his bed, I felt that way. Afterward, I counted the hair products and told myself, "You know what the bathroom clutter means."

Also, he'd rushed me out of his apartment by 8:30

A.M., claiming his assistant would be coming in by nine. I knew his "assistant" had to be a young and gorgeous woman he'd fucked or was fucking or had once and, after a brief intermission during which she'd hoped to push him into a commitment by withholding, was again fucking. I was falling in love, but not blindly. I saw exactly where I was headed as I allowed myself to tumble off the parapet into the moat filled with snapping crocodiles, all male, with their huge, spiny penises, unsheathed by condoms, menacingly exposed.

The phone had been ringing when I'd come in the door at 9:00 A.M., but I'd ignored it and headed straight for the shower. Now I had to deal with the twenty-two phone messages: five from David, becoming increasingly irritable as he repeatedly asked, "Where are you?" And "I'm respecting your need for space, but I'm here if you need me," from Tim, the geek, as if I'd ever have any use for the geek again. *Women Today* and *Bluebook* had both, "regretfully," killed the stories I was doing for them. Vinnie had better be increasing my salary by a significant percentage or the loss of the ladies' mags would put me in the hole. And, everyone from Morgy to my sisters was desperately trying to reach me.

I was just going to pick up the phone and return David's calls first when it rang beneath my fingertips.

"Where have you been?" he demanded. "It isn't like you to disappear without telling me. I know you were out all night, because I called at three in the morning."

"I was with that gorgeous photographer Charles." He *knew* that. If he'd called at three in the morning, it was only to determine whether or not a presumed afternoon delight had turned into an all-nighter. "How did you know I was out all night?" I asked. "I could have come home at 3:10 A.M. Doesn't Peggy (his wife) object to you calling female friends in the middle of the night?"

"The black one?" As if he didn't know! "I wouldn't

call him 'gorgeous.' He's too thin, and he has less hair than I do. And you know Peggy is completely without jealous feelings. Besides, she egged me on while I was dialing. You finally got laid?"

"Yes and yes," I said happily.

"He looked like a star fucker. Really, Carolyn, you're going to have to be more careful about whom you pick up now that you're famous."

"Oh, please! I'm not a star." I could see David smiling, his feet propped on the desk, his eyes on the entrance to HMV, smug at having gotten me to respond on cue. "He's not a star fucker. He's had a slew of models in his past."

"Was it good? Is he hung?"

"It was incredible. He *is* enormous. All these years I've been telling people that Kinsey says the average black penis is only point two centimeters longer than the average white penis. Last night I personally found the stereotype every white man fears exists inside a black man's pants. I love his big penis. How did I ever get by with less?"

"Typical woman, you say you don't care about penis size until a big one comes along."

"Yes," I agreed. "You're right. I'm doomed to spend the rest of my life comparing every one I meet to Charles's."

"Hmm," he said. David had often told me he is "the standard six, the best size, and proud of it." Oh, ha. Secretly, or not so secretly, every man wants to be a ten. "I'm glad you enjoyed yourself since your days appear to be numbered."

"You would have to bring that up. How long do you think they're going to keep this story alive?"

"Until there's a verdict in the La Passionata case. It makes better copy to imply a link between the three deaths and your imminent demise, which brings me to the purpose of this call."

"I thought you were calling to see if Charles had a big black penis."

"I assumed he didn't have a big white penis, Carolyn."

"Is there such a thing?"

"You're going to be insufferable if you get laid on a regular basis again, especially by this black super stud," he said, sighing theatrically. "Enough about your sex life. I have a wonderful story idea for you. I want you to write a piece for the magazine on La Passionata's death. Was it an accident? Or, murder? If he gets off, will he be getting away with murder? If he gets convicted, will it be because the jury is punishing him for his sexual perversity? It would give you a chance to do some real journalism. You could attend a few sessions of the trial, then interview all the key witnesses on your own, talk to the bondage expert for the defense, some shrink from the Violent Crimes Unit of the FBI."

"And it would be great publicity because the press would cover me covering this story."

"Right."

"Vinnie would love it," I said, getting straight to the point.

"Right." There was a pause while he gave me a brief chance to refuse the assignment. When I didn't, he asked, "Is it true what they say about black men?"

"Not true. He performs cunnilingus with skill and enthusiasm."

While I listened to David lecture on the statistical odds of a stereotype being true or not, I looked up Charles's number in the phone book. I sort of slid past David's condom question, but I don't think he was fooled. When he said goodbye, I pressed down the phone button until I heard the dial tone, then punched in Charles's number.

"Charles Reed Productions," a young and gorgeous-sounding woman said. "How may I help you?"

"Cathy," I said breathlessly as if I were searching through stacks of folders and piles of scrap paper on my desk for the precise piece of information I needed to share with her, "I believe we talked about prices yesterday for the Carlton shoot."

"I don't remember that," she said. "If you'll tell me what you need again, I'll be happy to go over the price list with you. My name is Barbara, not Cathy."

"Oh," I gasped. "Here it is. Wrong number!"

I hung up the phone. *Barbara.* The same Barbara who is white, twentysomething, married to someone else, and doesn't want kids, particularly one would assume, little half-black kids?

I closed my eyes and remembered him saying, "It ended. There hasn't been anyone serious since."

Resolutely, I opened my eyes again and looked back at the computer screen. Was it the same Barbara? Had he hired her before or after the affair began? Had it really ended? Would I ever know the answers to these questions and others?

At least, I knew just the letter I wanted to answer next and pulled it from the stack of recently opened mail on my desk.

Dear Superlady of Sex,

I'm sure my wife is having an affair with her boss. She has begun wearing her sexiest lingerie to work, including sometimes garter belt with no panties, which I have to beg her to wear for me. I pretend not to be paying attention while she dresses in the morning, but, believe me, I am watching. Also, she is working later and later. Do you think my suspicions are well-founded? Last week I drove past her office while she was working late. Her car and his were the only ones left in the lot. At the company holiday party, where spouses are invited, she and her boss seemed to have special eyes for each other. I've asked her if something is fishy there, but she says no. How can I make her tell me the truth?

Faithful Husband

Dear Faithful Husband,

Unless you are the sort who continually suspects your partner of infidelity with one man or another, you are probably right in assuming she's having an affair or is, at the very least, quite sexually attracted to her boss. Spouses either know these things about each other or suppress the knowledge. She's not going to "confess" until she's ready.

You can't make anyone tell you the truth, babe. I paused. Should I include a mini lecture on STDs?

If she is practicing sex without a condom, Old Faithful, she is putting you, as well as herself, at risk for STDs. And, should you be tempted to run out to the nearest low-rent bar to buy a cheap blow job in retaliation, you should know that herpes, chlamydia, gonorrhea, syphilis, and gonococcal farongitis can all be transmitted from the mouth to the penis. Most people worry about AIDS being transmitted orally—and worry *about AIDS is all most people do—when they should be concerned about getting a resistant strain of another STD this way.*

Was this lecture meant for the reader, Faithful Husband, or for Superlady herself?

For a few minutes, I considered getting David to hire Charles to shoot the La Passionata story, but sanity prevailed following a brief interlude of fantasizing about working with him. After a tough day of listening to court testimony about why some people can't reach orgasm unless they're so tightly bound breathing is a problem, we would climb into a limo together for the trip back to Manhattan and his apartment. We would toast each other with champagne. Then he would dip his fingers into his glass, sprinkle a few drops on my nipples, which I had exposed for him, and suck them dry.

No one had ever looked at my breasts the way he did, worshipping and consuming them all at once. My hand moved inside my leggings, down to my swollen flesh, tender from last night's lovemaking. I imagined his hands between my thighs, moving up and parting the moist inner lips. I felt him touching me, then licking me, faster and higher, until I collapsed with pleasure.

When my breath came normally again, I called David who agreed Tiffany should be the photographer accompanying me to the La Passionata trial. He called her, and she called me. She was thrilled to get the assignment, which would mean photographing some people entirely clothed, a new experience for her, in addition to the models who would no doubt be shot in tight bondage as additional illustration for the piece. Tiffany and I agreed to meet for dinner that night at an Indian restaurant in her neighborhood to discuss the story and its photo requirements.

The phone continued to ring throughout the day, because I was "hot." Everybody wanted to talk to me, except the one person whose voice I most wanted to hear. Other than David's, I didn't return any of yesterday's calls. Before leaving my apartment, I waited for Charles's call until waiting any longer would have meant keeping Tiffany waiting alone at a restaurant table for longer than the acceptable fifteen minutes.

Then, waiting for the PATH, I called the machine to see if perhaps I'd just missed his call walking those three blocks. I hadn't missed his call, only another call from Morgy. I felt guilty for not calling her back earlier. Two things happen to women as soon as they get into relationships: waiting and guilt.

"It's getting weirder with Georges," she'd said on yesterday's tape. "I need to see you for breakfast or lunch or something," she'd said today. "Call me!"

I felt guilty, but consoled myself with the thought that Morgy, in similar circumstances, would have kept the line open waiting for *his* call, too, leaving me to handle my own crisis with *him* for another twenty-four hours.

I spotted Tiffany immediately. Only a few of the tables were occupied, bad sign. No Indian diners at all. Worse sign. "Never eat in a Chinese restaurant if you don't see a Chinaman at a table," my father always told me. I still considered it good advice, applicable to any ethnic cuisine. Christmas lights were wrapped around two fake fig trees at the restaurant's entrance forming an archway. She was visible directly through the center of the arch, which probably had some meaning in new age holistic psychobabble terms. On the wall nearest her was a plaque of a brass female with many arms, long and slender and braceleted, the ubiquitous quasi-religious figure predating the American Supermom of the late seventies, whose arms were attached to briefcases, diapers, cooking utensils, and vacuum cleaners. Pink and purple plastic orchid-like flowers were tacked to the wall beneath the plaque. A cloying, smoky incense filled the air. I love Indian food, but I hate the incense and the decor.

"Were you recognized on the train?" Tiffany asked.

"I don't want to talk about it," I said, making a face in response and hugging her briefly before sitting down across from her. Maybe I had been recognized or maybe I was being paranoid, but I'd felt eyes on me all the way from Jersey City to the 14th Street PATH stop, where I'd gotten off and taken a cab across town to 26th and Lexington. And hadn't I seen that man again? I didn't want to think about it. What if he was Starred Man? Something I wanted to think about even less.

"You look fabulous," I told her, because that's what women say to each other, though Tiffany, whose social skills were limited, never returned compliments.

She was wearing a pale green gauzy loose blouse more suited to July than December, unbelted over jeans. Her unfettered breasts swung freely down into the folds of gauze. If she'd leaned forward at a thirty-degree angle, they would have been resting on her knees. Multitiered brass earrings, like miniature tacky chandeliers, hung from her lobes. Streaks of gold highlighted her overdone eyes, but her face was radiant, rested, and relaxed. Tiffany in her goddess mode. She exuded a sexual warmth as if she were wearing a gauze skirt to match the shirt and golden sandals, no underwear, her legs open to a breeze catching her musky scent. It was hard to understand how the *Directory of Adult Films* had ever called her: "Not one of the top female erotic performers of all time, but the kinkiest."

Tossing my black and leather fox jacket over the chair, I felt overdressed in black sweater pants, matching v-necked sweater, and black cowboy boots. I was glad I hadn't worn a bra. A pot of herbal tea was steaming in the center of the table, flanked by two small white porcelain cups, the kind in which the tea grows quickly cold.

"They have wine," she said.

"Thank goodness."

I signaled the nearest waiter and ordered a glass of

Chablis, the only option. It would be the cheapest California jug wine, but it was better than herbal tea. I asked for a glass of ice. Cheap white wine is better iced.

"Is that real fur?"

"It's real leather," I said, dodging the question, not wanting a lecture on animal rights, even in Tiffany's soft, sweet voice.

We ordered appetizers: chicken livers with poori bread for me, vegetable fritters with chutney for her. She filled me in on the progress of the Goddesses and Sluts all-day seminars, the first of which had been held the day before. She'd charged six women forty dollars each to spend a day applying makeup and trying on costumes and accessories gleaned from thrift shops, costume supply sales, and Tiffany's past. Seemingly everything she'd ever worn was stuffed into the two closets in her apartment or under the bed in boxes, or in the broom closet and the high shelves of kitchen cabinets. Her end tables were actually boxes filled with clothes and covered with some Eastern-looking fabric.

"I decided against the before and after shots for the future," she said, "because they all looked too much like the before shots when they left the transformation salon. Then again, maybe they should look the same when they leave," she mused. "I told a reporter from *Paper* the seminars are a safe way for women to explore their fantasies in dangerous times. Maybe they're safer if they leave looking like they came, their fantasies back inside.

"Now, I plan to take three polaroid photos of each woman, one as a slut, one as a goddess, and a 'tits on head with Tiffany,' shot, their head beneath my bare breasts. I'm going to do the tits on head at the book party for everyone who buys a book, too. Don't you think it's a great idea?"

"Great," I said, signaling the waiter for more wine

and a main course, vegetable curry for her, shrimp curry for me.

"I want you to come to a Sluts and Goddesses seminar," she said. "You won't have to pay."

I nodded encouragingly. Tiffany had taken my picture once, and I'd looked like a Las Vegas madam with an unusually good haircut. In two beats, I was prepared to get on the real subject, the assignment. Then, interestingly, it was she, and not David, who gave me the important news of the day.

"Have you heard about the internal investigation and reorganization at the magazine?" she asked. "Clarissa told me this morning. Vinnie's new money man is examining all the expense accounts, reevaluating the salaries and department budgets, whatever that means, and it probably means people are going to be fired and David won't be able to pay us as much anymore. Clarissa is afraid it might affect her. She's really worried, with the new baby coming and all."

"Uhm," I said, not wanting to admit I hadn't heard. Why hadn't David mentioned this in one of our four conversations of the day? Wasn't it more important than his learning if Charles performed cunnilingus or not? "Well . . ." I said, letting my voice taper off significantly and shrugging my shoulders eloquently, implying I might know more than she did.

"Do you think David won't be able to pay us as much as he does now?" she asked. "This is the first time in my life I've ever made so much money for my work."

"I don't know what it all means," I said, but really I did. It meant big trouble for David, who could be replaced at half the salary, and that couldn't be good news for those of us who were his chosen few. When editors go, so go the free-lance writers and photographers. Every new editor brings in his or her own favored people with whom to share expense account lunches. Can you blame them?

"We'll probably be fine," I said reassuringly. She looked so worried, I reached across the table and took her hand. Her fingers, covered in cheap rings, felt small and cold, like a child's. "They won't cut the fees too much if they do cut them."

She suggested I walk the three blocks down Lexington back to her apartment and look at some recent bondage photos of Vera to see if they'd work in the La Passionata article. It happened midway between the restaurant and Tiffany's building. Out of the corner of my eye, I noticed a slight figure in pants, heavy jacket, gloves, and baseball cap pulled low over the face. Man or woman? Boy or girl? Whichever, whoever was coming up fast alongside us. Then he or she seemed to notice me noticing him or her and dropped back a few paces. At the same time I was suddenly aware of another figure, larger, definitely a man on the other side of the street crossing against traffic coming toward us. I knew this man. He'd followed me from the PATH train to my apartment building only a few days before. I was extending my left arm out to touch Tiffany's sleeve, prepared to suggest in an urgent whisper that we sprint for her lobby, when it happened.

I felt the thud in the center of my back, followed by the slow dripping of heavy wet liquid down my back. I'd been hit. Tears flooded my eyes; I gasped, not from pain, but from humiliation.

"Oh, no!" Tiffany screamed. "You don't have the right to do that, no matter how you feel about animals!" she yelled after the running figure well behind us now. She turned to me and asked, "Are you okay?"

"I don't want to turn around and look," I said, grabbing onto her arm. Sticky red globs were falling behind me on the pavement, landing with sickening plops. Looking down, I could see them through my legs.

"I got it on film," said the man in front of us. He was the figure I'd seen moving across the street, a big, beefy tabloid photographer, the man who had probably been following me for days.

"She got you good, didn't she?" His mouth was curled up, either in his version of amusement as copied from old gangster movies or from a tic. "Hey, you know it's only paint, it's not blood. Vinnie will probably buy you a new coat."

"You were following us, weren't you?" Tiffany demanded, but, ignoring her, he stepped out into the street to hail a cab.

"Has it ever occurred to one of you guys to stop a crime in action instead of photographing it?" I yelled, but he ignored me, too. "That asshole would have shot the picture just the same if I was being stabbed," I said to Tiffany.

"Let's go inside and see what we can do about it," she said, patting my shoulder.

"I love this coat," I said. I'm ashamed to admit it, but I felt like bawling over a silly clump of fur. "I've had it for two years. My first fur coat. I bought it for myself."

"Oh," she said, her eyes filling with tears. We hugged each other on the street.

"At least it didn't get on the rest of your clothes," Tiffany said. She'd insisted on making cups of an anemic greenish tea of unidentifiable herbal origin, which we were sipping at the table in her dining alcove, photos of Vera bound filling the space between us. The coat was lying on top of plastic cleaner bags on the kitchen floor. We'd tried wiping the paint off and succeeded only in rubbing it in. The poor thing looked like an animal which had died in childbirth.

"I'll loan you something to wear home," she said.

"Maybe the cleaners can get the paint out," I said. She nodded enthusiastically. "This really isn't their part of town, is it?" I asked.

"Whose?"

"Animal rights protesters who throw paint. Don't they keep mainly to the Upper West and the Upper East sides?"

"You're right. I think they do." Her forehead wrinkled in thought, she absentmindedly traced with her right index finger the crucifix hanging from Vera's nipple ring in one of the photos. I didn't think the crucifix would work in the layout we were planning. "And, they usually work in groups, pairs at least. I've seen them on the street uptown."

"There's something wrong with this, isn't there?" I asked.

I stared into the framed photograph hanging over the table, Tiffany and Vera, arms wrapped around each other's waists, dressed in matching bustiers, stiff crinolines, mesh stockings, and five-inch heels. In red print at the bottom of the frame the caption read: "THE TRANSFORMATION SALON!!—Sexual evolutionaries Tiffany Titters and Vera want you to have a good time." Beneath their makeup masks, their faces were set in the smiling lines preferred by generations of homecoming queen candidates.

"Maybe there is something wrong with it," she said.

We were silent for several minutes, looking at each other. Like most New York apartments heated by steam, this one was now too warm which would undoubtedly alternate with too cold throughout the night. A drop of sweat trickled down between my breasts. Released by my warmth, my perfume rose in a gentle cloud filling my nostrils. I felt my nipples become erect.

Her eyes, blue and green with flashes of yellow, wide with innocence and deep with wisdom, grew softer. She reached across the table and laid her hand on top of mine.

"You don't have to carry that coat home on the train," she said. "There's a good cleaner in my neighborhood. I'll take it to him tomorrow."

I left Tiffany's apartment after politely refusing her offer to spend the night, either in her bed or on the living-room futon, where many luminaries of the sexual underworld had slept when between apartments. The famous writer, Octavio Juarez, had died there, nursed by Tiffany through the last horrible months of AIDS. Swathed in a scratchy woolen cape of many colors that made me feel like a runaway from a white slave camp, I had every intention of going back home to Jersey. I took a cab to 14th Street, where I started down the steps to the underground PATH. I couldn't make myself put my dollar in the slot and go through the gate. I turned around and went back up the steps.

I'm unnerved, I thought, so I'll just get into another cab and pay the twenty or more he will charge to take me to Jersey. On the street, I walked directly to a pay phone and dialed Charles's number, which I knew by heart, having only dialed it once. Tiffany would have called that a heartsign, though all of her heartsigns pointed to women now.

"Babe," he said when he recognized my voice. "I just tried to call you. What's going on?"

"I'm a few blocks from your apartment, wrapped in something big and bright and wooly from Tiffany's closet. An animal rights activist pelted my fur coat tonight."

"Come over, babe," he said. "I'll make you feel better."

I walked into his apartment, into his arms, and we did not talk. He lifted the hair away from my face and kissed my hairline, then my eyelids, my cheeks, and finally my mouth. As he kissed me, he opened my legs with his thigh. My heat enveloped us.

"I told you I was going to want more," he said, leading me to the bedroom.

We lay side by side, naked, touching each other with healing strokes. I ran my hand along the curve of his hip and, cupping his buttock, drew him closer to me. He lowered his head to my breast and took the nipple in his mouth. I cradled his head while he sucked me and thought of how it would feel when inevitably he put his mouth to my vagina. Shivering in anticipation, I reached for his penis and squeezed it gently.

"Make me come," I begged.

I was thick and wet from wanting him. Without taking his mouth from my breast, he put his hand between my legs, his fingers sliding back and forth in and out of me while his thumb massaged my clitoris. The orgasm which began almost immediately was so strong it seemed to suck his fingers inside me. I came around his hand, the spasms shaking my whole body.

"You are so incredible," he said.

As he had the night before, he pulled me up and into the center of the bed. Sitting with my legs over his, I moved my hips toward his penis. Holding my back firmly with one hand, he guided it inside me with the other hand.

"Hard," I said. "I want you inside me as far as you can go."

My urgency released his passion, which became as

insistent as my own. Growling deep in his throat, he lifted me off the bed in an act of penetration so deep and so total that I lost awareness of everything except his penis thrusting repeatedly inside me, claiming me, owning me. I came over and over again. When he ejaculated, I almost lost consciousness.

"I love you," he whispered, licking the sweat from my face. "I didn't hurt you, did I?"

"No, God, no, you were wonderful. I wanted you so much."

He held me tight against his chest. We stayed that way, without speaking, until we'd stopped panting. Then he laid me back against the pillows, fluffing them before he put my head down, and stroked my vagina until I was writhing, my hands over my head, grasping the headboard.

"Do you want me to eat you out?" he asked.

"Please," I begged. He lowered his mouth to my body as if he were about to partake of a sacrament.

I'd told too many men it was the best sex I'd ever had when it really wasn't. The male ego being what it is, they'd all believed me. Well, who wouldn't believe in his superior sexual prowess while lying beside a woman capable of thinking herself to orgasm? Now I really was having the best sex I'd ever had, and I didn't have any words left for the real thing. What could I say that I hadn't said untruthfully before?

I was limp. Orgasmic contractions, like the aftershocks of an earthquake, still shook my vagina. He was going out to buy the morning edition of the papers. I couldn't have gotten out of the bed for anything less than a large fire . . . directly *under* the bed.

"How can you go out into the cold?" I asked. "I don't have the energy to breathe."

"Babe, it's automatic. You're okay," he said, grinning affectionately at me and pulling the sheet up to my chin. "You have to see the picture of this person who hit you with the paint. I don't like the way it sounds at all."

I didn't like it either, and I liked it even less when he handed me the *Post* ten minutes later. They had me on the front page, coming and going, in a split page double photo. On the left-hand side Tiffany and I were walking toward the unseen photographer, the assailant framed behind us in the space between our heads. On the right-hand side, the paint was being flung by a startled woman, who had turned to face the camera just as he'd taken the shot.

"Do you recognize the woman?" Charles asked. He handed me a photographer's loop in case I needed to magnify her face for closer study. I didn't. "You do, don't you?"

"Elizabeth Thatcher. She tried to strangle me a few weeks ago on the 'Olive' show."

"Fuck!" he said, slamming his hand on the dresser, causing his mother's photo to collapse. "Fuck! I knew this was no animal rights protest when you told me about it. They don't hang out on Lexington Avenue in little India. We're going to call the cops."

I wouldn't let him call the cops. If I'd recognized Elizabeth Thatcher, so would someone else. The cops would be calling me, and I was in no hurry for the conversation, which would be too much like the one I'd had in Chicago. *Now, what did you say to her just before she tried to strangle you? I'd like to hear that again.* The New York cops would probably ask me if I'd wiggled my finger at her before she threw the paint.

We slept spoon fashion, his back to my chest, my hand around his penis, his hand around mine holding his manhood. I woke sometime in the night. He had an erection, and his hand had moved past mine so that both our hands were wrapped around it, like hands around a baseball bat. There was room at the top for another hand.

Chapter Nine

I wasn't the only one who'd recognized Elizabeth Thatcher as the paint thrower. So had someone at the *Post.* The later morning edition carried the same split page photos, but had replaced the front page headline, "New Enemy For Superlady!" with "Olive Choker Strikes Again!," making it sound as though Olive's necklace had a life of its own and had either bitten her or someone else, perhaps turning to violent crime to get her attention away from the competing jewelry in her wall safe. Having inwardly sneered at the headline, I was reading the article while waiting for Morgy to join me for breakfast at David's Pot Belly Stove restaurant on Christopher Street.

"Would you like another cappuccino?" the waitress asked from her hovering position over my left shoulder. I knew she was there before she spoke. The air around her smelled like the stuff that smells just like Giorgio, and why would anyone want to smell just like Giorgio?

The cup was half full, so I waved her away. Reluctantly, she took a few steps backward, reducing the almost Giorgio content of the atmosphere enveloping me. This member of a typically inattentive staff, who had needed half a dozen requests to replenish my cappuccino only the week before, was treating me like this was my last breakfast. If I kept on reading the *Post,* I might believe it was.

After relating the paint incident as the photographer had seen it, the *Post* article claimed:

Ms. Titters, who is herself a vegetarian, said, "Carolyn and I both thought something wasn't right about the whole thing." Ms. Steele could not be reached for comment. Elizabeth Thatcher's husband, Phillip, a lawyer, was on his way from Memphis, accompanied by Mrs. Thatcher's therapist, Dr. Roland Legerdermaine, who had no comment. At the Memphis airport, Thatcher said, "Obviously this crazed sex lady, who clearly is not a lady, has driven my wife temporarily insane. We are considering filing suit for damages against her and that magazine."

In an accompanying sidebar, titled "Faking Zelda," they played up, and not for the first time since her death, the great discrepancy between who her readers thought Zelda was and who she really was. This time they identified Clarissa as the current ghostwriter and accurately listed everyone who'd written the column before her. Who outside the magazine could have told them all this?

Zelda, of course, had never written a word of her own advice. Her name and her face had sold a lot of magazines in the early days. Beneath the sidebar, the *Post* ran the familiar *Playhouse* photo of her as a gorgeous busty blonde, taken twenty-five years ago, next to a candid pose of her in her final days—bald, her three hundred pounds stuffed into jeans and a plaid lumberjack shirt. It was a rather startling contrast. Hadn't any of these faithful readers thought to notice there was something odd about a woman whose face hadn't changed in a quarter of a century?

"Which woman would you tell your sexual troubles to?" the cutline asked.

The lie of Zelda made it all the more important that

I have "a very public existence," Vinnie had said in our last phone conversation. Readers were calling the magazine every day to protest the faking of Zelda and often to question my existence. They couldn't be madder if Zelda had been faking in their very own beds all these years, according to David, who handled most of the calls.

"Could you throw this away?" I asked the waitress, who was, I knew without inhaling deeply, still within hearing range. I thrust the folded paper in her direction without looking at her.

She took it from me and scurried to the back of the room in the direction of the kitchen. David's Pot Belly Stove is only about twelve feet wide, shaped like a bowling lane, and packed with tables on either side of the narrow center aisle. You have to go through the kitchen, passing dangerously close to the grill, to get to the single stall unisex restroom. On a bad day the smells of urine, Pine Sol, and grease hit you just as you turn right past the stove.

At 8:00 A.M. on a weekday morning, David's wasn't crowded. The West Village doesn't wake up early. Few of the people who live down here have "regular" jobs. They have "creative" jobs which are performed at home or, if in an office, then a nontraditional office, which opens for business after ten or eleven and where the furnishings are cheap, but the plants are awesome. A renegade corporate type who has chosen the West Village for his home would quietly breakfast in that home before slipping even more quietly off to the subway. Two lone male diners, probably musicians who hadn't been to bed yet or early rising writers, their attention captured by their copies of *The New York Times,* were the only other people in the room.

"I hate this place," Morgy announced loudly, two feet from the table. "If I weren't desperate to talk to you, I wouldn't be here."

What she meant was if she hadn't been too sleepy to argue when I'd called her at 7:00 A.M. from Charles's apartment, we'd be somewhere more decidedly upscale. She was only willing to endure downtown in the later afternoon when drinks were part of the package. Unassisted by alcohol, she couldn't abide anything below 57th Street, except her Wall Street office. Tossing her black leather Vuiton briefcase and matching handbag on the bench beside me, next to Tiffany's cape, she hesitated before placing her mink coat on top of it.

"What's that?" she asked.

"It belongs to Tiffany. Good morning to you, too."

"Oh," she said, pulling the coat back and tossing it over her chair across from me instead. Dragging the floor was better than touching that which had touched Tiffany. She sat down. "Oh, damn, I hate life."

"You look terrific," I told her, and, of course, she did. Dressed in a designer black wool coatdress with dark stockings, Bruno Magli pumps, and a small fortune's worth of real gold at her earlobes, neck, and wrist, she made a statement that read like the inflated bottom line of a glossy corporate annual report. "I don't know how you can look this good before noon."

"Well, you know the mess I leave behind to do it," she said.

Yes, I could picture Morgy's apartment, especially the bathroom, which typically looked like twenty-seven models had used it to prepare for a fashion show. It was the kind of mess that left one wondering how a perfectly coiffed, attired, and made-up beauty could have come out of this place, rather like a perfect child coming from the womb of a total loser with bad teeth, split ends, and no sense of style.

"Oh, Carolyn, what am I going to do?"

"Get the maid to come in every day instead of three times a week?"

"Coffee?" the waitress asked her. "Another cappuccino?" she asked me before Morgy had time to answer.

"Yes, to both," I said, waving her away again.

"Well, she's a skinny little thing," Morgy said, looking after her with distaste. "Anorexic."

"Every woman looks like that in Tennessee until she has her first baby," I said irritably. I knew Morgy was being snippy because the waitress was ignoring her while behaving obsequiously to me.

"Is she from Tennessee? I couldn't hear an accent."

"It's behind her vowels and consonants fighting to be heard. Obviously she's an aspiring actress on voice lessons."

"Oh. We should order when she gets back and get that out of the way because I don't have much time."

I nodded and picked up the huge menu listing plates of food which would also be oversized and in most cases came with hush puppies. There was a headache developing in the middle of my forehead. I wanted to be on the train back to Jersey because I had a lot to do at my apartment before returning to the city in the afternoon for Clarissa's baby shower. And, most of all, I realized I didn't want to hear about Morgy's latest romantic disaster, which wouldn't be much different from the one before it and the one before that and so on. I'd rather be taking a nap.

"There's something different about you," she said, after we'd placed our orders: waffles with Häagen-Dazs chocolate ice cream for her, a spinach and Swiss cheese omelet, with accompanying hush puppies, for me.

"It's probably the reflected glow from Tiffany's cape."

"Well, it does look a bit radioactive. No, really, there's something different about you."

"I can't imagine why there would be," I said, surprised at the strength of the angry feelings bubbling up inside me. "That crazy Elizabeth Thatcher attacked me last night and ruined my coat. I'm getting threatening letters and phone calls. The *Post* is doing a countdown of my last days. I've finally met a man who actually fucks instead of talking about it, but I think he's involved with a couple dozen other women, too. I didn't make him wear a condom, so I'm probably already harboring some new resistant strain of an STD. And, according to Tiffany, Vinnie's new money man is examining the numbers with an eye to slashing the budgets. Maybe we'll all be replaced by j school grads.

"Why wouldn't I be the same carefree old me?"

"Oh." She paused to be sure I was finished. "No, it isn't that. It has more to do with me, I think." Then, looking around for the waitress, she said, "This coffee's cold already."

While we waited for the waitress to return with hot coffee, we looked uncomfortably at each other. Why was so much of my irritation directed at her? And how did she, who rarely recognizes any feeling not coming from her own gut, know it?

"I'm sorry I didn't call you sooner," I said contritely. "I was swept away on a tide of passion. You know how it is."

"You'll have to tell me about him," she said. "It's Georges."

"No, I'm not seeing Georges, Morgy."

"You know what I meant."

I knew what she meant. Everything was always all about her. Any interest she had in other people was minimal and with a voyeuristic and/or critical bent. Why did I consider this woman my very best friend? Oooh, I was feeling mean and nasty.

"I don't know what to do about Georges," she said, the tears beginning to slide gently down her cheeks, where they would no doubt not even streak her makeup. She allowed the tears to slip all the way to the edges of her face before dabbing at them with her napkin just as the waitress, who finally noticed her, put the plates down in front of us.

"I'm afraid he might be, like you know, really a pervert. He's agreed to talk to you. He says he has a lot of respect for you, and I want you to talk to him. Will you do that for me?"

I wanted to throw my omelet in her face, but I smiled. No, I didn't say, "Yes," but I smiled, which was almost as bad. I didn't say, "No."

Why do I consider this woman my best friend? I asked myself.

I was sitting on a nearly empty car of the PATH train headed toward Jersey. It was a little after 9:00 A.M. No one goes to Jersey in the mornings. They leave from Jersey in the mornings to work in the city and don't go back again until after five. Anyone who was going back to Jersey in the mornings had their reasons and wouldn't be bothering me.

Why can't she just stand up at a Forum meeting and say, "Excuse me, my lover wants me to be his slave. Would that be giving away my power or not?" I asked myself. Surely they could tell her what to do.

I was in no mood to deal with Morgy and her made-up problems. The guy was a jerk. He wasn't satisfied with spanking her before anal sex. Tying her to the bedframe with silk scarves no longer titillated him. Now he wanted her to wear leather restraints, five-inch heels, and nothing else as she knelt before him to receive his sexual orders every evening. What a little prick, and, yes, I would have bet he had a little prick, especially since Morgy hadn't said otherwise. And wouldn't anything a man could "sort of slip" so easily into an anus have to be small?

Do you know what really irritated me about this

situation? I knew exactly what Morgy would do. She would play the game as long as it stimulated her. When she'd had enough, she'd drop him. And I knew that Morgy knew exactly what she would do, too. All this wringing of hands and begging, "What should I do? What should I do?" was only part of the game.

I'd been inside my apartment less than five minutes when Charles called. His voice, like a length of black satin being wrapped around me, smoothed out all the rough edges. Smiling, I flopped down on my bed, the half that wasn't covered with books, magazines, newspapers, research Cynthia Moore-Epstein had sent over on the lives and deaths of Tanya Truelust, Madame Zelda, and La Passionata, and letters to Superlady.

Two minutes into the conversation, his call waiting beeped, and Charles put me on hold. I hate call waiting. In that moment, I made up my mind to cancel my own call waiting and never to have it again. I could afford now to be eccentric.

Waiting for him, I glanced at the top letter, which read:

Dear Superlady of Sex,

I recently saw you on TV and God spoke to my heart to send this letter to you. Harvest time is here and God wants you, your family, your friends, and those sick people who write to you to believe in Him. I am looking forward to spending eternity with you, but this cannot happen if you do not repent now. Read the Bible and repent.

A list of recommended readings filled the rest of the page and a second one. If God Herself wanted to reach me, wouldn't She dial direct? Would She trust Her message with some nut who thought She was a man and would couch Her wisdom in cryptic terms like "See Matt. 7:7?" No, She wouldn't. I wadded the letter up into a ball and tossed it into the wastebasket, reducing the bed clutter by two sheets of paper and one envelope. The more threatened I felt in daily life, the more junk I piled on my bed. When things were really bad, as they were now, the usable space for sleeping was the width of a nun's cot.

"Babe," he said, coming back on the line. "I've gotta run, but I wanted to touch base with you this morning. Would you like to get some food later? I'll be flying out to L. A. in the morning, and I won't be back for ten days. I want to be with you tonight."

"I'd love to," I said, but the smile was gone. Ten days? He would be gone for ten whole days? "What time?"

"Come on down whenever you're finished with your baby shower," he said, chuckling.

Charles had found the idea of a baby shower for a lesbian "father" quite amusing when I'd told him about it that morning. In fact, Charles found many of the details of my life amusing. His eyes lit up when I told him about WIP lunches, fact checkers who don't comprehend penile thrusting, and letter writers with messages direct from God. What would I do to entertain him when he became as familiar with the bizarre as I was?

We talked for a few minutes about absolutely nothing; when I hung up the phone, I was smiling again, even with a corner of Fay Weldon's *Life Force* sticking in my back. I pulled the book out from behind me and settled back into the pillows. How I wanted a nap. Only fifteen minutes, I promised myself, I have so much to do.

Forty-five minutes later, the buzzer woke me. I clutched at the comforter in the same way another woman, in the next block perhaps, might grab her gun or knife when startled into waking. A lot of good a handful of feathers was going to do me. Repeatedly someone downstairs was banging the buzzer. I went into the hallway, pressed the talk button, and said, "Yes, who is it?"

"Messenger from Mr. Mancuso," he said.

"Could you wait a minute while I turn on the TV and check you out?" I asked.

"Sure thing," he cheerfully replied.

My hand wavered. Would an antiporn attacker cheerfully encourage me to check him out? Would a man be an antiporn attacker in the first place? No. A mad rapist. He would be a mad rapist, and would a mad rapist invite me to preapprove him on closed circuit video? Sure, why not? He's mad, isn't he? Figuring it was a lose/lose situation, I almost pressed the Door Release button, but didn't.

I hurried back to the bedroom, turned on the TV, punched in the closed circuit channel with the remote, and studied the man outside my front door. A medium-sized black man with a neatly trimmed beard, he was dressed in a green uniform, carrying under one arm a large oblong and relatively flat shiny black box, and waving directly at the camera. If I let him in and he killed me, at least he'd be on tape. I went back into the hallway, my hand hesitating over the buttons. What did I know now that I knew what he looked like? Was an informed choice possible with such limited information?

"Okay," I said, releasing the door with a bit of trepidation.

Security wasn't a perfect concept, especially when the word was applied to a system that basically depended on me deciding from four floors up if the doors should open or not. And some people buzzed in anyone who hit their bell, assuming, without checking, it was a neighbor with full hands or a forgotten key. Is that how my tormentor had gotten the letters under my door? I needed a doorman. I needed, I suddenly realized, to move to Manhattan so I could cut some of the daily risks I faced by staying off both the New York City subways and PATH trains.

The messenger had climbed the four flights of stairs quickly. He was knocking at my door. I looked through the peephole. Same guy. Same smile, the wave smaller this time, meant for the confines of the peephole.

"Hi," I said, opening the door. "Sorry I was being so overly cautious."

"Hey, Superlady." He handed me the large box. "If I was you, I'd be careful, too. I probably wouldn't have let me in the door in the first place."

I signed for the package, secured the deadbolts behind him, and took the box to the bedroom. Gold letters proclaimed Antoine's, the name of a far better than acceptable New York furrier. Vinnie had replaced my coat after all. Opening the box, I gasped. Vinnie had more than replaced my coat with this full-length Blackglama mink. It was exquisite. I held it to my cheek, where it seemed to lovingly return my caress, as I read his note: "Carolyn, May this bring a smile to your lovely face. With sympathy for your loss and enormous gratitude for all you do for the family, Vinnie."

Now, how could I complain about laying my life on the line for a man like that?

Any normal woman after being pelted with nasty red paint only the night before would not have worn her precious new fur coat on the PATH train to New York that very afternoon, especially if she was carrying an oversized box stuffed with Winnie the Pooh, Eeyore, Tigger, and Piglet and wrapped in disgustingly cute nursery patterned paper. Any other woman might have considered the package alone increased her visibility level to the potentially uncomfortable point. But I sometimes take the Superlady appellation to heart, and this was one of those days. I wore the coat. The PATH wasn't crowded. The three riders in my car, middle-aged Puerto Rican women, glanced derisively at my fur, then looked away, not meeting my eyes. I got off at Christopher Street and grabbed a cab uptown.

David's office had been commandeered for the shower. When I arrived, the other Women In Porn were already there, except Clarissa, who'd been sent on a fool's errand to the art department, and Bobby, who would be stylishly late. David was out getting ice for the champagne buckets. A sheet cake decorated with two well-endowed naked mothers, whose long flowing pubic curls entwined together, and one curly-haired baby sat in the middle of David's desk, surrounded by presents. There were also presents on the floor.

"Oh, my God, my God, I love it," Stephanie squealed, referring to my coat. She pinched the rich fabric between her fingers appreciatively. "David told us you were getting it, but we had no idea it would be *this* good. It's truly choice. Can I try it on?"

Everyone gathered around, stroking the coat, as they helped me out of it and articulated their feelings about Elizabeth Thatcher's paint job. They were all talking at once. The conflicting advice and opinions bounced painfully off my body.

"Vinnie says she's been remanded to a psychiatric hospital, so I wouldn't worry about her anymore if I were you."

"They'll keep her a week, and she'll be back."

"But home in Memphis, sedated."

"She'll palm her pills and sneak back to New York."

"She can't hurt you anymore."

"That woman is a problem."

"I really believe she's going to try to kill you."

"No, not kill. It was paint, not blood."

"But red, symbolic. Symbolic of blood."

"Stop!" I shrieked.

I put up my hands, and the babble stopped. Coat removed, I was wearing a snug black minidress in a wool knit with long sleeves and a square neck showing the top of my cleavage. Every woman in the room, except Tiffany, was wearing a black minidress. Only the sleeve lengths and degree of plunge varied from one of us to the other. Tiffany wore a v-necked hot pink fuzzy sweater, a push-up bra heaving her breasts up and almost over the top of it, and a blue jean skirt, sort of the outfit every high-school boy once dreamed of finding his date in when she met him at the door on Friday night.

"I told you about turning your back on women in silk dresses," Gemma reminded me.

Vera, looking stern and worried, stood behind her, nodding in agreement.

"Did anyone think to invite Miriam?" I asked, because I just wasn't up to talking about the incident.

My life had become a series of public incidents; all I wanted was to talk about the simple things, like was the cake white or chocolate, and were we really going to play pin the baby on the lactating boob as Tiffany had said we were?

"Oh, Miriam," Carola said, dismissing the gestating mother with a flip of one beautifully manicured hand, nails done in the French manner. "She is no fun."

"She doesn't really like us," Vera said, crossing her arms over her heaving bosom. Not being liked wounded her more than it did the rest of us; none of us were impervious to the strong reactions, often of pure hate, we elicited in other women. "Miriam thinks what we do is very sleazy. She told me she wouldn't 'sell out our sex' like we do."

"She can afford to have her prissy principles," I snapped. "Clarissa supports her."

"No, I think she just doesn't know how to handle being with a lot of people at once," Tiffany said. "She's shy."

Shy. Then I noticed on the wall where the tattooed penis usually hung the huge blowup photo of Miriam, nude from the waist up, her pregnant boobs enormous, but taut. They looked like they would burst on contact with anything, even a filmy nightgown. She'd filled out so much with pregnancy, the snake tattoos on both breasts appeared to have been recently fed large white rats. *Shy.*

"It's for pin the baby on the boobs," Tiffany said. "Here's the baby." She picked up an art department rendition of a baby who resembled a cherub on a Victorian Christmas card. "They don't exactly go together, do they?"

"I think the snakes are going to scare the shit out of baby when she arrives," David said from the door. "Look how their heads point down into the nipples. It will be like being nursed in the zoo."

I went immediately to hug him, surprised at the strength of my need for his reassurance. If we'd been alone, I would have bawled in his arms.

"Nice coat," he said, returning my hug. "I think you are definitely higher on Vinnie's list than anyone else at the moment. Congratulations. You deserve it." Softly, he said to me alone, "Vinnie has personally assured me Elizabeth Thatcher will be stopped one way or another."

"Oh, honey," Bobby said, filling the doorway David had just vacated with his arms akimbo, fanning out his own huge fur coat, a raccoon he'd saved from an incipient insect infestation in a vintage clothing shop. "Uhm, uhm, uhm. That coat is the most delicious thing I've ever seen. I'll bet you no woman ever got anything like that out of Vinnie without swallowing a lot of his come. You did it, honey, you made it on your own."

I didn't have a chance to reply to that. Cynthia and Rhumumba led Clarissa into the room, followed by the caterers, young men dressed for the occasion in black satin bikini panties and gossamer white frilly aprons, bearing trays of finger food. Dressed in a man's brown suit, white shirt, and brown shoes, Clarissa burst into tears. If the guest of honor hadn't been dressed as a man and the party favors piled in a basket on the floor hadn't included vibrators, flavored body paints, and ben-wa balls, one might have mistaken it for any baby shower in New York City, where the women, regardless of profession, tend to wear a lot of black.

"Let the raucousness begin," David said, opening the first bottle of champagne, and so it did.

Later, Vera and Gemma were spinning Clarissa blindfolded, the cherub in her hand, when Tiffany said, her arm resting lightly across my shoulder, "I've had sex with every woman in this room except you and Clarissa." After pausing to give me a chance to respond, which I didn't, she added, "Clarissa really is very old-fashioned, you know. She wouldn't cheat on Miriam."

"I agree with Vinnie," Charles said, signaling the waiter for the check. "Let him help you find an apartment in the city while he's in the mood to do it. He's feeling like he owes you. If you want my opinion, he does. Take advantage of it."

"Uhmm," I said, sipping my cappuccino. "Well, I didn't argue about the car and driver. It's a tremendous relief to have a chauffeur at my disposal."

"You're out there taking the heat, while his magazine reaps the publicity benefits. Take everything he'll give you. It's yours. You're paying for it by risking your life." I winced, and he reached across the table for my hand. "No, not your life. I don't mean that. Somebody just wants to scare you, not kill you."

I nodded, discouraging further conversation. Charles and I had already debated before over whether that "somebody" had "juice," meaning money and connections, which would explain how he or she could have gotten into my building or obtained my phone number. He didn't quite get it. I'd been on so many talk shows, my phone number and address passed through the hands of so many assistant producers, I might as well have been listed, or my apartment building marked with a neon sign. You lose your privacy when you have a public life. It's a basic concept most people don't get until it happens to them. Maybe I'd end up like Vinnie someday, unable to move without a phalanx of bodyguards, the memory of the shooting of *Hustler*'s publisher always in mind.

We'd just finished a delicious dinner at Claire's, a turquoise-hued oasis, the closest thing to Key West in Manhattan and only a few doors down from Charles's apartment on Seventh Avenue. His red snapper and my catfish had been superb; coming from Mississippi River country, I knew catfish. The service, however, was well below average, and Charles was getting irritated. He kept checking his Rolex and frowning. I was surprised. It was the first time I'd seen Charles express impatience, which is something I naturally express all the time.

"When Vinnie called me at the office this afternoon to tell me he wanted me in the city as soon as we could arrange it, I was shocked," I said. "Shocked that he would think of it. I'd already been thinking of moving someplace where I'd have a doorman and wouldn't have to take subways anymore. But do you think any broker Vinnie uses will know how to find an apartment I can afford?"

"Sure," he said, stretching out one long arm to physically stop a passing waiter.

"Tell our waiter if I don't have a check in two minutes, I'm leaving without paying," he told the disinterested, would-be actor he'd halted.

"I'll probably be living here before you get back," I said.

"I'll like that," he said. Endorsing the check which had suddenly materialized on the table in front of him, he smiled without looking up at me. "Come on, let's get out of here. For a minute there, I thought Vinnie'd have you relocated across the river before I could pay for dinner."

I wanted to hold hands on the street, but Charles squeezed the hand I slipped into his, then let it go. He didn't go in for public displays of affection. I couldn't decide if he didn't want to call attention to the obvious racial difference or if he didn't want to appear connected to me in case we walked past one of the other women in his life. I was convinced there were others, and who knew how many? And why did I care so much? I was thinking like a typical woman, expecting him to "commit," by which we usually mean carnally forsaking all others, because he and I had sex a few times.

Inside his apartment, he played back the answering machine tape while I used the bathroom and slipped out of my clothes and into his maroon silk robe. With the door shut, I could still hear the low melodic melange of women's voices running together, the well-modulated, accent-free voices of professional women who could be black or white, twenty-five, thirty, or forty. Were all his clients women?

When I came out, he was lying on his side across the bed, naked, his head resting on one elbow, the opposite hip thrust out.

"You have a gorgeous ass," I told him, taking a gentle bite of it.

"I'm glad you think so," he said, smiling indulgently at me. "Take off that robe and come here."

It was only our third night together and climbing into bed next to Charles already felt like coming home. He took me in his arms, and I was happy. Happier than I'd been in longer than I could remember, since long before Roger came into my life and went out of it again.

We didn't speak. For several minutes, he just held me, touching my face and looking into my eyes. I took his hand and pulled it to my mouth, kissed his fingers one by one, then sucked them each in turn. Unhurriedly, he lowered his head and kissed the top of my breasts, then licked in wide circles around each nipple. I shivered and moaned.

"You're so responsive," he said. "I've never known anyone like you in bed."

He turned me over on my stomach and ran first his hands then his mouth up and down my back, all the way into the crevice of my ass. I ground my lower body into the bed, seeking pressure against my clitoris as he continued down my body, caressing and kissing my hips, the back of my thighs, the backs of my knees. Then he ran his hands up my inner thighs.

"Touch me," I begged, arching my body to elevate it from the bed.

He slid one hand in the space between my legs and with the flat of that hand masturbated me. In seconds I rode him to orgasm. I heard him breathing heavily, nearly as heavily as I was. He grasped my hips and entered me from behind, all at once in a hard and satisfying thrust. I began to come again.

"I love you," he said. "I love you."

We made love fast and quick and deep. I wanted to believe his words spoken in passion so much that I did. He loved me.

* * *

I was drifting into sleep when I heard a familiar voice on his machine.

"I'm looking for Carolyn," she said. "Carolyn, it's important. Georges is here with me, and we need to talk to you. Please call."

I pretended not to hear, but I felt Charles watching me. A little later I heard him slip out of bed and go into the next room where he picked up the phone and made a call. I couldn't hear the words, except for "babe," but I recognized the tone. It was exactly how his voice sounded when he talked to me.

Tears filled my eyes. Why are women such fools for love? Or, is that fools period?

Chapter Ten

Dear Superlady of Sex,

Last night I caught my husband masturbating in the bathroom after he thought I was asleep. I have been suspicious of him many times in the past when I heard him getting up on tiptoe to go to the bathroom after he thinks I am sleeping. I asked myself, What could he be doing in there? The answers I could come up with were not good. My worst fears were realized when I opened the door and caught him with Playhouse *in one hand and his thing in the other. Worse, I caught him just in the act and some of it spurted onto my foot. Why would a man turn to self-abuse when he has a loving wife in bed beside him who would satisfy his needs whether she wants to or not? I blame you and your magazine for this.*

Dear Reluctantly Willing Wife,

Why would a man masturbate when he could enjoy the sexual indulgence of his willing, if not eager, wife?

There are, Reluctantly Willing Wife, many reasons for an occasional preference for masturbation over intercourse. Perhaps he wants quick release and nothing more. Some men tell me their wives need so much stimulation to reach orgasm that intercourse is something they only undertake when they are prepared for the arduous task of lovemaking. Or, maybe masturbation is a forbidden sexual treat for him, which, of course, makes it more desirable. Since you disapprove so strongly of his solitary pleasuring, this may be the case in your marriage.

Many people, men and women, married and single, report their orgasms are stronger during masturbation than intercourse. This is because they are not distracted by the other and can thus surrender totally to the private sensations of orgasm. Really, you should try it. You might like it. I personally enjoy masturbation whether I have a partner at hand, pardon the pun, or not.

Meanwhile, I suggest you leave your husband to his pleasures if you are having intercourse with him as often as you like. If not, why not suggest a mutual masturbation session? I'm betting he'll get so turned on watching you masturbate, he'll fuck you.

I switched off the computer and shut the light in my new spacious office. On the way to the bedroom, I stopped to examine the contents of boxes, opened but not unpacked. I was reacquainting myself with my favorite things as though our separation had been a long one, not a matter of hours. I touched a leather book and fondled a recently purchased ceremonial mask from the Yoroba tribe in Nigeria. The face was painted white, the lips bright red, black markings like fish hooks through hearts on either cheek. On its head, a couple sat side by side. Was it a wedding mask? Was it meant to be a mother whose children were driving her crazy?

The mask led me to wonder if the Yorobas, like many African tribes, performed clitorodectomies on their young girls, removing the clitoris, the site of sexual pleasure, in an attempt to keep them pure before marriage and faithful after. That led me to wonder why

Americans are so hung up on masturbation, that most wholesome and natural of human behaviors. Haven't we, for most of our existence as a nation, attempted to perform psychological clitorodectomies on our women?

Each generation of Puritanical descendants has had their own language for condemning the solitary pursuit and their own methods for discouraging it. The prohibitions have been applied to both sexes, but more strongly to females. Eighteenth century mothers made their little girls sleep in gloves. Nineteenth century mothers forbade all children sleeping with the hands under the covers. Kellogg invented corn flakes, which he thought would deaden the masturbatory drive in pubescent youths.

My guess is neither cold hands nor cold corn flakes stopped the truly lusty from touching themselves even if they did fear blindness, hairy hands, or warts would result. Today's woman—and don't accuse her of prudishness!—has her own explanation for why masturbation is bad for us. Anything which detracts from the "intimate" relationship between man and woman is bad for us. Each sexual urge should be tied to an equally strong intimacy urge. His own penis or her own clitoris, for that matter, should never come between them and their feelings for each other. People, especially women, irritated me so much with their pious, judgmental sexual attitudes it's no wonder I stuck my favorite finger out at Elizabeth Thatcher on the Olive Whitney show.

Wearily I climbed into bed. With little conscious encouragement from me, the same finger was moving down to my netherparts. It was my first night in my new apartment, and few things in life are lonelier than first nights in new apartments. I touched myself for reassurance as I looked around the huge, by New York standards, bedroom in my Upper West Side apartment. It was sixteen by eighteen feet, a luxurious amount of space which dwarfed my possessions. I couldn't wait to buy more things, and I could have my sister ship the oak wardrobe with the delicate hand carved flower petals decorating the doors which I'd stored in her attic.

More than that, I couldn't wait for Charles to come home in two days. Closing my eyes, I saw his big black penis, a being of beauty and perfection if there ever was one. It rose majestically over his prone body, waving like a magic wand beckoning to me. I touched myself and surrendered to it.

He was fucking me slowly, and we were sitting, as he preferred, in the center of his bed. We watched his penis as he moved it out to the tip then pushed it all the way back in, over and over until I thought he had to come, couldn't stop himself from coming, but he did stop, at the brink each time, his body convulsing as he pulled it back from the edge. We watched his penis, a life apart from us, connecting us, dividing us, giving us both more pleasure than anyone can reasonably expect to feel in bed in this imperfect life.

I stroked the sides of my clit, harder, faster, watching in my mind's eye as his penis, wet with my juices, pulled all the way out, then went all the way back in, farther than any man had ever gone inside me. I was going to come and suddenly I remembered the night before, my last night in the Jersey apartment, masturbating and looking up to see the security guard on the roof looking into my window watching me. He was black like Charles, and I'd smiled at him, thrusting my pelvis forward, giving him my orgasm; his eyeballs and teeth glinted white like exotic pale streaks in an ebony statue. As I rode my hand to orgasm, I could see him watching me and Charles in the middle of the bed.

The orgasms kept coming in irregular intervals over the next hour, often with no help from my hand. Everything, the world it seemed, was centered in my genitals. They were singing, alive with desire again the moment they were satisfied. I was aware of nothing around me. There was only the sensation of orgasm, coming again and again, Charles's penis in my mind's eye pushing in and out of my vagina, creating pink and red whirlpools in its wake.

The fantasy was so real, I could smell the way we smelled after sex when it was over. It was hard to believe he wasn't in the bed beside me. I fell asleep with my hand in my gluey crotch.

When I awoke many hours later with the familiar feeling of dried stickiness between my fingers, I was naked from the waist down and wearing a worn gray sweatshirt from the Gap on top. My ass was cold. I looked around the room, momentarily confused at the space. Then, I remembered where I was. Home, on West 74th Street in a prewar apartment, four spacious rooms with wood floors, a working fireplace of oak and marble, and architectural details, including wide woodwork that was intricately carved above the doorways, a stained glass window in the bathroom. I had a doorman twenty-four hours a day. Smiling, I regarded even the semi-unpacked wardrobe boxes standing outside my walk-in closet with affection. *Home.* I looked at the clock. 7:10 A.M. I wrapped myself in the peach comforter prepared to go back to sleep when I remembered that a car was picking me up at 8:30 A.M. Tiffany and I were going to New Jersey to attend a particularly interesting session of the La Passionata trial.

It would be a major photo opportunity for the tabloids, who'd pretty much left me alone since the pelting incident. Sleepy as I was, I suppressed a sigh. I was trying to break the sighing habit.

"She had been trimly and symmetrically bound, with blue tape around her wrists and elbows signifying shackles and white tape around her forearms," said Dr. Fred Durwood, the forensic psychiatrist brought from Washington, D.C., to testify for the defense of Anthony Spiker in the death of Domina Rodriguez, alias La Passionata.

Regarded as the nation's leading authority on bondage deaths (Do you suppose there's a lot of competition in that field?), Dr. Durwood spoke in a well-modulated voice expressing class, education, and sophistication. He sounded like a British lord explaining the intricacies of the English school system or perhaps the game rules for cricket. He held a copy of Alex Comfort's *The Joy of Sex,* from which he had just quoted to prove that bondage is a far more common sex game than the average American realizes. Tiffany, sitting next to me, seemed quite taken with him. So did the members of the jury, surely a plus for the defense.

"The bindings were elaborate, excessive for the purpose of merely rendering her motionless. They were among the form of restraints favored by regular bondage participants."

He described other typical forms of restraint favored by the serious bondage artist, which go far beyond the simple method of attaching limbs to bedposts by silk scarves, the game with which most of us have some familiarity, either through personal experience or going to the movies. I half listened, my notes here turning into the questions Tiffany had posed on our drive to New Jersey together. She was convinced that a conspiracy might exist to kill the women of porn. Pondering the possibility was more entertaining at the moment than listening to Dr. Durwood explain bondage. I knew all about bondage.

Perversely marking each one of my questions with a five-pointed star, I listed them:

*What if someone or ones did drug Anthony Spiker's

champagne and pushed the gag deeper into Domina's mouth until she suffocated, then set the fire?

*What if someone or ones did push Julie [aka Tanya Truelust] down those fire escape stairs?

*What if the same or a related someones also killed Stella [aka Madame Zelda]?

I was writing the what-ifs in my notebook. Vera, not surprisingly, favored the WWAWAW membership directory as the primary suspect source list. And who's to say, given my own experiences with Elizabeth Thatcher, that she couldn't possibly be onto something?

"Domina Rodriguez was wrapped as neatly as a Christmas package," Durwood said, bringing me back to the here and now.

The jurors, seven women, five men, perhaps with thoughts of their own Christmas packages wrapped tightly and stacked under their trees, squirmed. With seventy-six feet of adhesive tape wrapped around her, twenty feet of it around her head alone, Domina/La Passionata must have resembled no gift I ever wrapped on the way out the door to delivering it. I never can find a new role of Scotch tape and am always making do with the last inches on one that's lost most of its stickiness.

"Such tight wrapping," he continued, "is characteristic of serious bondage."

"He's kind of cute, don't you think?" Tiffany whispered to me.

"Uhm," I said. I didn't exactly think he was "cute." Tall, dark, and reasonably handsome, he had a mustache slightly reminiscent of Hitler's. Probably he was one of those men who couldn't grow much of one, but then why bother? I couldn't help looking at it and wondering if his penis was likewise foreshortened. Yes, I know hand and foot sizes are considered the likely indicators of penis size, but some men fool you. And some give it away in their chosen mustache styles.

I was getting bored, so I began diligently taking notes of the major points he was making for my story.

1. If Anthony Spiker had used bondge as a cover for murder, he wouldn't have used so much carefully aligned tape.

2. The death by asphyxiation could certainly have been accidental, as between five hundred and one thousand accidental deaths occur during sexual bondage each year, most through asphyxiation.

3. The surviving partner panics and tries to cover up what happened.

4. Starting a fire is the most common form of covering up.

"What have you got?" Tiffany whispered.

I crossed my legs higher and tilted the notebook in her direction making it easier for her to read. Without consulting each other in advance, Tiffany and I had both worn black leather, mine a suit with a miniskirt, hers a dress borrowed from Vera. If she leaned over, her breasts would fall out. Two male jurors, casting covert glances in her direction every five minutes, seemed to be waiting for that to happen. She was wearing thigh-high black suede boots, which almost met the top of her dress. I had selected three-inch black slingbacks, just the thing for the northeast in the winter, if you're being chauffeured.

With one long red nail, tipped in gold, she pointed to the questions she, via Vera, had posed earlier. She arched her eyebrows, which were largely pencil lines, at me quizzically. I shrugged my padded shoulders, careful not to encourage her.

If the crazy women of WWAWAW had anything to do with La Passionata's death, when had they come onto the crime scene? I couldn't imagine them knowing how to tape the victim nor could I picture her sitting willingly as they wrapped the seventy-six feet of tape around her. Had they been hiding in the bushes until the taping was done, the gag in place? Then, had they sprung into action? Not likely.

Or was it? Research into male paraphilias, or perversions if you prefer, show a strong correlation between sexual perversity and religious extremism and intolerance. As Dr. John Money says, Scratch a rigid, Republican, born-again Christian and you are more likely to find a foot fetishist, masochist or sadist, or pedophile than you are if you scratch the skin of his politically liberal, non-churchgoing neighbor. Could the equation hold equally true for right-wing women?

Maybe. Mentally, I drew lines through Tiffany's questions anyway. The scenarios I had to conjure to put the WWAWAWs at the scenes of the crimes were improbable, at best.

"Let's skip the afternoon session and go out to the scene," I suggested, and her eyes lit up.

Tiffany left the courtroom before the morning session was over, so she could be in place to photograph the principals on their way out. Other photographers were already waiting outside to photograph her photographing the principals. Covering this trial, Tiffany and I were like a movie within a movie, a soap opera on a soap opera. I slipped out a side door and met her at the car, thereby avoiding the tabloid press until the last moment. Had I realized they would run the shot of me climbing into the car, all legs and ass, I might have done otherwise. You just can't cheat the tabs out of their share of your fifteen minutes of fame.

Driving out to Fort Lee, Tiffany and I went over the background material we had on La Passionata.

"Look," I said, "I side with the defense. She was a willing participant in a bondage game gone wrong. He probably got drunk and passed out while she was wrapped. She choked on the gag. He came to and staged the fire. Maybe he's even telling the truth when he says he doesn't remember anything until he smelled smoke. He could have been in shock when he carried her out to the garage and started the fire.

"What I don't see is any reason to connect the WWAWAWs or anyone else with her death."

"He was seeing other women," Tiffany said, "and she didn't like it. Maybe he did kill her."

"I don't see how the fact that he was clearly a lying, womanizing scumbag makes a difference," I said, dismissing the whole thing. "The only interesting part of this story is what the jury's going to do about it. Will that white bread group be able to grasp the concept of tight bondage and acquit or not?"

While Tiffany put up her argument for murder, either by Anthony or the WWAWAWs or all of the above, I mentally went over the facts on each of the three "mysterious deaths." None of them added up to murder. I sighed. It was proving to be a hard habit to break, like biting one's fingernails.

"I know," I said, brightening, "I brought the mail. Let's find something to laugh at."

I flipped past a letter from a woman who said her husband was bringing home strange underwear which he'd claimed to be pulling from trash cans. She wanted to know if I thought he was lying. *(Honey, does it look and smell like garbage?)* Another from two guys, "best buds," who said they measured more than a foot and wanted to know what to do with their things. *(Guys, stand facing each other, tie them together, and use as a jump rope for girls you want to impress.)* And a letter from a wife whose husband wouldn't eat her out. *(Cheat.)* Then, I found it.

"Okay," I said. "Here it is. A twenty-page letter, beginning, 'Dear False Goddess.' "

You call yourself a sex expert, but I am telling you how spiritually ignorant you are about the sexual function of human beings. You know nothing of sex as God intended for it to be used. When God created Adam and Eve and their first relationship led to insertion, He insisted they get married. The advice you give is the same they gave in Sodom and Gomorrah. It caused David to lose the Ark and the Covenant. It has brought on the epidemics of AIDS and broken hearts and destroyed minds. You encourage blacks and whites to mingle their sex when you know Cain married a black Neanderthal female animal, better known to the human race as the black people who continue to act like animals and think they are human beings. Do you wonder now why Hitler destroyed the Jews?

"Why do so many of these people think I'm Jewish?" I asked. "I'm always getting hate mail from Christians who assume I'm Jewish. Don't they look at my picture? What self-respecting Jew would have this hair?"

"I don't know," she said. "Did you know I am Jewish?" I admitted I didn't. "Well, I wasn't raised Jewish, because I was adopted. Do you know something that's been bothering me about this whole thing?" she asked, pointing to the research on the three dead women neatly piled, and just as neatly ignored, on the seat between us. "Stella never knew who her father was. Julie, who was also Jewish, but was raised by a Protestant stepfather, ran away from home when she was fourteen. Domina's mother left her when she was a baby."

"So?" I asked. "I don't get it. Why would that make them victims of murder?"

"The point is we don't know a lot about them because their pasts are gone."

She talked about the three women and what was known about their pasts in her dreamy wispy voice, the kind of voice Jackie Onassis would have if she'd spent her life in porn instead of marital money.

Tanya never had an orgasm during sex with a man,

on camera or not. Like Tiffany, if for different reasons, she'd given up on men and turned to women as lovers. She got into the video business because she believed X-rated films should show women having real orgasms so the men watching would learn something.

La Passionata had in life as well as on film been a bondage devotee, and the major details of Zelda's life had been common knowledge among those of us in the know. Was I beginning to get any pictures? Tiffany wanted to know. No, I wasn't.

"They had in common disadvantaged childhoods, porn pasts, and atypical sexual appetites," she said.

"Oh," I said, trying to sound like it all made a difference in factual terms, though I didn't believe it did.

"We should research Elizabeth Thatcher, that's who we should research."

"You may have a point," I said, largely because I wanted to put us back on common ground.

But, after I thought about it a while, I decided she did have a point, though what it had to do with any other point she'd been trying to make, I didn't know.

The scene of the crime, a classic sixties tract house in quiet, residential Fort Lee, was a disappointment. Only the charred edges of the garage door indicated anything untoward had ever happened there. In the cold clear December sunshine, one could shut one's eyes and not be able to envision a nude woman bound tightly to a chair, burned beyond recognition behind that very door. No. All you would be able to picture in that neighborhood was an electrical fire caused by old Christmas tree lights.

Dutifully Tiffany shot her pictures, but I could tell she was as bored as I was, maybe more so. When you're accustomed to looking through a lens and seeing juicily interacting body parts, how can you get excited about a concrete driveway, evergreens, and a picture window? We both almost fell asleep in the car on the way back to Manhattan and seriously considered dropping our initial plan of stopping at the office in favor of returning to our respective apartments for naps.

"Oh, let's go by the office and see if Miriam's had the baby," Tiffany said, and I agreed because I didn't want to admit I was in no mood to care if Miriam had the baby.

Back at the office, however, we found more than baby news. Starred Man had dropped by for a visit while we were in Fort Lee.

"It was awful," Clarissa said, wringing her hands which had just delivered a Polaroid of Starred Man into my own reluctant hands. "Like worse than you ever thought he would be in your wildest dreams. His chest hair was sticking out between the buttons of his shirt all the way down to his stomach. Like he buys his shirts too tight, I guess. It was gross. Hair like steel wool cleansing pads. You can't imagine," she said, shivering for dramatic effect.

I looked at his picture. He was white, but darkly complected. His skin looked muddy, and his eyes looked vacant. The hair of which he was so proud stuck out everywhere, even from his nose and ears. He needed a shave, beginning below the eyes and ending somewhere in the vicinity of the protruding stomach.

"Clarissa is extraordinarily repulsed by chest hair," David said, "but she does have an aesthetic point. Even a lover of chest hair might find his too much."

"His shirt was most certainly too tight," Cynthia Moore-Epstein, ever the stickler for details, added.

I put my hand on my forehead where a headache was beginning. It threatened to spread to my entire body. Why was this happening to me?

"I wouldn't worry about it," David said, putting his arm across my shoulder. "He won't be back."

"Oh, and why not?" I asked.

"How did he get upstairs anyway?" Tiffany asked.

"Oh, he didn't get upstairs," Clarissa said. "We all went downstairs to watch while security held him for the police. Cynthia brought the camera so we could take pictures for all the other security guards in case he comes back—" She caught David's menacing glare. "Which, like, he won't. I know he won't. We scared him off for good. And, Vinnie's lawyer is getting a restraining order now, so he won't be permitted anywhere near you. And, like, if he violates it, he's going to jail for a real long time, so he won't."

"How did they know who he was?" I asked. "Did he sign himself in as Starred Man?"

"Carolyn, he wasn't wearing a coat," David said.

"And he didn't smell nice," Cynthia added.

"So, like, of course," Clarissa finished, "they knew something was wrong."

"If he's shown up here, isn't it likely he's been sending the letters?" I asked.

"The first letter was sent by express mail," Cynthia said. "I can't imagine he could figure that out."

"Vinnie's P. I. doesn't think so," David added. "I'm not sure why, but maybe he has a lead on someone else."

And what none of us knew then was this: Someone called a *Post* reporter at approximately the same time the security guard was dialing the police.

Miriam's water broke as we were huddled in David's office discussing the ramifications of Starred Man's sudden appearance at our building. Her frantic call to Clarissa got our minds off Starred Man. Tiffany, with a video camera borrowed from the art department, rushed off to the hospital with Clarissa. David sent everyone else home early, mostly, I think, so he could ride back to my apartment with me, sprinkling so many reassurances into his conversation I felt like Mary Poppins had taken over his body. Terminal illness and death rarely take the edge off David's delightful ability to be caustic and amusing at the same time.

When I got as far as my bed, I crashed. I didn't wake up until almost midnight. The phone was ringing.

"Picture this," David said. "The front page of the *Post* is a photo inside a huge cookie cutter star. You are climbing into a car. Exercise does pay off, Carolyn, dear. Your ass does look good enough to nibble, but may I suggest in the future that you enter automobiles with some grace and not headfirst?"

"Oh, shit," I said.

"The headline reads," he continued, " 'Behind The Bondage Trial.' "

I wanted to pull the comforter over my head. I never wanted to get out of that bed again. I wanted him to shut up and go away, but I knew I wasn't going to get what I want, ever. Relentlessly, he read the latest chapter in my doomed life, according to the *Post*.

> *While the Superlady of Sex, Carolyn Steele, attended a session of the sensational La Passionata bondage murder trial in New Jersey, one of her fans was stalking her at the* Playhouse *offices on Broadway. Ex-con Lamont McDermont, known to Steele and the* Playhouse *staff as "Starred Man," because of his practice of identifying each paragraph of his fan letters written from prison with a meticulously drawn five-point star, announced to a security guard, "I've come for Superlady. She's expecting me."*
>
> *The security guard, Arlen Shepherd, noted McDermont's general appearance, including that he*

was not wearing a jacket or overcoat, and became suspicious.

He says, "I told McDermont, I would call her down if he'd wait there in the lobby. He agreed to this, and I pushed the silent alarm, the buzzer is on the floor beneath my desk, calling for backup and also called upstairs to ask Mr. David Keltner if Miss Steele would be expecting a big guy who smelled bad and didn't have an overcoat. Mr. Keltner asked what color he was, which is white, and said, 'probably not.'"

Keltner denies making a racially oriented comment. He says, "I asked what color his shirt was, thinking he might be a messenger from one of the local courier services. Ms. Steele frequently receives review copies of books from publishers."

Within seconds additional security guards surrounded McDermont, who was held for the police. When they arrived thirty minutes later, several Playhouse *staff members were watching the proceedings from a safe distance, photographing Lamont and openly speculating over whether he was the person behind the threatening letters Ms. Steele has been receiving. They identified "Starred Man" by his chest hair, which was protruding from his shirt and by his shouted insistence, "Superlady wants me because of my manly hairiness!" Copies of his letters to the Superlady of Sex were handed over to the authorities.*

Meanwhile, Steele, accompanied by former porn star, Tiffany Titters, heard expert testimony on sexual bondage practices by Fred Durwood, MD, forensic psychiatrist from Washington, D.C.

According to Durwood, sexual bondage aficionados typically use extensive forms of restraint, such as the seventy-six feet (see accompanying articles on pages four and five) of tape used on La

Passionata. He also said it is not unusual for the "survivor" of a bondage accident incident to stage a fire to cover up the true cause of death.

"Survivors will go to almost any lengths to protect the victims' secret from discovery," he says.

McDermont was recently released from New York State Prison in Albany after serving five of a fifteen-year sentence on aggravated assault and armed robbery.

Ms. Steele could not be reached for comment.

After hanging up with David, I went to the kitchen to pour myself a glass of chardonnay. The phone rang. I hoped it was Charles, but I thought it was David calling back.

"Carolyn," the now familiar voice said. "Do you remember I told you you had your chance and blew it?"

Chapter Eleven

Dear Superlady of Sex,

Pornography has become increasingly aggressive, violent, and abusive. It harms relationships and encourages the subjugation of women. When you tell a woman in your column, as you recently did, to say to her man, "Fuck me," when she wants sex, you are really telling her to ask him to subjugate her into submissiveness. Shame on you! Every fiber of my being revolts against you. What you are doing is worse because you are a woman. Did your great-grandmother own slaves, and did she beat the women hardest? Or was she content merely to force them to submit to the rape of the white masters? Perhaps she enjoyed watching. Some day this is going to come back to you, and you will find yourself at the mercy of violence. . . .

Only 5:15 P.M., but the editorial offices of *Playhouse* were empty, except for me. It wasn't the kind of place where people felt compelled to stay late to prove their commitment to the job. David set the tone for the staff, and the tone was, "Let's keep everything in perspective here, people, this is a sex magazine, not a surgical amphitheatre, be out by five, latest."

I was only there because I wanted uninterrupted time

on-line with Nexus, the exhaustive computer research service plugged into nearly every newspaper and periodical published in the country. No, I didn't think I'd find the answers to my critical question—*Did someone murder Tanya, Zelda, and La Passionata and was that same someone coming after me?*—by punching up, Porn Pretty Killer, on the screen and entering the command, Search All Files. But after learning that Zelda, too, had received cut and paste threats on the same cheap typing paper before her death, I was desperately looking for a way to link those brief missives to a person or a group.

I put the letter from the woman who equated "fuck" with "subjugate into submissiveness" into the "Dangerous" folder, but was it really dangerous or just plain nutty? And why didn't we have a "Plain Nutty" folder? Clarissa suggested going through the hate mail looking for a "thread." That had sounded like a good idea, but what thread could one find in hate mail besides hate?

So, here I was, alone in the office checking hate mail, both mine and Madame Zelda's, against published antiporn diatribes, looking for possible connections. These women tended to be highly repetitious. Perhaps I would find the threats were phrases pulled from longer letters. Or maybe I could match an anonymous letter with a signed letter to the editor appearing in an esoteric lesbian journal or right-wing Christian newsletter.

I picked up another letter.

Dear Madame Zelda, You Cunt,

Perhaps you are familiar with Surgeon General C. Everett Koop's warning against pornography, issued in May 1988. He said, "Men who see such material [violent porn] tend to have a higher tolerance for sexual violence. And we suspect that, for men who are even slightly predisposed to such behavior, this material may provide the impetus that propels them from fantasy into the real world of overt action."

Perhaps you are also familiar with the similar conclusions reached by Donnerstein, Linz, and Penrod . . .

This had fallen into the hate pile because of the greeting and salutation, "Dear Madame Zelda, You Cunt," and the closing, "May your clitoris be ripped out without anesthesia." Definitely from a WAP. No WWAWAW would use the word "clitoris." The findings mentioned coincided exactly with those listed in a letter to the editor recently published in *The Cleveland Plain Dealer* by a WAP member. I found it on Nexus and wrote the woman's name in pencil on the letter as "possible author."

But, having found it, what had I found? I could probably have proven in a few hours' time that half or more of the hate mail came from established antiporn groups largely composed of women. I knew that already.

Sighing, I went back to the stack of letters, typed and printed on word processors, hand written in block print and script ranging from Palmer perfect to nearly illegible. So many people, the majority of whom were women, with so much anger directed at us. How much happier would they have been if they'd taken their hands away from their writing tools and placed them on their own bodies where they could do some real good?

And what was the thread linking them together? Fear of sex? Fear of pleasure? Fear of losing control? Everyone was looking for threads. Tiffany had been obsessively combing the lives of Zelda, Tanya, and La Passionata, looking for the connecting links. When she found them, they were exactly what you'd expect them to be. High-school dropouts all, they had sold what they had to sell for the best possible price. Had she really expected them to have come from happy, reasonable, functional families? Or to be graduates of Vassar?

I smelled the presence of someone else in the office

before I heard anything. It was a subtle shift in the air as though someone were blocking a draft. I took my hands away from the keyboard and sat very quietly, listening hard. Nothing.

Maybe it was my imagination, I told myself, like a Gothic heroine, determined to proceed up the dark and narrow staircase to the attic in search of some truth. I picked up another letter. Well, what else could I do?

Dear Porn Queen Steele,

According to my hypothesis of what makes a woman sell out her own sex as you have done, I know who you really are. Like all porn queen types, you were abandoned by your mother, either physically or emotionally, and overstimulated by a father who both wanted and hated you . . .

I felt it again. A diffusion of the atmosphere behind me, directly behind me. I put my hands on the desk in front of me and tensed, as if bracing myself for an imminent crash. If someone was going to shoot me in the back, I didn't want to turn around and catch it in the face. Or, if someone was going to bring a heavy blunt object down on my head, I didn't want to see it coming, did I? Maybe if I didn't turn to look, nothing bad would happen after all.

"Like, what are you doing here?" Clarissa yelled.

I turned, partly in relief and partly in fear. Was it Clarissa who meant to bludgeon me to death? She had suggested a computer search for the missing links.

"Working," Rhumumba replied in the slow and low mumble that made it hard to hear what she was saying once she got past single word replies, which, come to think of it, she seldom did.

"What is everyone doing here?" I asked, walking to the doorway to confront them.

"Carolyn!" Clarissa said. "She was spying on you. I

saw her. I couldn't believe it. I didn't know who was in the computer room, but it was you. Like, she was standing there without moving and watching you!"

"Why were you watching me?" I asked Rhumumba, who remained silent.

"I decided to come back to do a little work since they wouldn't let me stay at the hospital, but I want to go back again for the evening visiting hours," Clarissa said, talking fast, her eyes on Rhumumba, who kept her eyes on me and her mouth shut. "You know I said there was something not right about her all along, didn't I?"

"Why were you watching me?" I asked again.

Rhumumba turned and walked out of the office, making remarkably little noise for someone who was built like an armored vehicle. Clarissa and I looked at each other. We couldn't have stopped her even if we'd wanted to try, which we hadn't.

"Well," Clarissa said, clasping her hands together in front of her body and rubbing her palms together back and forth until the dry raspy sound irritated me. "I think it's time we found out who she really is. I've always thought she was hiding something. Remember the rest of you thought her secret was a simple one. And, like, when we saw the hormone pills on her desk and knew she was a transsexual, everybody said, 'Well, that's it,' and I said, 'It's not going to be something so simple as this.' "

"How much more could a lesbian transsexual body builder have to hide?"

"Did you read the *Post* today?" Clarissa asked. We were waiting in the hallway outside Miriam's hospital room, the personal contents of Rhumumba's desk in three large gray envelopes in our arms, two for me, one for her. "What's a sitz bath anyway?"

"I hope the *Post* didn't say I was sitting in one."

"No, Miriam is. The *Post* has decided Anthony Spiker didn't murder her, that it was a bondage accident. I think they've taken that path because they couldn't find any way of connecting the porn pretty deaths, don't you? Like if they can't have a clean sweep of murder, they'd rather be bold and go with bondage accident. It gets the bus driver readers all agitated."

"A sitz bath is when you immerse your bottom in warm water to make your stitches feel better," I said. All that fisting and she'd still needed stitches? "In my day, it was alternated with heat lamp treatments. I still went through massive amounts of Tucks, but then I changed them every time they got dry on me."

"I have a headache," Clarissa said, visibly paling at the thought of what was happening to Miriam's vaginal area.

"She'll be all better in a few weeks. The stitches are catgut. They just fall out."

"Oh, gross!" she said, clamping one hand on her ear. "Carolyn, if I'd wanted to know about this stuff, I would have gone to Lamaze classes."

"I think you're right about the *Post*. Once this trial is over, they'll stop plotting my demise."

There were no chairs in the hallway. I pulled off my four-inch black slingback pumps, hiked my black wool skirt a little higher, and sat down on the floor, legs crossed in front of me. I tugged on Clarissa's trousers; she sunk down to join me. Wordlessly, we began going through the material in the envelopes.

"They have a magazine just for lesbian bodybuilders?" I asked.

"Why not?" she said, glancing at the cover. It was someone who looked enough like Rhumumba to make me fear she was a type in her own world. We both added, "Not my type."

She hadn't filled out the insurance request forms in

the company information packet she'd received upon hiring. Everything was still neatly in its pockets. I pointed that out to Clarissa, who merely raised her eyebrows.

"Fliers from health food stores, her gym membership card, hormones, and vitamins, what did we expect to find anyway, her old penis in a jar?" Clarissa asked, shoving everything back inside the envelope.

"That wouldn't have told us anything we don't know," I said, putting my share of Rhumumba's stuff back into the envelopes.

And then I did know. The picture on Rhumumba's desk, a 3 × 5 photo in one of those plastic frames that curves to make its own stand. I saw it clearly in my mind's eye. It had bothered me when I'd looked at it, but I didn't know why, had blamed my vague feeling of discomfort on the woman's bad haircut. Now I knew exactly who she was. And knowing who she was also explained Rhumumba. Why hadn't we brought that photo of the little tank's special someone with us?

Thanks to my driver's ability to move that limo through traffic as easily as if it were a motorbike, it took me less than twenty minutes to go to the office, retrieve the picture, and get back to the hospital. I slipped into Miriam's room, behind the back of an Oriental nurse who'd told me she already had her quota of visitors, two, and I'd have to wait outside. Some experiences are universal. This was no different than visiting any member of the Junior League back in Easterville, following the birth of her child. The rooms of new mothers were always standing room only. There was as much sneaking around to get inside those rooms as there would be later to get inside someone else's spouse's bed, after the babies were older and the thrills were gone.

Dressed in what was either a long sweater or a very short sweater dress, royal blue, shot with lurex threads, deep v-neck, Tiffany was cooing over baby Zelda in her crib beside Miriam's bed. A plump nine pounds, six ounces, Zellie, as we were all going to call her, had skipped the isolet in which many newborns typically start life and gone straight to Miriam's room. In five-inch stiletto heels, electric blue with ankle straps, Tiffany towered above baby like an East Village version of the good witch from *The Wizard of Oz.* Clarissa was seated on the bed, holding Miriam's hand and managing to look like she was the one who'd suffered.

"Carolyn, come look at her," Tiffany said. "She has so much hair."

I leaned over the crib. Zellie did have a lot of hair, tight fuzzy black ringlets, which set off her *café au lait* skin. The hospital had taped a pink bow to her adorable fuzzy little head in case someone failed to get the picture drawn by the pink receiving blanket wrapped around her. Why hadn't anyone told me the sperm donor was black?

"She's beautiful," I said truthfully. Isn't it nice when we can honestly say that about other people's babies? I lightly touched her cheek, baby skin, like nothing else on earth. Instinctively she nuzzled in my direction. "So beautiful," I cooed.

"Isn't it great she didn't come out red like white babies do?" Clarissa asked. "Like, I never thought about skin very much until I saw her, and now I think she's the best color to be."

Tiffany and I gurgled shamelessly over her for fifteen minutes before we had to leave for Tiffany's book party. It doesn't matter how babies get here or how strange their parents may be, they are little miracles of love and hope, the great levelers, turning all of us into the kind of people who lisp in nonwords.

We kissed Miriam. She looked truly awful, which is

another reason women her age shouldn't give birth. They don't look "wan but luminous" like younger mothers do. No, they just look plain awful after putting their bodies through something they shouldn't have to endure. And what were stretch marks going to do to the snake tattoos on her boobs?

Clarissa walked us to the door. I pulled the photo out of the deep pocket of my fur coat.

"Recognize her?"

It took a few minutes for recognition to dawn, but when it did, they were almost simultaneously spitting indignation. The woman who occupied the space of beloved honor on Rhumumba's desk was the thin blond WAP who regularly harangued us on the street corner, waving her placard of a torture victim in our faces as she shrieked, "Women, what are you going to do about this? Men are masturbating to this every day. They're masturbating to it right now. What are you going to do about it, women?"

"Rhumumba is a WAP!" Clarissa hissed. "If her lover is a WAP, she has to be one, too. Like those people don't intermingle. Right in our midst. No wonder she didn't fill out her insurance forms! She's a spy, a plant . . ."

"A killer?" Tiffany finished.

David and Charles were already at St. Mark's Bookshop in the East Village when Tiffany and I got there. They were standing, paper cups full of wine in hand, at opposite ends of the room, a group of thirty or so people between them. Blowups of several of the photos from Tiffany's book, *The Erotic Journeys of Tiffany T.*, were mounted on flimsy wooden easels along the walls.

Some of the photos were startlingly good. I particularly liked one of a nude couple: the tall, muscular black man holding a soft white woman whose body was rigid at a fifteen degree angle to his body. Her ass was too wide, and his penis was hidden. But, I liked it anyway.

It was a definite improvement over the party David and I had experienced recently at a Tribeca gallery where a writer's girlfriend had her first art exhibit. The writer hadn't told us his beloved only painted insects. Yes, bugs. Roaches, spiders, flies, caterpillars, bugs of indeterminate, to me anyway, species. The smallest canvas appeared to be three feet by four. The largest, a fly with many eyes, was bigger than the floor of a typical New York studio. They hung from the thirty-foot ceilings like the backdrops for a horror movie. Waiters handed out crystal flutes filled with champagne and offered guests dried beetles from glass and brass boxes. We had declined the beetles. Yes, this was a better party.

Eyeing the distance between them, I didn't think David and Charles were going to be friends. For a moment, I hesitated. Whom did I hug first? Charles, whose flight had landed only hours ago and for whom I was desperately horny, or David, my dear friend. David, of course. My mother always said brains outlast beauty. If she'd added friends outlast lovers, she would have given me everything I really needed to know about life. Anyway, I'd learned the last part on my own.

"Carolyn," he said, returning my hug warmly. "Were you and Tiffany helping each other get dressed? Is that why you're late?"

"We were looking for threads," I said and then I quickly and quietly filled him in on what we now knew about Rhumumba.

While he went to find a phone to notify *Playhouse* security that Rhumumba was no longer permitted on the premises, I connected with Charles, who wasn't amused at being second.

"I thought you didn't see me," he said, pulling back from my embrace.

"I had to tell David something important," I said and then told him what was going on.

"Babe," he said, putting his arm protectively around me. "That's frightening. You don't think she's behind the calls and letters and the paint throwing, do you?"

"The cards and letters, yes, it's possible. But, not the paint. She and Thatcher would never collaborate on a political action even if they do share the same side of the porn fence."

While he massaged my neck, I tried to explain the difference between WWAWAWs and WAPs. Whatever else she may have done, Rhumumba couldn't have been in league with Elizabeth Thatcher, because the WWA-WAWs want lesbians to have orgasms even less than they want heterosexual women to have them. They were two separate groups with agendas which dovetailed nicely on only one point.

David joined us, and they chatted briefly about photography for a few minutes. Why do two men instinctively pick a subject the one woman won't be able or willing to converse upon? I excused myself and went over to Tiffany, who was standing with her arm around Vera's waist in animated conversation with the other WIPs.

"I told them about Rhumumba," Tiffany said to me, encircling my waist with her other arm. I have to tell you my waist is a lot smaller than Vera's. She's expanded considerably since the cameras lovingly caressed her bound torso.

"I knew there was something weird about her," Vera said, but who hadn't known there was something weird about her?

We never did figure out where to rank her in the hierarchy of terrorists that night, because Tiffany's "special guest," her friend Angelo, formerly Angela, arrived.

"Oh," she squeaked to him, once her. "You look so delicious."

Truthfully, Angelo didn't look bad at all until he unzipped his pants. He was close to six feet, broad shouldered, with prominent cheekbones, a thick headful of blond, probably not natural, hair, styled close to the face and full in back, curled down to his shoulders. His jaw was a little weak for a man, but couldn't the same be said of a lot of men? It was the penis he pulled out of his pants which spoiled the effect.

"It's still a little raw-looking," he said anxiously. "The doctor told me the red might not disappear for several more weeks."

"Oh, it's beautiful," Tiffany said, reaching out to pat it, which, thank the Goddess, didn't cause it to fall off.

There were murmurs of polite assent among the women. Speechless, I smiled down at it. I felt like a mother had just lifted a deformed baby from its stroller and thrust it in my face for my admiration, something I might have been able to pull off with advance warning, but not without. Looking closely at it, I could see why male to female transsexual surgery was more common than female to male. It must be easier to slice off a penis and fashion a crude opening that could appear enticing, especially covered at the entrance by hair, than to create one by pulling the skin from the vagina outside and fashioning it around tissue taken from various parts of the body.

It was three to four inches long, maybe two inches wide, bright red in places, mottled red and purple in others, creating a patchwork skin effect. The hole in the head wasn't quite centered. The head, for that matter, wasn't quite a head, merely a slightly thicker part of the whole. And it was lumpy-looking throughout its inglorious length. I glanced at the other women looking at it and knew they all, with the exception of Tiffany and Vera who are kinder and gentler than the rest, shared my thought, *Not in my vagina, you don't!*

"Does it work?" Carola asked.

"Sort of," Angelo said proudly. "It doesn't get too hard, and it doesn't ejaculate, but I feel orgasms in it already."

Several people were peering discreetly into our little circle to see what the thing was in Angelo's hand. Charles was one of them. Judging from the expression of gentle distaste on his face, he wasn't quite sure what he was looking at, but he knew it wasn't pretty. Tiffany moved outside the circle, opening a space so everyone who wanted could come to admire Angelo's new organ.

That's why so many of us were standing bunched in one place when a figure dressed all in black from stocking cap to boots, and wrapped in a coarse black wool cape, opened the door to the bookstore and tossed something inside. A package wrapped in plain brown paper fell inches from us. We did not move or even, with the exception of Stephanie, scream. She started quietly enough, but her scream crescendoed until, at its peak, it began to rise and fall rhythmically. People looked at us as if they thought perhaps this was our version of the famous faked orgasm scene in *When Harry Met Sally,* and nobody wanted to intrude.

Luckily nothing worse than smelly smoke (in shades of yellow, green, and orange) emanated from the package. Tendrils of it curled up into the air surrounding us like party streamers. While Stephanie continued to scream and the rest of us began to cough, David rushed over, grabbed the package, opened the door, and threw it onto the street.

"Do we agree no police?" he asked, rejoining us.

We did and only Charles, camera in hand, got the shot.

"Rhumumba?" Charles asked.

"Not possible," David said. "I talked to Vinnie only minutes ago, and he said Rhumumba had been taken to police headquarters for questioning about the letters and phone calls. His P. I. has found someone who saw her on Wayne Street near Carolyn's apartment on the day one of the letters was delivered."

"Then who?" Charles asked.

"The WWAWAWs," I said. "Definitely their style. No wonder Vinnie seldom goes out."

"If you hadn't been ignoring me all evening, you would have noticed I was taking pictures," he said, and he was pouting.

It was hard to pay close attention to him now either when a short distance past my bare feet a woman was lowering her mouth over a penis, not as big and fine a penis as Charles possessed, but a nice one.

"What am I, the enemy now, too?" he asked. His eyes were stormy; I wanted to kiss his face, but I didn't want to touch him yet. "You think I'm going to sell that shot to the *Post?* You think I'd stoop so low? Or maybe you think I paid somebody to toss a stink bomb into Tiffany's celebration?"

"Of course not," I said. But did I mean it? I didn't trust him, though it was his wandering penis I suspected of endangering me, not his camera. "I'm just being paranoid. You know I've been through a lot lately. Does that turn you on?" I asked, pointing to the screen.

"Don't get paranoid with me, babe."

He considered the action on the screen. The woman's face was contorted by the penis in her mouth. There was a bead of sweat on the end of her nose; she was stroking her clit as she sucked her lover. He was calling her by name, Amanda, and thanking her for fellating him even as she was doing it. We were looking at the first feminist porn video produced by Vera and Gemma's joint venture, the Red Hot Mamas.

"It's hot," he said, putting his hand between my legs. "Does it turn you on?"

"Yes," I said.

I lied. It didn't turn me on. Like most of the woman-produced porn I'd seen, it was a little too politically correct to be arousing. Did he have to thank her so profusely? And, earlier, with equal politeness, he had asked her if it was okay to tie her to the bedposts while he ate her out, which he explained he only wanted to do so he could pleasure her more. Vera and Gemma wanted me to invest in their company. I was considering it, but only if I could have some creative input.

Charles turned me on. I tried to say his name, but I produced only a gurgle in my throat. The days and the miles and the distrust between us all came together like spaces suddenly compressed, and we fell into each other's arms, collapsing walls of feelings and flesh melding together. If I thought I'd wanted him before, it was nothing compared to how I wanted him then. I'd gone beyond having a strong sexual appetite for him. This was a hunger so intense, so active, I wanted him all at once, simultaneously in every orifice, his hands on every inch of my skin.

I was on my back, completely open for him. Our pelvises were locked together, and he was deep inside me. We moved together, slowly at first, he tried to keep it slowly, the movement contained. But I couldn't wait. I tightened my thighs around him, squeezed and pulled him inside me faster, deeper; soon he couldn't wait either.

I cried his name and screamed as the first orgasm began. He moaned and grabbed me fiercely to him. I felt him ejaculating deep inside me, a place where no one else could reach; I buried my face in his neck, inhaling his scent. He was all I wanted. I wanted him over and over again.

"Babe," he whispered, "I love the way you do this."

We lay together on our sides, still locked, his penis firm inside me, panting. Moving slowly, he stroked my clitoris lightly with his hand, bringing me to orgasm again. He kept it up, making me come over and over. I dozed and woke to him caressing me, entering me before I was conscious of wanting him. He lifted me up, guided his penis in with one hand so he was only partially inside me. And suddenly I was moving toward him and coming again. With each spasm of orgasm, he pushed in a little deeper until he was all the way inside me.

I touched his face. His eyes filled with tears. And I pulled him deeper into me, fiercely pulling his penis, all of him to safety inside me. My body entwined around his, I fell into a deep and grateful sleep.

In the middle of the night, I woke to the sound of static on the TV. The Red Hot Mamas' first video had played itself out hours ago. Charles was sound asleep, facing me, his arm across my body, his leg over mine. I pressed my nose and mouth into his chest. I licked his skin. It was salty. Knowing it would never happen, I thought I could be happy for the rest of my life with this man in my bed at night.

Then I felt it, the slow drip of a thin bitter liquid seeping out of my vagina, a liquid that was neither semen nor vaginal secretions.

I went to see my ob-gyn the next morning and asked her to culture me for chlamydia. Having had it once, I recognized the thin, faintly dark discharge. It smelled vaguely unpleasant when I put my fingertips to my nose.

"You're lucky you have a discharge," she said. "Most women don't."

Right. Lucky was exactly what I didn't feel with my feet in the stirrups, my diseased parts exposed to the air. Stupid, maybe. Why hadn't I made him wear a condom?

"You might have gotten it even with a condom," she said reassuringly. "People don't realize so many of these STDs can be spread during foreplay. There is discharge present in his seminal fluid or your vaginal secretions, you touch each other's genitals before putting on the condom, and what can I say? You've got it."

I sighed. Hopeless. It was hopeless. Sex was hopeless. She said he would have to be tested and treated, and we should consider agreeing to a monogamous relationship so this wouldn't happen again next month. Oh, Charles might *agree* to a monogamous relationship, but he'd never actually keep his penis to ourselves. Hadn't he made his position clear on our first day together when he said he was on a quest to implant his sperm in any suitable vagina?

"He's probably had it for a long time without knowing it," she said, patting my shoulder. "Men aren't tested for it unless they ask to be."

She sent me away with a pamphlet explaining chlamydia, its method of transmission, treatment, and the consequences of leaving it untreated: In women, Pelvic Inflammatory Disease; in men, infection of the testes leading to infertility. In fact, the neatly printed little words told me: "Untreated chlamydia is the leading cause of infertility in men and women today." If he'd been carrying the disease for a long time, his odds of being infertile were good, the ultimate irony.

The test came back positive. I got my prescription for Floxin filled and left the pamphlet with a note for Charles with his doorman. He was not amused. Then I went back to my apartment where a message from Vinnie was waiting for me.

Rhumumba had confessed to sending the letters and making the phone calls, to feeding information, including who really wrote the Madame Zelda columns, to the *Post.* But she swore she hadn't killed Zelda and had no intentions of harming me. Neither his P. I., who had been on Rhumumba's trail even before Clarissa and I caught her in the office, nor the police could find any reason to connect her, or the WAPs, with Zelda's death.

"It's over, Carolyn," Vinnie said. "She meant to scare you and to cause the magazine as much discomfort and embarrassment as she could."

The WAPs had posted her bail, but Vinnie's lawyer had slapped a restraining order on her prohibiting her from coming near me. If she did, she would be arrested immediately. With both Rhumumba and Starred Man kept on leashes, I should have felt safer, but I didn't.

It was over, Vinnie said. But it wasn't.

Chapter Twelve

Dear Superlady of Sex,

I notice most of your letters are from men who want to put more excitement in their sex lives with their wives and girlfriends. Well, I am a woman with a man's problem. When I started seeing my husband four years ago, I wasn't surprised he only penetrated me, had an orgasm and that was that! He was a twenty-five-year-old virgin and didn't know any other way. I am a few years older than he and began having sex at the tender age of fifteen so you could say I had been around the block and knew he wasn't up to speed. I loved him anyway because I knew he would be a good provider and father and we were married. But it's four years later and he still does it that way. I've tried to show him new ways and new ideas, but he says he prefers the "traditional" way, in which unfortunately I don't have enough time to come. Sometimes I take his hand and make him masturbate me but he feels uncomfortable doing that. What can I do with him?

Dear Patient Wife,

You have been patient far too long. He sounds like a very sexually repressed man who would benefit from counseling. If you can't get him to see someone with you or alone, make an appointment for yourself. You can at least get professional advice on how to deal with your marital situation and perhaps suggestions on how to get him into the therapist's office. Meanwhile, make it clear that you consider sexual satisfaction your right as well as his. He's treating you like a prostitute by taking his satisfaction quickly with no thought to giving you anything in return. Next time, tell him lovemaking has to last long enough for both of you. If he won't touch you, masturbate yourself. And don't let him inside until you're almost ready to have an orgasm. Finally, have you considered an affair? If you want to keep the marriage together and he won't or can't change his sexual attitudes and behaviors—a lover is the answer for you.

I was glad I didn't write for *The Ladies' Home Journal.* They would never have let me advise a wife to cheat. This was not the kind of advice Dr. Rita would give either. I smiled. Then the disease thought intruded as it did so often. Should I warn poor wife to have an affair with a married man who was only seeing her and absolutely no one else and whose own wife was too repressed to look outside the marriage for sex and still get tested twice a year? Yes, I should. One should be responsible about advocating potential disease-risk situations. I hate the nineties.

"What are you so mad about?" Morgy had asked me when I'd told her about my chlamydia, which had all but ended my relationship with Charles. "It isn't AIDS. Like you aren't going to die. So, you take antibiotics for a few weeks. It's gone, isn't it? I can't believe a sophisticated sex advice writer is getting so hysterical over a piddly little STD."

"And then I get it back and take more antibiotics until eventually I get a strain so resistant to drugs I have to stay in the hospital for a few weeks and take them intravenously!" I screamed into the phone at her.

We hadn't seen each other since the breakfast at David's Pot Belly Stove Restaurant. She was mad at me for ignoring her pleas to talk to Georges. I was mad at her for what . . . for being Morgy?

"Georges says you're overreacting," she said. "He thinks you're not as sexually liberated as you pretend to be."

"Oh, well, if Georges thinks so . . ." I said, enunciating each word as if I were spitting out ice chips.

Like every conversation I'd had with her lately, it hadn't gotten us anywhere. Christmas was only a week away. She would be flying back home to the Midwest in five days. I would be on a plane to London the same day to spend the holidays with my kids. What were we going to do about the annual gift exchange if we weren't speaking?

I sifted through the pile of mail, looking for a letter to balance the one I'd just answered. For example, I tried to follow a letter from a more or less typical husband or wife (i.e., one who isn't getting fucked enough) with a question from a swinger, fetishist, or a woman who was fantasizing about having sex with her priest or her husband's sister. You have no idea how many Americans are fantasizing sex with their in-laws, particularly, and this surprised me, men with their wives' mothers.

Each month I covered one letter in-depth, running the entire letter and answering it in five hundred to a thousand words and then twenty "Quickies With Carolyn," shorter questions and answers. The whole section took up six pages in the magazine. No wonder I felt like I was always tending to the mail.

I picked up a letter from a woman who didn't know how to tell her husband she wanted him to spank her.

Too bad she wasn't married to Georges. I put it in the back of the pile.

Where did Morgy get off telling me chlamydia was no problem? Wait until she found out someday, as she inevitably would, that she'd been infected with it for so long it had destroyed her ability to reproduce. You can bet she'll want a baby as soon as she finds out she can't have one. I was tired of people telling me every new threat to my health and happiness wasn't AIDS or some other life-ending catastrophe. It's only chlamydia. It's only hate mail. It's only threatening calls. It was only paint on my fur coat. Only a stink bomb, not a real one. *Only.*

Not to worry about Elizabeth Thatcher, everybody kept saying in disgustingly cheery tones of voice, because she got two months commitment to a mental health facility. In two months, they can do wonderful things, can't they? And so what if Starred Man is still loose? They recognize him at the security desk now. And Rhumumba? Her job is history. The WAPs will be paying her legal bills for so long, they won't have the cash to replace that placard her lover waves when it falls apart.

Everything that had happened to me was just an *only* event.

Even the *New York Post* had lost interest in me as a potential victim. Their series on the porn pretties ran out of steam when they couldn't find a single compelling reason to continue hinting that the deaths of Zelda and Tanya had been anything but freak accidents. The verdict in the La Passionata case, just handed down, had been involuntary manslaughter, with Anthony Spiker most likely to serve approximately a year of real time on an anticipated two-to-six-year sentence. My article was almost finished, ready to be sandwiched between Tiffany's strange collection of photos, shots of the principals that made them all look like relatives of the *American Gothic* couple and old bondage photos of Vera before the fat.

I put down the letter I was scanning from a man who wanted his unwilling partner to have his name tattooed on her ass *(What makes women so selfish as to deny their men the smallest pleasures?)* and picked up the *Post.* A mob killing, a society divorce, and the second newborn baby to be found in a dumpster in the Bronx in two weeks had taken my place. Only Tiffany seemed to think all was not yet quite safe in the world for me.

Even David had said irritably just the day before when I expressed a feeling of continued unease, "Carolyn, darling, don't you think a certain amount of this goes with the territory? You're not Dear Heloise, Queen of Household Hints, for God's sake!"

I found the next letter.

Dear Superlady of Sex,

I really like older women, and would rather bang them than the girls in their twenties my own age. An older woman gets it off faster and easier. She's grateful for you doing her. It's the perfect relationship for me, mutual lust and mutual gratitude. This is how sex should be. So, how do I get my mother's best friend into the sack? I've wanted her since I was in puberty.

I was contemplating my answer when the intercom buzzed, and the doorman announced Charles was downstairs.

"Send him up," I said reluctantly, in part because I was wearing a sweatsuit, black at least, and no bra, so my nipples, which always seemed to have an erection, were visible. But, still, a *sweatsuit!*

When I opened the door and saw him standing there, trim and elegant in a gray suit, white shirt, discreet though clearly expensive maroon and navy striped tie, a black cashmere topcoat over one arm, I got a lump in my throat. The lump was lust. I swallowed; it quickly traveled to my groin swelling my vaginal lips and making them sweat.

"Why are you so sure you got this from me?" he said, pulling the pamphlet on chlamydia from his inside jacket pocket and throwing it down on the glass coffee table. His eyes, so dark brown they were almost black, were glowing with indignation and hurt. "Do you think the other men you've slept with are cleaner than I am? What do you think, Carolyn? Are black men dirtier?"

I folded my arms across my chest, because I wanted to reach out and touch him so badly. We stood looking at each other, the anger and pain and desire palpable in the space between us. I breathed; the air was heavy with it.

"I asked you a question. You leave this pamphlet with a note telling me I've given you this disease. Did you leave everybody the same message?"

"There aren't any other bodies," I said softly. He looked at me incredulously. "I haven't been with anyone else in months, not since I had my last gynecological exam and got tested for STDs, as I routinely do twice a year. I didn't have chlamydia then. I have it now, and I've only been with you. What would you think if you were me?"

"I don't believe it," he said. I looked away and dug my nails into the palms of my hands to keep from crying.

"How many women have you been with in the last few weeks, Charles?"

"I told you I wasn't involved with anyone when I met you."

"I don't believe it!" I yelled. "You have enough hair care products in your bathroom to open a salon. Your phone machine is always filled with women's voices."

"Do you check my pockets for phone numbers and love notes while I'm sleeping?"

I almost told him about the night I'd heard him tenderly talking to some other "babe" on the phone in the other room while I pretended to sleep in his bed, but I bit it back.

"Charles," I said, tears welling in my voice, if not my eyes. "Why can't you just be straight with me? I know I'm not the only woman in your life. Why can't you just admit that?"

"I'm not a slut," he said.

Yes, he actually said, "I'm not a slut," before turning around and walking out my door. I stood there for several minutes, watching the door, though I certainly didn't expect him to walk back through it. Maybe I was watching it because I believed almost everything I wanted in a man—a huge penis and amazing lovemaking skills—had irrevocably passed through it, never to return. Finally, I started crying. I picked up the pamphlet and tore it into pieces and tossed them into the air like confetti.

"Men!" I said to Tiffany.

We were sitting at her little table, its chipped gray formica top an exact match, in my memory at least, to the one my sister, Billie Ann, had tossed away many years ago. A pot of scented tea in an unappealing shade of pale brownish green with specks of leaf floating on the top sat between us. I couldn't look at it without thinking of a dying man's last diarrhea, so I couldn't possibly drink it. I had stopped at Balducci's and bought a picnic dinner, apples and cheese, French bread baguettes, vegetable pâté, cold sesame pasta with shrimp, and a bottle of white wine. I was drinking the wine. Tiffany didn't drink.

"I know," she said, putting down her needlepoint and reaching across the table to cover my hand gently with her own.

She was embroidering a sampler that would read, "Sex is my spiritual discipline, expertise, politics, favorite subject matter, source of my income, foremost conversational topic, and the key to my health and happiness. I live as if I were making love every moment." Vera had written the words on the cloth for her in a flowery script. I wondered how many hours it would take her to trace the letters in rich red thread, given her apparent ineptness with the needle. Lucky she'd chosen red to hide the many drops of blood she would undoubtedly spill.

"I'm adding an ecstasy facial event to my Goddesses and Sluts seminars," she said. "It's optional. For another ten dollars they can have a sensual group facial and mud pack. I know this wonderful herbalist feminist facialist who will come in and do it."

"Oh," I said, imagining the description of this "new event" on one of Tiffany's Xeroxed pink fliers. There would be a star at the bottom of the page before the words, "Bring your own towels, washcloths, and a way to tie your hair back." Every one of Tiffany's creative ideas was quickly assigned a monetary value and trumpeted on pink paper with her signature "Tiffany," topped by a heart radiating lines at the bottom.

"Tell me about your video," I said.

Tiffany's most serious creative project, an ongoing effort, was a video about women and sex. Only Vera had seen it. The rest of us had been titillated with occasional erotic details. Now that it was almost finished, I was impatient. I wanted to see it before the other women did. If I couldn't be first, I would be second.

"I'll show you what I have so far after dinner," she promised. "You tell me about Charles first and then I'll tell you what I've learned from my investigations. I think I'm onto something."

If she really was "onto something," was this good news or bad? After inwardly railing about my new status as neglected minor victim that morning, I'd abruptly adjusted to it. Yes, it was rather nice after all not having the fat guy from the *Post* waddling around town in my wake, especially since I knew he'd photograph me being stabbed to death, rather than putting his ample flesh between me and an attacker.

"There's not much to say about Charles," I said. "He's a lying, womanizing sleazebucket. He gave me chlamydia, and he doesn't believe I couldn't have gotten it anywhere else. The man is a jerk, a stereotypical jerk. I only fell in love with him because he fucked me, which is a stereotypical woman's reaction."

"Had you told him you hadn't slept with anyone else before today?"

"No," I admitted. "What's that got to do with anything? If I'd told him sooner, he would have thought I was trying to pressure him into a relationship or something."

"Probably," Tiffany said. "But you have to admit, it would be difficult for most people to believe a sexy woman like you hadn't been fucking for the past several months, especially since you were dating." She put up her hand. "I mean I believe you, of course, but I can see where he might not. You don't believe him when he says he isn't involved with anyone, do you?"

"That's different! I know he is."

"How do you know?" she asked, sipping her tea.

I told her about the phone calls, the shampoos, the conditioners. Carefully she said they could be considered "circumstantial evidence," but that's what happens when you take an impressionable porn star to a murder trial. Tiffany was applying this principle of all men being innocent until proven guilty, but I wasn't buying it. I didn't have to catch Charles with his face in another woman's pussy to know the score.

"You're probably right," she said. "That's one of the reasons I only make love to women now. Men do always seem to end up being liars. Why do you think that is?"

Sitting under the poster of Tiffany and Vera in their matching corsets, I nevertheless felt as if I were back home in some other woman's kitchen, sitting across the table from my sister, Jenny, or my friend, Barb, preparing to launch into the latest chapter of *My Troubles* and knowing sympathy would be dispensed with the tea and wine. It didn't matter that Tiffany was dressed in leopard printed tights and a black bodysuit. It didn't matter that Morgy considered my growing closeness to the WIPs "neurotic." She was a snob, a shallow person who would always choose people from the outside in. Tiffany was woman, friend, confidante, source of warmth.

"I think men are liars because they know women are seduced by words," I said. "If women want to attract a man, we dress a certain way. If we want to seduce him, we undress a certain way. They are primarily visual. We are primarily verbal." I took a large gulp of wine. "Charles does this really insidious little thing. He drops 'we' into the conversation, almost from the beginning. Before he's fucked you, he's telling you 'we' are going to do this or that. It's very seductive."

"Couple talk," Tiffany said, dreamily stirring some honey into her tea.

"Sex lies." I drained the wine in my glass and poured more. "Lies, lies, lies. I hate it when men lie to me."

By the time we moved to the sofa, Charles, as a subject, was finished. I was slightly drunk. Tiffany was going to tell me what she had discovered in her research. But something happened to end all conversation, and I started it. I don't know if I meant to start it, but I did.

Tiffany put my wine glass and the bottle on the table in front of me, bending at the waist so that her ass was angled in my direction. I put out my hand and tentatively touched the wide expanse of flesh covered by clinging leopard spots. My fingers sunk into her. She held still for several seconds, perhaps waiting to see if I would extend the hand to the crack between her cheeks or the place between her legs. When I didn't, she poured more wine into my glass, then slowly stood up and turned to face me. I dropped my hand as she did. Her eyes were warm and glowing and fuzzy around the edges, as if they were slightly out of focus, the look of lust, no different in a woman than a man.

Did I reciprocate the feeling? I don't know. She sat down beside me and took my hand in both of hers.

"Did you ever feel a woman's breast?" she asked. I nodded no. "I want you to feel mine. It feels like yours."

She put my hand over her breast, which felt nothing like my own. The flesh wasn't taut inside her skin. I ran my fingers over the skin and felt the breast move separately beneath it. Her nipples were huge and rosy pink, not brown like mine. As I stroked her breast, she opened my black silk shirt and put her hands inside. I wasn't wearing a bra. She adjusted her body so she was closer to me and lowered her head to my breast. When she began to suck, I wanted . . . if not exactly her, I wanted androgynous, clean and pure and almost anonymous sex and I wanted it with her.

Without moving her mouth, she unfastened my silver studded belt and unzipped my jeans. I arched my back and lifted my hips off the couch so she could pull the pants down. My body was warm and ripe with desire, desire without discrimination, its center in my clitoris, burning like a beacon. I understood what it must be like to be a man, undifferentiated desire filling the penis that must be sated. She slid her fingers around it; I sighed and moaned. The orgasm came suddenly, intensely, almost out of nowhere, surprising her.

Tiffany sighed happily for me. Of course, I knew what I had to do next, give her something in return. I just wasn't quite sure about how to do it.

"Come into the bedroom," she said. "We'll take off all our clothes."

As Tiffany stripped off her bodysuit and tights, her smell enveloped me. It was a comfortable smell, like something herbal and musky, mixed with the greenness of Jean Naté. Nervously, I removed my own clothes and, following her lead, lay down on the bed. I looked at our bodies together side by side. She was fleshy, overly generous in every curve, but her back was thin. Her collarbone protruded. Her caves were trim if her thighs were not.

My own body, in contrast, was far less lushly defined. My hips are as slim as a trim young man's, my ass is high and firm. My back, though, is thicker, more muscled than hers. Propping my head with one arm, I turned on my side, thrusting out one hip, adjusting my body, as I automatically do at some point in bed with a man, to create the illusion of a more curvy hip, a more tightly cinched waist. I pulled up one leg and angled both my feet, toes pointing down, like a dancer posing.

"You don't have to do that in bed with a woman," she said, touching my body in long sweeping strokes from breasts to knees, like an artist preparing a canvas. "Relax."

I reached for her breasts again. When I lifted one up, I felt a line of sweat, which had been trapped beneath it and now trickled to the side of her body. Her breasts were things of great curiosity to me. I only knew mine, which being nowhere near the size of Tiffany's, had a far less active life of their own. How far could they go without me?

"I'm going to eat you out until you come and come and come," she said. Reaching under the pillow, she pulled out two white silk scarves. "Put your hands over your head." When I hesitated, she said, "You know you can trust me. I want you to let go completely."

Trembling slightly, I put my hands above my head. As she gently tied each one to the iron headboard, she ran her tongue from my wrist to my armpit. The trembling grew stronger.

"Relax," she repeated. "This is my tongue, not a whip."

I closed my eyes and pushed my body against her tongue as she lapped my cunt like an eager kitten at a dish of milk. With my eyes closed, she was anyone, a man; she was Charles, his long extraordinarily pink tongue exploring my inner crevices, moving surely toward the clitoris. When I opened my eyes, she was Tiffany, her big ass like a mother moon hung low over the bed. She was Tiffany with one hand in her cunt, masturbating herself as she tended to me. I closed my eyes and surrendered to the sensations until, as she'd promised, she made me come over and over and over again. She untied my wrists and kissed my palms.

When it was my turn to lick and suck her, I was too liquid to be tense. She lay on her back, legs obligingly opened wide, her face eager. Sex was communication to her; she was looking at me expectantly, as if she anticipated me making a clever remark.

I applied myself to the licking and sucking of her genitals and found it was curiously easier than performing fellatio on a penis that I may have found only minimally appealing. I didn't have to open my mouth so wide. She tasted sweet and salty at once, like a honey covered nut. Going down on a cunt is like eating and drinking at a Junior League tea party. You take little bites, and you don't talk with your mouth full. Her orgasms were accompanied by loud shrieks and moans and thundering sighs and even sobs.

When it was over, we lay side by side, sweaty in a companionable silence. She stroked my hair. I patted her thigh. Because I had no desire to be held in her arms, I didn't stay the night in her bed as she wanted me to do.

Instead I went home alone and cried myself to sleep. That had nothing to do with Tiffany. It was about Charles. Having sex with someone else only made me want him more. I felt as if my whole body were sexual, but every touch to it, no matter how hotly desired, would within hours leave me aching for him. I wanted him, hated him, not one more than the other.

The next day, I took the coward's way out on Christmas gifts, leaving with their respective doormen both Morgy's gift (a pair of handmade beaten gold earrings shaped like doves of peace) and Charles's gift, a bottle of Dom Pérignon with a note reading, "For you to share with that special someone who might make your baby on New Year's Eve." Corny as it sounds, I more or less meant it. Clearly he'd already had plans for New Year's Eve, since he hadn't invited me out, even before the disease scene. If he had plans he might as well start something other than another case of chlamydia, which, I would have bet, he still had.

Charles at the urologist getting tested for an STD? Having his fertility tested? No way. It would take all the romance out of his life.

I dragged Vera with me on my gift-giving rounds. We were on our way to Tiffany's for the Women In Porn Christmas luncheon. She'd suggested we go together since she was planning to be in my neighborhood that morning, and four hands were better than two at picking up the last-minute food items we'd both promised to contribute to the celebration. I was glad for her early morning call. I would have felt a little uncomfortable walking into Tiffany's alone the day after having sex with her. So, we cabbed our way around town together, finally arriving at Tiffany's slightly later than the "around eleven" we'd promised as helpers.

Tiffany didn't answer the bell.

"That's strange," Vera said, getting visibly nervous after the first series of short jabs failed to produce a response.

Tiffany's building had no doorman, so we had to stand in the lobby outside locked doors waiting for her to respond to us and release the door. I put down my Balducci's and Grace's Marketplace bags next to the bags Vera had dropped containing more food and both of our exchange gifts. I leaned on the bell. No response.

"She probably went out to pick up something she'd forgotten," I said. "We might as well wait here. As soon as we pick all this stuff up and go somewhere for a cup of cappuccino, she'll be back."

"You're right," she said, but she sounded worried.

My feet in four-inch black suede heels were tired, so I took off my shoes. The tiled entranceway felt cold on the soles of my feet. Vera put her large black vinyl carryall on the floor and sat on top of it, with her knees pulled close to her chin. The view of her ass, almost totally exposed by the pulled-up miniskirt, was awesome, but her legs were still fabulous.

Ten minutes later I put my shoes on and walked to a phone booth on the next block, while Vera stayed with the bags. I dialed Tiffany's number and got the machine with her standard outgoing message spoken against an Indian music backdrop. If she'd had to leave suddenly, she would have left a new outgoing message telling us what was going on. Walking back to the building, I knew something was wrong.

"Nothing?" Vera asked, her darkly penciled eyebrows raised in a solid thick cloud of concern.

"No. Let's buzz the super."

He wasn't anxious to let us in until he saw us. His eyes visibly lit up when he got a glimpse of our heels, miniskirts, and black stockings. He agreed not only to take us upstairs so we could knock on the door, but to open it with his master key should there be no response. Any two women in short skirts, black stockings, and high heels could have their way with any super in this town.

We put down the bags again in Tiffany's hallway. When the bell and loud knocking produced no response, he turned his key in the lock. He stood back so we could enter, which Vera did first. When I heard her scream, I knew Tiffany was dead, but seeing the body was still a shock.

She was lying on the floor between the sofa and the coffee table, fully clothed in her leopard tights and an old black sweatshirt, her limbs splayed open and pointing in four different directions. Her eyes were popping out of her head; they were so bloodshot, the irises appeared to be swimming in blood. Her neck was red and black and blue around the white silk scarf constricting it so tightly it was cutting into the flesh. A heavy purple tongue protruded from her lips.

It was the tongue that bothered me most.

Part Three

FEMALE SUPERIOR POSITION

Chapter Thirteen

Dear Superlady of Sex,

I am sorry to read of the death of your close friend, Tiffany Titters. I hope you are keeping yourself safe while the police search for her killer . . .

I thought about the piles of condolence letters that I'd received following Tiffany's murder as Vera read an erotic death poem, written in tribute to her "best friend, in sex and out." They had surprised me, those letters coming from every part of the country and Europe, Japan, South America, Australia, even from a brothel in Hong Kong, the words varying little from one writer to another. *Sorry. We are so sorry. Be careful.* They had been waiting for me when I got back from London, neatly arranged in stacks lining the walls of David's office by his secretary, Gwen. When I'd seen them, I'd burst into tears.

"Last night with warm inspiration on my hand, I began an erotic poem," Vera read, pausing at the end of the line to look at us, her enormous brown eyes made bigger and more luminous by thick black eyeliner, layers of mascara, and a veil of tears.

The Women In Porn were all gathered for the private ceremony at Vera's apartment. Everyone was wearing black, even David and Charles, the invited guests, and

Mike O'Reilly, my bodyguard, one of the three Vinnie had hired to give me twenty-four-hour protection. If Tiffany had been at her own memorial service, she would have dressed in purple or red or something hot pink and fuzzy.

"I wanted to write of your body, familiar as my own," Vera continued. She was wearing a black corset with garters that laced up the front with black fishnet panty hose. It was covered from waist to the top of the thigh by several black crinolines. "But, I could not. Death has changed your body . . ."

Oh, yes, dramatically changed. I shivered at the memory of Tiffany in death. Charles put his arm around my shoulder, squeezed lightly and kept it there. I was grateful for his touch. The night of Tiffany's murder, I'd called him. He'd taken me back to his apartment and tenderly cared for me until he put me on the plane for London, and he'd been waiting at the Kennedy International Airport on my return.

I would have been glad to see him, even if my visit with my children had been an unqualified success, which it wasn't.

"Everyone knows who you are," Matthew, twenty-one, had said through tight lips only seconds after our initial hug.

"It's true," Kate, twenty, said, "but he doesn't have to be such a big butthead about it. I keep telling him it's not your fault your business associates got murdered."

"My roommate knew who you were before you made the news here," Matthew said, ignoring her warning scowls. "He came in one day with the British issue of *Playhouse* and showed me your column. He showed it to other guys. Somebody is always wiggling his fingers at me and asking, 'How's Supermom?' "

"Oh," I said, getting the significance of the wiggling fingers. "It was about masturbation?"

My own son winced at the word, and his face looked like his father's had years ago when he'd told me he didn't think it was "very womanly" of me to touch myself during sex. All this before we had the luggage stowed into the trunk of Kate's Ford mini. There were many such moments sprinkled liberally throughout the visit.

I tried to talk to them about the pervasive American fear of sex, because I wanted them to see me as a sexual revolutionary engaged in the noble work of enlightening an ignorant populace. They didn't. Kate looked sympathetic, her beautiful, innocent face open to possibility but not convinced. Matthew simmered and seethed—and spit contemptuous remarks at me, disguised as humorous barbs.

About Tiffany, he said dismissively, "How could you be friends with someone who held a mirror to her twat as part of her performance art?"

"A speculum," I corrected. "She invited male members of the audience to use a speculum so they could see her cervix."

"That's not art," he snapped. "It's disgusting."

"No," Kate admonished him. "It's just too clinical for me to consider it art. But I think it has something to do with feminism and protest, doesn't it, Mom?"

Charles was a very welcome sight at Kennedy when I landed. But even his consoling presence now beside me couldn't drive the memory of Tiffany in death from my mind as Vera spoke about her body. Her tongue, large, purple, swollen to three times its normal size; her tongue had haunted my dreams these past weeks. What a cruel irony for someone who had given so much oral pleasure to end her life with her lovely tongue horribly mutilated.

Though she must have felt the same way I did on discovering the body, worse because they had been so much closer, Vera had held herself and me together. At first I'd stood beside her, unable to move while the super called the police. Then, after the immediate shock of finding Tiffany dead had left my body like rigor mortis abruptly letting go, I had wanted to run to her and force the tongue back into her mouth and hold her lips shut so no one else would see what we had seen. Vera had kept me from touching Tiffany by holding me tight to her body, her arms like straps around me, until we both started crying. She'd made me understand I couldn't touch anything.

"You are no help, you cannot help as I try to conjure visions of flame-tongued nights and am left with ashes in my mouth," Vera read, her voice catching on the last word.

The ashes were a point of bitter contention between Vera and Tiffany's mother, who'd had her cremated as soon as the autopsy was completed, and then returned to Milwaukee the same day with Tiffany in an "urn," which is a funeral home word meaning "cheap square brass box with nameplate attached." Hers had said, "Linda Sue Mitten, 1952–1988." Vera thought the ashes should have stayed with her. She wanted to put them in a Chinese vase and keep them on her night table, where the proximity would help keep her friend alive.

On the other side of me, David grimaced slightly at the mention of the ashes. Unable to overcome his Catholic upbringing at such times, he thought Tiffany should have been given a "decent burial" in one of the old scenic cemeteries in the Bronx. If she'd wanted to return to Milwaukee, he'd reasoned, especially as Linda Sue Mitten, she would have done so long ago.

"That death could pull you from my nipples before our suckling was through . . ."

Mercifully, Vera dissolved in tears. Carola, resplendent in a black velvet suit and black and silver beaded bustier, stood, walked to the podium, and led her back to her seat. We'd rented the podium and folding chairs from a party rental service. Vera had borrowed vases from everyone and filled them with white gladioli. Her L-shaped studio apartment was alive with death flowers. We may not have had a body, but we had the appropriate floral displays and an enormous catered spread sent by Vinnie. For several minutes, we sat in silence, looking at the flowers, the plates of food, the champagne flutes, trying to avoid each other's eyes.

Recognizing the need for someone to take charge, I stood and asked, "Does anyone have anything else they'd like to say about Tiffany?"

Bobby rose dramatically from his chair. He was wearing a floor-length black velvet dress that fit his body like thick, soft skin. It was cut to the navel. Rhinestones in exuberant floral arrangements began at the shoulders and trickled down the sides, following the slit to the navel, by which point they looked like delicate fallen petals from the succulent blossoms on top. His breasts heaved theatrically as he spoke. Bobby could have had a career in opera, if he'd only had the voice.

"I know almost everybody here has made love to Tiffany," he said. "But I consider myself the luckiest of you all because I had the privilege of loving her as a man and as a woman. I had my penis inside her, and later she made me come all over both of us by playing with my breasts. I never felt like a whole woman until Tiffany did that for me. Nobody loved like she did." The tears gathered in the corners of his eyes. When he spoke again, he sounded as if they were falling inside, too, down into his throat. "The beautiful thing about Tiffany was she accepted, she accepted whoever you are but she also believed you could be whoever you wanted to be. She accepted at the same time she was helpin' you change."

He sat down. I waited a few minutes and stood again. Almost everyone had said something. David had called her an "undiscovered genius, a woman whose intelligence and talent were rarely given their due." Only Charles, who didn't know her well, and Clarissa, who wasn't able to overcome her embarrassment at her own emotional response to our loss, had not delivered a eulogy.

"I think Tiffany would like it if we'd open Vinnie's expensive champagne now," I said. "She might not have been a drinker, but she always loved it when Vinnie spent his money on us."

Charles and David stood at once, reaching out to touch my arms from either side.

"I certainly could use a drink," David said. "The thought of Vera with those ashes in her mouth has made me thirsty."

I knew it was what he felt he had to say to keep us all from crying again.

We stood in little clumps of two and three, nibbling on shrimp and pâté and caviar, and speculating about who had killed Tiffany. Most of our speculation centered on Rhumumba. She was our murderer of choice. The police investigation, however, was focused on Tiffany's sex life because the cops were sure it was a "sex crime." They pointed to the white silk scarf around her neck and hinted it was a bondage game gone wrong, another La Passionata story. They didn't quite get the principle of bondage; restraint typically applies to ankles and wrists, not choking to death. Each of us had been interviewed; we'd heard her other "known" sex partners had also been contacted.

"If they investigate everyone Tiffany ever slept with, they'll be doing interviews for years," Gemma said, pulling up the wayward strap of her lingerie-style black silk gown. "That's so crazy. She wasn't in the middle of sex when she got killed. How many people have to tell them Tiffany never did it with her clothes on before they'll get the picture?"

"They asked me if I thought she might have been having her partner choke her at the moment of climax to heighten the sensation," Stephanie said. She was wearing a tiny black leather strapless dress with a black leather rhinestone studded collar and five-inch heels. "One of the assholes who questioned me said I should know about such techniques, being a working girl and all."

So far the only information the police had uncovered had been about us. We now knew that both David and I had been to bed with Tiffany. He was as shocked to learn about me as I was him.

"Carolyn," he'd said, uncharacteristically raising his voice over the phone when he confronted me. "You, too? I can't believe this. What were you thinking?"

"Well, what were *you* thinking?" I'd asked.

"It was only once."

"But I thought you had never cheated on Peggy. You told me that, and I believed you. Why would you lie to me?"

"I never have cheated on Peggy," he said, and it sounded like tears in his voice. "Being with Tiffany just that one time didn't feel like cheating."

He paused, waiting for my forgiveness, which wasn't coming. I counted on him to be happily married. He and Peggy had married as teenagers when she got pregnant. They had grown up together and stayed together and had, what I'd believed to be, the one perfect marriage of two independent people willing and able to give each other space as they remained intensely connected to each other.

"Carolyn, you know it's been hard for me, editing a sex magazine without ever having been with any other woman. You know my curiosity has often been cruelly aroused."

"It was only once for me, too," I said, still not willing to let him off the hook. Besides, hadn't his vicarious experience of my sex life been enough for him?

"Would you have done it again if she'd lived?" he asked.

Tiffany had died the next day, but if she hadn't, I don't think I would have had sex with her again. But who knows? I let him wonder.

"It's a good thing you and Vera found her together," Clarissa said between bites of caviar, which she was spilling on the jacket of her shiny black menswear suit, a new thriftshop find, "or they would have pinned it on whoever came in first."

"Only in the movies," David said. "And that suit," he told Clarissa, "looks like it might be harboring moths. Don't put your hands in your pockets."

"Ha!" Stephanie said. "Where do you think they learn how to do their job? They watch bad movies."

We circulated around the room, forming and reforming little groups, saying the same things over and over again. Mostly what we said was: Rhumumba murdered Tiffany. She was strong enough. The Goddess knows, she was mean enough. And she was about the only person none of us could picture Tiffany fucking under any circumstances, which would certainly explain how she ended up dead with all her clothes on.

I'd told each of them about Tiffany's intention of telling me what she'd "discovered" before our last evening together turned into a sexual encounter. I blamed myself for that. If I hadn't touched her ass, would she have told me what she'd found? Could we have done something with the information which might have saved her life?

"What do you think it was?" Clarissa asked.

Everyone had asked the same question. I didn't know, couldn't even guess.

"Surely it had something to do with Rhumumba," Vera said.

"Are you ready?" Charles whispered in my ear.

Even in mourning, my body responded to his presence. We would be the first to leave, but I didn't care. I could have sent him on his way alone, but I wanted to be with him. I said my goodbyes.

Since the murder, he had held me, stroked my face, gently kissed me, and consoled me. He hadn't fucked me, which was what I wanted and needed now. As we were making our goodbyes at the door, Bobby handed us each a creamy white envelope sealed with red wax.

"A lock of Tiffany's pubic hair," he said. "I had it saved from the time she let me shave her. It didn't seem right to keep it all to myself." Again, his eyes filled with tears. "I thought we should all have a piece."

"Oh, Bobby," I said, putting my arms around his neck and hugging him hard. He smelled as wonderful as he looked. "I love you."

"Girl, I love you, too," he said, brushing his thick luscious lips across mine.

Charles extended a hand to shake. Bobby grasped the hand in both of his and held it briefly. Mike stood between us and the door, watching the scene, as if he thought we were all a little strange, but was too polite to point it out to us.

"I don't get him," Charles said. We were in the limo, with Mike on the seat across, facing us. "If he wants to be a woman, why doesn't he go all the way and have it chopped off?" Mike winced, and Charles grinned at him. "Yeah, I agree. But he's got breast implants. Why does he want both?"

"A breast and a penis aren't synonymous," I said.

"These ain't your typical people," Mike said, shrugging his shoulders. A big Irishman in his early thirties with red hair so thin his freckled scalp peeked through, Mike had been working for Vinnie for ten years. "You get used to seeing anything with these people. That pubic hair thing, that didn't even faze me. When I started working for Vinnie, my jaw was on the floor about half the time." He nodded in my direction. "She's almost normal, the most normal one of the whole bunch I've met so far. I don't know what she's doing in this crowd, but I guess she knows."

"Sometimes she knows," I said.

"Don't get me wrong," Mike said. "They ain't bad people. I would never say that. Quite the contrary. You get to know them, they're good people. I couldn't ask for a better boss than Vinnie Mancuso."

"Well," Charles asked me, "do you get him? Does Bobby make sense to you?"

"Do I understand why he wants to live as a woman, but keep his penis? Not exactly. It's his choice."

"He's not a homosexual, right?" Charles asked.

"Right. I think he's bisexual, but I don't know it for a fact. He's not a transsexual, because he doesn't want his penis removed. If he were a transsexual, he'd believe he's a woman trapped in a man's body, and he'd be anxious to make the body completely female. So, you're asking me to explain why he has gone further than most transvestites by having the breast implants and dressing all the time as a woman . . . and I can't. It's just what he wants to do."

"Like he said back there when he was speaking, you just accept it or you don't," Mike said, raising his eyebrows and lifting his hands in a "what-can-you-do?" gesture.

"Bizarre," Charles said. I got the feeling he wasn't as amused by the bizarre as he'd been a few weeks ago.

Nevertheless, he put his arms around me and pulled me close against his chest. Being there was all I wanted for the moment. Tiffany's death had changed me. I was going to take love where I found it, whether or not it held the promise of tomorrow, or came with the seal of sexual good health.

Mike checked the apartment, including the closets and under the bed, for a lurking stranger—like Rhumumba would have fit under the bed—then pulled the shades and left us alone while he sat on a chair in the hallway outside my door.

"It's dark in here," Charles said.

"I may not be the next victim, but my plants stand a good chance of dying if the killer isn't apprehended soon." I put my arms up, and he came into them. "Thank you for coming with me today. Having you there made a big difference to me."

"It's okay, babe. I told you I'm your friend. You're the one who treats me like the enemy."

"Please stay awhile."

"Sure, babe. Come here," he said, taking my hand and guiding me to the sofa, though I would have preferred the bed. I didn't care if he still had chlamydia and I'd have to take antibiotics for another ten days, I wanted to make love to him. "Stretch out on the couch and let me rub your neck."

I kicked off my black heels and laid facedown on the sofa, my head resting on my folded arms. He began massaging my neck and shoulders, his fingers soothing and warming my muscles. Knowledge about Charles was working its way into my body at the same time. He had changed, too. This was kindness, not lust.

He'd been intensely interested in me in the beginning, plying me with questions about myself, talking in the "we" terms. The first several times we'd made love, he'd almost demanded I get involved with him on a deeply emotional level. But, like every true romantic, he'd cooled down. He would have, no matter what I'd done. It was tempting to say, "If chlamydia hadn't come between us, things would have worked out." Tempting, but wrong. That's what I was thinking now. I was sure I felt his loss of desire through his fingertips on my skin.

"You don't want me anymore, do you?" I asked him, raising up and turning to look into his eyes.

"You think I don't want you?"

He ran his hands down my back and let them linger on my ass. I put my head back down. Was I wrong? And why was I always so unsure when I was with Charles?

"I want you, babe, but I don't want to hurt you. If you think you got something from me, I don't want to put you in that position again."

"Charles, did you go get tested?"

"No," he said, a pout creeping into his voice. "Nothing's wrong with me. I don't need a test to tell me there's nothing wrong with me. If my dick were leaking, I'd know it."

"But, your dick wouldn't necessarily leak if you had chlamydia," I said, raising my head again. "In fact, it probably wouldn't."

"Babe," he said, taking his hands away from my body. "There is no point in talking about this."

I rolled over, rubbing my thigh against his as I did. My black silk sarong skirt had attached itself to the leather sofa, and hiked up even farther when I twisted it loose as I turned my body around. Now the skirt was barely covering my crotch. I watched him look at my crotch and then my breasts. I was wearing a black silk bodysuit, no bra. Taking his hands in mine, I put them on my breasts.

"You know I love your breasts," he said; his eyes were liquid with desire. "Don't do this to me, Carolyn."

I sat up, and he moved back against the sofa. I sat on his lap and kissed him. He touched my breasts through the silk. I felt the heat again in his hands, his mouth, but it was different between us now. Had I been the one to hurt him?

"I want you," I whispered in his ear, my tongue finishing the sentence for me . . . fuck me, I want you to fuck me.

"I don't want to hurt you, babe. I'm afraid of hurting you."

"I don't care. I want you to make love to me."

"Do you want to come? I'll make you come."

He pushed the bodysuit back from my breasts and ran his tongue around my nipple. His other hand moved down my body to rest between my legs. I tightened the muscles around it. With his thumb, he flicked open the snaps of my bodysuit and rubbed against my clit through my panty hose. I wanted him to pull my clothes off. More than anything, I wanted his penis inside me.

"Please," I said.

He moved his thumb against me expertly. In seconds I had an orgasm, which left me hungry for more. I wanted more of him, and I wanted it now. Moving him aside, I yanked off my panty hose.

"Carolyn," he said, sitting back against the sofa again, his hand resting on the huge bulge inside his pants. "Don't."

I climbed on top of him and reached beneath my own body to unfasten his belt, unzip his pants. He kept his hands on my hips, firmly pinning me down, so that I couldn't move high enough to center myself on his penis. But he kept guiding me with his hands, moving me so that I rubbed the side of his penis against my clit. He let me use his penis to masturbate myself; I came again and again, but he never did.

Collapsing against his shoulder, I started to sob.

"It's okay," he said, smoothing my hair, kissing my neck. His penis was still hard between us. "You're gonna be okay."

Embarrassed, I stood and pulled the skirt down over my body, sticky with my own residue, not with his.

"You'd better go," I said.

"Okay, babe." He kissed the top of my head and ruffled my hair. "Take care of yourself. You know you can call me if you need anything. I love you."

I cried for a few minutes, then took a shower and dressed in jeans, a black silk shirt, and boots. While I furiously scrubbed my body clean and dressed it, I promised I'll never do this to myself again. Never humiliate myself by practically begging a man to fuck me. *Never.* Grabbing my mink and the keys, I hurried out the door without looking at the sofa where Charles had refused to make love to me. I could smell him in the room.

"We're going back to Vera's," I said to Mike, who was sitting outside my door.

"Jeez, do they still have food left?"

Everyone was still at Vera's, and there was a lot of food left, which made Mike happy. Miriam had brought the baby over, too. Vera was holding her when Mike and I walked in.

"It was not the reunion of your dreams," David said after taking in my red eyes.

"Fuck off," I told him, collapsing onto the futon beside him.

"He's not worthy of you," David said, putting his arm around me.

"A big penis is a big penis," Gemma told him. "When a man has a really big penis, he doesn't have to be worthy because his penis is."

"Right," I said. "That's why both the men I've known who had big penises were such jerks."

"You women are disgusting," David told us, shaking his head as if he sincerely meant it. "You tell men not to worry about how big our penises are when all you really want is a big one. No wonder we don't believe your pathetic little reassurances."

"We don't really mean it," Gemma said, her eyes sparkling mischievously. "Why should you believe it? We're trying to inflate your pathetic little egos so what you have doesn't give out on us when we need it."

"Oh, I think a big penis is overrated," Stephanie said.

"Well, you would! You just want to get them in and out with as little complications as possible," Gemma teased. "I see your point, of course, but you're looking at the penis with a professional distance."

"I think big ones are overrated, too," Vera interjected without taking her eyes off Zellie dozing against her bosom. "If a man has a really big one, he doesn't think he has to do anything else except let you look at it and shove it in."

"I wonder if Rhumumba had a big one," I said. What I didn't say was, "Not Charles. He didn't just let me look at it and shove it in. He used everything at his disposal, not merely his major penis." If I'd said that, I would have started bawling.

"I doubt she'd have removed it if it had been a spectacular specimen," David said.

"I agree with you, honey," Bobby said. "You don't see me cutting mine off. When you've got a good thing, you hang on to it because you never know when you're going to decide to put it to use."

We all laughed. David got up to pour some champagne in a rented crystal flute for me and replenish the others' glasses. Vinnie had sent enough Cristal for two or three drunken memorial services. We sipped our champagne quietly for a few minutes, watching Zellie sleep. Would she grow up to be ashamed of her parents as my son now was of me? And would he outgrow it when it occurs to him someday that my embarrassing work helped pay for his education? What did we ever do before Clarissa and Miriam had Zellie? Every group of adults needs a baby to watch.

"What do you suppose Tiffany thought she had found out?" Carola asked no one in particular. "It keeps nagging at me. Suppose she did stumble on something that led to her murder or proved Zelda or Tanya had been murdered. I don't see how La Passionata could fit into the mix. Her death seems pretty straightforward to me."

We all agreed it did. No one had a clue about Tiffany's secret discovery.

"It was probably nothing," David said, but his voice lacked conviction.

We kept asking ourselves, What *did* Tiffany *know?* Maybe Mike got tired of the question, because he was the one to propose a means of finding the answer.

"Easiest thing in the world to get into her apartment if you want to go through her things," he said. "Was me, that's what I'd do."

"The police have it sealed," David said.

"Which means they have a piece of yellow tape across the door," Mike explained. "You lift the tape, pick the lock, put the tape back when you're finished."

"Are you offering?" I asked.

"Why not?" he said, and stuffed two shrimps in his mouth at once, chewed three times, and swallowed. "Beats sitting around here listening to you guys wonder what she knew that you don't know. Who's going with me?"

Clarissa, Vera, and I stood first, so we got to go. More than four, Mike said, would be a "crowd action."

Getting past the locked lobby doors proved so easy I wondered why they bothered to lock them. Mike buzzed an apartment at random, said, "Hey, it's Mike downstairs. I forgot my key and my girlfriend must be in the shower because she doesn't answer." In seconds, the click of the door release sounded, and we were in.

"Sometimes it takes a few apartments before it works," he said. "We got lucky. A man answered. Women aren't so quick to let you in."

Upstairs, he lifted the tape and picked the lock before anyone came into the hall and saw us. Inside Tiffany's apartment, I felt panic rising in my throat. I could smell her death. Sweat broke out above my lip and under my arms.

"Take short breaths for a few minutes," Mike said, his hand on the back of my neck. "Then breathe deeply."

I did what he said, and it worked. Vera and Clarissa, both pale, seemed to be following the same advice. Within minutes, we were able to move around the apartment without fear of vomiting, but what were we in search of?

"Any idea what we're looking for?" Mike asked, scanning Tiffany's refrigerator which was covered with photos, copies of her pink Xeroxed fliers, and cards, newspaper clippings, everything but drawings made by children. "What was she looking for anyway?"

"Okay," I said. "She kept talking about connections between Tanya, Zelda, and La Passionata. She was looking for missing links. That's all I know."

Mike and I took the living room; Clarissa and Vera, the bedroom. They found copies of the research Cynthia Moore-Epstein had sent me about the three deaths on one of Tiffany's bedside tables. Since I already had the material (and hadn't found it enlightening), we left it.

"We'll make a copy of your copy for everyone," Vera said, putting the pile of papers carefully back down inside the dust outline around them. "Maybe you've missed something one of the rest of us would see."

We combed the apartment for almost an hour, each team taking the other's territory in the second half of the search. We found nothing.

"She's got a lot of videos here," Mike commented. "Anything in that?"

"She was getting into producing her own," Vera said. "So, she had a lot of them for study purposes. I don't see how they could have anything to do with anything else."

"Like, we're missing something really obvious or someone got it before we did," Clarissa said.

"The police or the murderer," Mike said, ushering us to the door. "Anyway, we tried."

He put the yellow tape back, and we got out of there without running into anyone in the halls again. Breaking and entering is actually a lot easier than it looks on TV.

Back at Vera's, Mike's replacement was waiting his turn to guard my life. A tall, muscular, and noncommunicative Jamaican, Samuel inspired great confidence in me, even if he wasn't as much fun as Mike. Who could possibly get past Samuel? His hands folded across his chest, he nodded impassively when we came in. It would never have occurred to him, I'm sure, to ask where we'd been.

"The changing of the guard," Mike said, kissing my cheek. "See you tomorrow, Superlady. Sleep tight to-night."

We stayed at Vera's talking until almost 3:00 A.M. Clarissa and Miriam were sleeping with the baby on the futon, which Vera had opened up for them, when I left. I was so tired that Samuel picked me up and carried me to the waiting car. Bodyguards and chauffeurs are wonderful people to have in your life sometimes.

I fell asleep in the car and barely woke enough to get myself to bed. That's why I didn't listen to the messages on my phone machine until morning. The last was from Mike, who'd called shortly after leaving Vera's the night before.

"I know how you girls can get your answers," he said. "Don't know why I didn't think of it sooner. Get yourself a meet with Otis Campbell and Steven Cohen, Vinnie's P. I. team. You girls ain't their favorite bunch of people since you busted Rhumumba before they was ready to point the finger at her. But I think they'll help you anyway. If Tiffany did know something, these are the guys who could find out what it was."

"Girls!" He called us "girls"?

Chapter Fourteen

Dear Superlady of Sex,

My erections are never rock hard anymore. I am thirty-seven and hate to think of myself as a sexual seen-better-days guy, but maybe it is true of me. Sometimes I can only penetrate a woman if she sits on me. After we fuck awhile, I can hold it inside her in any position. Before I shoot, I feel good and hard, at least to myself. But recently my partner has said she doesn't feel me as good and hard at this point. Then she reassures me she doesn't mind. If she doesn't mind, why does she bring it up? Is there a standard for hardness—and how can I tell how far off I am from the male norm for my age?

Why are men so obsessed with measurements? They want to know how long sex should last, how long orgasm should last, how big other men are, how many times a week other people do it, and how hard other men get. The person who invents a method of measuring penile hardness will become a billionaire. ("Hey, honey, I hit an 8.2 on the Smith and Barney Erectile Quality Scale tonight. You know the average guy my age is lucky to come in at 7.0.")

For men, sex, like sport, should have a set of statistical standards by which they can judge their performances. Why can't they be more like us and obsessively compare their bodies to each other's? Or why can't they just pore over *GQ* and privately agonize because their thighs aren't as good as the model's?

I was formulating an answer to poor "Mr. Sexual Seen Better Days" in my head when the phone rang again. Did David take all these phone calls when *he* had this job?

"Want me to get it for you?" Mike asked.

"No, thanks," I said, and he went back to his newspaper. Mike liked my new job, replacing David as Editor-in-Chief of *Playhouse.* He got to sit on the sofa all day, look out the window in search of celebrities going into HMV, and see the unretouched photos of the girls of *Playhouse* as soon as they hit my desk. His favorite was the one of Miss May, a voluptuous Hispanic beauty, before her overflowing black bush was trimmed into shape by waxing her inner thighs.

"Madame Editor, how's it going?" David asked.

Why did he sound so smug and self-satisfied as if he knew it couldn't possibly be going as well as it had when he was doing it? I wasn't comfortable talking to him in the office, our positions reversed as it were. Look, the missionary position had worked for us for a long time. He'd said he didn't care about me climbing on top, but what if he did? I knew he did. David was competitive.

"Did you answer your own phone when you did this?" I asked him. "I can't remember."

"No, but I always took your calls."

"Don't call me 'Madame Editor.' I still think of myself as Superlady." I sighed. "It's frantic. I don't remember ever seeing you work. There was nothing on your desk. How did you pull that off? I hate this job. We both know Vinnie only hired me for the PR value of having me here. He didn't expect me to do anything, did he?"

"It was easy," he said, giggling. His giggles sounded

forced and smarmy now, not real. He was laughing *at* me, not *with* me, all the while pretending nothing had changed between us. He no longer trusted me enough to admit it had. "I didn't work. You promoted Clarissa, didn't you? She should be doing everything now. She did it before . . . for a lot less money."

"Uhmm," I said, a nonword I'd taken to using on the phone to indicate to the person on the other end: I can't talk now. This never happened to me when I worked at home.

Cynthia Moore-Epstein was standing in my office door, a pile of blue line copy in her hands. Her eyebrows were raised in that "We have a problem" thin line, which made me automatically cringe. Everything on her body from her jaunty breasts to her carefully aligned prim little black ballerina flats was pointing needily in my direction.

"I'll call you back in fifteen," I said. "I promise."

"Call me back. I'm having an anxiety attack."

He was having an anxiety attack? I pictured him in his big Jackson Heights co-op, Peggy off to work, the last of the kids still living at home in class at NYU, his feet propped up on his own desk. Motioning Cynthia inside, I was suddenly consumed with envy. I wanted to be David, fired for fiscal mismanagement, and sent packing with a year's severance pay. At last he could write the novel he'd said he'd write if only he'd had the time to do it. He'd sworn he was "delighted" that I was getting his job. Peggy was "thrilled" that he would be the housekeeper/cook now; she completely believed in his ability to write a potential best-seller by the time the severance package was spent.

Lies. But why shouldn't they be delighted and thrilled? I was being paid about a third less than he'd received to do the same job, and he was free. And Peggy no longer had to share the household chores which she considered more onerous than he did. I was, however, still getting a separate check for Superlady, which put me slightly ahead of where he'd been on the financial scale, not that *I'm* competitive about these things.

Accepting Vinnie's offer had seemed like a good idea at the time. I hadn't realized how much I would dislike getting up every morning and going to an office. Okay, I got here at ten and left shortly after four. It was restrictive nonetheless, especially since I was only permitting myself business-related lunches. Even Mike was bored with the lunches with advertisers, writers, photographers, publicists, and members of the staff. And playing dress-up and wearing heels all day, every day? I hated that, too. I missed my jeans and sweats. Today I was wearing a cobalt blue wool fitted jersey dress with matching stockings and shoes. The plunging v-neck was anchored with an antique silver brooch in a diamond shape. The swingy long silver earrings that coordinated with it were making my ears tired. It was the kind of outfit I loved wearing for two or three hours, not six or eight.

The only part of the job I liked was assigning articles. I had, for example, a female writer trying out the new intercourse position, Coital Alignment Technique, invented by a man, which was the latest version of how to give your woman a no-hands orgasm. Presumably a man and a woman could align themselves so he gave her clitoris sufficient stimulation during intercourse in the missionary position to bring her to orgasm without additional clitoral stimulation. After trying it with three men, my writer reported, she could only achieve alignment by having her partner move so far up her body, his chin was hitting the top of her head as they fucked and his penis felt hooked inside her.

"Another letter from the main pervert," Clarissa said, barging in past Cynthia, waving a letter on yellow lined paper.

Starred Man was still writing to me. Rhumumba and

Elizabeth Thatcher might be spending the winter on the same Caribbean isle for all I knew, but Starred Man was in town and careful to keep me updated on a weekly basis about his comings and goings—all within the confines of the restraining order which kept him out of my sight. Sometimes I wondered if he'd killed Tiffany because he suspected she was a rival for my love.

"Like, I mean, wouldn't you think he'd give it up?" she said. "I called a publicist at Doubleday for you. They have a book on obsessive love, and I told her you needed a free copy because it was happening to you."

"Great. I hope you made it clear I am the obsessee, not the obsessor. I can just see the item on Page Six now."

"Oh, sure," she said, throwing Starred Man's letter down on top of the general chaos which was my desk. "Cynthia, I told you not to bother Carolyn with this little stuff. Take it all back to my office, and I'll be right there."

She started out the door, came back, and tried to retrieve Starred Man's letter, but I caught her hand.

"You don't have to deal with this," she protested, but I waved her away. "I'll read, copy, and file for you."

"I love you, Clarissa," I said as she and Cynthia departed.

"I know," she said, smiling benevolently at me on her way out the door.

Reflecting on how much fatherhood had changed her for the better, I picked up the phone and forgot whom I meant to call, and therefore which numbers to push, and put it back again. In seconds, it was ringing. Twenty minutes later, I returned David's call.

"Have you settled in yet?" he asked.

"Not entirely. I still have to replace your tattoo collection with something more me. Clarissa gave me a picture of Zellie for my desk, so I have a start."

"Maybe you can have them shipped to me. I'd love to keep those photographs."

"No way." The silence on his end was muted rage. I knew it was. This was like a divorce. He would make me pay for keeping his photographs. "I'm sorry. Vinnie is feeling punitive toward you today." I paused. "But I could stack them up behind my desk and leave them there for a month or so. No one will notice if I send them to you then."

While David defended his fiscal excesses yet again ("It was the eighties; everybody did it."), I scanned Starred Man's letter. Being out of prison had not opened up his creativity. He still began with, *"Do you like chest hair?" Now, however, he had an address and phone number where, he said, I could reach him whenever I was ready. I put the letter on top of the Out basket. Clarissa was right; I wasn't going to read his missives anymore.

"I envy you," I told him. "You get to do what you want."

"But if I can't do it, then what?"

We were both holding our breath. Neither spoke, possibly consumed by the same thoughts. Before I had known him, David had a past life I couldn't comprehend. When the kids were small, the family had been on food stamps while David was six months between editorial jobs and Peggy was too ill from complications following the last birth to teach. They had owned a male cat they couldn't afford to neuter, and he'd urinated in all the corners. While I was busily presiding over the Junior League, David had lived in a drafty old house which smelled like cat piss.

"I never made money until *Playhouse,*" he reminded me peevishly. "If you will recall, I got this job because Vinnie's sister, who was charged with finding the new editor, went to college with my cousin."

"How did you manage to run this magazine without

alienating your kids?" I changed the subject to one in which he had the clear advantage. "My son would give up his earring and long hair for a mother who edited *Good Housekeeping.* Things are so touchy between us. You don't know how jealous I am of the closeness between you and your kids."

"He'll get over it," David said, but his reassurance lacked a certain degree of warmth. The softness of voice, to which I once could lean back and relax, was gone. "My kids have been through hard times. They never had the luxury of taking a moral stand on where the money's coming from, but they take their moral stands on other issues, which irritate me. I can't go to the grocery store without buying an item the consumption of which constitutes committing some sin against nature. Carolyn, he'll come around," he said, brushing off my concern as if it were pettiness on my part. "It's not easy for a young man to have Superlady for his mother. You're the older woman all his friends want to fuck. You see his point?"

"I'm going to get everything off my desk today," I told him, interrupting another one of his speculations on how long the world of print porn had to go before near total fiscal collapse, being squeezed by the antiporners on one side and the video market on the other, "so I have to hang up."

"Put it in a box and dump it on someone else's desk."

"Actually, I had planned on several boxes. Why should one person have to do everything?"

I did something very bold then: I told my secretary to hold all calls, except from the A list—David, Morgy, the WIPs, and Vinnie's elusive P. I. team, Campbell and Cohen, who were in no fucking hurry to get back to me. I'd been trying to get one or the other of them on the phone for a week. They didn't seem to return calls or they weren't returning mine. My secretary, Gwen, said their secretary was "nice" and Cohen was "a sweetheart, but out of town a lot," but Campbell, the top man himself, she thought, appeared to have an attitude. How she got this without actually talking to him, I don't know.

When the phone rang, I was hoping for one of the elusive dicks and got Morgy instead. After she'd dumped Georges with a speech I'd helped her prepare and advised me on negotiating a sign-on bonus which I'd invested in Red Hot Mamas, we had achieved a rapprochement. Having discovered a murder, I was changed somehow in her eyes. She didn't know how to treat me. Now she was spending a week in California recuperating from Georges. It was day two of the healing experience, and, if I'd thought about it, I could have predicted this call.

"Carolyn, I've met someone," she said, her voice breathless.

"That's nice."

"Well, don't sound so discouraging," she said crossly. "He is nice . . . for a change. I met him yesterday. He took me for a three-hour drive down the coastline. We had dinner on the beach. We'd been kissing all day and holding hands, and I, like, really got weird on him. Do you know what I did?"

"Refused to sleep with him because he won't respect you if you give in so soon?"

I could hear her pouting in the silence. She didn't like having her game analyzed, but what did she expect? She typically followed a disaster like Georges with either a celibate period or a brief relationship with a suitable man, whom she attempted to control by the timely dispensing of sex. It was, she thought, what good women do to get led down the bridal path, a path she occasionally decided was greener than her own. Talking to Morgy about men was like returning to the nostalgic days when girls talked about boys at slumber parties.

Uncomfortably, I realized I'd enjoyed the conversations up until only recently.

"Well?" I asked. "Isn't that what happened?"

"He wanted to rent a room, and, like, I go, 'I'm not sleeping with you tonight. I think it's better if you wait for sex.' And he goes, 'I've done it both ways, having sex right away and waiting for it and I don't think that influences how things will go, but I'm willing to do it your way.'

"So, I wouldn't let him get the hotel room though I wanted to go to bed with him. We drove back and I stayed the night at his place. He loaned me a T-shirt and shorts. We kissed and I masturbated him and gave him a blow job and then he masturbated me, but we didn't have sex. In the morning, he seemed a little confused about what to do, so he made a big breakfast. When we finished eating it, he announced he had a lot to do today.

"Do you think he'll think I'm too neurotic to see again?"

I stopped her by pleading "the I have to be in a meeting" excuse, one of the good things about having a real job versus working at home where no one thinks you're really working. After hanging up with her, I buzzed Gwen and told her to move Morgy down from the A list to the B, which meant she wouldn't automatically get through to me in the future.

I felt a little mean about it, but don't executive women have to make some hard decisions? Besides, our little separation had convinced me Morgy and I would only be able to remain friends if we saw less of each other. She was fun once, twice a month. Beyond that, she seemed like work. Was I being smug in believing I'd outgrown her?

Guiltily, I looked around my office. I had one old friend's job and didn't want to take another old friend's calls. I sighed. Mike looked up, offered no verbal encouragement, looked back down at his magazine. I picked up my pen and a packet of post-it notes.

In less than an hour, I had the work on my desk divided into little piles littered with sticky notes meant for other people's desks. I felt good about myself again for accomplishing something. Vaguely I had a plan about this job, which was "Do it for a year or so, put the money away, then quit." I could handle it for that long, and print porn would probably survive another year, too.

I felt only a momentary satisfaction at my clean desk before thinking about Tiffany's unsolved murder. Every one of us had been questioned; Bobby several times. The cops seemed to be talking to all the wrong people. Yet, a month had gone by with no arrest being made.

"Try Campbell and Cohen again," I told my secretary. "Why do they keep avoiding me?"

This time she got Otis Campbell on the line.

I was waiting for Otis at the Museum Café on Columbus and 78th. Samuel, my bodyguard, was sitting at the next table, rather too conspicuously I thought, but then again how can a stunning, big, black man ever be inconspicuous?

With a name like Otis, I considered the odds were good he'd be black, too. Did I want him to be black? I did. Blame it on missing Charles, who was now nothing more than an occasional phone caller in my life. Perhaps to be sure a phone call wouldn't lead to an immediate tryst, he rarely called me when he was in New York. I heard from Charles when he was on assignment in Detroit, L. A., Chicago, wherever far away. True, we sometimes mutually masturbated while tenuously connected by long-distance technology, but that was the extent of my sex life. And, since Charles, I had only fantasized about black men. Why did I care if Otis was black or not? He was a man, approximately my age, rumored to be unattached. If he fit the description, I also wanted him to be black. White men didn't look good to me anymore.

Morgy said my fantasies about black men were the result of a shrewd unconscious appraisal of the marketplace, not longing for Charles's master organ. White men over forty consider a younger woman the status symbol of choice, she said. Or, if they don't, they are geeks, losers, nerds, or too poor to afford a status symbol. Black men over forty want white women on their arms. Was Morgy right? Were my fantasies of black cocks inspired by dating realities, not Charles? I'd dated other black men before Charles, and none—in spite of the familiar adage, "Once you have black, you don't go back"—had left me dreaming only black dreams. I had been younger then.

"Ms. Steele," he said gently, as though he were trying to awaken me without startling me. How had I not noticed him walk into the café and stop in front of my table? "I wouldn't expect you to know who I am, but, of course, I know who you are."

He was tall, very black, and handsome. Unlike Charles, he had hair; tight little curls, slicked down so they appeared to grow in wavy rows. His hand, extended for my grasp, was reassuringly large. But the eyes were the best part. He had large hazel eyes that glinted with lights, flickering information about him like blinking signs. The man sent constant sparks from his eyes. He had to be smart, inquisitive, sexy, and warm. Would those eyes lie? His history was written in his eyes, and I was reading them like a palm reader.

"Otis Campbell," he said, not breaking eye contact as he held my hand far longer than was necessary.

"I'm so glad to meet you at last," I said, allowing a

touch of sarcasm in my voice, knowing it would be offset by my widest, most winning smile.

One good thing about being born blond: People don't automatically give you credit for being smart enough to be mildly caustic. You almost have to pour verbal drain cleaner all over some people, especially men, before they realize the words are truly coming from the mouth of a blonde. It gives us a tactical advantage in these verbal times.

"You're prettier than your picture," he said, "even the ones taken by Charles Reed."

I batted my big blue eyes at him, but it would be, I knew, to no avail. The man was on to me. I would bet he'd done his homework well enough to know about me and Charles. He gave me a shrewdly appraising glance, sat down, signaled the waiter, and ordered a Heineken on draft.

"I would have guessed that would be your drink," I said.

"Well, your glass of white wine isn't exactly a surprise choice, Ms. Steele."

"Please call me, Carolyn."

"Is that what you really like to be called—Carolyn, not Caro? You can call me O. My parents handicapped me with Cleotis after my grandfather, and I've spent my life shortening it to something I could live with. I think I'm finally there."

"Anything but 'babe.' You don't call women 'babe,' do you, O?"

"Only if they've really earned it," he said, laughing.

I liked the way he laughed, throwing his head back as he did. He had beautiful even white teeth and a lovely tongue. But, as easily as he'd let himself go, he reigned himself back in again. I got the impression he'd liked me immediately, but was not all that pleased he did.

"Okay, Caro, let's get this business cleared away," he said. "Vinnie wants us to listen carefully to what you have to say, then talk you out of doing any investigating on your own. He says you're high on Rhumumba as the killer. I don't see that. Neither does my partner, Steve Cohen. He had the lady fingered as the letter writer, but a killer—No. You women"—he said, wagging his finger at me, but he got points for saying "women" and not "girls"—"should have stayed out of it. Finding poison pens is a specialty of Cohen's. He had the case all but made against Rhumumba when you stepped in. Any idea how many poison pens are operating inside corporations using inside knowledge to frighten or blackmail people into giving them promotions and such?"

"No," I said, and, at this point, I didn't care. Those nasty letters were the least of Rhumumba's sins. "Why not Rhumumba?"

"It doesn't fit her psychological profile. Also, she has a pretty good alibi. She was at the Clit Club. Somebody like Rhumumba doesn't get missed at a lesbian club. About thirty total strangers said she was there."

"You're sure they were total strangers and not WAPs protecting her?" I asked, taking a sip of my wine and watching him closely over the rim of the glass. Maybe he didn't take the WAPs as seriously as I did.

"WAPs, WIPs, WWAWAWs. Don't you women know how to organize anything without a W in the acronym?" He reached across the table and patted my hand in what could be construed as a patronizing fashion. "No, I don't think they were protecting her. A buddy in homicide let me read the interviews. I'm sold. Steve is sold. Besides, Caro, why would Rhumumba kill Tiffany, who was basically a lesbian at the time of her death? Come on, it doesn't make sense. Do you know how likely it is a lesbian will commit a violent crime anyway? Not likely."

"I don't think of Rhumumba as a lesbian. She's a transsexual lesbian bodybuilder. It's a little different."

"Do you know the guy at the next table is listening to

everything we say?" he asked, his voice dramatically lowered. "Not that anyone could be blamed for eavesdropping on *this* conversation. Happens to you a lot, I guess, doesn't it?"

"Yes, I always talk about sex and murder in restaurants," I said, taking a larger sip of wine so my mouth wouldn't set in some little hurt line. "He's my bodyguard Samuel."

"I should have realized you'd need a bodyguard. That's the shits."

He softened toward me then, and the sudden empathy in those beautiful eyes touched me. I reached for his hand. He met mine halfway across the table, and we held hands. After telling me their clients were largely corporate and the work often entailed ferreting out industrial espionage, he promised he and his partner would take another look at Rhumumba anyway. If Vinnie didn't mind, they would see if they could come up with some other leads in Tiffany's murder, which, he emphasized, was a job for the police. He was humoring me, undoubtedly at Vinnie's request. Had Vinnie been kind enough to send him to me because he was black and beautiful? Or had he wanted to meet me himself? Or, most likely, had his partner, who would have been stuck with this minor job, been out of town again?

"Now that we've got the business out of the way," he said, "there's something else I want to ask you."

"Okay, ask."

"Are you only interested in me because I'm black?"

I picked up my wine goblet again. It was a fair question, and I wasn't going to answer it with a suitably respectable middle-class response, like, "Are you accusing me of being a racist?"

"I am more attracted to black men now than white," I admitted. "I'm not sure why that is, but being black wouldn't be enough. For instance," I said, lowering my voice and indicating a rotund black man a few tables away, "he doesn't do it for me."

"Why are you more turned on by black men now?" he asked, refusing to let me make light of the issue. "I have to tell you, Caro, I'm tired of women looking at me and seeing something I don't even know if I am. Black women want me because I wear a suit to work and make decent money. White women want me for the cock. What do you want?"

"I have dated all colors, black, brown, white, even a man who was born in Cuba of a Chinese mother and African father, then adopted by a Jewish family in Brooklyn. It was like fucking the U. N. Give me a break. I've earned the right to state a preference. Why do some men prefer blondes? Or big breasts? Or fat butts? Men make choices based partly on a woman's age or body type or hair color, and we don't question them. Why can't I be aroused by the sight and touch and smell of black skin?"

Softening the lecture, I stroked his hand, lifted it to my face, inhaled his scent, then kissed him. He caressed my chin, then put his thumb in my mouth. Briefly, I sucked it, and I saw him swallow hard.

"I suppose if the condition persists, I could go back into therapy," I said.

"Will you have dinner with me tomorrow night?"

"I can't think of anything I'd rather do."

We liked each other. The lust was mutual. He'd asked me for a date, and I'd accepted. Ignoring the fact that his distrust of my color preference loomed like a boulder in my romantic path, I was hugging these basic facts to me in the car going back to my apartment. They made me feel as warm as my beloved mink did.

"We got a date with the man tomorrow night?" Samuel asked from the seat across from mine.

"Yes. Did you like him?"

"Seems okay. No reason to worry about him. You like black men, don't you?"

"Yes, I do. Don't tell me you didn't hear that part?"

He grinned and ducked his head. Another week of sharing my life and he would be asking me if it was true black men had bigger cocks. My relationships always evolved in the confessional direction.

After checking the apartment and listening to my phone messages, Samuel settled down on the sofa with a science fiction paperback. I only asked my bodyguards to stay outside when I was having sex; there hadn't been much of that lately, unless you count masturbation. After a month of having the men around, I was so comfortable with them, I closed the bedroom door to masturbate, but I didn't ask them to leave. In fact, it titillated me to know Mike or Lennie or Samuel—especially Samuel—were listening in the other room.

I went back into the bedroom to change into my sweats and start on my homework, viewing erotic videos. In the last week I'd been through ten; most of them had excited me only briefly. Does anyone ever watch these things all the way through? Surely, one either masturbates or grabs one's partner somewhere in the first ten minutes. My observations of the films were recorded in a fat steno book. I planned to have Gwen transfer all my notes to a computer file. I couldn't put erotic sizzle into the Red Hot Mamas without studying the competition, could I? And, speaking of that, why weren't they more interested in what I had to say? They'd taken my check, but they didn't seem to want my creative input.

"We've been doing this a while," Gemma had snapped when I'd told her I wanted to get together to go over my ideas. "Maybe you should study the products and the process before you tell us how to make a video. It isn't as easy as being a celebrity editor."

Celebrity editor. That had stung. They weren't taking my promotion any better than David was. I suppose I could see their point. Their asses had been literally on the line for years, and now *I* was the acknowledged Queen of Porn. I could see their point, but I wasn't, however, ready to concede it.

The first film I put into the VCR was *Behind The Lilac Door,* a classic from the late seventies. It was Tiffany Titters at midcareer, not typical of her work. No fellatio. No tit-fucking. I also recognized Gemma in the girl gang bang sequence, where Tiffany did it to six girls, one after another, each writhing in turn for her on the lavender and pink printed sheets. Except for nostalgia for Tiffany's comforting presence, I felt nothing but boredom. My mind was wandering from Tiffany to David and what he would do if he couldn't write that novel. Why not go into the feminist porn business with us? I had my hand on the fast forward button ready to move quickly ahead when I saw what might have been a familiar face. I freezed the frame. It looked like, but it *couldn't* be . . . a younger Elizabeth Thatcher?

"You're kidding," Clarissa said when I called to tell her what I thought I'd found. "Well, like, if you're not kidding, you must be mistaken. It must be someone who looks like she might have looked fifteen years ago. Well, like, don't you think that must be it?"

"You're probably right. But, there's something about her facial expression which makes me think it couldn't be anyone else. I'm bringing *Behind The Lilac Door* to the office tomorrow so you can look at it."

"Carolyn, you don't think Tiffany got the same idea?

She was doing the same thing you're doing, studying videos, before she was killed. Remember how many cassettes we saw stacked up in her apartment when Mike broke in? What if she thought she saw Elizabeth Thatcher, too?"

"What would she have done about it if she had?"

"I don't know." Clarissa paused, and, in the pause, I heard a whine, either hers or Zellie's. "I see what you're getting at. She wouldn't exactly have called her and said, 'I'm on to you.' So, how would Elizabeth Thatcher have known to come over and kill her?"

"Right. How? If Tiffany had contacted Elizabeth Thatcher about anything, she would have told one of us, especially Vera."

We agreed she almost certainly would have. When we hung up, I was still in the familiar state: clueless. But the memory of those stacks of videocasettes in Tiffany's apartment nagged at me.

Samuel didn't know how to break into an apartment, so I had to wait for Mike, whose shift that day started at midnight. I had to bribe him by promising he could have all the shots of Miss May he wanted before he'd agree to break and enter one more time. When we got into Tiffany's place, most of the videos were gone. We grabbed the half dozen or so that were left and got out of there.

"Cops probably took them," Mike said. "Think what a temptation that would be. Can't really blame them, can you?"

No, I couldn't—only myself for not being smart enough to take them with me the last time I was there.

Elizabeth Thatcher, or her young look-alike, didn't appear on any of the cassettes, which I scanned immediately after getting back to my place. Maybe David would know what we should do next, if there was a way of positively identifying an actress from an old porn flick. In the morning, I'd call him from the office. I was bleary-eyed from watching naked people cavort and ready to fall asleep when Charles called.

"Babe, I miss you."

"I miss you, too." His voice was thick and rich, and I wanted to lie back on the bed and let it pour over me. "Where are you?"

"Seattle." I pulled off my sweat pants. "Ever been to Seattle?"

"Last year." I put my hand inside my black silk string bikinis, the kind he liked because they showed my ass to good advantage. "I loved it."

"It's okay. Too much rain for me."

"Can't sleep?"

"No." His voice grew even huskier, and I knew his hand was around his cock. My mouth watered for it. "You gonna help me sleep?"

"What are you wearing?"

"Nothing, babe. I'm lying on the bed, naked. The sheets are white. I remember you said you liked to see my black ass on white sheets."

I had a vivid memory of him naked on my own white ruffled sheets, lying on his side, his head propped up on one arm, in the position Tiffany said women didn't need to assume for other women. His hip had been thrust out. I'd bent over to kiss it before climbing in bed with him. Had he been posing for me?

"Charles, I'm touching myself. My legs are raised. I'm on my back. I'm playing with my clit."

"My dick's standing straight up in the air. I wish you were here to sit on it, babe."

"I can see your hand wrapped around it, moving up and down. Close your eyes and pretend it's my hand."

My voice broke, and he asked, "Are you coming already? Come for me, babe. You know how I love it when you do. Nobody comes like you do."

My hand was still against my clit. Silent tears were running out the corners of my eyes and down my temples, into my hairline. I let him think I'd come. It was the first orgasm I'd ever faked in my life.

"Only once, babe?"

"I'm tired, Charles. It's been a long day."

Chapter Fifteen

Hey, Superlady!

You could call me a cocksman, and proud of it! Women say they don't care about size. They claim they want sensitive men. They swear they don't care that much about orgasms, just touching and holding and satisfying their man is enough for them. It's the "closeness" they want, or so they say. Balls! Women want cock. They want it big, thick, hard, and long lasting, and handled by a real man. They're just too nice to say so. Don't you agree with me, Superlady? I've got a bet on your answer with some buddies who think what women really want is good lickin' and suckin'.

Cocksman,

I was not surprised to see the Texas postmark on your letter. But, how could you have failed to tell me how much you measure? Though few men are so besotted with their penises as you seem to be, your attitude of penile superiority is a common one. I surmise you are no fan of "lickin'" and "suckin'" unless, of course, someone else is doin' it, and your penis is the object of the oral attention.

I'm not sure how this will affect the settling of the bet, but I say women want it all. They want to be licked and sucked, then fucked, or sometimes in the reverse order. Since 65%–75% of women do not reach orgasm by intercourse alone—something you should know if you're a regular reader of this column—either oral or manual clitoral stimulation is typically necessary for orgasm. Yet, I do believe most women enjoy the experience of intercourse, of being filled by a hard cock. And, yes, some women do prefer it big. I *prefer big.*

And I, too, have never been convinced by women who say they really don't need an orgasm to be satisfied with sex. Maybe occasionally that's true for some women. But on a regular basis? No!

Why don't you call it a draw and donate the bet money to the Tiffany Titters Foundation for Sexual Transformation? You can send your check made out to the Foundation in care of this magazine. Your contribution will help those who are trying to change their lives through their sexuality, including transvestites and transsexuals, former prostitutes and porn stars struggling to launch their own erotic businesses, and video producers and directors in need of funding for their films. Unfortunately, this is not tax deductible.

I closed the file on Superlady and reapplied my lipstick, sort of a matte peachy-beige, not the color anyone ever said I should always wear. Between the column and editing the magazine, I was spending more time working than I would have preferred. My car was waiting downstairs to take me and Mike to a WIP luncheon at the overpriced and overrated Mesa Grill on lower Fifth Avenue, my choice. Mesa does Southwest cuisine the way they do it in California, which is not particularly good eating—food designed more for atmosphere than pleasurable consumption. I was putting lunch on my expense account. Today was the first of

February and I wanted to pretend I was in California and had taken everyone there with me; not, I suspected, that the everyone in question, David and the WIPs, really wanted to be with me. Eating at the Mesa Grill where everything on the menu looked like a pile of grilled vegetables arranged on effete forms of lettuce was the closest I could manage to a beach. Buying lunchtime companionship was the only way I could get it.

I needed something to cheer me up. Nothing did that like spending Vinnie's money on food none of us liked. There is a perverse satisfaction in signing an inflated expense account check after a mediocre lunch, washed down with pricey pitchers of margaritas.

Unfortunately, if things kept going the way they seemed headed, we'd be spending our brand-new Foundation's piddling funds on a legal defense for Bobby, when we'd been hoping to contribute something to Angelo for the additional surgery his penis required. Bobby was "talking" to the police at their "invitation" on such a regular basis, the *Post* was calling him the "lead suspect" in Tiffany's murder.

"Ready?" Mike said, jangling the keys in his pocket as if they were the keys to "our" car, and he was going to drive us to the mall. Our relationship had settled into something akin to a sexless marriage. He hurried me along, told me my skirts were too short, and frequently suggested I learn how to cook. "We got the car double-parked down there, you know."

Of course, we had the car double-parked. In Manhattan, it's the only way to park. Other cars have been holding the legal parking spaces since 1969.

"Coming, dear," I said, and he was so into the role he didn't blink.

Mike was doing a double shift because he needed personal time off tomorrow. I kept looking at him for signs of sleepiness, but there were none. Apparently he got a good night's sleep on my sofa while I scanned videos, faked a phone sex orgasm, and cried over Charles. In the beginning, he'd been alert at all times. But since Tiffany's death and the unmasking of Rhumumba as the poison pen, I'd received no more threats on my life. My bodyguards no longer behaved like I was a high-risk property.

On the ride downtown, he told me my gray cashmere dress was too short and suggested I "do up a few more buttons." I ignored him. The dress buttoned all the way down the front, but I'd chosen to leave the buttons undone into my cleavage and, from the bottom, inches beneath my pussy. Too bad if it made him nervous! My underwear and panty hose and suede pumps were gray, too. I was the epitome of classic good taste for my circle.

"You got a date tonight?" he asked, and I nodded affirmatively. "With that new black guy?"

"How'd you know about him? I only met him last night."

"Samuel told me. Look, I'm not nosy or anything. If I'm supposed to be protecting your life, I have to know who you're doin', don't I?"

"Sure," I said, shrugging, "but we made a date for dinner, not necessarily for 'doin'.' "

"Yeah. The fellas will be on the chair in the hall tonight. You like black guys, don't you?"

"Yes, I do."

"You don't think there might be something funny about that, a white woman liking black guys as much as you do?"

"Are you trying to psychoanalyze me, Mike?"

He ducked his head and the question. Why not Mike in the therapist's chair? Who wasn't questioning me about black men today? Date two black men in a row and you have a problem. Nobody ever asked me, "Why white guys?" I'll bet nobody ever asked a man, "Why blondes?"

"Don't get defensive," he said, as if he could read my thoughts, which I'm sure he could by now.

Everyone else, including David, whom we'd made an honorary member at Vera's suggestion to ease the pain of his firing, was at Mesa Grill when we arrived. The maitre d' had seated the group in the window at a section of small tables, which he'd pushed together—probably because the reservation was in my name. In New York, fame, no matter how it's come by, brings one sure reward: the best and/or showiest tables in restaurants. I should have been flattered the Mesa Grill wanted me on display in their window, but I wasn't. Celebrity was getting old, much the way a diet of chocolate covered eclairs would.

"We should get this party moved out of the window," Mike said.

"Carolyn, it's good to see you," David said, kissing my cheek perfunctorily, his lips pursed almost in distaste, after I'd kissed him first.

"This window is a liability area," Mike said. "I'm gonna call the maitre d' and get us moved."

"You're the one who's looking good," I said to David, while putting my hand on Mike's arm and shaking my head no. The loss of his expense account had encouraged David to develop better eating habits. He was losing weight and working out at the gym. "My God," I said, "you've even cut your hair. Will hair spray sales ever rebound from the loss?"

"When you reserve, you should always ask for a table in the back against the wall like the Mafia does," Mike said.

Since I refused to have everyone moved to another

table, he had them rearrange the seating so that Bobby and I were at the end, our backs against the partition separating this dining section from the entrance area. Then he put his chair at the corner of the table behind me. If the other diners didn't know who we were when we came in, they probably did by now.

"Don't you love it?" Gemma asked. They were all fawning over him. "David has allowed himself to go natural. No more silly hair mat over his bald head. He's much sexier now."

While I took my place between Clarissa and Bobby, whom I hugged hard, the women exclaimed over David's new look and Bobby's gray flannel miniskirted suit over a peach lace camisole and his fabulous gray suede heels. You wouldn't believe the selection in shoe stores catering to cross-dressers these days. Nobody told me I was looking good.

Reluctantly, Mike sat down. More drinks were ordered. And, after the first flurry of conversation, the silence landed on our shoulders like big soft flakes of snow. Vera's eyes filled with tears.

"Our first meeting without Tiffany," she said, and I reached for Bobby's hand. He still loved me. Clarissa only sucked up to me.

"We have to find out who killed her," David said, "because nobody else is going to." He looked at Bobby, then quickly glanced away. David avoids even the near occasion of sentimentality. "I have more free time than anyone now. I propose we develop an investigation plan of our own today, and I'll be the legman."

"He's right," I said. "We owe it to Tiffany. She would be devastated to know Bobby, who loved her so much, is under suspicion. We have to get moving on this on our own."

"I don't like this," Mike said.

After ordering several variations of chicken or shrimp rolled in blue corn flour, grilled, and served under piles of things that were good for us, David appointed Clarissa recording secretary and began listing our leads: they added up to Rhumumba. And shouldn't I have been the designated appointing person now? What kind of feminists were they, deferring to him as if he were a god?

"Do all roads really lead to Rhumumba?" David asked irritably. "This isn't very original of us."

"The cops aren't original," Bobby said.

"I think you all want it to be Rhumumba because you don't like her," Stephanie said.

"Who else could it be?" Clarissa asked. "Tiffany had no enemies. Everyone loved her. She also had nothing to steal. No drug connections. She didn't pick up strangers in bars. For the last few years, she was only having sex with friends, mostly women friends. Who but a crazed antiporner would have killed her?"

I told them about my discussion with Otis and his promise to give Rhumumba "another look" though he didn't see her as a murderer.

"You like black men, don't you?" Carola asked, but I ignored her.

"If we rule out Rhumumba, what does that leave us?" I asked.

"I'm not suggesting we rule her out," David said, enunciating his words with exaggerated care, the way he used to talk to Clarissa, "only add more people to the list."

The waitress brought our food and another round of drinks. As we ate, Clarissa told them about *Behind The Lilac Door.* She'd viewed it in the office that morning and also thought the woman could be a young Elizabeth Thatcher. But how could we find out?

"I'll see what I can do," David said, his face growing animated. "I don't think this has anything to do with Tiffany's death. But, Carolyn, what a great story for the magazine if we can prove the head WWAWAW was a porn actress in her youth!" He said my name with insincere warmth. Where was he going with this? "You could do a tremendous piece for the magazine. The publicity would shake the WWAWAWs to their core. Why, you could even have *me* write it!"

"Could I?" I asked. *Should I?* Did I want to give him that assignment? If I could give David assignments, I'd feel less guilty about having his job. On the other hand, if he kept being such an asshole, I'd feel less guilty about having his job anyway. I felt coerced, with the eyes of the WIPs, like the metal tips on cat-o'-nine-tails for the hard core, biting into me.

"Of course. Why not? By the time it appears, Vinnie will have forgotten he hated me, and it will be too good for him to do anything but praise us both anyway." David was pushing hard.

"Hmmm," I said, knowing he was right about that. The wrath of Vinnie was reputedly short-lived. But what about the hurt feelings of Carolyn? How long would they remain tender to the touch?

We ordered another round of drinks and then another. I was signing the check when I realized the only item Clarissa had on her list after Rhumumba was "Check out the sex clubs. See if anyone knows anyone who didn't like Tiffany." Lunch hadn't accomplished much beyond allowing David to reassert his authority over us.

"That is not a good idea," Otis said, frowning, but he looked good, even with a furrowed brow.

"Why?" I asked.

We were having dinner at Bayamo, the big and funky Chino-Latino restaurant on lower Broadway which I loved. The waitress had seated us upstairs beneath the enormous multicolored dragon. Sipping my white wine and looking into his big eyes as he lectured me, I was thinking about his cock. How long? How thick? How hard? I was not having a knee-jerk feminist response to his "macho protect the woman" stance. Nor, was I having a knee-jerk feminine response. There are some good things about being forty and comfortable with sexuality, both male and female.

"The sex clubs are raunchy, depressing places, Caro." He reached across the table and took my hand. The touch of his skin against mine elevated my heart rate and body temperature. "Considering your level of celebrity, I definitely don't think you should be hanging out in them."

"I wasn't planning to enjoy myself," I said, focusing on the "depressing" part of his objection and not the implied: You might find yourself followed home by a star rapist, which is even worse than being pursued by a star fucker.

"Amateurs are not equipped to conduct murder investigations, dear," he said in a tone I would have considered smug had it come from the lips of any other man. I liked his lips. "You must read too many novels."

He was wearing a black silk T-shirt, black jeans, and expensive black cowboy boots, a surprising look for him. I loved it. Looking at him was a pleasure. Surreptitiously, I'd already checked out other men in the same age range in the restaurant. Downtown middle-aged white men are less likely to be fat and accompanied by women half their age than the men you see uptown in Lutèce, for example. But Otis was still a standout in this, or any, crowd. I also agreed with him about the sex clubs being no place for Superlady these days, but I couldn't readily concede the point, could I? If I did, he would think he'd persuaded me of his viewpoint too easily.

"Well, one could legitimately call investigating the sex clubs part of my job, couldn't one?" I asked.

"Don't give me that 'one' bullshit! You're the one we're talking about, and we both know it. So, why do you have to call yourself 'one'? If you want me to help you with your little private investigation, you will stay out of those places. Send some other 'one' in your place if you want a story for your magazine. Have you got that?"—*Have you got that?*—"I'm not going to worry about you getting kidnapped, tied up, and whipped across your nice little butt . . . or worse."

"This isn't your way of telling me you think I have a sleazy job, is it?" I asked, suddenly feeling defensive.

"No, it isn't. I don't think you have a sleazy job. I admire you. Not many people can carve out a life for themselves on their own terms and do it as nicely as you have. You're a hustler, Caro, and I like that." He smiled warmly at me. "Black men are natural born hustlers. We gotta be. You don't see the white man making a space for us in the club steam room, do you? I like that about you, the way you take the status quo and make it work for you. I've read Superlady; she's got a smart mouth.

"And you do have a nice little butt," he said, squeezing my hand.

Our food arrived: a huge burger with jalapeno jack cheese and green chiles for me and a more healthful steamed pot of spiced chicken, rice, and vegetables for him. He let go of my hand so the waitress (dressed in the table waiting uniform of the lower east side, black tights and oversized white shirt) could serve us. I missed his hand. At the next table, Samuel was also having the burger.

Over dinner he told me about his life. Mine, of course, was an open tabloid newspaper. A Midwesterner, he had gone to college at the University of Missouri, on a football scholarship. He graduated, moved to New York City, and became a cop. He quickly hated it. He went to work for a private investigator, and eventually opened his own office. He took on a partner, Steve Cohen, who had left law school in his third year to earn money as a P. I. and found he liked that better. They had worked their way ever higher up the client scale, until now they only handled corporations. Anybody who wanted his wife tailed had to be a *very rich* entrepreneur. He was thirty-eight and the father of two sons, fourteen and fifteen.

"How long have you been divorced?" I asked, dreading the answer no woman wants to hear: less than six months or, worse, I'm only separated.

"Never been married," he said, attacking his steamed pot with vigor. "That's a real white question, you know. I wasn't married to either one of the mothers of my children."

"Have you been involved with the kids?"

"What is this?" he asked, putting down his fork. "Yes. I didn't know about the first one until he was three. His mother is a white girl. When we were together, I told her I didn't want kids. And if she got pregnant, it was her problem." He put up his hand to silence the expected attack. "I know. I was a jerk. She went away without telling me she was pregnant. When he was three, she needed money, so she showed up at my apartment one day with him. When I opened the door and took one look at his little face, I knew he was mine. I was living with a black girl, and we had a two-year-old. It wasn't a pretty scene, honey. But, yes, I've been involved with both my boys. I support them, and I'll send them to college. Okay?"

"I'm glad. I walked out on a man in a restaurant once after he told me he didn't pay child support and hadn't seen his six-year-old in four years."

He laughed, throwing his head back the way he had the night before.

"Do you want to get married?" he asked when he'd

stopped laughing. "Have another baby? Is that why all the questions?"

I told him I'd had a tubal ligation years ago because I believed two perfect children were all anybody could ever be lucky enough to have. Why not quit when you're very far ahead? Then, changing the conversation lest he think I wanted the marriage if not the kids, I told him about *Behind The Lilac Door* and how I was certain Elizabeth Thatcher's naked, and plumper, little body had graced its torrid scenes. He didn't seem to think it was worth checking out until I told him David was pursuing the possibility the spokesperson for WWA-WAW was once an X-rated starlet. Then he decided maybe he should see what he could learn. As my daughter says, "If you want a man to do something, you only have to tell him another man already is."

We finished the meal with cappuccino and hand-holding.

"I want to go to bed with you," he said, lifting my hand to his lips. "I am put off by this thing you have for black men, but I want you."

"I want to go to bed with you, too."

"He stays outside, doesn't he?" he asked, indicating Samuel.

"What do you think I am? A voyeur or something?" Samuel asked.

He put his arm around me in the car going back to my apartment, but, in deference to Samuel's presence, he didn't kiss me. It was all I could do to keep my hand off his thigh. If I'd put my hand on his thigh, it would have moved of its own free will toward his penis. I knew his wouldn't be as big as Charles's, and really that was fine. Charles had a bit too much, or at least I would console myself for the rest of my life with the excuse that Charles really had a bit too much. Most likely his penis would be significant; he had the hands and feet.

"You look lost in thought," Otis said. "You aren't still thinking about going to the sex clubs, are you?"

I insisted I wasn't. He hugged me. Did he hug all his clients when they accepted his guidance? Samuel caught my eye, and I could have sworn that he knew exactly what had been on my mind.

Back at the apartment, Samuel went through his standard security check, including playing back the messages on my machine. I could tell by Otis's eyebrows pulled together in a tight line, he found it needlessly intrusive. I popped the cork on a bottle of Moët & Chandon. When I brought the bottle and two champagne flutes into the living room, Otis, who had been sitting on the sofa, stood. His black leather jacket was tossed across the coffee table. He'd taken off his boots and socks. There is something appealingly vulnerable about a man's bare feet, even large ones like his.

"Let's drink in the bedroom," he said.

"I'll be outside if you need me," Samuel said, passing us in the hall and quietly closing the door behind him.

"Would you like to watch *Behind The Lilac Door?"* I asked, setting the glasses on the dresser and filling them.

Yes, what an inane question. Now that we were alone in my bedroom, the familiar feelings began to bubble inside me, like the champagne in the flutes. I wanted him close, didn't want him close. I wanted to pull him close and push him away, all in the same motion.

"I should put some ice in a bucket for this," I said.

"No. The last thing I want to do is see that video. I'll take it with me and view it in the office on Vinnie's time."

He stopped me as I was going back toward the

kitchen by planting his body directly in front of mine. I watched him look at me and saw that his breath was coming ragged, his hands were curling nervously at his sides. The feelings stopped shifting back and forth inside me. I wanted him close, wanted him inside me, wanted him so much I felt the bottom dropping out of my stomach when he swallowed. There was no ambivalence.

"Forget about the ice for now and take off your clothes," he said. His eyes grew soft. "I want to see you."

I kicked off my heels, unzipped my dress, and let it drop to the floor. Just as I finished, he pulled me into his arms. I felt his stomach muscles tense as he kissed me. I put one hand on the hard ridges of his belly and held it there as his tongue explored my mouth. He unfastened the gray silk bra and took one breast in his hand.

"You have beautiful breasts."

I brought his mouth back to mine and kissed him, searching him with my tongue, as I ran my hands under his shirt, up and down his back. He was lean and hard; I guessed he got his body from free weights, not the machines.

He pulled the silk T-shirt over his head and threw it on the floor. I tossed my bra on top of it. He embraced me, then led me to the bed. We laid down side by side; he pulled off my panties, and panty hose. He ran his tongue inside my thighs as his hands caressed my hips. Then standing beside the bed, watching me watch him, he took off his jeans and white briefs. His penis was magnificent, not as large as Charles's, of course, but absolutely beautiful. It stood a good seven or eight inches in length; thick, very erect, and deeply, purely black. I liked it immediately. I wanted it inside me.

I opened my arms, and he got back on the bed. Lying side by side, facing each other, we kissed and caressed, learning each other's bodies by taste and touch. I wanted him now. Putting my leg on top of his hip, I angled my pelvis and pushed down on his penis, forcing it inside me. The jolt of the connection shot through both our bodies simultaneously. Moaning into my mouth, he grasped my buttocks with both hands and thrust in and out of me, his body hungry, not yet finding a rhythm. I opened my eyes, and his were already open. My orgasm began immediately, and its beginning established his rhythm.

He was sure of himself, of his erotic power over me. I saw the change in his eyes. I kept my eyes open the whole time we made love, letting him see into every corner, letting him have me completely and without reservation. When he came at last, I felt him surging into me and saw his eyes stop churning and grow calm like a quiet sea.

I woke with my breasts flattened against his back, my hand around his penis and the feeling he was in no hurry to leave. It was a good feeling.

"I could be late, honey," he said, and I moved my hand gently up and down.

He reached around and masturbated me with his hand. Within a few minutes, I was on the verge of orgasm, and he was on top of me, making love to me, with his body and his eyes. After bringing me to orgasm again, he pulled out and buried his face in my cunt. I gasped, my hands involuntarily clasping his head, guiding his tongue deeper into me. He manipulated my clit with the bridge of his nose while his tongue pushed inside my vagina as deeply as it could go. I came again. He pulled his face away from my cunt and mounted me. I wrapped my legs around his waist, and we came together. When it was over and he was lying in my arms, trying to regain his breath, I kissed his eyelids.

"You're gonna make me fall asleep again," he whispered, "kissin' my eyes like that."

He rolled over on his side, and pulled me against his chest. We slept till almost noon, ignoring the phone, the sunlight streaming in the windows, and Mike, who came in to make a routine check and pulled the comforter over our naked bodies, like a mother tucking his charges in. When I woke again, we were a tangle of limbs, an artful blend of black on white, white on black. Would I ever be satisfied with a white man again?

"It was that good?" David asked, pushing for details. My new lover had put us temporarily back on safe ground. "How was it so good? What was so different about it? Carolyn, there are only so many ways to fuck."

He said the last in pure exasperation. David envied me the sexual experiences of my life as I envied him the stability of his. His first several months at *Playhouse* had been very hard on him. Maybe it was time I forgave him for his one lapse with Tiffany. And, maybe I would have, if he'd forgiven me for taking "his" job.

"It was better than that good," I said, recrossing my legs so that my green wool knit dress crept a little farther up my thigh.

David and I were waiting for O and Steve Cohen to join us for dinner at Swing Street Café, my favorite midtown restaurant on East 52nd Street. The food, American bistro, is good, not overpriced, and the staff is warm and friendly. We'd agreed on Swing Street because they were working on a job at a corporate headquarters in the neighborhood. He didn't give me any details, not that I really wanted any. Why would I care about corporate espionage when I was looking at proof of Elizabeth Thatcher's past life in porn?

"Better than Charles?" he asked.

"Better."

"Not bigger, I hope."

"No, just better," I said, and I meant to withhold the details from him, a first in our friendship. "Intense. Emotional. Physical. No holding back. Just better. That's all you're getting, okay? It's private."

"Your sex life is private? All I have to do is wait a few months until you write a piece for the magazine on 'my black nights.' Everything you do turns up in print. Sometimes I don't know which comes first, your life or writing about it."

"Not this time."

"You hear from Charles?" he asked, sort of changing the subject.

"He calls me when he's out of town."

"Phone sex?" He nodded wisely, like he knew something about phone sex, which I doubted he did. His wife didn't travel often. "Well, you can't blame him, Carolyn. It isn't entirely his fault. Here the man is in possession of the mythical huge black penis. Do you think you're the only woman after that? The only white woman? Interracial sex is the last taboo."

"Uhm," I said. "Do you think I'm interested in black men because it's the last taboo?"

"Why are you interested in them specifically?"

"Because the only good white men my age are married, gay, or would rather be dating my daughter. The men who are left don't want to fuck or if they do, I don't want to fuck them. I hate having to lift up a man's stomach in search of his penis, particularly if it turns out to be a little one."

"Well, there you are. Do you think the possessor of such a prize organ as Charles has can be expected to save it for one woman only?"

"You're saying he's not responsible for being a lying

asshole because he has a big black penis? What, his penis makes him do it?"

"I hope you realize you sound like the typical woman when you say things like that," he said, and I winced, because he was right. "Did you use condoms with the new man?"

I maintained a dignified silence. How could I describe the longing I felt for a man inside me, with nothing between us? How to explain how much I love the feeling of him ejaculating strongly inside my vagina? There was no way I could say those things without sounding like some man who was too big a jerk to use a condom.

"I thought so," he said.

"The truth is, David," I said irritably, "I hate the damned things, too. And don't give me your safe sex lecture. I wrote it for you."

Seeing O come in the doorway, I broke into a smile that felt like it was cascading over my whole body in warm waves. David's appraising eye and twisting mouth couldn't make me hide my happiness because O had walked into the room. But, and I sensed this immediately, O was returning my smile at less than half the wattage.

"Caro," he said, brushing his lips across mine.

The introductions were made.

"I feel like I know you already," Steve said. He was short, maybe 5′6″, with the kind of thick curly chestnut hair and long eyelashes women would kill for. A plus, he had a beard, light brown shot through with red and flecked already in gray, though he couldn't be much past thirty. He was adorable, if you're into younger white guys. "I've been reading you for years."

"A fan," I said.

"I didn't say I was a fan. I said I've been reading you for years."

He grinned, softening the implied critique. We all shook hands, ordered drinks, white wine for me, Heineken on draft for O and David, coke for Steve. I shoved the material that David had given me across the table to O.

"Where did you get these?" O asked David, indicating the publicity still shots of a young Elizabeth, totally nude. They were bland, the poses formulaic; her back arched off the bed on one, her hand coyly held over her pussy in another. She had been interchangeable with any number of young women who come to New York or L. A. each year, seeking fame or money or salvation at the end of a camera.

"At Movie Star Photos in Times Square," David said, clearly proud of himself. "In addition to the standard old studio stills, they have a lot of stuff from the independent photographers who were more apt to have shot the porn starlets. Nobody's asked to look at these photos in years. I gave the kid at the desk a twenty dollar bill to let me look through drawers, and I found her. She called herself Liz Larue. If it's not her, it's a relative."

O compared the nude stills with the recent publicity photo of Elizabeth in her silk dress representing WWAWAW. He nodded his head and passed them to Steve, who also nodded his head in agreement. Men validating men. Then he picked up the Xeroxed sheets from the *Encyclopedia of X-Rated Films.*

"She only made three films?" Steve asked, scanning the information sheet in O's hands.

"As far as I can tell," David said. "She may have done some others, even smaller budget films. Or she may have used a different name. It's hard to be sure. I could only find Liz Larue in three places. Tiffany was in two of the three films she made. Could that be a coincidence?"

"You think Tiffany remembered her, and that's what got her killed?" O asked.

"I don't," I said, but they ignored me.

"It's possible," Steve said.

"What would make Tiffany suddenly remember her?" I asked. "And why, if she remembered her at all, hadn't she put *this* Elizabeth and *that* one together a long time ago and told us about it?"

"Because, Carolyn," David began in his voice of patient explaining, "she would have no reason to connect the two in her mind. But, while reviewing videos for her own project, she could have seen the old Elizabeth and suddenly put the two together."

"I agree," O said, smiling apologetically at me. "And besides," he added, picking up the most damning evidence of all, "if these three women aren't all the same women, I'll be surprised. It fits too tight. Elizabeth Thatcher's psychological fingerprints are all over these other two personas."

Oh, yes, woman number three. He was holding a Polaroid photo of her leaving a meeting of Love and Sex Addicts Anonymous in Memphis. Though she'd identified herself to the group as "Lia," she was clearly Elizabeth. The picture had been sent to David by a reporter on the Memphis paper, who also wrote erotica under a pen name, after David had called her to see if she had any "dirt" on Elizabeth Thatcher.

The note accompanying it read, "David, We had a tail on Elizabeth for a few days after she got out of the hospital just to see if she would head for New York again. When she didn't, we had to drop the tail, too expensive for no results. The only interesting—strange!?—thing she did during those two days was go to three meetings of Love and Sex Addicts Anonymous. A woman who'd attended one of the meetings said she'd called herself 'Lia' and alluded to a dirty sexual secret in her past. We figure she probably had an orgasm once. What do you think?"

"I think she might have killed Tiffany," David said. "She's just crazy enough to do it."

"It shouldn't be hard to establish her whereabouts for the time of the murder," Steve said. "I'll get on that."

"I don't think she killed Tiffany," I said. "Wouldn't someone have figured out she was in New York at the time of the murder if she had been? I mean, please, the woman is high visibility, thanks to 'Olive.' "

"Not if they aren't looking for her to have been up here," O said. "You forget, the cops are real busy with Tiffany's sex life. And, Caro, she's not that high visibility, no matter how many times you see her photo in the *Post.* She looks like thousands of other pretty but banal women."

"He thinks all white women look alike," Steve said, and David laughed heartily.

"Okay," I said, "I'm not convinced, but David's right about one thing. This will make a hell of a story for the magazine."

"We need to send a woman down to Memphis to infiltrate her support group," he said.

"One of the WIPs?" I asked.

"It has to be someone who won't stand out in a crowd, which rules out everybody except—"

"Clarissa!" I said.

"Clarissa? I was going to say Stephanie."

"Clarissa, if we can get her to dress a little more like a woman, you know in the kind of pants suits my sisters would wear. Stephanie?" (He secretly lusts after Oriental women.) "You don't think a beautiful Oriental woman would stand out in a Memphis crowd? Clarissa. Absolutely. She's the only one who could pull it off."

He cringed. What an idea! David and Clarissa coauthoring the article of the year.

Chapter Sixteen

Dear Superlady,

I want more sex than my wife does. I also want more variety. From reading your column, I gather this is a common state of affairs between the sexes. Sometimes I wish I were a gay man so I wouldn't have to deal with women. My wife's solution was to see a therapist together. After four weeks we are still discussing such hot topics as how to prioritize our intimacy. What bullshit! But my wife is into it. If I hang in for the sessions she wants, will it make things any better in our bedroom? No improvement in that department yet, I must say. If not, what do you suggest?

I was formulating an answer that would be neither dishonest nor wholly discouraging when Gwen buzzed me that Clarissa was on line one from Memphis. I lunged for the receiver, banging my solid gold link watch from Cartier, a welcome aboard gift from Vinnie, on my desk. She had left yesterday morning, and this was her first contact with us. Miriam hadn't heard from her, and she was driving us crazy phoning the office, me at home, and David at home. We didn't even know where Clarissa was staying; neither did Miriam who didn't seem to function well without her. I was beginning to think the WWAWAWs had confiscated our undercover journalist at the airport.

"Carolyn," she said, more exuberant than I'd heard her sound since Zellie's birth. "I feel like a spy, like, I'm looking over my shoulder even though I'm in my own motel room now. I love this. Do you think Otis and Steve might take me on as a third partner? I could learn to handle a gun, I know I could."

Wearily, I shut my eyes. I could picture her: an orange chenille bedspread draped around her shoulders as combination cape and fire protection, in case she had to leap from a first-floor window to safety, should someone throw a bomb into her room. I felt a headache coming on. Now I understood why David had been so cranky when he was editor.

"Clarissa, what's going on?" I asked, taking off a heavy gold earring to get the receiver closer to my ear. She was speaking softly. "Why haven't you called sooner? We've been worried. David's called Otis twice to suggest he send someone down to look for you. What do you mean, handle a gun? I hate being the boss here."

"I'm in deep cover in Memphis. What did you expect? Hourly bulletins? I'm out in the cold, Carolyn."

"Yeah, right," I said, toying with the band of my watch. This dispatch from the front was coming in slowly. "What have you been doing down there in the cold?"

"I've been to four LSAA meetings. You know Steve was right when he said people who are, like, heavily crazed into these groups go all over town to meetings. I keep seeing the same people. One woman has been to all four of the meetings I've been to and another half dozen have been to three meetings and . . ."

"Have you seen Elizabeth?" I interrupted. You know, Clarissa, the object of your search, I added silently to myself, internalizing the things David would have said out loud.

"Lia, oh yeah. She calls herself Lia, but it is definitely Elizabeth. She's lost a few pounds, definitely not looking good. There's a crazy look in her eye."

Clarissa had a talent for understatement. She had once labeled "a little weird" a letter from a man who'd described masturbating to orgasm while his wife gave birth. Afterward the new parents had eaten the placenta together or so he claimed.

"What, a crazier look than she had when she tried to choke me to death?" I asked.

"Crazier. I think she might be ready to break." *Ready to break?* "I've seen her at two meetings. I can tell she's a regular in the one group and an occasional visitor to the other. But I have a list of nineteen groups here—"

"There are nineteen of these love and sex addict groups in Memphis alone?" I asked. "Don't these people have jobs, families, lives?"

"Yeah, you wonder, don't you? And, like, all the people who go to them say the same things. And you aren't supposed to give anyone advice about their lives, it's like group therapy without the leader or the therapy. But after they share, everybody kind of nods their head, like, yeah, you're a sex addict. This fat guy blubbered all over himself because he had phone sex with a wrong number, and these women said—"

"I know the lingo," I said. "Remember, I briefly dated a recovering drummer? What does Lia say when she 'shares' with the group?"

"Well, here's the problem, not much."

Clarissa and I sighed simultaneously. We were hoping, of course, that Elizabeth would announce she'd gone to New York City as a teenage runaway and made three porn films. Clarissa would have that on tape and catch the next plane home. It wasn't going to be so easy.

"Well, tell me, exactly what does she say?"

"Okay, I have my notes transcribed from the tapes. That little tape recorder hidden in my jacket pocket is the coolest. Here it is: 'Hi, my name is Lia and I'm a sex addict.' Then everyone says, 'Hello, Lia.' Then she says, 'I haven't had an addictive episode in many years, but I am still haunted by that time in my life when my lust led me down a sick and twisted path to perversion.' Then, she goes on the same way, where she basically says she did terrible things for her lusts, but she doesn't say what they were. And, at the end of her spiel, which she delivered almost word for word at both meetings, she says, 'The man for whom I had insatiable shameful lust forced me to do things so evil, the memory of them burns like acid inside me.' "

"Has the ring of poetry to it, doesn't it?"

"Yeah. Like, I'm sure she's been saying it since she started going to meetings. But, like, here's the interesting part. A lot of people really go off on pornography in these meetings, but she doesn't say much on the subject. Does that make sense to you?"

"Maybe she's trying to keep her WWAWAW connection quiet. They surely wouldn't want their PR director describing herself as a 'sex addict,' would they? I wouldn't say anything about porn if I were her either. What would it take to get her to elaborate on her story? Doesn't anyone try?"

"Not really," Clarissa said, a note of dejection creeping into her voice. "Everyone is thinking about what they get to say on their turn when other people are talking. Do you want to hear my cover story?"

I didn't, but she told me anyway. Clarissa was posing as an ex-nun who'd been forced to leave the convent because she couldn't control her lascivious thoughts about the other nuns. The people in the groups loved it, she said, especially the part about her masturbating during mass to thoughts of the other nuns' breasts.

We agreed that Clarissa would attend as many groups as she could in the next week until her presence was so familiar, she could risk questioning Lia without arousing suspicion. Under the guise of a religious helper, she could perhaps draw Thatcher out from behind the thicket of rhetoric hiding her. I took down the name of the motel, the phone number, and Clarissa's room number. And I made her promise to check in at least once every day.

"And call Miriam," I ordered. "She's driving us crazy."

"Wives," Clarissa said, her last comment before hanging up.

Then, before I could get back to work and answer the letter from the poor man whose wife was trying to prioritize their intimacy, which sounded a lot like alphabetizing the spices, Gwen buzzed me again. Vera was on the phone. We went over the plans for the evening. She and several other WIPs were going to the sex clubs to talk to people about Tiffany. I had decided to stay home. I knew Otis was right when he said my celebrity would get in the way. The WIPs had enthusiastically endorsed this position, too. I planned an early dinner, then I would go over my notes for the Will Douglas show the next day, and fall asleep early.

I was truly looking forward to a quiet evening alone.

"LED BY SUPERLADY, SEX STARS TAKE OVER SEX CLUBS!!!!"

Without comment, Mike had handed me the *Post* when he came on duty at eight in the morning. Until he did I was feeling sane and healthy, rested and virtuous. I was sitting at my white tile kitchen counter eating a bowl of whole grain cereal and fruit and drinking vanilla almond coffee from my Virginia Woolf mug. The headline was enough to make the milk on my cereal curdle.

"What the hell?" I said.

"Yeah, I showed it to Samuel, and he was just as surprised as you are. He says you two didn't leave the apartment last night. They've got your name attached to somebody's behind on the picture inside."

I opened to page three, a picture of Vera, Gemma, and Carola climbing into a limo. All you could see of Carola was ass and legs—and a very fine view it was. They were indeed identified as mine. We've all got to take climbing into car lessons from the Princess of Wales.

"I'm flattered," I said.

"Yeah. I would hate to be standing here if they'd mixed you up with Vera."

The article was brief.

> *Why was a team of aging sex stars doing the sex club scene last night? They were asking questions about Tiffany Titters. Questions, like, "Do you know anyone who didn't like Tiffany?" Are the Women in Porn trying to solve the murder of one of their own without help from the police?*
>
> *The women hit the club scene hard. They were spotted uptown at Brothel, Brothel, a triplex where posh rooms are rented on the half hourly basis. From there they headed downtown to clubs ranging from lesbian to S&M. Music stopped at the Hungry Pussy when they came into the club. At the Hellhole, Superlady stepped in something and left with it clinging to her shoe.*
>
> *None of the women would comment on their motives for the whirlwind tour of the underbelly of life. When informed of their investigation efforts, Homicide Lieutenant Michael Reardon, in charge of the case, said, "We cannot stop private citizens from going into public clubs and asking any questions they want to ask of anyone they want to question. But we*

can't guarantee protection for these women either if their questioning gets them into trouble."

Did they learn anything? Nobody knows.

"Aging sex stars!" I said contemptuously, checking the byline. Allison Kemp. "Wouldn't you know it's written by a woman. She's probably twenty-seven and hates porn."

"Yeah, well, you know I think you girls look damned good for your ages," Mike said. "Vera's got a little too much meat on the hoof, but she's still a good-looking dame. What do you suppose Carola stepped in that ended their evening prematurely, so to speak?"

"Thanks, Mike, for the compliment," I said sweetly; he smiled, genuinely believing in my gratitude. "And I shudder to think what she might have stepped in at an S&M club. I've been to Hellhole once, with David, for research. Some women were manacled to the walls; a few women were lethargically whipping men. The smell of urine and feces was strong. We both got nauseous and had to leave."

"Yeah, she most likely stepped in shit. Hell, I wouldn't pay $50 to get in somewhere like that. You can step in dog shit on the street for free."

I'd finished my cereal and put the bowl and coffee cup in the dishwasher when Otis called. He was furious, in a controlled and professionally distant way, of course. I held the phone away from my ear while he yelled at me about "risking" my "silly little neck" to ask "even sillier questions" of people whose answers, if they even had any answers, "wouldn't impress a judge because they have slightly more credibility than a street junkie."

"Why, Otis, I think you care. I really think you do," I said. I don't know why I said it, because I didn't really believe he did. He didn't give me time to explain I hadn't been there at all.

"Caro," he said. The pause between the saying of my name, in that tone of voice the dumper typically uses with the dumpee, and the clearing of his throat told me all I needed to know. Being a sensitive man, he had to say it anyway. "I care, but not quite in the way you think I do."

"Otis . . ."

"No, Caro, I have to say this. I'm not going to see you again, and you deserve to know why. I like you, but I can't get past this black thing of yours. I'm not comfortable being with a white woman who's into black men the way you are. It makes me feel like something you bought off the auction block. Do you understand that?"

"No, I don't understand why men are allowed to have physical preferences, but women aren't."

"There's something else going on here, too. You know I work for Vinnie first. His interests and yours are probably the same, but, if they're not, I have to be on his side."

"Why wouldn't his interests and mine be the same here, Otis?"

"Look, Caro, I can't fully trust David with the rumor going around that he's seen a lawyer about filing a lawsuit against the corporation. It may not be true, but . . ." He paused, clearly waiting for me to defend or criticize, confirm or deny. I wasn't going to let him know this was the first I'd heard of that particular rumor. "I'm sorry you don't understand. I'm sorry to be hurting your feelings. I . . ."

Everyone who has ever rejected another person has been sorry. Not wanting to hear him wallow in his sorriness, I slammed the receiver down so hard on the wall phone that the plastic cracked right down the seam from ear to mouthpiece. Tears smarted in my eyes, but

I brushed them angrily aside. Was he so put off by my attraction to black men or was he just another one of those guys who fuck you like an angel then never call again?

And what was David doing behind my back?

"I hate men," I told Gwen when I walked past her desk on the way to my office. She was surrounded by plants in fussy little ceramic pots and at least a dozen photos of her two-year-old son, a dishwater blond like her. "If they aren't geeks, nerds, losers, jerks, or lying assholes, they have other problems."

"Yeah," she said, following me as I stormed into my office. Gwen was tiny, not five feet and under a hundred pounds and meek and mild until she put a phone to her ear. The phone turned her into a dynamo, capable of getting rid of any caller without alienating him or her. David always said she gave the best business phone in the business. "You got another letter from the Starred Man. Clarissa says not to bother you with them, but she's not here. Should I leave it in her box?"

"Fine," I said. "Call the *Post* and tell them they misidentified the ass of Carola Rogers. I was not in the sex clubs last night."

"Sure," she said, tidying up my desk for me.

"And get me Steve Cohen—Steve, not his partner—on the phone. Don't put anybody through but Clarissa or him. I've got a lot to do this morning."

Forget Otis. I was working with Steve. He was a fan. I would have bet he'd masturbated to my columns; the words, not the picture. Steve was a man of words, and the words I wanted from him were the ones that would tell me what David was doing.

I wasn't coming back to the office after lunch. A limo was taking me straight from lunch with an advertiser to the Douglas show where Carola, Gemma, and I were appearing live that afternoon. Subject or so we had been told: Feminist Porn. Afterward, it looked like another early night. Should I notify the *Post?* Or should I lure young Steve into my lair and between my thighs to get back at Otis?

Clarissa got me on the car phone on the way to lunch. She'd had a "breakthrough," if you define a breakthrough as something achieved by hitting a person who is reluctant to talk with the equivalent of an emotional sledgehammer. Clarissa had told Elizabeth Thatcher she knew who she was—both then and now.

"But, like, I did it real cool, like I said I know I've seen you somewhere. I remember you from the past, I know you were in an old X-rated movie I saw—*Behind The Lilac Door!*"

"Did you tell her you'd rented it on one of those rainy Saturday afternoons back at the convent when there wasn't anything else to do, the prayers had been said, the bread baked, your panties washed by hand?"

"Carolyn, if you're going to make fun of me, I'll hang up," she said in her pouty voice. "I got enough of that from David. I handled her perfectly, which you will soon realize. Do you want to hear the rest or not?"

"Sure," I said, already dreading telling David. "I can't afford not to hear it, can I? I'm the one who's going to sign your expense vouchers for this trip."

"Well, she was so shocked I knew about it that she said yes. Then, I pressed my advantage and asked if she wasn't that woman active in one of the antiporn groups, and she said, yes, again. I have it on tape." She faded out, then came back in again. I hate car phones. "I'm a fucking genius! I acted like I really admired her for what she was doing. Then she told me she'd been forced to do those films by the man she was with, like he sexually enslaved her. I told her she should come clean and admit who she is because denouncing porn after you've been in it would be even more effective."

"You didn't!"

"I wanted her to trust me, which she does. She isn't going to come out and tell the world about her shameful past. Her husband doesn't know. Anyway, I have to go because we're getting together for coffee this afternoon."

"Clarissa, be careful. Get all you can out of her today and then come back to the city as soon as possible. And sit in a public place with her at all times. Don't take her back to your motel. And, Clarissa, be prepared to get choked, okay?"

She laughed. Obviously, she thought I was kidding. I wasn't. While I couldn't see Elizabeth as Tiffany's murderer, I knew she was definitely the type to indulge in a little spontaneous choking when her emotions got out of control.

"Here we have three women who are going to tell you there *is* such a thing as feminist porn, a form of pornography or erotica, if you will, which arouses women and doesn't degrade them," Will said, sweeping his arm in our direction, the gesture indicating a unity we did not have.

"And over here, we have two women who will tell you there *isn't,* that all porn is by definition exploitive of women," he said, pointing at the opposition. It included Marsha Foster, a thin lesbian lawyer with bad hair, who was trying to get a tough antiporn law passed by Congress, and Rosalie Anderson, a very fat lesbian writer whose bad hair was totally overshadowed by her general ugliness. But we were playing by TV talk show rules and could not say the word "lesbian" as descriptive of their life-styles on national TV, because they were not "out." Outing them would have violated their rights.

Rosalie was, perhaps, the ugliest woman I'd ever seen except for Rhumumba, the kind of woman who gives feminism a bad name. I consider myself, and anyone who believes in equal pay for equal work, a feminist, but I understand why the women of the twentysomething generation don't want to be identified by the word "feminist." Women like Rosalie have taken it over. She wouldn't let the makeup people put foundation over her pimples or powder down her oil. What did these women do with the money they didn't spend on hair care products, makeup, or disposable razors?

"Boy, oh, boy," Will said, "have we got a disagreement here."

The audience laughed. He fiddled with the cards in his hand. This was not his favorite show. He would rather have presidential candidates debating the issues or, perhaps, former President Jimmy Carter philosophizing on how building houses helped build America. This was a feminist issue, which meant he was just a bit more excited than he would have been introducing a group of male strippers; one of whom would probably set his jock strap on fire as part of his act. In other words, the kind of mindless show that gets the ratings.

"Uhm, let me see, uhm," he said, arranging the cards. "Here we have Carola Rogers, a former X-rated video star, who started her own production company ten years ago, and considers herself the founding mother of feminist porn. Have I got that right, Carola?"

"You have, Will, but I prefer the term 'feminist erotica,'" she said. Why had it taken me so long to notice how arrogant she was? "My erotica is aimed at women and couples. It has all the elements necessary to female arousal, including a romantic storyline, tenderness between the partners, and attractive settings. The women are certainly not debased and degraded—"

"I would have to challenge that," Foster said. Me, too, on different grounds.

"Okay, okay, you'll get your chance to challenge," Will said. "Right now I'm introducing the women on this side of the issue. We'll get to you. Just be patient. This isn't a courtroom."

The audience laughed, though Will certainly wasn't as funny as Olive.

"Women are only renting your videos to please their men," Rosalie said.

"All right!" Will almost yelled. "You'll get your turn." Pointing to Gemma, he said, "Here we have Gemma Michaels, also a former X-rated video star, publisher of *Great Sex!,* a sex magazine some people consider raunchier than *Hustler,* and owner of her own feminist porn production company.

"And, next to her," he rushed on, to get the introductions out before the polemics began in earnest, "is someone you may recognize because she's certainly had more than her share of publicity lately. Carolyn Steele, the Superlady of Sex, now the executive editor at *Playhouse* magazine, and a new investor in a feminist porn production company these three women have formed, called the Red Hot Mamas!

"Tell us about your new company, Carolyn."

Knowing my partners were seething under their makeup to hear *their* company labeled *mine,* I smiled into the camera and launched into my product spiel. They dutifully waited a respectable amount of time before cutting in on me. All those years of faking orgasms had taught them how to be polite.

". . . and women are shown in these videos as being

the sexual initiators," Carola was saying. "We know, Will, that's true in real life as well. Studies show women are initiating up to fifty percent of the sexual encounters in their relationships. And their fantasies have become bolder, too, reflecting their new reality."

Stifling a yawn (these women were boring, all four of them) I indulged in a mini fantasy of my own. Dressed in garter belt, stockings, heels, and a mask, I was riding astride first Charles, then O, flying high in the female superior position. I picked up my whip and snapped it across each man's nipples as I rode him. Now I was on Charles. His penis grew and grew so big I had to leap off it in mid orgasm or it would have split me in half. I rode on the side of the giant penis, my legs wrapped around it, my heels digging into it, until it detached from his body and shot up, like a rocket into the sky. After a while, I brought it back down to earth, to O's bed, where it deposited me in his arms.

The whiny voice of Rosalie brought me back to reality. Anyway, in real life, O would have said, "You only fell out of the sky into my bed because I'm black. Please go back up into the clouds."

"All forms of male to female genital interaction," she was saying when I rejoined the program in progress, "are acts of aggression. If a man loves a woman, he should not even let her see him with his penis exposed."

The last shot going into commercial captured my look of pure disdain.

"Are you there, caller?" Will asked. "I'm glad you waited," he said, even before the caller spoke.

We were past the half hour point, and I was seriously bored. Will had vigorously run up and down the aisles, working the audience, saying, "Help me out here, people," and "This is a talk show, let's talk," whenever they flagged in their enthusiasm for the debate. Gemma, Carola, and I had stood up for heterosexual sex. Foster and Anderson were against penetration, and that probably included male tongues and fingers. Why then, I've always wondered, are so many lesbian women into dildos? Will, a man clearly on the side of feminism, had hedged his bets. He seemed to favor the ugly broads, but, on the other hand, he'd been courteous, sometimes deferential, to us. Maybe in his heart he really liked a woman who liked a penis, good and hard. But everything any of us said had been said before on TV talk shows, often by one of us. What was the point? Did the audience really care? I didn't really care. I was tired of being on TV. Where would I rather be? Riding a giant penis into the sunset.

"I just want to say, Will," the caller said, "your giving equal time to those three sluts in their short skirts bothers me. Pornography against women is a serious issue and should be treated as such."

"Okay, caller, does that mean you only want to hear one side of a serious issue, the side you already agree with?"

"Yes," she said, "I believe—"

"Thank you, caller," he said, cutting her off, "and I would like to remind you that labeling these women 'sluts' because they're wearing short skirts or because they have a different opinion than you do is a form of prejudice."

The audience applauded lukewarmly, but still they did applaud. Maybe they were merely endorsing our decision to shave our legs. Who knows? I took the opportunity to recross mine, making my skirt pull up a little higher. Out of the corner of my eye, I saw Carola suppress a smirk. This is how old girls fight.

We went into a commercial break. The makeup person patted down the grease. A thin woman in her late twenties with long brown hair, she looked like she would be walking down the aisle of a church in a New Jersey suburb all dressed in white any day now, never to return to this life again. She made a wide berth around Rosalie. I wished I could. The truth is, Rosalie smelled like she needed a bath.

Coming out of commercial, a clip from one of Carola's videos was on the monitor. A couple was undressing each other, their passion tempered by the need for political correctness. For each piece removed from her, a corresponding piece had to be removed from him, so they would be nude at very nearly the same time. The action stopped when they were in their tastefully sexy underwear.

"Okay, the woman in that clip seemed to be the sexual initiator to me. Am I right, Carola?" Will asked. She nodded affirmatively. How could you be wrong about something so obvious, Will? "Okay, then what is your problem with that, Rosalie, Marsha?"

They, of course, had many problems with it and shared them all with us. Listening to them speak, with frequent interruptions by Carola and Gemma, I thought what fun it would be to read aloud from Rosalie's works on national TV, not that she had written anything which could be read aloud for long on national TV. How far could I go into a graphic scene of fist fucking before I got bleeped?

"We'll be back in just a moment," Will said, heading into the final commercial break. "And the Red Hot Mamas will tell you what's new on their agenda."

Maybe it was the word "agenda" that did it. I came to life on the word. "Agenda" seemed to bite me like a bug pulling me out of the stupor I was in. After the commercial, Gemma plugged our new line of videos, still in production, and Carola sounded off about censorship. Then I issued a veiled threat to the WWA-WAWs.

"I'm glad you asked about new projects," I interjected. "At *Playhouse,* we're in the process of uncovering a major scandal connected to a prominent figure in the antiporn movement. Our story will deal a death blow to one of these groups. I can't say any more than that at this time, of course, but—"

"I thank you, I thank all of you for your contributions to this program," Will said over the rising theme music.

Samuel had come on duty during the Douglas show, relieving Mike in the green room. The two of us rode back to my apartment in relative silence. I liked that about Samuel. He never found it necessary to comment on my skirt lengths or critique my TV appearances. When I got tired of playing Mike's wife, I could pretend I was Samuel's lover. But I was wearying of the bodyguard thing. The unmasking of Rhumumba had ended the threats on my life. Maybe there was no reason to believe the person who had killed Tiffany would be coming after me at all. Maybe the person who had killed Tiffany was a random nut who would never surface again. I made a mental note to call Vinnie tomorrow and suggest we terminate the bodyguards. I wanted to be alone again.

After Samuel had checked the apartment and listened to my messages, none from Otis telling me he'd suddenly developed a lust for white women, I went into the bedroom. Hugging my sadness close to me, I changed into my favorite old jeans, washed so often they were soft and shredded at the knees, and a gray cashmere sweatshirt. I sat down on the bed. For the first time in months, I remembered Tim the geek's favorite question: *How does that make you feel?*

O's rejection had made me feel wronged. How dare he walk away from me because I was drawn to his blackness? Has a blonde ever walked away from a man because he desired her blondness? On the other hand, maybe my attraction to him wasn't healthy. Was David right when he said O was just my way of having Charles? I did still want Charles. I rubbed my temples. My sudden and intense interest in only black men made me uncomfortable, too. Maybe Otis was right: I'd treated him like a piece of particularly tasty meat.

I paced the floor, shifting my focus to my anger at David. What was he doing behind my back?

"I'm not a fan," Steve said. "I didn't even know you were Superlady until that woman choked you on 'Olive.' I never checked out the picture. I liked the column, the way you answered letters. You really put it to those pervs sometimes."

He pronounced "didn't" like "dint." It was kind of cute.

"Sure," I said. "Whatever."

We were sitting beside each other on the sofa, with at least two feet of space between us. He was on his second Coke; it was my third glass of champagne. What I knew about him so far: He was very smart and knew it. He was quite attractive and didn't have a clue. His romantic history was filled with women who had mistreated him and moved on. But the question *"Have you heard the rumors about David?"* remained ignored by us like a silent fart.

"So, have you heard anything about David?" I tried again.

"Did you invite me here to pump me for information or to get back at Otis?"

"What do you think?"

"I think he's not comfortable with you because you write about sex." He took a long sip of his soda. "A little of both, information and revenge. I don't know anything about David," he said, finally relenting, "except that he's talked to a lawyer about the possibility of suing the corporation for defamation of character. He claims he didn't steal anything. He is just not a very good manager."

"How American of him," I snapped. "Defamation of character."

"Maybe he doesn't want a cash settlement. Maybe he wants his job back. Did you ever think of that?"

"Maybe his wife wants him to get his job back. David hates working."

"Don't you?"

I poured some more champagne into my glass. When I leaned back again, I closed some of the distance between us. Though I was slightly drunk, I could see well enough to recognize an exceptionally large erection nestled inside his jeans. If he had a big cock, I could have him. Men with big ones were always looking for excuses to take their treasures out and play. Is this why well-endowed men aren't monogamous?

"How old are you?" I asked.

"Thirty."

"Too young."

"I like older women."

He was grinning. Too young, I thought, sipping my champagne. Then he pulled off his sweater, exposing a very hairy chest. I'd forgotten how much I liked white male chest hair. Those long, silky strands, sensuous beneath the fingers. He took my champagne away and kissed me softly at first, his lips almost softer than a man's should be; then hard, pushing his teeth against mine, but it felt good. His hands on my back, my breasts, he lifted up the sweatshirt, moved it up until it was bunched around my shoulders. I pulled it over my head and threw it on the floor. He kept kissing me, not letting go of my mouth, until we had removed all of our clothes.

"Do you always leave your eyes open when you kiss?" he asked, his tongue flicking my eyelids.

I resisted the urge to say, "If I didn't, I might forget who you are."

His penis was at least as large as O's and more solid than any piece of flesh I'd ever held in my hands. And he was clearly proud, penis-proud. Who could blame him? And who would have thought such a magnificent organ existed on a short white man? I stretched out on the sofa beneath him and opened my thighs. Grasping my hips, he pushed his cock inside me. We fit perfectly, his body not too large, his penis wonderfully so. We moved in sync. No emotional interference to throw us off our stride. He wedged his fingers between my legs and held them steady against my clit. I fucked his hand and his cock; the orgasms began in short, distinctive, little blasts and grew and melded together until my mind was blank. I felt him come inside me in a spray deep and hard, the ejaculation of youth. As he came, he growled.

I woke in the middle of the night and took his penis in my hand. The weight of it thrilled me. I held it loosely and watched it move against my palm, edge up toward my wrist. He moaned and closed his hand around mine, forcing me to hold it tight. I climbed on top of him and guided his penis inside. He held onto my ass and pumped into me, without coming fully awake. I angled my body to take him harder, deeper. In the moonlight, our bodies were like a moving sculpture covered in a fine mist. White on white. I came.

Chapter Seventeen

Dear Superlady,

I would love a woman occasionally to make love to me. Take me into her arms, kiss me passionately, and lead me into the bedroom. From there, slowly remove my clothes, kissing and caressing each part of my body as the clothes come off. One time a woman did something like that to me. She started at my feet, kissing and sucking my skin. Up she went, past my calves and knees and in between my thighs. I had an incredible erection. She went past my genital area and started at my navel and worked her way down. I was going crazy. Finally, after a good while, she grasped my penis in her hand and started kissing and sucking. It was all I could do to keep from coming. Now, that is foreplay!

My question: Why don't more women make love to a man? Why do they think foreplay is something we're supposed to do for them?

Dear Enthusiast,

Foreplay is a negative word, don't you think? It has come to mean the sexual work men do for women to prepare us for intercourse. The assumption is that he *doesn't need any preparation. Ask the typical American what foreplay is, and he or she will tell you it's the time she holds him off while he revs her up. Maybe that was true when we were all sixteen. Maybe. It certainly doesn't work for adults. Men like to be touched, and the older they get, the more they* need *to be touched to become aroused . . .*

I didn't realize how caught up I was getting in the answer until I heard myself moan. It was O's body I saw in my mind, and my hands and tongue were moving up and down him, lavishing liquid attention on every part of him. It was O's beautiful body responding to my kisses and caresses, the ridge of his stomach muscles tightening with his initial excitement.

He was lying on his back, and I was kneeling at his side. I took his penis in the palm of my hand and ran my tongue the length of the shaft and around the head. No, it wasn't O's penis. Definitely, this organ belonged to Charles. I took his penis into my mouth and slowly moved down to the base and back to the head again. O was beginning to writhe and pant under my ministrations. I kept fellating Charles's penis until O was so excited, his body gave off the scent of heated flesh. Repeatedly, I flicked my tongue across the ridge behind the head of his penis. Then I ran my tongue back down to the base and up again. When I knew he was ready to come, I sucked the head of his penis, drawing his sweet come from his body into my mouth.

Moaning, I pressed my hand against my clit and let the orgasm go free. It felt so good, like old times, me alone with my computer and my hand. Why was I fantasizing black men when the personal messages on my answering machine were all from Steve? He'd let me know he was the kind of guy who, having had sex with a woman, wanted to continue having sex with her and nobody else. At last I'd found a serial monogamist, and he was sure to wake up some morning and realize I was looking decidedly too old.

Fortunately, I was working at home today, and I was gloriously alone. I'd persuaded Vinnie against his better judgment to discontinue the twenty-four-hour bodyguard. We'd agreed on a compromise: He had a state-of-the-art alarm system installed in my apartment, and I'd promised I wouldn't go out in public without a bodyguard. I only had to dial a twenty-four-hour number to have some big guy at my side, which made spontaneous trips to the deli for frozen yogurt problematical, but think of the calories I'd save if I had to ask myself every time, Is this trip worth calling for security backup?

I got up and walked around the room, plucked a dead leaf from a hanging basket of Swedish ivy, and straightened the magazine pile on the ottoman upholstered in heavy turquoise silk that I was using as a coffee table in my newly decorated office. My apartment was entirely redecorated, and Vinnie had paid for everything because *People* magazine was coming in two days to photograph it. The office was my special delight. I had a huge solid oak desk and matching computer stand; built-in oak bookcases on three walls; an antique kilim rug in shades of faded green and blue and an orange, so old it had turned peach; a white sofa, filled with floral pillows in shades of peach, turquoise, and green, most of them handmade, many in the shape of flowers; also "curtains" of hanging plants.

"You've arrived," my son had said, when I called to tell him I was going to be the focus of a *People* story, which indicated I now had a measure of mainstream acceptability. He was pleased.

Once in my life, and not so long ago, I would have loved being in *People.* Now I wasn't impressed, only glad to have the points with my son. Vinnie wanted the article and photo spread because publicizing the editor-in-chief of *Playhouse* as a pro-sex feminist was good for the magazine. I had to agree, because the Red Hot

Mamas needed the publicity, too. Though I'd only had a small portion of fame as compared to Michael Jackson or Madonna, I was tired of media attention. Welcoming the inevitable slide back to oblivion, I couldn't wait for my fifteen minutes to end.

Do you know what fame is?

Fame is having a small part of you known or, more likely, misperceived by a large number of people. Give the public a few details, and they'll fill in the rest, drawing from their large community storehouse of "What They Say" and "What Everybody Knows." Fortunately, most people get all they need of celebrities on "Entertainment Tonight" or in ten-minute reading doses in the doctor's office or the privacy of their own bathrooms. Only the few and the sick are truly fascinated, hungrier for more than the famous could ever give them. And only the sickest are angry enough to overreact when they don't get enough, because we haven't got whatever they want to give. The possibility is always there. That's fame.

And Steve was too excited about my fame.

I walked into the living room, another indoor garden, with sofa and matching chaise upholstered in a print bursting with red and white flowers, and more greenery. The antique pressed back rocker had green cushions, and the single chair was done in red. The side tables were antique, oak, and expensive, one covered by a patchwork quilt over a hundred years old, and the Eighteenth Century distressed pine common table, used as a coffee table, came from England. I had built-in oak bookcases on two walls and palm trees which reached the ceiling.

Stretching out on the chaise, I contemplated a nap before my lunch date with David and Clarissa to discuss the WWAWAW exposé. I planned to let David know over the first glass of wine that I knew he was toying with the idea of suing to get his job back. Let him wriggle off that hook under Clarissa's watchful eye. Then the phone rang. It was Rhumumba. Yes, Rhumumba. She had, she said, something very important to discuss with me.

"Like, you can't really let Rhumumba come to your apartment, she's dangerous," Clarissa said.

She was midway through her first large Sfuzzi, a slushy drink made of frozen champagne and peach brandy, the house drink of the restaurant of the same name on 65th and Broadway. I took a sip of my own Sfuzzi. David was drinking a draft beer. I don't know what kind. I'd lost interest in listening as the server gave him the rundown twice.

"I agree with Clarissa," David said, rolling his paper drink napkin into a cylinder and tapping it against his glass. "Seeing Rhumumba in your apartment alone is too dangerous. I'll go home with you."

"I'll have a bodyguard there. I've already called and arranged it. He can hide unobtrusively. If you're there with me, she might not be so willing to talk." I paused. "Like you care." I was glaring directly at him, but peripherally I saw Clarissa's eyes widen. "With me out of the way, maybe you won't have to sue to get rehired."

"Still too dangerous," he said, ignoring everything after the pause.

"What are you talking about?" Clarissa asked, fiddling nervously with the knot in her tie, on which naked buxom blondes cavorted in muted tones.

"Which bodyguard?" David asked, staring intently into his beer.

"Mike."

"She could take him out in seconds."

"What's going on?" Clarissa asked.

"Anyway, it's arranged," I said. "She's coming. He's coming. Too late to back out now. We'll talk later," I said to Clarissa, and to both, "someone tell me what's happening with the article."

"Since you promoted it on the Douglas show, we've been besieged with threats, requests for more information, offers of information for a fee . . ." David began.

"Yeah, yeah, I know. You forget I work there."

"It's easy to forget this week. You haven't been there much," he said.

"I'm bored with the office," I admitted. "In fact, even before I was told to look out for Trojans on horseback, I've been thinking of ways to get out of my contract. I'm getting a decent advance for my book of collected "Superlady" columns. If Vinnie takes the column away from me now, the book will still support me for a while."

"The print porn business is dying anyway," David interjected. "The growth lies in videos and phone sex lines, not print. Soon the magazines will exist only for advertisers of videos and phone sex lines. They will have no editorial integrity whatsoever."

"You mean take the money and run?" Clarissa asked, her eyes lighting up. Since she'd come back from Memphis, she wasn't as excited about her job either. Maybe she could sue to get fired. Maybe we both could. That last chatty coffee date with Elizabeth had clinched it for her: She saw herself as a P. I. "I like it. You know, I really like it. We could both get out at the same time. Miriam would love it if I could spend more time with her and Zelda."

"Then what will you do?" David asked me, ignoring her.

"I'll get more involved in the Red Hot Mamas, put my book together, maybe start a heterosexual feminist erotica quarterly if I can find a financial backer . . . and I can always write a novel, can't I?"

The waiter came to take our orders: the grilled chicken salad for me, little pizzas for them, and a bottle of chardonnay for the table.

"You'll miss the expense account," David said, still not meeting my eyes as he pulled his WWAWAW folder from his briefcase.

I took the folder and flipped through his notes. He'd found two women who remembered Elizabeth from her Liz Larue days. The first, Allison Nash, a divorced mother of three living in Cleveland, also had a bit part in *Behind The Lilac Door.* Like Elizabeth, she'd been a pretty blond teen runaway with big boobs and a vacuous look in the eyes.

Reading over my shoulder, David said, "Allison's best memory of Elizabeth is the time they watched Macy's Fourth of July fireworks display together from the roof of an East Side apartment building. They'd been invited to a party by a photographer. Typical early seventies party; marijuana, alcohol, group sex. Elizabeth wanted to get away because her legs were sticky from some guy spilling his seed on her. The bathroom was being used by a couple fucking, and someone had vomited in the kitchen. So they took bottles of club soda to the roof and Elizabeth poured them down her legs while they watched the fireworks."

"That's kind of sad," I said. "I was hoping for incriminating stories of her bestial nature, not poignant little tales to harden the reader's heart toward the life of porn."

"Life of porn, hell! That was life in New York in the seventies. We'll leave it out if you think it generates reader sympathy for her. And the best news is she was definitely eighteen when she made the films, which takes away the possibility of her being elevated to victim of child porn status."

I flipped the pages. The second woman, Chiquita Sanchez, was married to a successful Mexican businessman and demanded anonymity and some cash, in exchange for her memories of Elizabeth, which were much more promising. Also heartening, for an additional fee, she was willing to go on talk shows in silhouette, sharing her remembrances of Elizabeth in the old days with the electronic world.

Allison had known Elizabeth toward the end of her New York period, just before she'd returned home to face the wrath of her sanctimonious parents and cleaned up her act for good. Chiquita had been there at the start when Elizabeth was living as a "sexual slave," her own definition, to Rudolfo, the South American lover she'd told Clarissa had forced her to act in three porn films. Chiquita remembered it differently. According to her, Elizabeth did the porn films in an effort to turn him on and keep him interested when it was obvious he no longer was.

"Chiquita remembers her as a sexually depraved young woman who would do anything her lover wanted even before he thought to want it," David said. "Too bad Rudolfo died of AIDS a few years back. You knew he swung both ways? He would have made a great interview. By the way, she had a pubic ring."

"I know," Clarissa said, moving the bread plate aside so the waiter could serve her pizza. "And she wasn't at any of the meetings the day Tiffany was killed. Otis is looking into where she might have been."

"She was probably at the mall shopping for Christmas," I said.

Even though she'd tried to choke me to death, I couldn't see Elizabeth Thatcher as the woman who had strangled Tiffany. I'd seen Tiffany's body. That had taken strength, more strength than I'd felt in Elizabeth's hands when they were around my neck. They had not seen Tiffany's body.

While we ate, I looked through Clarissa's notes, which were even more interesting than David's. Elizabeth/Liz/Lia had described in riveting detail her life as a "sex addict." She had allowed herself to be fucked both vaginally and anally with the end of a nightstick. For Rudolfo's amusement, she'd fellated his buddies. Not only had she been orgasmic in her encounters with Rudolfo, anally, orally, and vaginally—she'd even reached orgasm during oral sex with "those sluts" in the movie.

"Did she ever specifically say Tiffany made her come?" I asked Clarissa.

"No, but it was obvious, don't you think? Like, I mean, the whole film is Tiffany doing it to women. Elizabeth only did three films, and she had oral sex performed on her in one, with Tiffany. We don't need Sherlock Holmes for this, do we?"

"Clarissa might need a bodyguard when this article comes out and Elizabeth realizes who did it to her this time," David said, looking at her for the first time in my memory with respect in his eyes.

Would *I* find warmth in those eyes again if I quit my job?

Waiting for Rhumumba to show up while Mike hid behind the closed kitchen doors, I should have been elated about the article, which promised to bring the magazine tremendous publicity and deal a sharp body blow to the WWAWAWs, but I wasn't. In spite of what Elizabeth had said to Clarissa, others remembered her as a willing participant in three porn films. She wasn't led to the set in chains. Nobody ever saw or heard Rudolfo beat or threaten her. In fact, he was remembered for his growing indifference to Elizabeth, no matter how tightly she wrapped her net of sexual complicity around him. I should have felt good about it all, but I kept picturing a girl of seventeen or eighteen washing semen off her leg with club soda while she watched the Fourth of July fireworks, which made her not so different from millions of young women who go along sexually without getting much from the experience.

If Elizabeth were really smart, she'd seize the advantage and go public with her story before we could. Then she had a better chance of selling her version, WWA-WAW in sexual bondage. She could be the new Linda Lovelace, and the media was always looking for a new somebody. How many times has the ghost of James Dean been invoked in the initial reviews of young actors' performances? The first version of any story has the ring of truth to it, no matter how big a lie it is. But Elizabeth had not struck me as very smart.

"The bitch is late," Mike said, opening the door a crack to make a face at me, his gun held firmly in his right hand, high against his chest, and pointing at the ceiling. "Think she's not gonna show?"

"She'll be here."

"Think it has something to do with Bobby being in the clear?"

"I don't know," I said.

Only that morning Bobby had called to tell me he was no longer an official suspect. His "date" the night of Tiffany's murder, a man Bobby had forgotten being with, had finally come forward and given him an alibi. A married Wall Street executive, Bobby's date had agonized for weeks before stepping forward and clearing him. Bobby hadn't known his name or remembered much about him even after seeing him again face-to-face, except the size of his penis, very small, and his wallet, respectably large.

"Honey, you know I only remember the important details," Bobby had said, shrugging off weeks of being a suspect as if it had never happened, his own invaluable self-defense mechanism.

"I don't know what she wants," I repeated to Mike,

"but I'll bet she shows. Don't fall asleep on your gun."

Twenty minutes later the buzzer sounded. The doorman announced Rhumumba, and I swallowed down panic so real it left an aftertaste in my throat like bile. When I opened the door to her, I was more afraid. She looked like she was spending six days a week at the gym.

"I know you hate me and you think I'm a killer and everything," she said when I'd seated her on the couch and was facing her from the red chair. "I don't care if you think that. I came over here to tell you something for your own good in exchange for a promise from you that you won't expose me."

"Expose you as what?" I asked, unable to resist looking at the patches of muscled skin exposed by the holes in her jeans.

"You know what, as a transsexual. I know you're doing a big story exposing a member of an antiporn group. And I know your detective has been all over my life. So, you know why I'm here. I don't want Leanne to know I was addicted to porn when I was a man."

"I see," I said, suppressing the urge to giggle. How had Otis and Steve missed her past porn addiction if they'd been all over her life? "But she does know you were a man?"

"That doesn't bother her, but the other would. She couldn't forgive it. What do you think she'd do if she read I masturbated to those magazines she's trying to destroy every day?"

"How did you know you were a porn addict?"

"My girlfriend told me. She was right."

"What, or who, are you willing to trade to keep it a secret?" I asked. I wasn't going to touch her last question.

"Elizabeth Thatcher."

I didn't say anything for a while. She fidgeted a bit, rubbing her mechanical cheeks against the sofa in an alternating rhythm. I almost expected her to make sparks.

"Okay," I said, "what about Elizabeth Thatcher?"

She told me, of course, everything I already knew about Elizabeth's past as porn starlet and her present as a secret sex addict. But how did she know it? Had they run into each other at a Sex and Love Addicts Anonymous meeting? Or was Rhumumba spending her afternoon, upon leaving the gym, as an amateur detective? When she'd finished, I asked if she could prove her accusations.

"Enough of them. Mostly, I learned it under confidential circumstances." They *had* been at the same group meetings, probably when Elizabeth was in New York on her paint pelting binge. Addict groupies never miss their meetings, even when traveling. "But you've got that big black dick to help you with the rest."

No point in telling her I now had a big white dick to help me with the rest. I pressed her for more, but she didn't seem to have anything more than we already knew. Finally, I agreed to her terms. *Playhouse* would drop the WAP exposé and go for the WWAWAWs. We shook on it.

As I was walking her to the door, she said, "Elizabeth Thatcher is a dangerous woman. We think she killed Tiffany."

"Who's 'we'?"

"Me and Leanne and the women in our group."

"I don't suppose you have any proof of that?"

Well, of course, she didn't. How could she?

Before she could get away, I put a hand on her formidable arm and asked, "Were the WAPs responsible for the stink bomb at Tiffany's book party?"

"Yeah," she said, and, I swear, she almost seemed to blush. "Sorry about that. Later, we learned we damaged some of the bookstore's stock."

After Rhumumba was gone for a minute or two, Mike came out of the kitchen, shaking his head.

"I don't like this at all," he said, putting his gun inside his shoulder holster.

Neither did I. In place of a confession, she'd given me something I already had. I felt like I did when I unwrapped those "gifts" advertisers send in the mail. A woman needs only so many vibrators and sets of ben-wa balls or body paints. And I was starting to believe maybe Tiffany *had* been killed by a stranger. It wasn't difficult to picture her going out for a box of tea bags, befriending some woebegone person of either sex, and inviting him or her up to share the tea.

I was going to call Clarissa to report on the meeting with Rhumumba and fill her in on what was going on with David when the buzzer sounded again.

"Miss Stephanie is here," the doorman said.

"Send her up," I instructed, wondering what Stephanie wanted and why she hadn't called ahead.

I opened the door to Elizabeth Thatcher. She was wearing a shiny red rayon raincoat over a vertically striped silk dress of many colors. In addition to looking chilled to the bone, she looked rather awful. Makeup would have helped.

"How did you know to use Stephanie's name?" I asked, when I should have slammed the door in her face.

"She's one of your group. I took the chance you'd let her in whether you were expecting her or not."

We stood facing each other; me wavering on whether or not I should let her in the door; her standing firm, as if she could will me to open the door wider. Apparently, she could, because I did. She came inside.

"What do you want?" I asked. In reply, she pulled a

handgun from her purse, pointed it at me, and held it steady.

"I think you should be found dead in your own bed," she said.

Thank the Goddess for Elizabeth's love of the polemic. She wasn't going to kill me until she had thoroughly explained to me why I had to die. She ordered me to strip first. I was to die in the nude, a photo the *Post* surely wouldn't be allowed to run without putting discreet black bands in the proper places.

"You are just as responsible for what happened to me as the men who made me do it," she said, holding the gun firmly in steady hands. She was probably a member of the NRA.

"What happened to you?" I asked, my fingers trembling at the wrist buttons on my long sleeves.

"Take off your clothes!" she said, her voice rising, sweat beading above her lip.

She waved the gun at me, so I complied. Sitting on the edge of my bed, I began to remove my clothes. Though my hands were still shaking and my body felt stiff, I forced myself to put an erotic twist to every action. I pulled the back of my pumps off first, then slid off the shoe, my toes pointed, foot arched. Maybe I could arouse her sexually and somehow get the gun away from her. And then what?

"You know what happened to me," she said sharply, her face aglow with the crazy blaze burning in both eyes. "Did you think I wouldn't figure out that ex-nun was your spy? Women like you think women like me who lead good Christian lives and stay home with our children are stupid. I'm not stupid. I figured it out and followed her back here."

"Does your husband know where you are?" I asked.

I would never have believed I'd ever ask any woman *that* question.

Lifting my hips off the bed, I pulled my black silk skirt off and laid it gently beside me. My legs apart and open, I sat facing her dressed only in panty hose and a black silk bodysuit.

"Take off the rest," she said, clearly evaluating my thighs, and giving them grudgingly high marks, in spite of herself. Hers had to be fat under those dresses with the defined waists and voluminous skirts which she always wore. "I'll go back home tonight after I've finished with you and rededicate myself to my marriage. Killing you will end this for me."

My eyes not leaving her face, I undid the snaps at the crotch of my bodysuit, raised my hips and slowly slid my panty hose down my legs. With my torso bent forward, I dropped my head briefly, looked back up at her, and met her glassy eyes. I sat up, sucking in my stomach and pushing out my chest as I did, and opened my legs again, wider this time.

"Tiffany turned you on like nobody ever did, didn't she?"

"Shut up," she said. Her face was flushed, her lips moist. "Finish undressing."

"I turn you on, too, don't I?"

Really, I wasn't so sure I did. Probably the prospect of shooting a hole through my body was making her eyes glaze over. I pulled the bodysuit over my head and laid it on top of the skirt. Naked now, I rested my hands on my thighs and looked at her. I was calm. The fact that I had seen Mike silently open the apartment door seconds before helped.

"You're wrong," she said. "It was Rudolfo."

"Rudolfo turned you on? Then why did you leave him? Or did he leave you?"

"I had an orgasm with Tiffany, and I'm ashamed of that, but he was the one. I was thinking of him when I had it. I was sexually obsessed with Rudolfo. When I took Jesus into my heart as my personal saviour, I asked Him to take away my perverted lusts, and He has. Each day I ask Him to keep them away, and I thank Him for doing it. I promised Jesus I would get rid of smut."

"Tell me about Rudolfo. What did he do to you that your husband doesn't do?"

Well, I thought, the possibilities there are endless. What could that uptight little motherfucker she'd married do in bed that a two-inch vibrator without working batteries couldn't do better?

"He . . ." she began. Her voice was choked. "I can't."

"Did he have a big penis?"

"He . . ."

She lost her voice in a gurgle deep in her throat. Yes, I would bet he'd had a big penis, and she was remembering it now.

"Are you going to shoot me? Why aren't you going to strangle me like you did Tiffany? I don't believe Jesus wanted you to kill Tiffany or me either. Why didn't you make Tiffany take off her clothes?"

I was rambling to keep her from making her fatal move as Mike inched his way down the hall, Rhumumba behind him. Elizabeth looked at me like I was a particularly inept student, and I suddenly realized I was. Around her neck, she wore a long white silk scarf. The gun, of course, was a prop to frighten me into submission.

"I didn't make Tiffany take off her clothes because she wasn't the Superlady of Sex. I had to kill her, because she knew who I was, but I didn't need to take her dignity away."

"How did you discover she knew who you were?"

"Tiffany talked to someone about me, someone who is as ashamed of her past as I am, someone I knew in those days; that someone called me."

Now I understood what had happened. Tiffany had probably talked to one of our informants, who'd been selling her information both ways ever since. Chiquita? Allison? Or maybe Tiffany had found someone we hadn't found.

"I called her, and she said she wouldn't tell anyone until she talked to me," Elizabeth said. "She wanted to talk to me, because she thought I was sending you those letters. She thought I was going to hurt you. She said she wouldn't tell anyone who I was if I promised not to hurt you, but I couldn't trust her to keep her word. I didn't want to kill her. She didn't taunt me with her wantonness on national television like you did."

"I'm worse than Tiffany?" I asked, deliberately keeping my eyes off her face and not looking at Mike standing in the doorway, Rhumumba behind him. "Why am I worse than Tiffany?"

"You're so proud of your body," she said. "You should be found naked and crumpled. Tiffany got fat, and men didn't want her anymore."

"That's not true," I said. "Tiffany didn't want men anymore. They've always wanted her."

Mike kicked the gun out of her hand. I rolled off the bed onto the floor and scooted under the bed. That's why I didn't see Rhumumba rush past Mike and grab Elizabeth, who managed to break free. Rhumumba chased her through the apartment, out onto the terrace, and somehow Elizabeth went off the terrace, twelve flights down.

Held tight against Steve's chest, I was still shaking inside the white cashmere robe, which Mike had tenderly wrapped around me after pulling me out from under the bed. The police were camped out in my living room. Mike and Rhumumba had repeated their story, our story, and Mike was telling it yet again. I could hear him from the bedroom where O and Steve sat with me. Steve stroked my hair and kissed my face. O did not seem upset by this display of public affection. It was soon going to be my turn to talk.

Why had Rhumumba and Mike come back to my apartment? On her way down Columbus, she'd seen Elizabeth on the other side of the street and followed her back here. Mike had been following Rhumumba, because he still thought she had killed Tiffany and might come back to get me, too. They had stuck to the truth on this part of their official story.

"She panicked, ran past us, and jumped before we could stop her," he said. "Jeez, I never saw anyone move so fast. The woman was a major nutcase."

It was a simple story. Not much to remember. I could handle it. In the minutes following the murder, before the doorman could summon the cops, we had agreed on the basic details. Rhumumba had helped save my life, and it was Mike who suggested why shouldn't we save hers?

Rhumumba claimed Elizabeth had jumped. By the time Mike had reached the terrace, Rhumumba was standing at the wall, looking down at the ground. If he couldn't corroborate her story, he said, the police might assume she'd pushed Elizabeth off. And Elizabeth had killed Tiffany, and justice had been done, Mike had said.

"Why expose her to criminal speculation?" he'd asked.

Did anyone, even Rhumumba, really deserve the penitentiary for killing a crazed WWAWAW who would have killed me if she could have? Even in my state of shock, I wasn't fooled and knew Mike was doing what he deemed best for Vinnie. Would the publicity surrounding the questioning and possible arrest for murder of a former *Playhouse* employee be good for the magazine? No.

"How could she have been strong enough to kill Tiffany?" I asked Steve and O.

"Caro, crazy people have strength we can't imagine."

I told them what happened, sticking exactly to the truth until the very end, when I said I'd watched Elizabeth Thatcher wrest free of Rhumumba and throw herself off the terrace. Mike and Rhumumba had to make an official statement at police headquarters, something I'd been spared for another day, because I was still shaking. When they were all gone, I went back to bed, and O poured the three of us snifters of Courvoisier.

"You think Rhumumba threw her off, don't you?" he asked. I nodded affirmatively.

"But why would she do that?" Steve asked. "Panic? Gut reaction?"

"Maybe she thought Elizabeth's death would quash an antiporn article in *Playhouse* and probably also ensure her own secrets were safe. And maybe she wanted to avenge Tiffany, too. I don't know about that. I don't know how she felt about Tiffany, but everybody else loved her. Or maybe she didn't want a member of a group on the same side of the porn issues she's on being taken alive. Or she could be a little crazy herself. I could vote for that one."

What I didn't say was I also believed Mike had made it to the terrace in time to see Rhumumba pitch Elizabeth down to her hell on earth.

"I'm sorry you had to go through this, Carolyn," O said, putting his glass down and taking my hands between his. "I'm going now so you can get some rest." He kissed my cheek, then walked to Steve, clapped him on the back, and said, "Let me know if you need anything here."

"We have his blessing," I said, after the door had closed behind him.

"We don't need his blessing. I don't, anyway. Do you?"

He pulled the comforter off me and opened my robe then knelt over my body, his legs inside mine which were outstretched, and lowered his face between my breasts. I sighed and put my arms around him, running my hands up and down his body. He kissed me, beginning in the hollow of my neck and moving down. By the time his tongue reached my clit, I was consumed with heat. I pushed my hips up, pressing hard against him My legs were trembling, sweat forming at the backs of my knees. His tongue had only to flick me lightly a few times, and I was coming.

I fell asleep; his body, fully clothed, covered mine.

Chapter Eighteen

ANTIPORN CRUSADER LEAPS TO DEATH CONVERSATION WITH SUPERLADY LED TO SUICIDE

Elizabeth Thatcher, public relations director of Women Worried About Wantonness Among Women (WWAWAW) leaped twelve floors to her death from the terrace of Carolyn Steele's Upper West Side apartment yesterday. Thatcher first gained national attention on the Olive Whitney show last November when, enraged by Steele's graphic description of masturbating on a subway train, she attempted to strangle Steele. Security guards pulled her off as the cameras continued rolling.

Steele, the Playhouse *magazine editor-in-chief known as the Superlady of Sex for her advice column of the same name, told police Thatcher came to her apartment with the intention of killing her. Police say a gun registered to Thatcher's husband, Memphis lawyer Phillip Thatcher, was found at Steele's apartment. Elizabeth Thatcher's prints were found on the gun.*

Steele's bodyguard, Mike O'Reilly, and Rhumumba, a former Playhouse *editor, arrived at the apartment in time to stop Thatcher from shooting Steele. After disarming her, O'Reilly reports, he turned his attention to Steele, whom he thought might have injured herself falling off the bed. During this time period, Thatcher ran past him and Rhumumba, heading out to the terrace where she leaped to her death by the time they could follow her.*

"The lady was a real nutcase," O'Reilly told reporters and police.

Rhumumba, a member of Women Against Pornography, was recently fired by Playhouse *owner Vinnie Mancuso, after Otis Campbell, a private detective hired by Mancuso, identified her as the author of threatening letters sent to Steele.*

No charges were filed against Rhumumba in this case.

Neither Rhumumba nor Mancuso were available for comment. Police have not required Steele to make a formal statement yet on the advice of her attending physician. She is being treated for shock.

(See pages 5 and 6 for related stories.)

Masturbating on a subway train?!

The related stories included sidebars on a history of the WWAWAWs, an interview with the grieving widower, who was threatening to sue me, and "Who Did She Think She Was?" speculation as to why I'd ever opened my door to Elizabeth Thatcher in the first place. Somehow they made it sound as if I'd asked her in with the intention of luring her to leap off my terrace. No connection between her death and Tiffany's murder was made in any of the stories. But Vinnie had already heard from the producer of "Hard Copy," who'd told him "the buzz is Thatcher killed Titters."

"Why don't the papers identify her as Tiffany's killer?" Steve asked.

Wearing only a peach silk robe, I was in bed reading the morning papers; Steve, who was reveling in his role of nursemaid/bodyguard, was snuggled beside me. He had provided the new stack of reading materials on my night table. They included an essay from *The New York Times Magazine,* written by a black woman about how much she hated to see her "brothers" dating white women. (She claimed they only liked us because *a.)* we were status symbols, and *b.)* we were "more submissive than feisty black women." Bitch.) He had circled the good parts in red ink. That was on top of Terry McMillan's novel, *Waiting To Exhale,* which paints a grim picture of the black man as life partner. Other books on interracial relationships, with negative conclusions, and magazine pieces, with similar conclusions, completed the pile, quite an impressive, though one-sided, collection.

The phone rang. He, of course, answered it.

"Who is calling?" he asked. Covering the mouthpiece with his hand, he said, "You don't want to talk to Charles, do you?"

Wordlessly, I took the phone from him.

"He's a devoted little guy, isn't he?" Charles asked.

"I'm fine. How are you?" I asked, smiling, I hoped, enigmatically at the "devoted little guy," who wasn't missing a single inflection in my voice. Could he tell I was chafing under the hot blanket of adoration? No. Could Charles? Yes, he could tell.

"The *Post* reporter says his editor labels that an 'unfounded accusation,' " Steve said, continuing our conversation as if a phone receiver were not being held next to my ear.

"We're reading the *Post,"* I explained to Charles. "Thatcher threatened to sue if they printed anything intimating his wife is a murderess, and I don't think they would unless everyone else does. Labeling a leading conservative woman an 'alleged murderer' will seriously discredit a right-wing religious group, not something the *Post* wants to do. The *Daily News* and

The Times are 'investigating' the charge. I don't think they can buy into the idea of a good Christian wife and mother as murderer, though she did try to kill me on national TV. Can you blame them?

"I didn't believe she was the killer until she was holding a gun on me, so what can I say about them? It's still hard for me to give up on Rhumumba. She was the ideal suspect."

"She was built for it, babe," Charles said, laughing.

"Won't someone print the truth about Elizabeth Thatcher?" Steve asked.

"We will in *Playhouse.* Vinnie wants me to write my own story for the next issue. That, along with Clarissa's and David's piece on Thatcher's past, should zap the WWAWAWs."

"Are you going to do it?" Charles asked.

"I know about your story," Steve said. "I meant was anyone else going to print the truth?"

Steve knew about my story because he knew about everything. He was a snoop. I'd caught him reading the size labels in my clothing and the names in my Rolodex. He went into relationships the way women do.

"I would think you'd rather put the episode behind you and let somebody else write the story," Charles said.

"I'm proud of you," Steve said, stroking my arm. The electricity he generated caused my hairs to stand away from my skin.

I was writing my story in part because Vinnie had agreed to let me out of my contract as editor, without punishment. I would keep the sign-on bonus and all the gifts he'd given me, and the column for which I was getting a raise. A sweet deal. Also, he'd agreed to give Clarissa a six-month trial as editor-in-chief. I knew he was going to be very surprised at how well she would handle the job.

"This is my story. I don't want anyone else to write it," I said.

"I always thought Vinnie was using you, letting you take the chances for publicizing his magazine, risks he'd never take himself," Charles said. "But I guess I'm a little surprised you'd give up the job so fast. Why did you do it?"

"I'm tired of being hated," I said. He assumed, I'm sure, I meant hated by the general public. I meant hated by David and the WIPs.

"Nobody hates you, sweetie," Steve said, nuzzling my neck.

He put his hand under the comforter and clasped my bare thigh. Leading with his thumb, he inched his way up my leg. I wanted to see Charles's penis one more time, feel it inside me, and watch him as he visually took in every physical nuance of my orgasms. Nobody got as much out of watching the sex he was having as Charles did. On the other hand, Steve was here, his fingers at the edge of the honey pot. He was eager to play. So was I. Life goes on.

"Vinnie wasn't always protected by bodyguards," I said to both of them.

I hadn't told anyone the details of the negotiation when Vinnie had come to my apartment that morning. The last thing Vinnie had wanted to do was let me out of my contract now that my fame quotient had skyrocketed beyond his previous expectations. But I hated working in an office. I didn't want to be such a public figure anymore. Soon the media's interest in Elizabeth Thatcher's plunge to her fate, even the inevitable questioning of whether or not she'd killed Tiffany, would subside. If I stayed off talk shows as the representative of *Playhouse,* I could lead an almost normal life. Only the people who wrote to me as Superlady would give me a second thought. I was glad Vinnie hadn't taken them away from me, because, with the exception of the occasional Starred Man, I would have missed them. David would forgive me. The WIPs, whose collective powdered nose had been out of joint since I was crowned Queen of Porn, would be mollified.

I was proud of how I'd gotten what I wanted from Vinnie Mancuso, who initially had no intention of letting me go.

"The magazine needs you, Carolyn," he'd insisted, taking my wrist in his hand. "If you want more money and less hours, we'll work it out. Whatever you want. I'm a reasonable man."

"I only want out," I'd said, taking my hand from his grasp.

The deal clincher had come when I'd encircled Vinnie's wrist with the fingers of my hand, gently pressed down, and said, "Vinnie, I would never tell anyone you hired me to do the same job a man had previously held for one third less salary. Nor would I ever offer to testify in David's behalf if he chose to sue the company."

"He almost went to jail once in England on obscenity charges," I said to Charles on the phone and also to Steve in the bed with me.

"That's not the same thing," Charles said. His voice was beginning to sound very far away. He was receding in my mind, his penis disappearing in the mist of a nearer lust. "You could have been killed by any number of nuts, if you ask me. He didn't pay you enough for that."

"No, you're right," I murmured.

Steve's thumb was massaging my clit, and my breath was coming faster. I could have been killed, and Vinnie hadn't issued combat pay. But is there enough money to compensate for that? Is it his fault the fear of sex in this country is so great that anyone in the sex industry can be a potential target for violence? He isn't safe either. I like having a real life. It suddenly occurred to me: I was beginning a real life right now.

"I'm glad nothing happened to you," Charles said. "I care about you."

With his other hand, Steve touched my nipple through the peach silk. I swallowed a moan in my throat. Okay, I still would have wanted Charles if he'd been in my bed, but he wasn't. Could any woman who'd ever had him not want Charles again? He was the dream lover, the phantom lover, the fantasy man. Nobody had more invested in this particular fantasy than Charles did.

"Are you happy?" he asked. "Are you getting what you want from that little guy?"

I giggled, my first real giggle since I almost got killed. He started laughing, too. And so did Steve.

"Yes," I said.

"Are you sure this is what you want?" he asked, sounding almost peevish. "I never thought you knew what you wanted, so I don't know how you could be sure this is it."

"I want my life back, and now I have it."

I also wanted a monogamous relationship with a man I love and who loves me. I wanted tenderness and passion and mutual respect. With Steve, I could probably have the whole package, big penis and all, because he wanted the same things. His pervasive need to know was irritating. Being a woman, I knew where it came from. You're afraid they won't tell you what you need to know, as fast as you want to know. So you snoop, like I had done the day I'd called Charles's office and pretended to be someone else, merely to learn his assistant's name and attempt to gauge her youth and beauty quotient in a split-second sound bite. Would Steve relax when the other men in my life had said their last goodbyes?

"Is he as big as I am?"

"Who?" I asked. Had he been checking out Steve's

crotch and found the bulge as surprising as I had on first notice?

"The black dick, the one you did before this little guy. What, do you think I'm too dumb to know that?"

"Charles," I reminded him. "I am not alone."

"Just answer yes or no."

"No one is."

"Tell him you have to go," Steve said.

I hung up the phone. He replaced his hand with his mouth. It was good to be alive.

There were so many things I might have said to Charles, if I could have. Nestled against Steve's side, drifting in and out of a light sleep as he read the *Post,* his favorite paper, I thought about Charles. Why was it so hard to talk to him? I'd always edited myself with him. What was the inhibiting factor? Was it him, or me, or the combination thereof? I didn't have any trouble talking to Steve.

I'd wanted to say: I'm sorry. From jump, I knew you were a man who would always use romantic idealism as an excuse not to commit. You didn't promise me anything else, so who am I to feel cheated? You gave me great sex. As far as the STD goes, any adult who plays without protection is responsible for his or her own infection.

I'd wanted to say: Thank you for making love to me when I needed a lover, and you really were the only man in my life when you *were* in my life. And may you find the twentysomething woman of your dreams and may you not be infertile after years of harboring untreated STDs when you do. In my new expansive mood, I wanted the best for Charles and Otis, whom I no longer blamed for distrusting my interest in him. I even wanted the best for Johnny, and Manuel, and Tim, the geek, all of whom had sent flowers with fond notes.

All I had said to Charles was, "No one is." Being a man, he might have found that enough.

I kissed Steve's side and ran my tongue up to his nipple, which I nibbled gently.

"You feel like doing something?" he asked in a husky voice.

"Yeah. Bowling. I thought we'd go bowling."

"You're such a princess. Royalty doesn't bowl."

Princess. Queen. Countess. Superlady. Those were Steve's preferred terms of endearment. He wasn't the "babe" type. He kissed my eyes, licked my face and my nipples. His tongue swirled in and out of my belly button and ran down the line of fine, almost invisible, blond hairs leading into my pubic hair. I pressed myself against his face, and the pleasure rose inside me like a wind that seems to whip up from nowhere. I love sex.

Over the next three days, I only got out of bed when *People* magazine came to do their story. Steve, who had appropriated the extra set of keys, returned from the office each night bearing plastic carrier bags of necessities, like take-out Chinese. Clarissa, Bobby, and David were regular visitors. When they were over, Steve devoted himself to organizing my life. He had everything from my phone numbers to my menstrual cycle on computer.

Morgy stopped by once—to announce her wedding plans. She was marrying the man she'd held off in California, one of those high-tech new billionaires, with apartments in Manhattan, Paris, and Tokyo, a villa in the south of France, and a beach house in Malibu. They were getting married in Paris the following week.

"You'll like him when you get to know him," she said. "He's more than a techno nerd."

"I can't believe you're marrying someone I don't already know."

"Oh, Carolyn, I know. We let our friendship get away from us somehow. It's not all your fault. Don't feel bad. It's just like I had trouble with this thing of yours about black men. Oh, I know," she said, waving her hand at me to stave off another discussion about the low quality level of available middle-aged white men, "the guys your color in your age group aren't in your league. Do you have to tell me that? I don't think I'm prejudiced or anything. I went to bed with a black man once, and I remember I felt a little funny about all those tiny curly hairs on the soap, but that was it."

She smiled at me. Looking perfectly beautiful as ever, she was wearing a cranberry silk shirt and full matching trousers, black heels, and beaten gold earrings and a necklace that a pharaoh would have envied. She leaned over and patted my hand.

"Are you really okay?" she asked. "I worry about you. It isn't just the murder thing. It's all these people you spend so much time with now. I feel guilty about feeling this way, but I have to own up to my feelings so I need to tell you."

"Tell me what?" I asked in exasperation, distractedly pulling at a loose thread on my jade green silk lounging pajamas. She was giving me vertigo. Maybe I'd been in bed too long.

"I don't feel as close to you as I once did," she said, a blush creeping into her cheeks. "You've changed. I think it's these people, these sex people, their influence on you. I don't get it. Carolyn, they are so weird. I mean, what do you say to someone like Bobby, who has a penis and breasts?"

"I understand," I told her, patting her hand. What else could I say? Aren't most people uneasy with someone like Bobby, whose gender isn't specific? "I was a bitch. Look, I'm glad you're getting married. I know you'll be happy. And I'm happy, too. Why wouldn't I be happy since your future husband offered to fly me on the Concorde to the wedding?"

"I'm happy you have Steve. He's good for you. The age difference doesn't mean anything. You look young. He's the right size for you. The two of you are so cute together."

"It will mean something when he wants kids."

"Maybe he never will."

"Right."

"Shallow," David said when I'd finished telling him about her upcoming marriage.

"I've always said that about Morgan."

"We wouldn't be the least bit jealous of the riches she is about to acquire, would we?" I teased, and he giggled. We had gone back to the way we were, all of us: me and Morgy, me and David, Morgy and David being jealous of each other.

His notebook was open, and he was ready to go over the plans for the benefit premiere of Tiffany's film, *Woman: Slut and Goddess,* at the Gay and Lesbian Center in the West Village. All the WIPs, of course, would be there in addition to everybody who was anybody in the sex industry. We'd invited Charles, who had also gotten the photo assignment from *People.* Vinnie had agreed to provide the champagne and canapés. But the bulk of the tickets, also paid for by Vinnie, were being given away on a first come, first serve basis. We anticipated a large crowd from the lesbian community. This was to be a gala evening, tinged inevitably with sadness, because it was our true farewell to Tiffany.

David, as new president of the WIPs, was in charge

of the plans. We'd made him our president because, he said, being around us spurred his creativity. He was actually writing the novel, which superstitiously he believed he couldn't do without us. Did that mean we were all going to be characters? Probably, but who were we to deny him his collective muse, particularly since he planned to invest his magazine article fees into the Red Hot Mamas?

"You don't suppose we could get Morgy's new husband to invest, do you?" he asked. "I could be nice for a sizable investment."

I was sitting on the floor next to Steve when the lights dimmed at the Gay and Lesbian Center, a big old stone building, so empty and dismal inside, it could have been the setting for a Gothic thriller. Take a wrong turn on one of the winding staircases on either side of the building and surely you'll find the torture room. Gemma had failed to order a sufficient number of folding chairs, for which David would verbally flagellate her later. We, the WIPs, other dignitaries in the world of sex, and our invited guests were either sitting on the floor or standing along the sides of the room. We had found chairs for Miriam who was nursing Zellie and for Dr. Rita, who looked like a sequined elf and had made it clear she had no intentions of lowering herself, no matter how small a distance that was, down to ground level. In the semi-dark, Miriam's pendulous breasts gleamed white.

"It looks like worms are crawling down her breasts," Steve said. "What is that?"

I explained the snake tattoos, and he shuddered.

"The kid will be in therapy," I said. Steve didn't believe in therapy. What a relief!

None of us minded sitting on the floor because we felt Tiffany would have wanted the people, mostly women and gay men, who'd stood in line in a chilly drizzle for hours, to get the chairs. In the months following Tiffany's death, she'd become a cult figure. Her films sold out in video stores; her book was on *The New York Times* nonfiction best-seller list, a rarity for a photography book. Two biographies were in the works, one at Doubleday. The crowd tonight exceeded the capacity of the room; and hundreds more, who hadn't been able to get in, stood outside, waiting for the next showing. After seeing the crowd, David had decided we would keep screening the film through the night until everyone who wanted to see it had been given the chance.

"Tiffany is what she said she was," I whispered to Steve, "a goddess."

"Tiffany," he said, "was crazy."

His legs were crossed at the ankles, his knees close to his chest, his legs open and bent. He had his arm around me. I squeezed his thigh, then let my hand rest there, the fingers brushing against his cock, which immediately grew hard inside his pants and stayed that way for most of the evening. I loved that about Steve. An accidental touch in passing could make him harder than the average man gets from being skillfully fellated for ten minutes.

I was wearing a strapless hunter green leather minidress, darker green panty hose, and slightly darker green shoes. The room, filled with several hundred bodies, was warm, and I was glad for the bareness, for the feel of his arm against my skin. I sneaked a glance at O, wearing a black silk shirt under a gray Armani suit. He looked good enough to lick, head to toe. I still craved the feel of black skin, but not as obsessively as I had. Outside it was March, cold and wet, still cold enough for my mink coat, which I'd worn, and checked, despite Steve's dubious expression.

Bobby, dressed in a tight cerise knit dress, floor-length, but slit-up the front to the crotch, sat next to me.

When the lights went out, he squeezed my knee. Bobby, Clarissa, and David, of course, had become my best friends. In the last faint glow before darkness, I glanced again at O. His unavailability taunted me. Grow up, Carolyn, I chided myself. Time you started wanting the man who wants you, loving the one you're with, and so forth. I nibbled Steve's earlobe.

The soundtrack came up, and the screen filled with the first image: a huge pink and grainy expanse, its texture and outline unidentifiable. When the camera moved back from the surface, it became obvious we were looking at cleanly shaven vaginal lips. There was a burst of laughter as recognition dawned.

"I see myself as a sexual evolutionary," Tiffany's voice said. The lips, moist and parted, remained on the screen. And they seemed to undulate sensuously as she spoke.

The camera drew back a little more. Tiffany deftly sketched, in a June Cleaver voice, the details of her life, from porn star to New Age sex oracle. Suddenly, the lips parted a little wider and out walked Tiffany, coming out of the vagina as if she were stepping out of an elevator. She was wearing a baby pink sheath dress accessorized by a single strand of pearls. Her long hair was pulled back in a dignified bun. She was wearing plain white pumps with a modest three-inch heel. I couldn't hear her lines over the laughter.

Ninety minutes later, when the lights came back on, I glanced quickly around. Several people had tears in their eyes, from laughter and from missing Tiffany. I'd wanted her film to be good, but it was better than that. *Sluts and Goddesses* was brilliant. She had artfully parodied everything from her own movies to our female obsession with thin thighs, touching the major points of concern for women about sex as easily as if she were skimming stones across a smooth pond.

"I liked the part where several women were masturbating one woman, and her orgasm lasted for seven minutes," O said. He had joined Steve and me for the ritualistic champagne toast. He was Steve's partner. We would probably share the occasional toast with him for the foreseeable future. "That was a profound comment on sex, wasn't it?"

"You think she was doing a takeoff on the old wives' tale that the average man only lasts seven minutes?" I teased. "Not, of course, that I've ever known anyone who only lasted seven minutes."

"You would have thrown him out of bed if you had," Steve said, nuzzling my neck and growling softly in my ear.

"Was that a real orgasm or faked?" David asked from behind us.

"If it was a real one, sugar, it broke the world's record for a single sustained orgasm," Bobby said. "I know it's something a pussy can do better than a cock, but I'm not sure I'm believing you could do it that much better."

"You're the expert, Carolyn, real or faked?" David asked.

"Faked," I said. Then glancing around us, I saw them, Rhumumba and her skinny blond lover. "What are they doing here?" I asked.

Steve, Otis, David, Bobby, and Clarissa turned to look at them. They looked straight back, with none of us so much as nodding our heads to each other. What were they doing there?

"Like this is a very big thing for the lesbian community," Clarissa said. "You don't understand, but, like, Tiffany would be the biggest heroine if she had lived. I guess she still will be, dead or not. She'll be like Marilyn Monroe is to the straight world."

"They probably stood in line for tickets, like everybody else," David added.

They had turned away from us and were resolutely looking in another direction now. I know Rhumumba saved my life, but I couldn't exactly warm up to her. I was sure she'd thrown a woman off my terrace when sitting on her until the cops arrived would have been a better way of handling things.

"It's okay," Steve said, holding me close against him. "She isn't going to hurt you."

"I know that," I said. "I'm not really afraid of her. Repulsed by her, yes; afraid, no."

The rest of the WIPs joined us. Our circle expanded to include them and Vinnie, who was wearing black leather pants and a thinner black leather shirt and so many gold chains he almost clanked. We talked about Tiffany's work and her life, and no one mentioned her death. She would have loved that.

"What are the Red Hot Mamas going to do next?" Vinnie asked. "Anything like Tiffany's work?"

"We're mainstream," Carola said. "Tiffany never was."

"We're going to do a video for women who love penises," I said, "really love them. A hard and hot fuck video from a woman's perspective."

"Carolyn wants to do something a little less politically correct," Carola said diplomatically. "We decided to give it a try."

Not that they had a choice. I wasn't putting my money into one of those "please and thank you" productions. Sex is not politically correct, whether we are talking about positions or the type of people who arouse us. We have to deal with that.

We paused in our conversation to take fresh glasses of champagne from a passing waiter. As I reached for mine, I looked past him into Rhumumba's eyes. What saw in them did nothing to allay my suspicions about ow Elizabeth had really met her death.

The WIPs were having a private party following the remiere at Vera's, but Steve and I had opted out. We aid we wanted to have sex, not talk about it tonight. ruthfully, I wasn't yet ready to reclaim my position as ne of the girls. In time, but not then.

He opened a bottle of champagne, put it on ice, and arried it to the bedroom. I followed with two flutes in and. Then I noticed something unusual. The closet oor was standing open, and a man's outfits were neatly ung on the side I'd used for bottoms and tops.

"I brought some things over," he said. "You houldn't be alone nights for a while, and it's easier for ne if I don't have to go back to my place every day."

"Okay."

"I don't like the idea of you being alone, especially at ight," he said, unbuttoning his shirt as he spoke. "I now you think with Elizabeth Thatcher dead, you on't have to worry about someone trying to kill you nymore. You're probably right, but I don't like you eing alone. Otis agrees with me. You're still a celebrity nd will be for a while yet. Protecting you is looking fter Vinnie's interests, too, and Vinnie is a good cli- nt."

"Okay," I said. "Where did you put the rest of my lothes?"

"In the closet in your office. Did you think I threw hem on the fire escape?"

"We aren't moving in together or anything, are we?"

"Nah," he said, scratching his chest, to draw my ttention to his hairiness no doubt.

I felt a smile beginning in my own chest and moving pward into my face. What the hell. Every older woman should have an affair with a younger man at least once before it's too late.

He took off his clothes and jokingly ordered, "Come here, Superlady."